In The Interest of Justice

By the same Author
*Rogues' Gallery*

Watch for these future murder mystery novels
by Daniel Eller

*In Search of a Reasonable Doubt*
*A Case of Felony Murder*
*In the Heat of Passion*

# IN
# THE INTEREST OF
# JUSTICE

## Daniel Eller

Hollyhock Publishing, LLC

ISBN: 978-0-9801081-0-1

Printed in the United States of America.

Published by
Hollyhock Publishing, LLC
13865 Hollyhock Road
Cold Spring, MN 56320
www.hollyhockpublishing.com

"The quality of a civilization is largely determined by the fairness of its criminal trials, and of its other proceedings in which men may lose their liberty, their reputation, or their right to pursue callings of their choice. Our notions of fairness in the conduct of such enterprises have a long history, and are constantly developing. But these tenacious ideas about the protection of the individual before the massive power of the state are meaningless without independent and courageous lawyers to defend them, and to defend them without fear of reprisal."

Eugene V. Rostow, Dean, Yale Law School, March 7 1962.

*Dedication*

*For Danielle, Jack and Charlie—*
*the next generation of readers.*

1

"I can't believe that jury is still out! What's it been, six hours? I expected them to be back in an hour or so."

My boss, Noah, seemed to ignore my comment. He leaned back in his chair. With his index finger he packed the tobacco in his pipe, struck a match, inhaled deeply, and then looked up at me with a content stare. "Jackie, my dear, you've got to learn to relax," he said out of the side of his mouth as the smoke curled over his head.

"Noah, I don't think there was a person in that courtroom who thought the jury would find Clint guilty."

He eased the pipe out of his mouth. "Except . . . probably the jury," he said.

"No way! I didn't leave a loose end anywhere."

I looked at Noah for his affirmation. His gaze fixed on me. He blew a couple of smoke rings. "I told you from the beginning, you have two strikes against you: first, it's a rape case, an ugly rape case, and second, you have a dirt bag for a client. Those jurors are going to sit there and say, 'Even though the State's case is a little weak, why would that young girl lie, and, moreover, why should we care if we send this bum to prison?'"

"I can't believe that," I replied.

"You don't have to," Noah said. "But I've been doing this for forty years, and when a defendant looks like yours, and is charged with rape, believe me, your chances are as good as the proverbial snowball in hell. You may as well relax."

I couldn't relax, however. We were in the law library at our office while we waited for the call that the jury had returned a verdict. Unable to sit still, I had taken to pacing, walking circles around the conference table. Noah sat on a lounge chair in the corner puffing on his pipe, seemingly amused by my anxiety. The room slowly filled with the sweet smell of smoke. I started to feel nauseous. I tried to recognize the aroma—cherry. I opened the door to let in a little fresh air.

"You're taking this way too personally," Noah said. "I was like that at your age, too. You think if the jury comes back guilty, it's some reflection on your ability as a trial lawyer. If you do this long enough, you'll get over that. If you give your client the best defense you can, that's all anyone should expect. If the jury comes back guilty, that's not your fault. After all, maybe they're right and you're wrong. You know, Jackie, every time I had a client who professed his innocence, by the time we got to the day of trial, I wanted to believe him, too. That's the only way you can get in front of a jury and appear sincere. If you're trying to con them, just spouting words, they'll sense it . . ."

"But he *is* innocent," I interjected.

"Well, then, you aren't going to be the first lawyer to have an innocent client found guilty."

"I don't believe they'll do that."

Noah sighed deeply, pursed his lips and exhaled a big puff of smoke that drifted over his face. I continued pacing. Noah grinned. Now I knew he was enjoying himself at my expense. But he was right. Even though this was my ninth trial, and the most serious charge I had defended, I'd only had one not guilty verdict, and that one had seemed like a fluke. But this one was righteous; I deserved a not guilty.

The phone rang and I jumped. It was the court bailiff. The jurors had decided to eat in so the judge was having dinner delivered. Noah and I decided we had time to go eat.

"Let's go someplace I can get a drink," Noah said.

It was a warm evening and a crimson sun filtered through the clouds, appearing to balance on the roof of the bank building. Noah crossed the street toward Joey's, a bar and restaurant a block and a half from the office. The waitress found us a nice quiet table toward the back where we could see but not hear the big screen television. We each ordered a whiskey soda, not my usual drink. Noah had not said a word since we left the office. As soon as the waitress set our drinks in front of us, I grabbed mine and inhaled half of it. Noah smiled. "Liquor is to be enjoyed, Jackie, not simply consumed," he said.

I ignored his comment, finished my drink with a gulp, and ordered another. Noah took a small sip to accentuate his comment. He knew what he was doing. Noah is a slow, deliberate person; he was hoping a little of this would rub off on me. I'm the exact opposite, supercharged and always in a rush.

"You know what bothers me?" I asked. "If the jury finds this guy guilty, he goes to prison and, with this judge, it's going to be for a long, long time."

Noah set his drink down on the table with a loud clink. "Jesus, Jackie, if he's guilty, he *should* go to prison for a long time. He pulls this girl into his car, brutally rapes her, threatens to cut her breasts off, sticks a straight razor between her legs and threatens to cut her vagina out. If all that's true, he should never see daylight again."

"You're right! But this isn't the guy. Somebody did it, but not Clint. She just picked the wrong slob, and he's going to pay for it."

"Well, that's what you told the jury. Hopefully they'll believe you."

After the waitress returned for our order, Noah turned and glared at the television at the other end of the dining room. He sipped slowly on his cocktail. I looked at his face. The lines were like a road map of the forty years he had spent in court fighting for the losers. He had a reputation for being a scrapper, always willing to fight the unpopular cause, to represent the reprobate no one else would handle. That's why I went to work for him in the first place. Now, as I looked at him in the dim light of the bar, it was obvious to me that all of his scrapping had taken its toll. Although sixty-five, he looked much older. I knew his heart was bad, but he never told me how bad. He was told to quit smoking and cut down on booze. Maybe that's why he liked to savor each drink.

"Eiffel Tower," he said suddenly. I looked at the television screen. It was turned to *Wheel of Fortune*. Noah had solved the puzzle. A commercial came on and he looked back at me. "I never watch television at home," he said. "A waste of time."

"Did you know Dr. Morgan was in court for closing arguments?"

"No," he replied.

"Yeah, he was sitting right next to Cheryl, the complainant. Did you ever try to talk to him about his role in this matter?" I asked.

"Yeah, I did. He said the girl was referred to him to help her through the trial. He couldn't get into any specifics. Doctor-client privilege, you know."

"I was just curious," I said. "He seemed to spend an awful lot of time there."

"He's a good guy," Noah said. "I've known him since he came to town about twenty years ago or so. We've socialized quite a bit. I like him; he's got a good sense of humor. His wife's a really nice lady. She has a Ph.D. in English. She does some serious writing, specialized stuff for some company. I'm not even sure what it is. They're both committed to their careers."

Noah looked around the bar. "There was a time I would've known almost everyone in here." His gaze settled back on me. "I'm curious," he said. "Did you get any feeling that some of the men on the jury panel had some . . . problem, I guess, dealing with a female defense attorney?"

"I know where you're going, Noah. I'm not sure I want to go there right now".

"Well, you have to admit that you are an anomaly around here. There are only a couple female attorneys in town and they do family law. To my knowledge, you're one of the few, if not the only, female criminal defense attorneys in the state."

"There are a couple others in the Twin Cities. But you're right; we're few and far between."

"That's why I asked. Did you sense any . . . help me here."

"Male chauvinism?"

"Yeah. We can start there."

"Actually, Noah, I've sensed it as a cloud over everything I've done since I passed the bar exam. I've learned to ignore it. I keep thinking things will change; after all, it is the 1980's. Why do you ask?"

"I was there during the *voir dire* of the jury that first morning; it just seemed to me that a couple of those guys seemed a little flippant in their response to some of your questions."

"To be honest, Noah, I was pretty nervous when I started *voir dire*. I'm not sure my radar would have been attuned to that."

"I noticed it more when you were questioning that older, gray haired guy— I didn't catch his name. His responses to your questions were quite abrupt and seemed, to me at least, a little sarcastic."

"Yeah. I remember him. I kept him on the jury only because there were others who seemed worse."

"Most of the time picking a jury is a crap shoot. You just hope you're right."

I knew Noah was waiting for a response, but it really wasn't something I wished to discuss in my anxiety of waiting for a jury to return. I knew the attitude of some men toward a female attorney was something I would have to cope with, however. I had learned early on at my first court appearance that my gender, and whatever feelings it may engender in the opposite sex, would be a fact of life.

We heard a clinking of dishes and I turned. The waitress was making her way across the floor with a tray. She put our plates in front of us. Noah had ordered a t-bone steak, rare. I had ordered a hamburger and french fries. He asked the waitress to wait a second as he sliced it down the middle; bloody juice filled the bottom of his plate. "Just right," he said. "Thanks."

I looked at the golden droplets of grease floating in the juice, the translucent fat on the edges. "You're not supposed to be eating that kind of crap, Noah."

He took a big piece on his fork, started chewing it, saying, "Mmm." I grimaced at him.

"Listen," he said, swallowing, "if the grim reaper's gonna take me, I'm gonna go happy. It's too late to worry about that kind of bullshit now."

We'd had this discussion before. I wanted him around for a while, but he had a very nonchalant attitude about his death. He told me about a friend of his, another lawyer, who had died a little over a year ago from cancer. Noah spent a lot of time with him in his last month, watching his suffering with anguish. The experience convinced Noah that he wanted to go with a heart attack, like his dad. The doctor had told him that his father was probably dead before he hit the floor. Noah much preferred that to a long painful death like that of his friend. I remember him telling me that if it had been him on his deathbed, he would just as soon have been given a shot or some pill and allowed to quietly drift off.

I ate a couple of fries, took the top of my hamburger bun off and added a little ketchup, but I had no appetite. This was the fourth day of the trial. The jury had gone out a little before noon. I found that with each day I had less of an appetite. Pain emanated from different parts of my stomach. I knew it was just tension. Noah looked at me. "You gonna waste that?"

"Maybe I'll have her box it up for later."

"I could never eat during a trial either," he said. "In a case I tried years ago I lost a little over twenty pounds. My pants were falling down when I made my closing argument—but I won." He smiled as he reached for one of my french fries.

"How late do you think the judge will keep the jury out?" I asked.

"It depends on whether he thinks your client is guilty or not. If he thinks he's guilty, he'll keep them there until they return a verdict, even if it's two in the morning. It's funny how jurors can change their minds and reach a consensus when it starts to get close to midnight. I had a case ten or fifteen years ago with old Judge Wenner. It was in the middle of winter. It had to be twenty below zero. When it got close to midnight, he still wouldn't let the jury go home. They came back and found my guy guilty . . . at one-thirty. He should've let 'em go home at seven. The next day I found out some were holding out for not guilty but they started to worry about their cars freezing up and not starting. So, one by one they caved in, and the result is that my guy is found guilty, not because they unanimously believed he was, but because some jurors didn't want to freeze their butts off in the parking lot trying to get their cars started. That's what I told you, Jackie. Sometimes justice turns on rather strange events that you have ab-solutely no control over."

Another Noahism, I thought. Lessons learned from years of experience that were never covered in law school. Noah had taught me many things I had never read in law books. I could sit and listen to his stories for hours. Sometimes I would hit the bar with him after work. There'd be three or four other attorneys, old-timers too, and they would compare war stories. At first I did it just because I thought it was fun; then I realized there were some real gems of information in some of those stories, things I could use in my own career. So I made a point of tagging along. At first the clique was a little hesitant to let me into their circle—I was the first female attorney who was allowed the privilege. But I must not have seemed a threat. After just sitting there and looking pretty the first few times, they even started to direct questions to me. I remember the heat rising to my face while trying to give intelligent sounding answers. Before long, though, I was just another one of the guys. I enjoyed that.

By then Noah had finished his steak. He looked at me. "Well, I guess I might as well get home. Thanks for the company. I knew if I went home Maggie would have salad and whole wheat toast waiting for me."

"That's because your wife wants to see you around for a while. So do I. I'm going to squeal on you."

"If you wanna be buried in writing briefs for the next month," Noah replied, "you go right ahead." By then he had reached for his wallet to pick up the bill. He always paid the bill.

We left the bar and stood on the street corner for a couple minutes chatting about things that were coming up. Since he was going home, I told him I was going to walk to the courthouse and see what was happening. We said our good-byes and I made my way the three blocks to the old courthouse.

As I walked to my car, I turned to watch Jackie step up on the curb on the opposite side of the street on her way to the courthouse. For a moment I hesitated, thinking I should go back to give her some support, but I let the thought pass, knowing Maggie would be worried if I was any later. With mixed emotions I continued to my car. Having been in her position many times, waiting for a jury to come back, I knew what she was going through—sheer agony. It was worse when you really believed your client wasn't guilty. I also felt pride. She'd tried one hell of a case.

Jackie had shown up at my office months ago inquiring whether I was looking for an associate. I was always amazed that out of all of the attorneys she could have picked, she ended up at my office. Nor, given that she had been living in Minneapolis and practicing as an assistant public defender there, could I understand why she wanted to practice criminal law in St. Cloud. Most of the young attorneys I had a chance to talk to believed all of the real action was in the Twin Cities. She told me that from her first year in law school, all she thought about being was a criminal defense attorney. And now she believed she was ready for private practice.

I pondered the idea of hiring her for quite a while. I liked being by myself, not responsible for another attorney. But there was more. Now, looking back, I realize it was silly, or maybe a bit of male chauvinism, but at the time I thought she was much too attractive and appeared way too fragile to be a criminal defense attorney. The first time she sat across from me, explaining why she wanted to work with me, I couldn't help but try to picture her sitting in the holding cell at the jail with some dirt bag who had just beaten up his wife, committed a rape, or blown someone away.

However, when I broached the subject with her, she told me she thought she could handle it. So later I called the public defender's office where she worked and found out that she was no stranger to handling ugly criminal cases with ugly defendants; in fact, she did it quite well. Her boss didn't want to see her leave, but he could see why she wanted to get out of the public defender's office. In his opinion she had the potential to be one of the best trial attorneys in the state.

His opinion still wasn't enough to convince me to hire her, however. Then fate stepped in; I started to have chest pains. The tests showed that I had a bad ticker. The doctor put me on some blood thinner and a diet. He told me I had to cut out smoking, alcohol, and, hardest of all for me, fatty steaks. Every once in a while I would ignore his advice, like tonight, and have all three at one sitting, feeling like when I was a kid leaving a B-rated movie and wondering what Sister Carmichael would say if she knew.

So after the doctor talked to my wife, and Maggie told me either I hired somebody or I simply couldn't go to the office anymore, I called Jackie. Luckily for me, she was still waiting for my call. She started in my office two weeks later and has taken the pressure off. She's willing to take just about any case I want to throw at her. She handles herself in such a way that she gets very little crap from any client, and if one decides to give her some, she gives it right back, but I've had to step in a couple times.

There's a certain kind of guy she has a hard time dealing with; at first, I didn't know why. It's only happened twice where she asked me to take over the case, which I did. I tried to figure out why, out of all the clients that came through the door, she had trouble with these particular individuals. It took me a long time to understand.

Her former boss had told me that she was a very polished litigator. I thought he was just trying to do a little puffing on her behalf. The first day in the office, I gave her a burglary case, one that I considered a sure loser. Because it was the defendant's third offense, if he were to get convicted he would go to prison, so he wanted to take his chances at trial. It was already set for trial before I found out about my heart. So when I gave the case to her, I assumed the first thing she would do was ask for additional time. She didn't. Two weeks after starting, she was in front of a jury trying the case. I sat through a good share of it, much of the time in amazement. After forty years of practice, I had never managed to develop the polish in front of a jury I saw in her. I had the reputation of being sort of the country lawyer, at times even a little bit of a bumpkin. I had seen Jimmy Stewart in *An Anatomy of a Murder* in my formative years, so I used him as a role model. I wondered whom Jackie had seen in her formative years. It was nobody that I could associate with. Watching her was truly a unique experience. Her presence seemed to fill the courtroom, to demand attention.

After more than a hundred trials I still didn't feel comfortable in front of a jury to the point where I could relax. A kind of nervous twitch stayed with me my whole career. Sometimes it got to the point where I felt I had to explain it to the jury. I always believed it was because I took every case too seriously. I blamed my heart condition on that as well. Jackie seemed more at ease. She stood in front of that jury so self-assured, confident, not a note in her hand. She laid out the defense so calmly, plainly. I was impressed. The jurors must've been also. They found the guy not guilty.

As I watched, I tried to figure out what it was about her that seemed to make her so in charge of the situation. I suppose the fact that she was young, tall and attractive, a picture of femininity quite incongruent with the general perception of the rough and tumble atmosphere of the criminal courtroom, might have been part of it, but I concluded looks were only a small part. There was an attitude about her, an attitude of defiance that said: Here I am, give me your best shot. For some reason it seemed to enhance her credibility. After that day in court I started to watch for it more and more. I concluded that, for some reason, she had a chip on her shoulder, as though she had something to prove. I couldn't imagine what.

As I neared home, I started to feel even worse about abandoning her at the curb. I shouldn't have let her go back to the courthouse by herself. If that jury came back and found her client guilty, she might need a little support. She put her heart and soul into the case. I knew she wouldn't take defeat very lightly.

My wife, Maggie, was sitting on the front steps as I pulled into the driveway. She was wearing a loose-fitting dress, her arms wrapped around her legs with the folds of the dress tucked underneath. In the twilight the black spruce next to the house stood silhouetted against the red sky, like great spires of some old cathedral. The air was warm and damp. Dew had already formed on the lawn. As I walked to the steps, lightning bugs scattered like sparks from my feet.

Maggie laughed. "You look like you're charged up," she said.

"There are enough of them to get a shock," I replied.

I sat on the concrete step beside her. I had no more than put my hands on my knees when she said, "You've been drinking and you've been smoking."

"Worse than that," I added. "I had a steak."

She slugged me on the shoulder. "Noah, what's wrong with you? You wanna leave me a widow, don't you?"

"Ah, Christ, Maggie, old habits are just hard to break. I was waiting with Jackie for her jury to come back. She hadn't eaten all day so I went with her."

"That makes no sense," she said. "You hired her because of your heart condition and then you go out with her and aggravate it."

"Maggie, it was only a little steak. I had my pipe but I didn't inhale . . . and I only had two drinks."

"That's the problem with you, Noah," she said, shaking her head. "You've spent your whole life coming up with excuses for people . . . You're never going to change."

"I hope not," I said. "I like me."

She looked at me and smiled. "I suppose I might as well go in and eat my dinner," she said. "I'll save yours for tomorrow night."

"What was I going to have?"

"Tuna."

"Oh, I'm sorry I missed it."

"I bet you are. What'd you have? A New York strip?"

"Tenderloin. Less fat." It was just a little white lie.

I joined her at the table. "I suppose Jackie's a nervous wreck," she said.

"She was when I left. She slammed down a couple drinks. I hope she doesn't have to talk to the judge."

She looked up from her plate. "I know you're supposed to be her mentor. Does that include your bad habits as well?"

I ignored the comment. We'd been married for thirty-five years, and the only time she didn't complain about my drinking was when she kept up with me, drink for drink. If she wasn't along, though, I was a sot. The comment used to bother me, but like a lot of other things in life, it was no longer worth getting excited about.

"She's got the potential to be one hell of a defense attorney. I just hope she doesn't burn herself out. She really took this case seriously—too seriously for the kind of client she had."

"You should talk about taking things seriously," she replied.

"But there's something different about the way Jackie does it," I said. "I don't know; I haven't put my finger on it yet. Anyway, I told her to call me when the jury's back."

"Well, from what you told me," Maggie said, "I hope they lock this guy up. What that poor girl must've gone through…"

Her comment jogged my memory. "You know, Dr. Morgan's been counseling her."

She looked at me, stopped chewing. "What do you mean?"

"Well, I suppose the prosecutor wanted to help the girl through the trauma of it all, so he hired Chris to counsel her. I'm not sure what he was supposed to do, just get her prepared for court. I've seen it before. Jackie told me Chris sat through most of the trial."

"He never mentioned anything to you?" she added.

"Oh, I knew he was counseling her. But, you know, he would never say anything to me."

"Well, I suppose he can't talk about it," she said.

"He can't. I'm still surprised, though, that he remained so secretive through the whole thing."

We were both quiet as we considered it for a while.

"Well, I don't see anything wrong with it," she finally said. "After what that girl went through, I can imagine she needed some professional help. And, knowing Chris, I would think he would be good at that."

"After this is all over," I said, "maybe I can talk to him. I just get a little concerned sometimes that it goes beyond counseling to coaching. Some of these young women can be quite impressionable. I can see some of the prosecutors I've worked with attempting to embellish their case under the guise of counseling."

"Chris would never do that," she said.

I shrugged my shoulders. "I would hope not."

12

$3$

I was sitting in the hallway outside the courtroom when the judge's clerk hollered down the hall, "Jackie, the judge would like to talk to you for a minute."

It had been close to three hours since I'd left Noah standing on the street corner. I had paced the halls, read the evening paper, even did a little research in the law library. And now I had been sitting on an oak bench outside the courtroom for so long that my buns were numb. The whole time I had not seen another person. Through the trial it seemed the only one who cared about my client, other than me, was his sister. But she'd only been there one day to testify that he didn't own a car and didn't drive, and then I never saw her again.

I knew somebody was in with the judge because I could hear laughter. I assumed it was the prosecutor. It sounded like him anyway. He and the judge were old buddies. I would see them playing cribbage at lunchtime at a bar across from the courthouse. It was a serious game, a buck a point. They were doing that now as I walked into the judge's chambers.

This was the first trial I'd had in front of Judge Peter Savano, and the first trial I had with the County Prosecutor, Randy Becker. After four days of fighting with them, I considered them both pricks. During the trial I think it got to the point where they were having a contest to see who could be the most rude. They had every opportunity to do so. See, one of the arguments of my defense was if my client made her perform oral sex on him, why didn't she ever mention to the police that he had a big wart on the end of his penis? It just seemed to me the wart was something she couldn't miss. The judge and prosecutor had quite a time trying to decide how they were going to let me get that in front of the jury. They wanted to know if I had made him flash me at the jail. I told them I wasn't bashful about it. As far as I was concerned, I would have my defendant stand up in a jury box, drop his pants, and whip it out. I think my comment caught them both by surprise. We finally decided on a photograph, black and white, eight by ten, glossy.

They were sitting there, cribbage board out, dollar bills spread out in front of them. The judge looked at his watch. "Nine-thirty," he said. "I expected them back hours ago. You must've sweet-talked some of those men on the jury." He winked at me.

The prosecutor muffled a laugh.

"Your Honor, I would think it's been a long day for them," I said. "I would like to ask that they be allowed to go home and come back tomorrow morning."

"Oh, you would," he said. "What do you think, Randy? She would just as soon allow them to go home."

"I would just as soon play a few more hands of cards," the prosecutor said.

"Maybe you'd like to come in and join us, play some three-handed. We can take your money," said the judge.

"That's okay," I said. "I've got some reading to do."

"Suit yourself," the judge replied.

As I turned, I could feel their eyes leave my face, run down my chest, and follow me as I walked out. Several times when we were having in-chambers discussions, the judge was having a hard time keeping his eyes off of my breasts. I started to feel self-conscious and I would wrap my arms across my chest. I think he realized what I was doing, and why, but he didn't stop.

I stepped through the door of the judge's chambers, imagining what each of them was thinking, only to collide with the judge's court reporter, Frank. We each backed up a half step and apologized.

"I just talked to the bailiff sitting outside the jury room. He said there's a lot of screaming going on. It's going to be a long night," Frank said.

I shook my head. "What are they arguing about?" I asked.

"He wouldn't tell me that. The bailiffs always pretend they don't know, but we all know better. I've got a pot of coffee on if you want a place to sit."

I had never spent any time talking to Frank. He seemed pleasant enough. He had always kept to himself in his little cubbyhole off the courtroom. I would see him in there all the time, dictating.

Court reporters occupy a rather unique position in the judicial system. Unlike jurors, court reporters get to hear all of the closed-door stuff that accompanies a trial. And unlike defense attorneys, they normally know what the judges, and often the prosecutor, are thinking. So I had learned from experience that sometimes the court reporters could be a good sounding board for how the case was going. Besides, it beat sitting out in the hall on a hard oak bench again.

I followed him into his office. He offered me his secretary's chair, and he took a stool from the corner. He had a coffee maker on top of his file cabinet. He grabbed a white Styrofoam cup, filled it, and handed it to me.

"Looks like it's gotten a little strong," he said.

I looked at the coffee. It had a vague resemblance to motor oil. I knew if I drank the whole cup, I probably wouldn't sleep for a week. I took a sip and politely said, "No, it's good."

"This is your first trial in front of Judge Savano," he said, more as a statement than a question.

Before I had a chance to answer, he continued. "He likes to give women attorneys a hard time. You have to remember he was on the bench for probably over twenty years before the first female attorney appeared in front of him. At a hearing one day, he called her a 'lawyerette.'" Frank smiled. "He got a nasty letter from the judicial board for that."

"I've heard the story," I said. "Noah told me. A judge in St. Paul lost his seat over a comment like that. Some woman ran against him and beat him by campaigning against him as a male chauvinist pig."

I didn't make the comment as any kind of threat to the judge, just a statement of fact. But Frank seemed to take it more seriously than just a casual remark. I had learned that court reporters felt a certain allegiance to their judges. It might have something to do with job security. I was staring at him to the point I could tell he was feeling uncomfortable. He looked away.

"You know," I said, "if I were a man, we wouldn't be having this conversation."

"You're right," Frank interrupted. "I guess I'm to blame. There were just some times that I thought you felt a little . . . I don't know, upset, with the judge's . . . whatever. Let's change the subject. This is the first time I've seen you in a jury trial. You did a nice job."

"Thank you," I replied, a rush of warmth coming to my face.

"I didn't think they would be out this long," he said. "The judge's clerk, Judy, thinks they'll find him not guilty. I think they'll find him guilty."

His frankness caught me by surprise. "Why?" I snapped.

"That young lady just made too good a witness," Frank said.

"But she was mistaken about Clint," I replied.

"Well, she may have been, but then she did an awful good job of describing her assailant. Sure sounded like your client."

The room went silent. The only sound was the distant voice of the prosecutor, shouting, "I have fifteen-six and three for nine. That's the game. You owe me another six bucks."

Frank looked at me and smiled. "Those two need a life," he said.

Without thinking, I took another sip of coffee. It felt like castor oil going down my throat. "Didn't it bother you," I asked, "that it took her over two years to report it? I mean, this was supposed to have happened in the fall of '84 and it isn't until February of 1986 that she goes in and talks to the police."

"She had a reasonable explanation," replied Frank.

"Yeah," I said, "that she was too embarrassed to tell anybody. What about that therapist that she was supposed to have told right after it happened? Why didn't she bring her in? See, that doesn't make sense to me. She's supposed to have suffered all this trauma over the rape, ended up in the hospital on the psych ward, gets all this treatment, but she never talks to the cops. Then she's sitting in the shopping mall and she miraculously sees her assailant . . . then she finally decides to go to the cops."

"That's one of your problems," Frank replied. "You have to admit, the guy's appearance is very distinctive. There aren't many guys running around town, tall, skinny, stringy black hair."

"Yeah," I interjected, "but she doesn't even remember his most distinctive attributes: he's missing most of his front teeth and he's got a big wart on his dingy."

Frank laughed. "I don't think I've ever heard it referred to as a 'dingy' before."

The heat came back to my face. "Well, I didn't know what to use. But you'd think to be face-to-face with him, she'd remember the missing teeth and . . ." I hesitated. "I've already talked about the other part enough."

"Well, he does have an ugly mug," said Frank, "I'll give you that. But maybe she was too frightened to notice the missing teeth. Besides, we only have his word for it that they were missing."

"And his sister's," I said.

"The jury doesn't have to believe her," he said.

"What about the fact that he doesn't even drive, never owned a car? I mean, how can my guy drag her in the backseat of a car and rape her when he doesn't even own a car? Doesn't have a driver's license!"

"I'll grant you," said Frank, "those are all good points. You did a good job arguing to the jury, but you have to admit that when that young lady got on the stand and testified how scared she was, how he threatened to cut her up with that blade, and the pain she felt when he forced her into sex . . . I was concentrating on the words but I was watching those jurors' faces. Man, I'll tell ya, every one of those women jurors could put themselves right in that spot. A couple of 'em teared up."

"Yeah, I figured that," I said. "I didn't look. I was watching Cheryl testify. I thought she was bringing things out of the recesses of her mind, but I wasn't sure whether she was telling the truth or not. I think what was apparent to me was that she was so well coached. I noticed it got to the point where not a word changed from one time she told the story to the next."

"I know the prosecutor's got somebody in the office who acts as a victim's advocate, who's pretty good at sandpapering the witnesses, you know, holding their hands through the trial," Frank said.

"I think they hired Dr. Morgan for that," I said.

"Is that why he was sitting in the back?"

"Apparently."

"I heard the judge say something but I never paid any attention," he said.

We sat and talked for another hour or so, but not about the trial. I had learned that court reporters, if they want to, can tell you a lot about the practice of law in your area, what kind of cases everybody handles, who's making money, who the good attorneys are. So I made an effort to cultivate a good relationship with them.

"You're single, right?" Frank said.

"Yeah."

"Any boyfriends?"

"Why? You interested?"

This time it was Frank's turn to blush. "Nope. But Johnny Conners is."

"Really?" I said. "How do you know?"

"He's asked me about you a few times. In fact, I saw him earlier today in the hall. He asked me how you were doing. I told him, 'Great!'"

Johnny Conners was another lawyer in town. Probably in his mid-thirties, he was a little taller than me; I guessed six foot or so, good looking. He reminded me of a young Sean Connery, from the 007 years, the same face shape, close-cropped hair, dark eyes. Except Johnny had a little bit more sensuous mouth. Not that I had really noticed, though.

I said, "I tried dating another lawyer once . . . No thanks. It right away becomes a contest. Who's the brightest; who can come up with the most arguments; who writes better briefs. That kind of crap. Tell you the truth, Frank, I can't imagine spending the rest of my life talking nothing but lawyer talk, and that's what I envision if I got married to another lawyer. I'm not even sure I would want a professional of any kind."

"Wouldn't that be a little tough?" asked Frank. "I mean, you know guys like to believe that they're the big honchos in the house. You know, the breadwinners. Don't you think you being the professional would cause problems in the relationship?"

Actually, it was something I had thought about. It came up from time to time in the girl talk in the law school cafeteria. Greatly outnumbered, we formed our own little clique and had many chats. One of my friends was dating a carpenter. It never seemed to bother him that his future wife was going to be a lawyer. I guess I just concluded that I was going to have to find somebody who was pretty secure with who he was and what he was doing. I always assumed that there had to be some men like that out there, somewhere.

Frank caught my glance at the clock. "How late do you think the judge will let 'em go?" I asked.

"If they're having fun playing cards, I don't know. The latest I've seen is midnight or so."

"That's terrible," I said. "Doesn't he think about those jurors? We started this morning at 9:00. They've been at this for close to fourteen hours. I don't think it's fair to them or the defendant."

"Well, I suspect he's got other things he wants to do tomorrow morning," said Frank. "He doesn't want to have to come back here and wait around for the jury."

I shook my head as I stood up. "Well, thanks for the hospitality. I think I'll go roam the halls for a while." In truth, I had to get out of there before I said something that I would live to regret. I figured anything I said about Judge Savano would probably get back to him. In my fledgling career, I knew I didn't need to aggravate him any more than I already had.

Frank was right; it was close to 1:30 when the bailiff finally came up and said the jury had reached a verdict. When I heard the word "verdict," every part of my anatomy that could telegraph a sensation went to work at once. I could feel my body tighten and perspiration form under my arms and down the small of my back. The jury had been out for more than twelve hours. They hadn't even left for dinner. If the bailiff was being honest, there was a real fight going on. I couldn't imagine which side had won out.

I was pondering all the possibilities when I heard the elevator ding and the door open. The deputy stood there with my client. Clint was still shaking sleep from his eyes. I wondered how in the hell could he sleep. Easy, I thought, he doesn't have a guilty conscience. Frank's words came back to me: "An ugly mug." He was right. Clint was close to six-foot five, skinny and stoop-shouldered, with a protruding Adam's apple and long greasy dark hair that looked like a wig flopped across his head. He had the start of a whiskey nose with a red, blotchy complexion. When he saw me, he smiled instantly. I grinned back, not really in response to his, but because of something that crossed my mind. I had never thought of it before, but his top row of teeth looked like a seven-ten split in bowling. Again, I thought, how could the complainant not have noticed that?

They hadn't bothered letting him get dressed in his street clothes. He wore jail-issued baggy pants and shirt, both of which were too short for him. The pant legs hung just a little below his calves and the shirt rode high enough to reveal a protruding potbelly. He started to shuffle out of the elevator in his terry cloth slippers. His ankles were shackled.

"Just a second," the deputy said. "I'll take those off." He leaned down and clicked them open. Clint walked out, his hands cuffed behind his back.

"Would you take those off too, please?" I asked.

"Give me time!" he snapped.

"I have to talk to him alone for a minute before we go in," I said.

"Well, go sit in the corner!"

From the deputy's attitude I concluded he was one of the members of law enforcement who didn't believe that a woman had any place in the criminal justice system. My place was at home, barefoot and pregnant.

As I walked Clint to the corner, I said, "I don't know what's going to happen in there, Clint. I hope they come back not guilty, but if they come back guilty . . ." and I saw the remnants of a smile disappear from his face, "the judge is going to have to do a pre-sentence."

"How can they find me guilty when I didn't do it?"

We'd been through this before and I still couldn't answer him. I didn't want to answer him.

"It happens," I said. "Just don't get excited in there. Don't make it worse for yourself. We have some things we can do if they find you guilty."

He stooped over even further, his head hung down, his chin almost touching his chest.

I didn't think there was much more I could say to him. I wanted him to expect the worst and then if it wasn't . . . but I think I knew better.

I walked with him into the courtroom and stood behind our table. The judge was already on the bench, the prosecutor seated at his table, the clerk at her station to the right of the judge. The judge turned to the clerk. "Bring the jury in."

She got up and walked to the side door where the bailiff was standing. When he opened the door, there was no noise coming from the room. Nothing. Dead silence. Then the first juror, one of the women, appeared in the door. Her face was cherry red, her eyes bloodshot. She stole a glance at me; it was so brief I would have missed it if I hadn't been staring. She walked stiffly toward the jury box. Once she was several feet out the door, the rest of the jurors followed. By looking at their faces, I knew what they had done. Not one looked at the defendant. The last one out was a man in his early sixties. During the *voir dire*, I had hesitated to keep him on the jury, but he seemed to be better than some of the alternatives I had. As he walked by the prosecutor's table, I saw him wink.

When the jurors had taken their seats, the judge said, "I understand you've reached a verdict. Who's your foreperson?"

The winking man stood up. I remembered his name: Jerome Kaufman.

The judge looked at his notes, and then raised his head. "Mr. Kaufman, do you have the verdict?"

"Yes, I do, Your Honor."

"Hand it to the bailiff, please."

The bailiff took the verdict form and walked over to the clerk.

"The clerk will now read the verdict," Judge Savano said.

She stood up, her hands shaking a little. She read, "We, the jury empanelled in the above-referenced matter, to the charge of criminal sexual conduct in the first degree, find the defendant guilty."

I could feel the air go out of Clint. I thought he was going to sit down. I reached over to grab his right arm. The muscles were so tense it reminded me of grabbing an aluminum softball bat.

"I want to thank you, ladies and gentlemen of the jury. You've done a good public service in this matter," the judge said.

"Your Honor," I interrupted, "I would like to have the jury polled."

He looked at me with a cold stare, I assumed for the benefit of the jury, and said, "Certainly, Ms. Geroux."

He turned back to the jury. "Ms. Geroux would like to have you all polled, so I will go down the list of your names and ask you each if this is your verdict."

This was my first opportunity to really look at the jury since they had taken their seats. In addition to the first woman out, a Mrs. Judith Prom, several other women on the jury appeared upset. I had no way of knowing what may have happened. I watched each face as the judge called their name and asked, "Is that your verdict?" Each responded, "Yes," with no hesitation. Maybe I was seeing something that wasn't there.

When he was done, the judge turned to me. "Is that sufficient, Ms. Geroux?"

"Thank you, Your Honor," I said, as graciously as I could.

"Ladies and gentlemen of the jury," the judge said, "you're excused. I'm sorry for keeping you so late, but justice had to be done."

21

Once the jurors had all left the courtroom, the judge looked at the defendant. "You'll be remanded to the custody of the sheriff. We'll have a pre-sentence investigation . . . unless you wish to proceed to sentencing at this point, Ms. Geroux?"

"We do not, Your Honor. I do want a pre-sentence investigation, and I also intend to file some motions."

"I assumed you would," replied the judge. "You can take him back to jail, Deputy."

The deputy grabbed Clint by the arm and started dragging him from the courtroom.

I looked at him. "I'll be over to see you in the morning, Clint. There are some things we can still do."

I watched him shuffle out of the courtroom. The prosecutor was shoving papers into a briefcase. He glanced over at me. "Son of a bitch is going where he belongs," he said as he turned his back to me and left.

I closed my file and walked out. I was hoping to run into some of the jurors, but by the time I got to the jury room it was dark and quiet. The bailiff told me that they were all in a hurry to get out. When I stepped outside, the bailiff locked the door behind me.

I stood in the courtyard, in the dark. I could hear car engines starting in the parking lot across the road. I looked up at a full moon and, as loud as I could, I hollered, "Shit!"

My doctor and Maggie had pretty much put me on a meatless diet. So when I went off my routine tonight and had a steak and a couple drinks with it, I think my stomach went into a state of shock. I didn't get sick but I had that queasy feeling, making it difficult to sleep. Then when I did fall asleep, I had weird dreams. The most bizarre dream, which I seemed to be having more often lately, was that I was in court in the middle of a jury trial in just my underwear. I mentioned my dream to Chris one time and he analyzed it with a bunch of Freudian bullshit. I chose to believe it was just a way for my body and psyche to get even with me for the years of abuse.

Tonight I'd had the dream. I was about to make my closing argument to a jury, and when I stood up from the counsel table, I wore just white briefs. I heard a phone ring in the judge's chambers and the judge said we'd take a short recess. The next thing I knew, Maggie was shaking me, telling me Jackie was on the phone. I looked at the clock. It was quarter after seven.

As I crawled out of bed, I caught my reflection in the mirror on the dresser. I grinned. I didn't cut the same figure I managed in my dreams. The whole thing struck me as rather ridiculous as I walked into the kitchen and grabbed the phone.

"Good morning," I said.

"Noah, I'm sorry for calling so early," said Jackie, "but I wasn't sure what to do."

"Where are you?" I asked.

"At the office."

"What are you doing there at seven o'clock in the morning?"

"You were right, Noah, the judge kept the jury until they came back with a verdict, after one-thirty in the morning. Guilty! I was so angry I couldn't go home. I came to the office. I've been up in the library thinking about what motions I can file."

I was about to say that I was sorry and I knew how she felt, but she didn't give me a chance.

"I'm sorry to call so early," she repeated breathlessly, "but I've just had the strangest thing happen. I was sitting at my desk and I saw the light flashing on the phone, so I picked it up. You'll never believe it, Noah. It was a pastor from one of the local churches, and he had two of my jurors sitting across from him telling him that they wanted to change their vote."

"Hold it, hold it, Jackie, you're talking so fast."

"I know, I just can't believe it, though. I just got off the phone with him."

"Settle down for a second," I said. "What did he tell you?"

"Two women jurors were there . . . and I know who they are. I saw it in their faces last night. They were there early this morning. Apparently they couldn't sleep. They're both members of his parish. They said they didn't believe Clint was guilty, but the foreman forced them into voting guilty."

As I listened to her I had to just shake my head. Jurors were always a source of consternation, but Jackie's story topped anything I had experienced. She told me that these two jurors were from the same congregation, and during the course of the four-day trial they had become friends. When the first vote was taken, there were five jurors, three women and two men, who were voting not guilty. The foreman started out by trying to convince them they were wrong, and as the hours wore on, he went from cajoling to browbeating and finally temper tantrums. About midnight the two men changed their minds and started voting guilty, which left the three women. They wanted to talk to the judge but the foreman wouldn't let them. Finally, at about one-thirty, just to get out of there, they changed their vote to guilty. They didn't know what the procedure was. They didn't know they could say anything when they were called back into court. They told the minister that when they left the courthouse they talked for a while in the parking lot, agreed they couldn't let the verdict stand, and without knowing what to do, decided to visit him first thing in the morning.

"He felt obliged to call me right away," said Jackie. "What do you think we can do?" she asked.

"There's a procedure you have to follow," I said after thinking about it for a moment. "You have to file papers with the judge accompanied with affidavits by the minister, possibly by the jurors, and see if the judge would conduct a hearing to determine whether the verdict was improper. But what you're asking the judge to do is to allow the jurors, at least these two, to impeach their own verdict. Its not likely Savano is going to do that."

"No! You've got to be kidding," she cried. "You mean with what those women are saying, he'd let this verdict stand?"

"My honest opinion?"

"Yeah."

"There's no way this judge is going to give Clint a new trial. You're going to have to go through all of the motions and hope that an appellate court reverses the conviction."

I could tell that wasn't setting well with her. For the first time I could hear her breathing. I imagined flames shooting across the room.

"Then that's what I'm gonna do," she finally said, some resignation in her voice. "You don't suppose it would help if I went and talked to the prosecutor?"

"Randy, that lazy bastard? You think he's going to want to try this case all over again? You can go tell him and see what he says, but I wouldn't hold out any hope."

"What about the judge?" she asked.

"Don't waste your breath," I replied.

We talked for a while. I told her to get in touch with our investigator and have him get a statement from the minister, possibly an affidavit from at least one of the jurors, something we could use to support our motion for a new trial. When we were about to hang up, I remembered something. "So you haven't been home yet?" I asked.

"No."

"Get any sleep?"

"No."

"Why don't you take the day off?"

"No way!" she replied. "Too many things to do."

I hung up the phone and stood there for a pensive moment. That's something I would have done forty years ago, fresh out of law school, my adrenaline pumping from the idea of taking on the system. I often wondered why some people get such a high representing somebody like Clint, a down-and-out bum charged with a brutal rape.

Maggie was up and the coffee was brewing, the aroma filling the kitchen. She looked at me and I knew I had that distant stare that seemed to always upset her. She told me that she believed I used it when I wanted to block her out. There were times in the morning, having coffee, when she'd be talking and my mind would be miles away. She would say something outrageous just to see if I was listening, and when I didn't respond, she'd slam her hand down on the table to startle me out of my trance, and then she would get up and leave.

"What's wrong?" she asked.

"The jury found Jackie's client guilty. I figured they would . . . but then she finds out some of the jurors didn't want to find him guilty."

I gave Maggie an abbreviated version of what had occurred.

"What's she going to do?" she asked.

"She's going to go over and talk to the prosecutor. I told her it isn't going to do her any good. She's just going to have to follow the procedures, hope she can convince somebody along the way that Clint deserves a new trial."

I took a seat at the table and sipped my coffee. Maggie sat facing me. She took a sip of her coffee and set the cup down.

"You know, it's kinda interesting. From everything you told me about this case, her client, it would seem that the women should be voting guilty. Instead, you have the foreman going ballistic to get them to change their minds. I would've thought it would've been the other way around. What'd you have, seven men on the jury?"

"Yes." I replied.

"And you wanted more, didn't you?"

I didn't respond.

"And you thought Jackie could sweet-talk those men. Maybe wiggle her hips a little bit to get them to vote not guilty. Wasn't that in the back of your scheming mind?"

I snuck a peek at her. I could tell she thought she had it figured out.

"That's not true at all," I said. "I would've tried that case if it wasn't for my heart."

"Uh-huh," she grinned. "Well, I hope you've learned a lesson. Women are sometimes more perceptive about these things than men."

"So you've told me, dear," I replied.

I sat at my desk and pondered. I knew I had sprung this whole thing on Noah without really giving him time to think, but I expected a little bit more guidance from my mentor. I guess in my disappointment with the verdict, I was looking for a quick fix.

I looked at the clock, seven-thirty. I knew our investigator, Brownie, would be up sitting on the deck at his lake home having a cup of coffee. I dialed his number and he answered in two rings. When I told him what I needed, he said he would be at the office in about an hour.

Brownie had been Noah's investigator for probably five years or so. He retired as a deputy sheriff when he turned sixty. It was fun to listen to Brownie and Noah talk about what they considered "the good old days." Brownie would arrest somebody, then call the judge and tell him what he had. The judge would call the prosecutor and Noah. They'd all meet in the judge's chambers, and in fifteen minutes they would decide what the guy was going to plead guilty to and what his sentence would be. They had their own sense of due process. If there was some young kid who they determined needed some guidance, he normally ended up going right from the courthouse to the army recruiter. Once accepted by Uncle Sam, the charges were dropped. If there was some vagrant, some drunk who got himself in trouble, the sundown sentence was imposed: the judge would give him some jail time, but the sentence would be suspended if he was out of town by sundown. Noah told me his fee for being court appointed had been forty dollars, and sometimes he would give ten of that to his defendant for a bus ticket out of town and a couple meals. When Brownie and Noah would reminisce, they decried the fact that they couldn't have fun like that anymore.

At precisely 8:00, our secretary Linda came in. A punctilious woman in her forties, she'd been with Noah for close to twenty years. She was neat, precise, and entirely humorless, the exact opposite of Noah. I assumed that's why the two of them got along. If he had hired somebody exactly like himself, he would have never made a dime.

She gave me a perfunctory, "That's too bad," when I told her what the verdict was. I knew she didn't mean it. In her spare time, which because of proficiency was probably half the day, she kept busy by reading our files. She believed Clint was guilty and that his sentence should be castration.

Knowing I would never get any sympathy from her, I went back to my research to see if I could find any cases that would give me a precedent for my motion for a new trial. After going through the case digest for a half an hour or so, I started to realize why Noah had sounded so pessimistic about my chances. I couldn't find a case where the appellate courts allowed jurors to impeach their verdict; once the vote was made and it was unanimous, regardless of how they got there, the verdict stood. If I was going to get a new trial, I would have to make some new law.

I was daydreaming when I heard Brownie's voice from the outer office. "Linda, my dear, it's going to be a beautiful day. Why don't you and I go sit on my deck, watch the loons on the lake, drink beer and talk dirty? What do ya say?"

There wasn't any response. I didn't expect any. Linda didn't like Brownie. He was probably the most irreverent person I'd ever met. There wasn't too much he held sacred. "Linda, you need a man in your life," he continued in his raspy, guttural voice. Then he hollered, "Jackie, I hope you've got fresh coffee on," as he shuffled down the hall to my office.

I had filled a cup and handed it to him as he walked into my office. "Jackie," he said, "for having been up all night, you look absolutely lovely this morning. How about you? You wanna go sit on my deck and talk dirty?"

I grinned and shook my head. I was used to all of his abuse. At first it bothered me, but once I got to know him, I knew he was just a good-natured blowhard whose bark was worse than his bite. I suspect if I had said, "Sure, let's go," he probably would've had a heart attack right there.

He took the cup of coffee, smelled it. "Smells fresh," he said.

Brownie looked like he spent too much time sitting on his deck drinking beer. Stocky, a little paunch hanging over his wide western belt, he was probably forty, fifty pounds overweight, with a round face and a ruddy red complexion. The first thing you noticed, though, was his hair: a full head of silver gray locks combed neatly, *a la* early Elvis Presley. Today he wore dark brown dress boots, brown slacks, and a tan shirt, the buttons straining to hold it closed over his belly. He sat down and smiled at me. "Sounds like you've got a mess on your hands, hon."

I told him everything that had happened and how Noah told me to proceed. I gave him the sheet with the minister's name and telephone number and passed him the phone. Just as he was about to dial, he looked at me and asked, "Do I call him 'father' or 'pastor' or what?"

"Pastor, I think."

He dialed the number. While it rang, he looked at me and winked. "Good morning," he said. "Is this Pastor Michaels? Yeah, this is Brownie Dodge. I'm an investigator with the law firm of Schepers and Geroux. I'm at the firm now talking to Miss Geroux. You talked to her earlier. If you've got a few minutes this morning, I'd like to come over and take a statement from you . . . What's your address? Okay, I can be there in about twenty minutes." Brownie hung up. "You know what? I think I know this guy. The address rang a bell. A number of years ago some young punks broke into his church and stole some gold candlesticks from the altar. If it's the same one, he seemed like a pretty nice guy. Anyway, I'll get back to you."

As Brownie walked out of the door, I dialed Becker's office. I was a little surprised to find him in. I told him I'd be right over.

The prosecutor's office was on the ground floor of the courthouse. He had two full-time assistants and one secretary. I'd only been over to his office a couple times, but I could tell that his secretary, Mary, didn't like me. I only knew a little about her. She was married, three kids. Her husband was a mechanic. It seemed to me she treated me rather coolly. I felt she thought of me as some uppity young broad who didn't know her place. Because of that, I never tried to carry on a conversation with her. It wasn't any different this morning. She kind of pointed me to the couch with a grunt, and I sat reading the morning paper, waiting for Randy. I was reading the metro section when the prosecutor stuck his head out the door and said, "Come on in."

He was dressed casually. "I've got a tee time at 10:00," he said. "I've only got a couple minutes."

Now I knew why he had wanted to keep the jury there until finished last night.

"What's up?" he asked.

I told him about my call, my research, and took the rather bold approach of suggesting that he should join with me in a motion for a new trial. The words were barely out when a big smile came over his face. The only sound was Mary tapping away on the typewriter in the outer office. He stared at me, his eyes doing a once-over.

He made me feel uncomfortable. There was something lascivious in his stare. I never knew how to take him. I didn't dislike the guy, but he just seemed a little bit of a slime. He was divorced, with a reputation of doing a little philandering. In his late forties, he looked much younger. I tried to think of something to say as his bloodshot eyes came to rest on my face.

"If I had any inclination whatsoever, even a gut feeling, that your guy isn't the sick bastard who did this, I might give your proposal five minutes of thought. As it is, that guy is guiltier than sin . . . and the only thing I'm going to do is make sure that Judge Savano puts the bastard away for the rest of his life."

The forcefulness of his demeanor and comment took me by surprise. I didn't expect to have an ally, but I thought that as a prosecutor, some sense of fairness would dictate that Clint deserved another chance.

I said, "I can't believe that. Doesn't it bother you what happened?"

"Hell no."

"You think jurors should be browbeaten into a decision?"

"Happens all the time. I'll tell ya something," he continued with a smirk on his face. "I knew Mr. Kaufman was going to be the foreman . . . as soon as I finished my *voir dire*. I was really surprised when you didn't strike him. He had law and order written all over him. You need somebody like that to take those few bleeding hearts that always end up on the jury and whip 'em into shape. If you've got the guts to stick around in criminal law for a while, Jackie, you'll find out that's how the system works. So," he said, looking at his watch, "I've already wasted four days of my life on your client. I'm not going to give up a tee time.

See ya in court."

I sat there for a moment slightly stunned. I wanted to scream some profanity at him but I knew better. With as much grace and dignity as I could muster, I stood up, and in the sweetest voice, I said, "Well, Mr. Becker, it must be nice to live your life with such a sense of self-assuredness. Indeed, I will see you in court." I turned and purposely did my sexiest walk out of there.

At bag lunch that day in our conference room, I sat with Jackie and Brownie as he related to us his meeting with Pastor Michaels.

"The juror's name is Judith Prom, and the juror who came with her is Angie Ohmann. There's a third gal who also held out until the bitter end . . . Mrs. Prom called her, too, but she didn't want to get involved. It sounds to me like things got pretty ugly. Apparently this guy, Kaufman, walks into the jury room, tells everyone he wants to be foreman. I guess nobody else is interested, so he's it. The very next thing he says is, 'I think the guy's guilty and I don't think we should waste any time debating it.' Unfortunately for him, there are five jurors who don't agree, and things start to go to hell from there. I take it from Pastor Michaels that Mrs. Prom is a pretty levelheaded lady. Tough, not one for hysterics. But she couldn't tell him anything this morning without crying. It got to the point where this guy's screaming at 'em, calling them every name in the book. You know, dumb bitch, and shit like that . . ."

"I talked to the judge's court reporter, Frank, last night about nine-thirty," Jackie interjected. "He told me the bailiff said there was a lot of screaming going on, and when that jury came out with the verdict, these ladies' faces were bright red. They were obviously upset."

"Why do you think they didn't say anything?" I asked.

"Pastor Michaels asked them that," said Brownie. "They didn't think they could. Mrs. Prom told Michaels that the reason she was holding out was because she couldn't understand why this complainant—what's her name again, Jackie?"

"Cheryl."

"Yeah. She couldn't understand why this Cheryl, if she was raped the way she said, didn't report it right away, why it took her two years. And that was pretty much what the other two holdouts were saying as well. But then this guy, this Kaufman, he said, 'I had a daughter who was raped by a boyfriend, and she didn't tell me about it for a long time. She didn't tell *anybody* about it for a long time.'"

My eyes met Jackie's in midair, like two radar beams.

"Noah, I asked it," she snapped. "I asked every juror whether they had any family or friends who had been subject to a sexual attack or sexual abuse. Only one juror said yes, and she didn't want to talk about it in open court. So we went into the judge's chambers where she told us it was her daughter. She had been sexually abused by a neighbor boy. She said she didn't think she could be fair to Clint. She was excused. So, if what Kaufman told the jurors is true, he covered it up in *voir dire*, Noah."

I knew she was telling the truth. Before the trial, we had gone over a number of times all of the questions she was going to ask on *voir dire*. In any rape or sexual abuse case, this was a question you couldn't avoid asking prospective jurors.

"Was *voir dire* recorded?" I asked.

The room went quiet for a moment. Jackie leaned back in her chair. "I don't remember. I don't remember if Frank was there or not. Wouldn't they normally record it?"

"You never know with Savano," I replied. "He might've sent Frank out to pick up his dry cleaning."

"What difference is it going to make?" asked Brownie.

"If it was just a question of these two jurors wanting to change their verdict, there is little likelihood the judge is going to do it. But it seems to me that if this juror lied in response to a question on *voir dire*, one of such materiality as to whether somebody in his family has been raped, and then that person becomes the foreman and won't let anybody out until they all vote guilty, I don't think Savano has any choice but to grant a new trial."

I heard a sigh and looked at Jackie. She sort of sunk in her chair. She had been at this for over thirty hours. Knowing her, she probably hadn't slept the previous night when she was preparing her closing argument, either.

"Jackie," I said, "why don't you go home? There's nothing we can do today."

She shook her head. "I just can't believe this," she said. "All the time and effort that went into this trial, months of investigation and research . . . four days of trial. You do everything within the system to give a guy a fair trial by a jury of his peers and then one person, one person with his own vendetta, corrupts the process."

She gave me a piercing stare. "And you know the worst part, Noah? I don't think the prosecutor or the judge is going to give a damn. I talked to Randy this morning, told him about the two jurors. I asked him if he would join in a motion for a new trial. He almost laughed me out of his office."

As I listened to Jackie, she seemed to cloud over like a fog had settled in the room. I shook my head to clear it away and I felt dizzy. Sweat started to form on my forehead and around my collar. I opened the top button of my shirt, loosened my tie, hoping to catch some air. Suddenly I had this image of somebody standing in the way of a wrecking ball, then I felt this crush to my chest and I bent over in pain. I let out a grunt and fell to the floor in a fetal position, clutching my chest. I heard Brownie holler, "He's having a heart attack! Call 911!"

Everything became hazy. I fluttered in and out of consciousness. Jackie held my hand saying, "Noah, don't you dare leave us."

I realized what was happening. My heart had finally had enough. For a moment I thought I was dead. I had heard many times about out-of-body experiences at the moment of death, and I was waiting to have my own . . . anything to get away from the pain. My mind focused on the people I would miss. I wondered what they would say at my funeral. Then there was more commotion around me and I could feel myself being lifted onto a stretcher. Voices mingled, everyone talking at once, and then a needle poked me. I felt like I was in a pool of sweat. My eyes rolled back and everything went dark.

I awoke hours later in the intensive care unit. I had tubes and needles coming out from all over me. Even though I hurt everywhere, my first thought was, "at least I'm not dead." I could feel a presence. My eyelids opened like a stuck garage door. The flood of light hurt; I had a hard time focusing. I blinked and I could make out Maggie sitting in a chair with a rosary in her hand. The sight caught me kind of by surprise. She'd never been a religious person, but she must've been covering all bets. I was under a white sheet, and I raised my hand high enough to catch her attention. She got up and walked over, an instant smile covering her face. She leaned down and kissed my cheek. A wisp of Lily of the Valley settled over me, followed by a rush of memories. Softly she said, "Don't you ever scare me like that again."

I tried to answer but my tongue seemed glued to the roof of my mouth. Maggie noticed and reached for a glass of water with a straw sitting on the bed table. I took a sip. It was lukewarm. I let it roll over my tongue and felt it pry loose. When I thought I could talk and make sense, I said, "It wasn't my idea, believe me."

She put her hand under the sheet and took my hand, squeezed it gently, and said, "Just take it easy."

I closed my eyes and said, "You know what, Maggie? Your whole life doesn't flash in front of you." A warm feeling came over me and I drifted off again.

By the following afternoon I was going stir-crazy. They had done an angiogram. The doctor explained to me all of the gruesome details. He told me I was lucky. If it hadn't been for immediate help, I probably would have died. He also told me that short of getting a new heart, there was very little they could do for me. He kept me on blood thinners, and I would get a prescription for nitroglycerin to help when I got angina. Then the doctor gave me the same old talk about my diet, alcohol, and tobacco.

* * * * *

I think in forty years of practice, I had probably stayed home three or four days because I was ill. So I never knew how bad daytime television really was. Now that's all I could do to help pass the time. I started to rate the shows from bad to really bad. I knew Maggie liked to watch some of them, and I was teasing her about the waste of time when Dr. Christopher Morgan knocked on my door. I welcomed him in. He gave Maggie a big hug and said, "Elizabeth sends her best." Then he stood over my bed looking at me, shaking his head. In his early fifties, he looked every bit the psychologist. He wore baggy suits that always appeared rumpled, hanging loosely on his small frame. He kept his dark gray hair long, as disheveled as his clothes, but his beard of the same color was neatly trimmed. It all gave him a rather shadowy appearance. Never one to look particularly cheery, which I ascribed to the fact that, like criminal lawyers, psychologists saw the worst side of life, today I could tell he had a particular concern—more than just my condition. We exchanged pleasantries. I spent fifteen minutes telling him everything that had happened. He seemed distant. When I finished, he turned to Maggie and said, "Maggie, do you think I could have a moment alone with Noah?"

"This isn't going to be business, is it?" she asked. "You know he's still in a little shaky condition."

"Don't worry about it, Maggie, I'm fine," I said.

"It's nothing like that," said Chris.

She came over and kissed me on the forehead. "I guess I'll go have a cup of coffee," she said. "Chris, when Noah's home, why don't you and Elizabeth plan on coming over some evening. Maybe we can play some cards. I'm going to make him take it easy for a while." She hugged Chris again, waved to me, and walked out.

"Christ, if you could see your face, Chris," I said. "It's like you've seen a ghost . . . or maybe you have."

He seemed to hesitate for a second as if his mind was caught between two thoughts. He stared at my face momentarily, his eyes fixed to mine, and then he averted his gaze. I could see tears welling up in his eyes. He brought his hand up to wipe one from his eyelashes.

"Noah," he said, "I'm in trouble. I know I shouldn't be laying this on you now, but there's no one else I can talk to. My whole life, my whole career, my marriage, everything is at stake." A flash of pain crossed his face. "I don't want to jeopardize your health, Noah. If you don't feel like listening to me, just say so and I'll leave."

What could I say? I couldn't tell him to get the hell out of here, and then spend the rest of the night wondering what it was all about. Besides, Chris always had a way of over-dramatizing everything, especially if he thought it was important. I guessed this might be another of those occasions.

"No," I finally said. "The doctor said I'm going to be fine. And I can tell you're going to be a basket case if I send you out of here. How would that look, a psychologist going goofy?"

He managed a half smile. He pulled up a chair, sat next to my bed, inhaled deeply. "I've really screwed up, Noah." He looked out the window. "I had sex with a patient, a very sick, neurotic patient, and I don't know how it happened."

The words hit me like a thunderbolt. From his demeanor I hadn't been sure what to expect, but certainly not that. Chris would've been the last one I could see fooling around with anybody, much less a patient. When I caught my breath, I said, "You're kidding, right?"

"I wish I were. It's a long story, Noah. We don't have to go through it all now, but I just had a session with her today; I told her it had to end, but she wouldn't take that for an answer. She said she's going to tell everybody, starting with Elizabeth. She said she'd go to the prosecutor. If she does that, I'll end up before the state board." He fixed his gaze on me. "I'd be through, Noah."

"If it's true, maybe you ought to be," I said.

"Noah, there isn't anything you can say that will make me feel worse than I already do. But I came to you as a friend, as a colleague, as somebody I respect. I don't know what to do. I need your help."

Regretting my comment, I asked, "You think she's going to carry through on her threats?"

"I don't know. Elizabeth is at her publisher this afternoon, so at least she won't be able to talk to *her* today."

I laid my head back into the pillow, closed my eyes, and tried to think. For some reason I felt obliged to help him, but I couldn't do anything from a hospital bed. I needed time.

"I can deal with her," I said. "You're going to have to smooth it over with her until I get out of here; I'll see if I can't talk some sense into her. Can you do that?"

"Yeah," he said, his head drooping. "I'll do it right away."

"Use your head," I said. "What's her name, anyway?"

Our eyes met again. He squinted, glanced away. "You're going to be pissed," he said.

I was more than pissed, I was ready to get out of the bed and strangle him. His paramour client was Cheryl Moore, the complaining witness in Jackie's rape case.

I gave my blood pressure a few minutes to quiet down. "You have to talk to somebody else," I said.

He looked shocked. "I can't. You think if I trusted anybody else I'd be here, bothering you? If I talk to somebody else, it'll be all over town."

"No, it wouldn't," I said. "No attorney you talked to could say a word."

"Yeah, right. Remember, I've been at some of your impromptu bar meetings with all the war stories."

"Yeah, but we never mention names."

"You don't have to," he replied.

"You do what I said," I replied, a hint of resignation in my voice. "Let me think about it."

He stood, took my hand. "Noah," he said, "get me through this. I'll do anything you want."

"The only thing I want," I said, "is for you to use your goddamned head. I can't believe you'd be this stupid."

He rubbed his eyes with both hands. I could tell he was totally humiliated. It had to take everything he had to come and talk to me. I couldn't send him away.

"Just give me a little bit of time," I told him. "I'll figure something out. Now you'd better get ought of here before Maggie comes back. One look at your face and she'll know something's up."

"Thank you, Noah. I don't know how I'll repay you," he said. He came forward as though he was going to hug me, but I waved him away.

Within minutes after he left, Maggie walked back in. She took one look at me and exclaimed, "Noah, what happened? You're bright red. Should I get the nurse?"

I put my hand on my pulse. It didn't seem to be racing. "No, I'm fine," I said. "Chris has just got himself a problem that's a little embarrassing."

"He should know better than to come in here and bother you."

"Maggie, really, it's okay."

She shook her head as she took the chair vacated by Chris. "Jackie called. I told her they would probably let her see you once you're out of cardiac care. The nurse told her that only family members were allowed to visit. Chris must've used his pull to get by the front desk. She said that she and Brownie are working on the motion for a new trial. I'm to tell you they have everything under control.

You shouldn't worry."

I wanted to make some smart remark like, "If they only knew." But any clue of something out of the ordinary and Maggie would have never relaxed until she got the whole story out of me. Instead I said, "I'm sure they'll do fine," and smiled as I reached for Maggie's hand, dragging my I.V. tubes across the bed sheet.

It was almost a week before I was able to see Noah. By then he was out of the cardiac care unit and in a private room. I had called him earlier to tell him I was coming.

When I got there the door to his room was partly open, so I walked in without knocking. I caught him just as he reached his bed, pulling his hospital robe around his waist. I got a flash of his tush as he turned to sit on the edge of his bed. Not bad for a guy of sixty-five, I mused. I could tell he knew I saw; he turned a shade of red as he slid under his sheets.

"Boy, am I glad to see you," I said, as I took the hand he extended. "You scared the hell out of us."

"I think Brownie saved my life," he said.

"That police training came in handy," I replied. "Good thing you didn't have to rely on me."

It was nice to talk to him. He looked good, recuperated. He said the doctors had told him there was only slight damage to his heart. He was lucky. Now they put him on a strict diet and told him exactly what he could eat. He was also going to start carrying nitroglycerin pills. The conversation turned to the office. I told him about all the calls we had gotten wishing him good luck. Eventually we got around to Clint's case. "Brownie finally got an affidavit from the juror. She apparently had gotten a little reluctant to sign something. It sounds as if she's lost some of the enthusiasm she had the morning she visited her pastor."

"You could expect that," Noah responded. "As time goes by, her passion for justice is going to cool a bit, and pretty soon she's going to wonder why she ever opened her big mouth."

"Hope not. She signed a pretty good affidavit," I replied. "We'll just have to wait and see. I don't suppose they're letting a lot of people up here."

"No, they like to keep it kind of quiet, just family. Dr. Morgan's been up here a couple times and Maggie's been here most of the time. I sent her home this afternoon to get some rest. She says she can't sleep here . . . neither can I. It was fine when they were keeping me drugged up, but now I'm raring to go."

"I don't suppose you asked Dr. Morgan about Clint's case?"

Noah turned toward the window. The little smile he wore faded and he seemed deep in thought. I took it as a clue that he didn't wish to talk about it. "Oh, I almost forgot," I said, "Linda sent this for you," and I reached in my purse and took out a book. "She said you'd enjoy this. It's a mystery."

I leaned over and handed it to him. He looked at the cover and set it on the bed alongside his leg.

"I should be getting out of here in the next day or two," he said. "It'll be a couple more days before I feel like coming back to the office."

By the time I got to the elevator, pushed the down button, a real sense of relief came over me. Ever since Noah's heart attack, not being able to see him, talk to him, I had this feeling of dread. I had pictured myself closing the office, farming out his files, trying to find a new job. He looked good. In fact, he looked better than I remembered the day of our luncheon conference. Now I could throw myself back into the task of trying to get Clint a new trial.

* * * * *

Judge Savano had set the date for our argument on the motion for a new trial the same day set for Clint's sentencing. When I called Noah at home to tell him, he started to laugh. "That's a pretty ominous sign, Jackie," he said. "If the judge's considering granting him a new trial, it would be unlikely that he'd set the hearing date for that argument on the same day as sentencing."

"It seemed unusual to me, also," I said.

"I'm sure Savano's getting a kick out of it," Noah said. "He can be a perverse bastard sometimes."

"Noah, he has to give Clint a new trial. Kaufman lied in his *voir dire*. If that's not grounds, what is?"

"You and I may believe that, but if Savano believes Clint's guilty, which I'm sure he does, he'll send him off and let you worry about justice."

There was dead air as I pondered Noah's comments. He asked, "Getting any new clients?"

"A few are trickling in here and there. Nothing big, mostly drunk driving. I got another domestic assault case, though. I postponed the court date until you're back."

More silence. Finally I said, "Are you still there, Noah?"

"Yeah, I was just thinking," he said. "What's the date on Clint's motion hearing?"

"Next Monday," I said.

"Maybe you'll see me before that," he said. We exchanged our good-byes and hung up.

* * * * *

The following Monday I sat in a little conference room off the hall outside Judge Savano's courtroom. Clint sat across from me; the same dumb stare on his face. We had both just finished reading the pre-sentence investigation. Because of the severity of the offense, the agent was recommending a substantial departure from the sentencing guidelines. The guidelines recommended forty-eight months in prison. The report recommended two hundred and forty months. Clint couldn't understand how he could even get forty-eight months for something he didn't do, and I couldn't explain to him why he should either.

"Ya know," he said, "that dumb broad couldn't even describe me. How come that jury ever believed her?"

If the comment "dumb broad" had come from any other guy, I probably would've smacked him. From Clint, in his position, I considered it more pathetic than annoying.

"Clint, you have to understand," I said, "I told you when we started this whole thing, going to trial was a risk."

"Yeah, I know," he said. "But if you're innocent, how can they find a guy guilty?"

"A mistake was made," I said, "and if the judge doesn't correct it, we'll appeal."

"I don't know," he said, leaning back in his chair. He brought his arms up from his lap and set them down heavy on the table, the silver handcuffs clanging against the oak. "Sometimes I just wish I were dead. I heard what happens in those prisons, ya know. They're telling me over at the jail, ya know, some big black guy's gonna make a lover outta me. I'd rather be dead."

I didn't know what I could tell him, that he was too big and ugly to be somebody's lover, or that such things really didn't happen, or that he really wasn't going to go to prison. I had my suspicions, but I didn't know what to say.

Minutes later we were in court and the prosecutor was addressing Judge Savano. "Your Honor," he said, "I've had an opportunity to read the report by the probation agent and his recommendation for a substantial departure from the guidelines; I couldn't agree more. In all of my years of prosecuting criminals, I've seen some terrible inhumanities perpetrated on other human beings, but I don't think I've ever seen more vile or despicable conduct as perpetrated by this defendant on a defenseless young woman."

I jumped up. "Your Honor," I said, "it was my understanding that the Court was going to consider our motion for a new trial prior to sentencing."

"I have, Ms. Geroux," he responded. "I filed a written order this morning. Didn't you get a copy of it?"

"No, I didn't."

He opened up the file, took out a sheet of paper and handed it to the deputy, who walked across the courtroom and handed it to me. The order was one sentence: *Based on all of the files and proceedings herein, the arguments of counsel, the defendant's motion for a new trial is denied.*

I could feel the tension and anger building in me. I handed the sheet back to the deputy. "Your Honor," I said, trying to retain my dignity, "I believe I had the right to supplement the record with an oral argument before that decision was made . . ."

"Ms. Geroux," he interrupted, "you don't have a right to do anything of the sort. You filed your motion; I considered it and denied it. We are here for sentencing. You will have an opportunity to speak on your client's behalf. Mr. Becker has the floor."

I took my seat, suddenly feeling like a whipped puppy. I had labored over this great argument I was going to make, spending hours the night before in front of the mirror practicing this eloquent plea for justice on behalf of this wrongly convicted defendant. My argument rang with such phrases like "to let this con-viction stand," "given such a compromise of his right to a trial by his peers," "is a corruption of the entire system," and it was all for naught. The judge didn't care. He'd made up his mind a long time ago and nothing I said, or would have said, would change anything.

The prosecutor rambled on. "This defendant," he said, "should never again see the light of day. I asked Miss Moore if she wished to be here today, if she wished to tell the Court and this defendant how his attack has affected her life. She begged me not to make her do it. She said she hopes she never has to see this man again. I don't have to tell the Court what an experience like this has done to a young woman of that age . . . and I'm willing to bet that this defendant will stand here before you, showing no remorse, continuing to profess his inno-cence, which, to me, only demonstrates how irredeemable he really is."

With the prosecutor's voice an annoying whine in the background, I thought about what comments I could make on my client's behalf. I guess I was so con-vinced that we would get a new trial, it really hadn't occurred to me that I would have to argue about Clint's sentence. There wasn't much I could say. I knew the judge was going to commit him to prison. All I could ask him to do was follow the guidelines and give Clint the forty-eight months.

It ended up being a hopeless task and a rather pitiful performance. I reiterated my client's innocence, the injustice of what happened in the jury room, and asked the judge to follow the guidelines. When I was done, the judge asked Clint if he had anything to say. I reached over and grabbed Clint by the elbow, tugged on it to make him stand. He looked at me, bewildered. Then he turned to the judge and said, "Your Judgeship, I ain't never done nothin' like that. I don't know where the girl came up with that stuff . . . but it wasn't me. My mama brung me up right. She would've rapped me on the ears if I even thunk about such things. I don't belong in no prison, your Judgeship." His voice started to break.

I glanced at him. His lower lip trembled. It was an odd sight, this huge man stooped over, trembling with fright, pleading for his freedom, and I could tell it was all falling on deaf ears. The judge didn't even look at Clint. He was doodling on a sheet in front of him. The prosecutor was nonchalantly turning pages in his trial book. Me, I was wondering what I had done wrong. How had we ended up at this moment? I was sure it had to be something I screwed up. Clint shook his head to indicate he couldn't go on, and a tear rolled down his cheek and splattered on the polished oak of the counsel table. I fixed my eyes on the pinwheel-like pattern of the wetness and listened as the judge read his sentence.

"I've made certain findings as follows: That the defendant threatened repeatedly to cause the victim great bodily harm or death; that the defendant made particularly offensive threats of bodily harm to the victim, including while holding a razor against her breast, he told her he would cut off her breasts and throw them in the garbage; that while holding the edge of the razor inside her vagina, he told her he would cut out her vagina and throw it in the garbage; that the defendant did more than threaten the victim with a dangerous weapon, but he cut her with a razor several times; that the defendant forced the victim to engage in multiple and different acts of sexual abuse, including he pinched and twisted her breasts, he forced her to masturbate his penis, he penetrated her vaginally with his hand forcefully causing her great pain; that he penetrated her orally with his penis; that he penetrated her vaginally with the handle of the razor; that he penetrated her vaginally with his penis and he masturbated and then intentionally ejaculated on her chest, and while doing so he told her she was not even worth the only thing she existed for, which was sex.

"I find that the defendant was gratuitously abusive, in that he had subjected the victim to outrageously gross and vile physical and verbal abuse and that his conduct traumatized the victim, resulting in her need of specialized counseling to overcome her deep emotional injury regarding her capacity to relate to male persons in a normal way and to redevelop self-esteem and self-worth as a female person.

"Based on all of the above, I believe this defendant belongs incarcerated for the longest term possible." He looked up from his bench for the first time, his eyes fixed first on me, then Clint. It appeared to me he was enjoying himself. In a firm voice he continued, "I order the defendant be committed to the Commissioner of Corrections for a period of two hundred and forty months."

The judge glanced at me again, obviously pleased with himself. The courtroom was dead silent. Clint turned toward me; I could see the confusion in his eyes. When it was all over, there wasn't much I could say. I don't think Clint understood anything the judge had said. I don't think it really dawned on him that two hundred and forty months was twenty years, that he could spend most of the rest of his life behind bars. The deputy slapped the handcuffs on him again and led him toward the door. Clint followed like a trained bear at a carnival.

That was the lowest point in my short career. I'd watched all of the television programs and I'd been sucked in by the glamour of being this big shot defense attorney: the money, the notoriety, and the press clamoring for an interview after my latest victory. I never envisioned standing here, watching my client being led off in chains to spend most of his life in prison, and believing it was all my fault.

I didn't go back to the office. I went to my apartment, got out a bottle of wine I had been saving for a special occasion, and slowly got drunk. I couldn't shake my thoughts all night. I had terrible dreams. I tossed and turned and finally crawled out of bed feeling like I had been in a marathon wrestling match all night. My morning calendar was clear and I was in no hurry to get to the office. I put on a pot of coffee and turned on *Good Morning America*. I was about to gulp down a couple aspirins when the phone rang. It was Noah.

"Jackie," he said, "I'm at the office. Can you meet me at the jail as quickly as possible?"

"Sure. What's up?"

"Dr. Morgan's been arrested . . . for the murder of Cheryl Moore."

8

I never got a chance to talk to Cheryl Moore and she never got a chance to tell her story to anybody else, at least not in person. From what I could piece together that morning from talking to Chris and the detective, Cheryl had not been heard from for two days. It was believed that the last person to talk to her, other than the murderer, was the prosecutor, Randy Becker, when he called her to see if she intended to testify at Clint's sentencing hearing. That was early Monday morning. On Tuesday morning, after receiving a call from one of her friends at school, the caretaker of her apartment building went in with the master key and found her body sprawled on the bed. She'd been dead for some time. Detective Kropp told me the body had been mutilated and, in his opinion, then posed to make it look like some sort of ritualistic murder.

In the search of her room, hidden in a shoebox in her closet, Detective Kropp found a little wooden box. Inside was a diary with an account of every therapy session she'd had with Chris. Kropp didn't tell me the details but I could imagine. There was also a pack of letters wrapped in a red rubber band, letters that Chris had sent to her which verified almost everything contained in the diary. They found a monogrammed white shirt with the initials C.M., a small lipstick smear on the collar, probably the reason it was left behind, he surmised. They also lifted numerous fingerprints that were sent in for identification. Detectives went to see Chris early that morning. He refused to talk without me present, and they took him into custody.

* * * * *

I walked into the jail and picked up the phone. The guard behind the glass looked out. "Noah, it's kinda soon for you to be back at work, isn't it?"

"Good morning, Eddie," I said. "I guess there's no rest for the wicked. You

48

have a friend of mine in here."

"Dr. Morgan, I presume," he replied.

"Yes," I said. "I'm waiting for my assistant. As soon as she arrives, we need in."

"Sure, Noah," he replied.

I took a chair and picked up the morning newspaper. The story broke too late to be covered, but the press would be all over it today and the next edition would have it splashed on the front page.

The waiting room had big glass doors to the outside. I saw Jackie's car go by, and moments later she came running from the parking lot. She wore dark blue slacks with a light blue blouse. Her hair bounced on her head as she jogged across the road. She darted through the doors and stood above me. I motioned for her to sit down.

"What do you know about this?" she asked.

I told her what I had found out that morning. I also told her what Chris had told me at the hospital. Her eyes grew wider as the story unfolded. When I took a pause, she just shook her head. "That creep," she mumbled, as she brushed back the black curl that slowly slid over her left eye.

"That's not a good attitude for a defense attorney to have," I said. "You don't know the whole story."

"Screw the whole story," she said. "That . . . that . . . how could he do such a thing?"

"Jackie," I said, "he wants me to represent him. I have my doubts whether I should. But, if they make a case against him, and I take it, you're going to have to help. So put those thoughts aside . . . and keep an open mind."

She nodded in agreement.

"Now, let's go in, but keep the peace. As this plays out, you'll have plenty of opportunity to find out what happened. Okay?" She nodded again. I could tell she was fuming.

The jailer let us in and led us to the professional visiting area, a small cell with a wood table screwed to the floor, two chairs, and a little rectangular window barely wide enough to put your arm through. We both took a chair. It was quiet. The only sound was the clanging of steel doors somewhere in the belly of the jail. Then we heard an electronic latch open and soft steps on the tile floor in the hall. I stood up and looked out. It was Chris. They had him dressed in jail garb as loose and baggy as any suit he ever wore. His hair was messy and stood out in every direction. His face was void of color except for his eyes, which were red and raw. They had issued him cotton slippers that scuffed along the floor as he walked. I reached out my hand. He shook it without saying a word. We walked into the conference room and he was startled to see Jackie. He looked at me.

"You know Jackie," I said. "If I'm going to be involved with this, she's going to be involved."

He nodded in compliance and then quickly exclaimed, "I didn't kill her, Noah! I did exactly what you told me to; I met with her that afternoon right after I left the hospital. I told her she had to give me some time to work it out, that I would take care of her. If that meant leaving Elizabeth, I would do it. She was satisfied with that, Noah, really she was. I was going to do just what you said, wait until you could talk to her."

"I talked to Detective Kropp this morning," I said. "He told me about her diary and your letters."

He bent his head, shook it in disbelief. "How could I have been so stupid?" he mumbled. "She never told me about the diary. I thought she destroyed my letters."

"Chris, look at me," I said. "All I wanna know is one thing." He raised his head and our eyes met. "Did you kill her?"

"You know better than that, Noah. I could never do anything like that."

"Even in desperation?" I asked.

"I told you everything," he said. "I knew what the consequences would be. If you couldn't have helped me reason with her, I would've had no choice but to take the consequences. My punishment. I would've killed myself before I killed her."

I believed him. From that day in the hospital until the call this morning, it never crossed my mind that he would harm that young woman. But I thought many times that, rather than face everybody in his embarrassment; he could easily do himself in. Because it was something that came up with his patients, we had talked about suicide many times. In certain circumstances he didn't consider it wrong and even planned how he would do it quickly and painlessly. I relied on that conversation, once, to help a friend, but I never told Chris—I never told anybody.

"That's all I needed to hear," I said. "I never thought you did. Now I have to find out what the cops think they have. You don't talk to anybody, hear?"

"I know better than that, Noah."

I looked at Jackie. Her eyes were frozen on him. I could imagine what was going through her mind. I tapped her on the shoulder. "I guess you and I will go over to see Detective Kropp," I said.

She nodded.

"Chris," I said, "the prosecutor has to decide what he's going to do in thirty-six hours. So if he doesn't think they have enough to charge you by tomorrow at noon, you'll be cut loose. If they want an indictment for first-degree murder, it has to go to a grand jury. We should know by late this afternoon. I'll get back to you."

"Did you talk to Elizabeth?" he asked.

"Yes, I did. I called her. Maggie called her too. She went over to keep her company. I told Elizabeth there's no way you could've done this . . . but she doesn't understand any of it . . . neither does Maggie, neither do I."

We started toward the door and the thought crossed my mind again. "You're not going to do anything stupid . . . to yourself, I mean?"

"Don't worry, Noah." And he took my hand and shook it.

I could see the tears being held back.

As we made our way down the hall to talk to Detective Kropp, Jackie didn't say a word. She walked by my side, keeping her thoughts to herself.

"You're awfully quiet," I said.

"Noah," she said, "I'm really having a hard time fathoming how something like this could happen. What did that old geezer think he was doing?"

I had to grin. Chris was probably fifteen years younger than I. If he was an old geezer, I could imagine what she thought of me.

Detective Kropp was standing in front of his office as we rounded the corner. When he saw me, he immediately held out his hand and gave me a big, friendly handshake. "I'm glad to see you back, Noah," he said. "You gave us all a scare.

51

Not too many honest attorneys around anymore that we can afford to lose one."

He made the comment while looking at Jackie. Then he reached out his hand to her. "Jackie, nice seeing you again."

I could tell something else was on the tip of his tongue but he held back.

Detective Kropp and I went back years. Our first encounter was at an evidentiary hearing where I was attempting to get a confession suppressed because Kropp held the guy in custody too long before he got him in court. The judge agreed with my argument and the prosecutor ended up dismissing the complaint. Though it was embarrassing to Kropp at the time, he realized he had screwed up and that even though his collar walked because of his error, he knew he would never make the same mistake again. The next time we met it was obvious to me that he didn't hold any grudges, which told me something about his character.

Now in his early fifties, he had lost all of that curly blonde hair he had back then. His face was tan and leathery, his nose red and peeling from all of the hours he spent in his fishing boat. But he still carried himself like that young beat cop, tall and erect, muscular, not an ounce of fat. He had blue eyes that seemed to have grown tired with the years, or probably from the pain of dealing with all the crap he had seen. He was always honest with me, and I had a tremendous respect for him.

As we sat around the conference table, he got us a cup of coffee. He had several files on his desk, one marked "PHOTOS." As he sat down, he said, "The body was taken to the medical examiner this morning for an autopsy. The cause of death appeared to be a slit throat . . . just a question of what was first. The body was badly mutilated, like the attacker had really flipped out."

"Bob," I interjected, "you know Chris. He couldn't do anything like that."

He let out a deep sigh. "He's been involved as a therapist in some of the cases I've had over the years, and I guess I'd have to agree . . . but then I couldn't ever imagine he would do the things described in her diary, either. I have to look at motive, Noah. Who else would have a motive? Jackie's client, Clint? He's in jail. To our knowledge, nobody else was involved with her." He reached into a file and brought out a little red-covered notebook. "I'll read you her last entry." He turned the pages and stopped:

*Chris was here today. He told me that he had thought it over and that I was right, that we belonged together. He wanted me to give him some time. He was going to tell Elizabeth about us, then we would get married, move to California. I was so happy I started crying and then he hugged me.*

Kropp looked up at me. I had made a sound like somebody had kicked me in the stomach. My own words echoed, my advice to Chris, and now it may well be the one piece of evidence that would send him to prison for the rest of his life. I'd had my advice come back and bite me in the ass before, but this one took a real chunk. But it had never, in my wildest imagination, occurred to me that he would tell her he was leaving his wife. He must've been more desperate than I'd imagined.

"Are you okay, Noah?" he asked.

"Just a little indigestion."

"From what I've seen, this was one disturbed young woman," he continued. "I can't see Dr. Morgan deciding that he was going to spend his life with her, and if she's putting pressure on him, going public . . . well, you can imagine the rest. From what I read, I suspect his fingerprints are going to come back all over the place."

For a few moments we all sat silently. Then Kropp said quietly, "There's no one else out there, Noah. It was him."

"But why the mutilation, Bob? That's what I don't understand. If he wanted to simply kill her to shut her up, why wouldn't he just do it, you know, clean?"

"I have my own theory of that, too," Kropp replied. "At this point it's all been turned over to Randy. We're going to convene a grand jury. In the meantime, I think we have enough to charge him with second-degree murder."

It was one of those times where everybody knew the meeting was over. We all stood up without saying a word. Kropp gathered up his files, and the one marked "PHOTOS" fell from his arm onto the table, spilling Polaroid pictures onto the table in front of us. Jackie gasped. They showed a naked body lying on a bed, her legs spread-eagled, and her face contorted, twisted in an unnatural way. Where her breasts had been there were now just gaping wounds, and almost her entire body was pocked with stab wounds.

Kropp quickly gathered them up, then looked at Jackie and said, "I'm sorry."

Before that day in the jail I had only seen Dr. Morgan twice. The first time was when Cheryl Moore testified in Clint's trial, the second was when he sat next to her during closing arguments. Sitting next to Cheryl, he struck me as a strange little man, almost spooky. But in talking to other attorneys, I discovered he had a good reputation. He was, I was told, one of the few psychologists in town willing to deal with issues important to women, like domestic abuse. He volunteered many hours at the local battered women's shelter.

After meeting him at jail that day, my mind was overloaded. I told Noah I needed some time to think. I was so angry. I couldn't clear the pictures of Cheryl from my mind. I knew where Noah stood, and I was simply afraid that I would say something that would jeopardize both our professional and personal relationships. I had grown to love Noah. I respected his legal abilities, but more than that, he was a wonderful person. So I knew I had to trust his instincts, but it was tough.

I had no idea what all this had to do with Clint's case, if anything. He was already off to prison. I could proceed with my appeal and if we won, I assumed the state would have to dismiss. They no longer had a client. That was the first time the thought crossed my mind: maybe Clint had somebody who was out for a little revenge. But that was unlikely. It didn't appear that anybody even cared what happened to him.

Then I wondered what was in those letters. If we handled Dr. Morgan's case, what would I discover about Cheryl Moore?

Noah called me later in the afternoon. He asked me how I was doing. I told him that I was still struggling. Everything had happened so fast. We talked for a while and I started to feel a little better.

"I just got off the phone with Detective Kropp," he said. "They identified some of the fingerprints in her apartment. Many of them belong to Chris.

Kropp honestly thinks they have this thing sewed up. They're going to get him in court tomorrow morning with a charge of second-degree murder and then take it to the grand jury."

"You really didn't expect anything different, did you?" I asked.

"Not really, I guess," he said. "They certainly have motive, but I still can't see Chris doing such awful things to that woman. There's something rotten here, and we have to find out what."

I didn't have the same doubts that plagued Noah. I knew that a man in a rage could be capable of anything. I agreed to meet Noah the next morning in court a little before nine.

\* \* \* \* \*

As I pulled up to the courthouse the next morning, I knew immediately that we were in the middle of something. Numerous television vans were parked out front; reporters from all over the state were there. I could see the headlines: *"Prominent Doctor Charged in Brutal Slaying of Paramour Patient."* It had the necessary ingredients for a sensational story: sex and violence.

The hall to the courtroom was filled with people. I had to elbow my way through. When I got to the door of the courtroom, Frank was standing there surveying the scene. "Noah's in the conference room with your client," he said.

When I walked in, I was surprised to see another woman. She was small, much shorter than I, and dressed in a dark gray business suit. Her hair was combed neatly, tied in a bun, salt and pepper colored. She had a plain face; she wore no makeup and her eyes showed the pain. I knew she was the doctor's wife. We were introduced. She took my hand, and her hand felt limp and fragile, like I could have crushed it with no effort at all. Her lips broke into a smile. "Noah's been saying such nice things about you, Jackie. I just feel that Chris is in such good hands with you and Noah."

"We were just talking about bail, Jackie," Noah said. "I talked to the judge and the prosecutor this morning. They want a hundred grand. Chris is going to get a bondsman, put their house up as collateral. So we should be able to get him out today. The prosecutor will give me a copy of the file after the hearing.

It'll probably take the rest of the day to digest all of that. I'm suggesting we have a meeting tomorrow morning, first thing."

I nodded in agreement.

Noah stood up. "Well, let's go face the circus." He looked at Elizabeth Morgan. "You up to this?" he asked. "You don't have to come in, you know."

"I'm fine," she said. "How does the song go? Stand by your man."

Noah gave her a hug. I noticed her hands were trembling.

\* \* \* \* \*

Everything went as expected. Judge Savano read the charge: "Murder in the second degree—that on the 14th day of July, 1986, the defendant did cause the death of Cheryl Moore with intent to affect said death, but without premeditation."

Bail was set at a hundred thousand dollars. Following the reading of the complaint, the prosecutor handed Noah a file, probably three inches thick, and the parties agreed to set a new hearing date approximately a month out. Until bail was posted, Dr. Morgan was remanded to the custody of the sheriff.

We were about to leave when Noah grabbed my arm and motioned to Elizabeth. "If you go out there now, you're going to be swamped by the press," he said. "Let Randy have his big show. Let's stay in here a few minutes and hopefully we can avoid the commotion."

He turned to Elizabeth. "Did you have any idea any of this was going on between Chris and Cheryl?"

"I kinda feel partly at fault, Noah. I've been so busy at the office; I haven't been able to spend a whole lot of time with Chris. He talked about this . . . this patient a lot when we did get a chance to talk, but it was always how sorry he felt for her. He never really went into why, but I gathered he considered her pretty pathetic. I can't imagine him being seduced like that."

Seduced! That's an interesting term for her to use, I thought. I watched her, and she struck me as a rather pathetic figure. I could see her mind working. She'd already turned it around: poor Dr. Morgan was seduced by this jezebel. *He* obviously wouldn't have seduced *her*.

They continued to talk as my mind wandered. I was trying to imagine the kind of relationship Elizabeth and Dr. Morgan had. Both professional people, both bright, no children, consumed by their work, they probably didn't have much for personal lives. I could see Cheryl Moore, a young attractive woman, spending hours in therapy with Dr. Morgan talking over sexual matters, all the things she claimed Clint had done to her. Would Cheryl have seduced Dr. Morgan, or would she have relied on him to help her through the whole ugly ordeal? I had my own suspicion.

Noah handed me the file given to him by the prosecutor. "I'm going with Elizabeth to get him bailed out," he said. "You can take the file back to the office; we'll go over it this afternoon."

When we walked out of the courtroom, the hall was empty. As we got to the ground floor of the courthouse, I could see Randy Becker on the courthouse steps standing in front of television cameras, microphones being pushed in his face, and I could tell he was enjoying every moment of it. Several reporters saw Noah and Elizabeth and started to run toward us. I quickly did an about-face and went out the back door. As I left, I could hear Noah saying he had no comment.

I immediately went back to the office, told Linda I wasn't taking any calls, grabbed a cup of coffee, and sat down at my desk.

There was really nothing in law school or my brief legal career that had prepared me for what I was about to see and read. When the first officer arrived at the scene, he knew, from experience, that the smell emanating from the apartment meant a dead body. He found Cheryl's body on the bed, naked, legs spread-eagled. Her throat had been slashed from ear to ear, her body covered with stab wounds. The officer counted up to thirty and then stopped. Her breasts were severed even with her chest. Her body appeared devoid of blood.

In the file was an 8x10 envelope stamped "PHOTOS." I hesitated to open it, but I knew I would have to look at them again sooner or later. I placed the envelope on my desk, opened the lid and inserted my index finger, sliding out the first photograph as I felt my breath leave my body. My first thought was that I hoped he'd slit her throat before he did the rest. It was like nothing I had ever seen. I looked at the face in the photos. Her eyes were wide open, a smoky glaze over them. My mind flashed back to Cheryl on the witness stand, those eyes dark brown, animated, darting back and forth across the faces of the jurors, tearing up as she recalled the rape. I could hear her voice, almost hysterical, as she described to the jurors what Clint had done to her. The thought struck me that at the time she testified, I didn't believe any of it. I wondered, in fact, how she'd managed to tell her story with such sincerity when I believed it was all a figment of her imagination. My only urge was to crucify her. Now I felt only pity. I slid a few more photographs out. I had seen the worst. I turned to the medical examiner's report. He put technical terms to everything I saw:

*Present is a gaping 8 x 5 cm. incised wound that extends transversally across the neck, centered 19 cm. from the top of the head. When apposed, the same wound measures 10.0 x 0.2 cm. The superior larder exhibits a definite scalloped appearance. The slice severed skin, platysma, a superficial fascia; the right sternocleidomastoid muscle; the right anterior jugular vein; the right superior thyroid artery and vein; the right facial nerve, superficial cervical branches; the left strap muscles (all); the left internal carotid artery and jugular vein; the right internal carotid artery; the right internal jugular vein; the right vagus nerve; the left vagus nerve; the tyro-hyoid ligament; and the larynx.*

It went on in gruesome detail, outlining every puncture wound, every scrape and abrasion. The medical examiner couldn't pinpoint the time of death, but his best estimate was eighteen to twenty-four hours before she was found. The air-conditioning had been turned off; the apartment was warm, making time of death problematic.

By then I was less than a half of an inch into a three-inch pile of documents. As I read on, I started to get this sick feeling way down in the pit of my stomach. The records included medical reports of therapy sessions she had after an attempt at suicide. The attempt was at age sixteen. It followed a visit with her father whom she claimed she had not seen for years. What followed was a real shocker. She related that her father had sexually abused her as a child, beginning at age six or seven, until her parents got divorced when she was thirteen. She then moved in with an aunt who had a teenage son. She reported that the son raped her numerous times and threatened to kill her if she told anyone. At age eighteen she basically emancipated herself, completed high school, and entered college. In her discharge summary, after the suicide attempt, the doctor wrote:

*Patient reports being sexually abused by father. Psychological testing shows no thought disorder. Some depression indicated. Dealing with incest issue has been very stressful for her, culminating in thoughts of suicide. MMPI result suggests indications of someone who is possibly exaggerating her difficulties, perhaps in an attempt to impress upon others her need for help.*

I leaned back in my chair, my mind swimming in confusion. I had known none of this. There wasn't the slightest hint of any psychological problems in her background in the discovery I received in Clint's case, not a word. From what I knew, her allegations against Clint were the first time she'd ever experienced any sexual abuse. I couldn't help but feel sorry for her. I was even feeling guilty that I had given her a tough time on cross-examination.

I felt my whole body tense up as the anger swelled in me. Why do we always have to end up being the victims? I just couldn't believe it. How could her dad use her like that? And her cousin? Do some of us have "victim" written all over our faces? I was afraid *I* did. I had my own experience in law school, one that left such an impact on me that it still haunted me.

In my second year of law school I met a man, Steve, who was in his last year of medical school. For me it was like a dream. He was handsome, brilliant, from a wealthy family. He wanted to be a heart surgeon. The first time he kissed me, told me he loved me; I thought I had died and gone to heaven.

At the time I lived in an old house off campus with five other girls. My room was an eight-by-ten cubbyhole in what was once the fruit cellar. Steve talked me into moving in with him. I didn't need much persuasion. He had a nice two-bedroom apartment in a new high-rise complex a block from the main campus.

Our relationship started out beautifully, studying together, spending hours talking about our future, what we both dreamed of doing, the adventures we'd seek. Then, slowly, almost imperceptibly, he started to change. I had moved in with him in October. By Thanksgiving I realized he wasn't the person I thought he was, and by Christmas I had my first black eye. At first it was just little things. He would be upset with the way I ate, the way I combed my hair, or a comment I made when we were with his friends. I always brushed it off as the pressure of medical school.

Then one night we went to a local bar after we both had tests and met a few friends for drinks. I made a comment about a case I had read where the doctor was sued for malpractice. It led to an argument and in a huff he said, "Lawyers are just a bunch of leeches, living off all the other professions." His words were not said in jest. At the bar I quickly changed the subject, but when we got back to his apartment, he renewed it with a vengeance. When I tried to come into the bedroom to tell him it was no big deal, he pushed me out, told me to sleep on the couch, and then slammed the door, the doorknob catching my hip and knocking me into the hall as I cringed in pain.

I should have gotten out that night. I should have packed my bags and left. But I truly loved him, and it was easy to rationalize, to blame it on the pressure of medical school. After all, I should have known better than to open my big mouth about something that would be that sensitive to him.

So I slept on the couch, got up early, made breakfast and waited to be forgiven. That took several days. He came home from school three nights later with a magnum of wine. We had a candlelight dinner and made love. He told me he was sorry. My newfound bliss lasted for just a week. The next time we drank wine, he got drunk and turned mean. He said the most terrible things about me, things I never thought crossed his mind. Finally I'd had enough. I stood up, told him he knew where to stick it, and then waited defiantly, expecting some apology. I didn't see his hand coming across the table, but I heard the crunching sound of cartilage as he caught my nose. My head was spinning, my mind in a daze. I heard the tinkling of plastic buttons bouncing off the hardwood floor. I could feel the cool air covering my bare breasts, then his hand pawing at me. I tried to say something, but I was choking on my own blood. He lifted me off my feet, carried me into the bedroom and threw me on the bed. In my daze, I couldn't fathom what he was up to, but the bastard raped me. It only took him minutes to finish and he was off, out the door, slamming it behind him. I lay on that bed like Cheryl Moore, spread-eagle, my panties around my left ankle. I could feel the warm blood pooling up in my cheek to flow out over my lips and onto the pillow. I laid there swearing at him, calling him every name in the book but under my breath hoping that he didn't hear, that he was gone.

I couldn't believe it. In a matter of just a few months, my dream had turned to a nightmare. Why me? I had been so careful. I wasn't going to give myself to just anybody. I had to love him and I had to believe I was going to be with him forever. The bizarre part is that as I got up and looked in the mirror, saw my nose twisted, the left side of my face swelling, the blood running down my cheek onto my bare breasts, I still wondered what I had done wrong.

Steve was gone. I packed as quickly as I could and left. I moved in with one of my girlfriends from law school. She told me to turn him in but I didn't. Steve didn't know where I was. The next day as I left law school, he was standing in the street waiting for me. I tried to walk by him but he grabbed my arm. He was apologetic, crying, wanting me to give him another chance. For just a fleeting moment, I weakened. I was about to throw my arms around him when I felt a tug at my arm. It was my friend, Gina. "Come on, Jackie," she said, "we've got some studying to do. You don't wanna waste your time with a jerk like him."

The smile quickly disappeared from his face and I saw the anger, the meanness in his eyes I had noticed the night before, seconds before he hit me. I knew Gina was right, and I turned and walked away.

For the rest of the school year he haunted me. His split personality continued, alternating between sending me flowers, gifts, invitations to expensive concerts, to ugly notes with threats, and phone calls in the middle of the night. I had the constant feeling that he was behind every bush, every parked car, and every door. The intimidations didn't end until he graduated that spring and left for an internship in New York City.

The experience clouded every contact I had with men. On every date, I knew I was, consciously or subconsciously, conducting a psychological assessment of the guy sitting across from me, trying to determine if he posed any threat. This had a tendency to put a damper on any ardor I may otherwise have been inclined to display. I think some guys actually sensed some ulterior motive to my questions and I never heard from them again.

I worked hard to overcome my tendency to be too cautious, and I thought I had managed to do so, until the first time this guy came into the public defender's office and I had to represent him on a charge of assaulting his wife. He sat across the desk from me and, in his most syrupy voice, told me how he hadn't really hit her. What had happened is that they had been arguing, she came at him, her arms swinging. All he did was put his arms up in self-defense and pushed her away. The floor was slippery and she fell and hit her face on the edge of the table. That's how she got the big cut. After listening to him, without saying a word in response, I stood up, walked into the next office and told my boss, "You have to find somebody else to represent this guy."

When he asked me why, I told him that I was a victim of sexual and physical abuse and if this guy's defense was left up to me, I'd walk him over to court, plead him guilty and try to get him life. I had to admit that wasn't a very good attitude for a criminal defense attorney, but I was just being honest with him. He was very understanding, said he'd find someone else.

I shook my head to clear the thoughts, continued with the file in front of me, paging through until I hit a sheaf of handwritten pages. It was Cheryl's diary. The handwriting was like a child's, almost scribbling. The first entry I had was dated March 11, 1986. It was a month after Clint had been arrested. I saw Dr. Morgan's name mentioned. As I read, my heart raced, my eyes glued to the pages. Thirty minutes later, I leaned back, feeling like I may vomit. Her diary was a childlike recollection of her sessions with Dr. Morgan. She believed she would never be able to enjoy sex. She had been sexually abused by her father, then her cousin, and finally, after what happened with Clint, she felt dirty. She had never experienced one moment of joy from sex. She related how Dr. Morgan sought to convince her otherwise. She wrote:

*I like Dr. Morgan. He told me that I was wrong, that sex with somebody you love is beautiful, one of the true joys of life. He said he would help me overcome my dread. That my feelings weren't right, not healthy. When I told him he was wrong, he laughed. He asked me, 'Do you wanna go through life believing sex is painful? That what you've experienced to this point is all there is to it?' I told him I didn't. That I wanted to be married, to have children. He said he would help me and I believe him.*

It started innocently enough, I suppose, with Dr. Morgan ending the session by hugging her, making her feel comfortable in a warm embrace from a man. But it didn't stop there. Within weeks they were lying on the floor, their groins together. According to her, Dr. Morgan was going to teach her how to masturbate. She wrote:

*All men have ever wanted is to hurt me. Things they have done to me make me feel dirty. Dr. Morgan says I have to get used to a man hugging me, caressing me, knowing that it can be a joy, and he's going to help me reach those feelings.*

He helped her all right. A week later he's got his hand down her pants, rubbing her vagina, telling her, "See, you don't have to be afraid, it can be good."

She went on to tell how he kissed her breasts, then her vulva, and how she experienced her first orgasm. From that point, according to her diary, every session became sex. It got to where they would lock the door. One of the colleagues down the hall heard about the locked-door sessions and became concerned. Dr. Morgan was apparently able to convince him that as they got closer to the trial date, he had to spend more time with her to get her through the trauma.

After the trial, she wrote she would have never made it through without Dr. Morgan's help. She now knew they were madly in love. She said that he told her he was going to leave his wife, that they would move to California, get married, and he could start a new practice. Knowing she was young, naive and probably helpless, I assumed she believed it.

I don't think I had ever been so angry. I was angry at Dr. Morgan. I was angry at Cheryl. I was angry at myself, at my gender. How stupid do women have to get, I wondered, to fall for crap like that? Is it so ingrained in us that somehow we have to have a man in our life that we'll succumb to every flattery, every con job thrown our way? If Dr. Morgan had been there that moment, I don't know what I would have done. He had to be guilty of her murder. He had to know that if their relationship ever got out, the fact that he had psychologically conned a young, lonely, pathetic girl into performing with him every kind of sexual fantasy he had ever imagined, that his reputation, his career, everything, would be shot.

It was almost noon by the time I got back to my office. Jackie's door was closed and I knocked and heard a weak, "Come in."

She was behind her paper-strewn desk, her face flushed, her eyes weepy. It caught me by surprise. "What's wrong?" I asked.

"This!" she said with a wave of her arms over her desk. "This! This abomination. You're not going to believe it, Noah. I know Dr. Morgan's your friend, but if I had him here now, I'd kick him squarely right between his legs. He seduced that poor girl under the guise of healing, if you can believe it."

I had no idea what she had found in those reports, but I could tell it had torn her up. She gave me a brief summary while I sat there, stunned, shaking my head in disbelief.

Jackie went on. "Her head's messed up because of the sexual abuse by her dad, and Dr. Morgan cons her into believing that if she has sex with him, she'll realize sex doesn't have to hurt. Can you imagine that? And this poor girl is so lost and lonely that she believes that crap. She even starts to call him 'Daddy' and he calls her 'Sugar.' Read the letters, Noah, the letters between the two of them. They're sick!"

I listened without saying a word. When she was done, she leaned back in her chair, let out a sigh, and crossed her hands over her stomach, pain visible in her eyes.

Always the defense attorney, being the devil's advocate, I said, "Maybe it was therapeutic. Maybe there's a school of psychiatry that believes . . ."

"Don't even go there, Noah," she interrupted. "I already assumed that's what the good doctor will probably argue. If you can get anybody to buy that crap, you're a better attorney than I thought. The school of perverse psychiatry." She grinned and then clutched her stomach tighter.

"Are you all right?" I asked.

"My stomach is tied in knots."

"Do you want to go home?"

"I can't," she replied. "I have to be in court at 1:30 for a second appearance on a domestic assault. I wasn't sure if you'd be back so I agreed to stand in for you, but after today, the case is yours."

I didn't argue with her. "Let's go to lunch then."

"I couldn't eat," she said.

"Well, then give me the part of the file you're done with. I'll look it over."

"You can take the whole thing," she said. "I don't think I can take any more of this today."

I gathered the file and went back to my office. I poured myself a cup of coffee and started paging through, picking out a page here and there to read. When I got to the stack of letters Cheryl saved from Dr. Morgan, I could understand Jackie's disgust. If I hadn't known who had written them, I would have suspected that they were notes being handed over desktops in junior high. The language and imagery were juvenile. There were ten letters in all, the longest two pages, and the shortest about a half a page. In the earliest letters the sexual overtones were subtle, but the sexual context became more overt as their sexual relationship progressed. They started to read like a cheap novel.

Under his letters in the file was a copy of her diary. I started to page through. Jackie was right. Anyone reading the diary would conclude that Dr. Morgan slowly and methodically manipulated the sessions to get into her pants. I could picture the prosecutor, Randy Becker, standing in front of the jury in Dr. Morgan's murder trial, self-righteous as hell, cutting my client into little pieces.

As I leaned back in my chair to contemplate the mess Chris had made, I could feel my whole body tense up. I knew this wasn't going to be good for me. I was too close to it. But for the life of me, I couldn't picture Chris murdering Cheryl. I couldn't even imagine that he would do it in sheer desperation. Even though his behavior with Cheryl was despicable, he wasn't the first middle-aged man who started to think with his pecker and got himself into a life-shattering predicament. I had seen it before, many times, and it had never led to murder.

So if Chris didn't do it, somebody else did. But who had the motive? The manner of death spoke for itself. The killer must have been in a rage. Who would have been that angry with her to evoke such a vicious attack? I knew we had to start digging into her past, learn about boyfriends, her sexual habits, and her reputation. There had to be a clue someplace.

My mind was drifting rather aimlessly when Jackie knocked on my door. After I told her what I was thinking, I could see a film of disgust, verging on anger, cross her face. "I know Chris didn't do this, Jackie. We have to find out who did." The comment settled like cold fog in the room. Jackie's face flushed, her hands grasped the arms of the chair. "You don't agree, do you?" I asked.

"Have you read that file?" she asked.

"Enough," I replied.

"Can you imagine how embarrassing that would've been to Dr. Morgan if that all got out? Just the threat of the letters, making that public . . ."

"He's not a killer," I interjected.

She gave a "humph," leaned back in the chair, and eased her grip. "Noah," she said, "he's a doctor, a psychologist, for Christ's sake. He's supposed to be a mature, intelligent professional. Instead, he's writing letters to this girl in a language you wouldn't expect from a teenager in heat. If she threatened to release those . . ."

"Now, Jackie," I interrupted, "if he was going to kill her over that, why wouldn't he get the letters? Why would they still have been in her closet, hidden?"

That comment seemed to catch her by surprise. She was quiet for a moment. "There are all kinds of explanations," she said. "He could've thought she destroyed them. She could've told him she'd destroyed them. He could've murdered her and then looked for 'em and not found 'em."

"You believe he did it?" I said.

"Noah, the pathologist did a sexual assault kit . . . there was no sign of rape. No semen! If this was some sort of sexual assault gone bad, or some sexual pervert, you'd expect some sign of rape. Doesn't that seem to indicate to you that her murder was the motive? I don't see anybody else, Noah."

"Because you aren't looking. You've let his sexual indiscretions shadow your thinking. And just because there's no sign of sexual assault, semen, that doesn't mean anything. I've seen that before. You have to remember, sexual assault isn't just about sex, it's about power. But I'm not trying to justify what Chris did to her. When I read the reports I got just as disgusted as you, but I've seen the face of a murderer, many times, and I don't see that in Chris."

"No disrespect, Noah, but I don't believe that. People aren't always what you think they are."

Her comment made me pause for a moment. I knew she was right. People could always manage to surprise you. But this was more visceral. In my gut I just knew Chris hadn't done it. "Where does that put us, then?" I asked. "You and me? We have to defend him."

"I've been struggling with that, Noah. I look at those pictures, that mutilated body . . . then I think back to the courtroom. For all of her problems, she was a beautiful young woman. She didn't deserve to be dumped on, and she certainly didn't deserve to end up with her throat cut."

"I know that, Jackie. But what I'm asking is if you can defend him. Can you put your personal feelings aside? He's entitled to the best representation we can give him. At this point, until I'm convinced otherwise, that includes believing he's innocent."

She stared at me, the veins in her temple pulsating as she ground her teeth.

"You have to decide this right, Jackie. If you're serious about being a criminal defense attorney, you don't have the luxury of saying I'm only going to defend the innocent. You wouldn't have many clients. I believe you're familiar with the presumption of innocence. If the system's going to work, you have to make the State do its job, and that's regardless of how guilty your client is, or you think he is."

"I know all of that, Noah," she replied. "It's just that when you're reading it in the law books, it all seems so simple. Now that I put faces, real people on it . . ."

I knew what she was struggling with. Over the years, on numerous occasions, from grade school kids to friends of mine, including people I considered intelligent, I was always asked the same question: how could I represent somebody who has committed an atrocious crime when I know they're guilty? I had explained it many times in very simple terms: that's my job. For Jackie, given the circumstances she now found herself in, it appeared she hadn't quite reached that simple conclusion. Or, more to the point, if she had, she wasn't quite certain that was the kind of job she wanted.

I was about to say something when my secretary buzzed me. Jackie had a phone call from Johnny Connors and he said it was important. Jackie seemed surprised, and she said she'd talk to me later.

I went back to reading the file. After going through the medical examiner's report, I understood Jackie's feelings a little better. To her, Cheryl was much more than cold words on a medical examiner's report. She could recall a face, hear a voice, and picture her move. To me, it was just another autopsy report, like many over the years, which I looked at with an eye of a defense attorney: How does this report damage my client's case?

"This is Jackie."

"Jackie, Johnny Connors. I was wondering if you might have a few minutes free for a cup of coffee or something. I would like to talk to you."

My mind flashed back to what Frank, the court reporter, had told me, that Johnny had shown some interest in me. I wondered if this was a preface to a date. My mind was still reeling from the information in Cheryl's file and my discussion with Noah, but it seemed a good way to change the subject. "Sure," I said. "How about if I meet you at the O.K. Café?"

"That's fine," he said. "Ten minutes?"

"I'll be there."

I went into Noah's office. He was still paging through the file. He looked up, and for a moment I was startled. He looked like he'd aged years since I had left just minutes before. His whole face seemed to sag. "I'm going to have coffee with Johnny Connors. I'll be back in a few minutes. Is there anything you want me to do?"

"I think we both have to digest this a little bit," he said. "Let's talk about it tomorrow."

It took me several minutes to walk to the O.K. Café. As I walked I tried to imagine what was so important that Johnny wanted to talk to me right away and whether it was personal or business. I hoped it was personal. I needed a new diversion in my life. Half a block away, I saw him round the corner. He saw me and grinned. I hadn't seen Johnny since before my discussion with Frank and my first thought was that he was even cuter than I'd remembered. As he got closer, I couldn't help but stare at his dark eyes. He approached, reached out his hand, very formal, shook my hand and said, "Thanks for meeting me."

"No problem," I replied.

We walked into the café and he led me to a table in the back, the one farthest away from other diners. I was disappointed; this wasn't going to be a personal visit. We each settled in and ordered a cup of coffee. As the waitress left, he looked at me. "I've been meaning to call you before this just to talk, maybe to ask you to a movie, but things just kept getting in the way. Now something's come up and I thought I'd let you know."

The waitress brought our coffee. Johnny poured in a little cream and stirred it. The only sound was the clinking of his spoon against the cup. "I sat through a little bit of your trial. You really did a nice job. You didn't have much to work with."

I acknowledged the comment with a nod.

"I saw Dr. Morgan there. He was involved in a child custody case in our office several months ago. I just knew who he was. Of course, now I've read the paper, I know your office is defending him." He hesitated, as if he was trying to gather courage to tell me the real purpose of the meeting. "We got contacted this morning by a relative of Cheryl's. She wants us to bring a civil action for damages against Dr. Morgan for wrongful death." He looked at me, silently, waiting for some response.

My mind raced, trying to put it all together. A civil suit was not something I had thought of, nor did I have any idea why he felt compelled to tell me. Without being able to come up with a brilliant response, I simply asked, "Why are you telling me?"

"I know this seems a little strange, Jackie, but I . . . I've been trying to come up with the courage to ask you out, and now, being on opposite sides, adversaries so to speak, I guess I wasn't sure how to approach it."

He seemed to be squirming a little bit, and I found it rather endearing. "Who's your client?" I asked.

"I'm not at liberty to say at this point. Actually, another attorney, Ron, is going to be handling the case, but I'm going to be doing all the footwork. So, I just assumed we'd be clashing at some point, and I was hoping that wouldn't prevent us from being friends, I guess."

Now I was getting a warm feeling. I could tell that he had really agonized over his perceived predicament. It appeared to me, though, that this was leading to some sort of invitation. I had this self-imposed admonition about dating lawyers. The couple times I tried it in law school led to disaster. But I had been in town for quite a while and I had thrown myself into my work, taking files home every night. I had made no new friends and had no social life whatsoever. I could see Johnny Connors changing all of that, and right then I was all for it. For a moment, though, I was curious about the implications of what he was telling me. Why did he feel that his office filing a claim for money against my client—or Noah's client, really—would be some impediment to a relationship?

"I don't know what you want me to say," I replied. "If you're saying that because we may be on opposite sides I would have no interest in talking to you on a social or personal basis, that's not true. If you're asking me for a date, I think that can be arranged."

He broke into a big, warm smile. "Great, great," he said. "That's what I was hoping."

Feeling a little bolder now, I pushed on. "In fact, what are you doing tonight?" I asked. "There's a great movie I've been wanting to see. You know where the Riverside Apartments are?" I asked.

"Yeah," he said.

"Apartment 205. Why don't you plan on picking me up about seven?"

\* \* \* \* \*

It's surprising what the upcoming date did to my disposition. On the way to the café and my meeting with Johnny I had been down, totally depressed. Now things seemed a little brighter. At least I wouldn't have to sit in the apartment by myself, pictures of a dead body going through my head time after time.

Noah was gone when I got back to the office. I looked at my messages. One call on a DWI. I returned the call, made an appointment, and told Linda I was leaving for the day. She didn't even bother to look up from her book as I left.

I busied myself at my apartment in an attempt to keep my thoughts off the case. But I couldn't stop thinking about Cheryl. The pictures of her mutilated body were indelibly etched somewhere deep in my mind and would appear, without warning, in full color, at times so shocking I'd startle. In desperation, I turned to a book I had been reading. Prior to Clint's trial I had been totally engrossed in a novel, *The Detective*. I started where I had left off but my mind wouldn't focus.

I went to the refrigerator. There was one full glass of wine left from the bottle I had popped nights before. I took a glass of wine, filled the tub, turned on soft music, and slipped into the hot water. Within minutes I could feel the tension leave. Poor Johnny Connors isn't going to stand a chance, I thought. I pictured the different outfits I could wear, trying to imagine which one would have the greatest impact. It was warm out . . . so I could get by with something slinky.

* * * * *

"What did you think of the movie?" I asked.

"To be honest," Johnny replied, "I found it hard to concentrate. What's the perfume you're wearing?"

"Something called 'Desire.'"

"Very appropriate," he said. "It definitely had that effect on me."

I took a sip from my glass of wine and felt my face warm up. We sat at a small table in the corner of the bar. Because it was a weekday, the place was quiet. A couple of guys sat at the bar with the bartender watching Johnny Carson. I hadn't felt this relaxed in a long time. I had started the evening with a scheme to entice Mr. Connors with my feminine wiles and I could tell it had worked. Now I was wondering whether I had gone a little too far. My experience with men, particularly after Steve, had been limited. But even with my limited experience, I could tell Mr. Connors was starting to feel a little amorous, and if I didn't want to end up embarrassing him, because I didn't intend to end up in his bed, I had to steer our conversation in a different direction.

"How long have you been practicing?" I asked in a very businesslike tone.

"Four years."

"Do you do mostly civil work?"

"Yeah, they've got me doing personal injury. I've handled some of the smaller cases, tagged along with a senior partner on some of the bigger. That's what I'm going to do in Dr. Morgan's. I told them I wanted to do trial work and they're trying to give me as much as they can. How about you? How'd you ever end up doing criminal work?"

It had been a question I'd been asked many times before. The common perception was that lawyering was really a man's job and that criminal lawyering was exclusively for men. It was like sending a woman into combat—it wasn't done.

He looked at me quizzically, waiting for an answer. I tried to appear deep in thought, as though I was reaching for something profound, but I already knew the answer. I had given it before. "Actually, I have to blame a law professor," I replied. "The first year of law school there was a mandatory four credits of criminal law. I had Professor Schwartz. He did some *pro bono* criminal defense work for legal aid. He made it sound way too exciting."

"I had to take criminal law, too," replied Johnny. "But I didn't find it quite that exciting."

"Where'd you go to school?" I asked.

"Michigan."

"Good law school."

"I hear you went to the U?"

"Yeah," I replied. "Professor Schwartz had a legal aid club at the school. We'd meet in the evening to help do research and brief writing for some of the public defenders. In one of the cases I worked on we actually got a confession suppressed. It was an exciting time. We were coming off all those U.S. Supreme Court decisions, expanding the rights of the accused . . ."

"I don't know," Johnny interrupted, "if a guy's guilty, why are we giving him all these free legal services and everything? I think it's gone a little too far."

"You don't really believe that," I said.

"Yeah, I think we've gone a little too far in protecting the rights of the accused. I think you're going to start seeing a backlash. People aren't going to put up with it."

I took a sip of wine and stared at Johnny, trying to gauge him. He smiled at me. I think he knew he was getting my dander up and his smile was an attempt to redeem himself.

"What do you like about your practice?" I asked to change the subject.

"It's not a question of liking," he said. "It's a job, and like any other job, I wanna make money. Personal injury is where the money is, and if you're good at it, you can make big money. I intend to make big money."

"Think you're going to make big money in Dr. Morgan's case?" I asked.

"Should," he said. "He's got a big malpractice policy, but I suppose you know that already."

"Actually, I didn't."

"Yeah, Ron says it's $500,000. That's worth chasing."

"Kind of mercenary, isn't it?" I replied.

"I suppose it is," he said, "but it beats doing wills and probate."

I had started this conversation to give us what I thought we both needed, a cooling off period. For me, at least, it had worked better than I expected. I didn't like his attitude. Law, to me, had never been just a way of making a lot of money. I viewed it truly as a vocation, a public service. I guess I had Professor Schwartz to blame for that. But there was always something rewarding about putting yourself up against the system—at times even beating it—it should never be easy to lock people up.

I looked at my watch. "I have an early meeting tomorrow morning with Noah. I better get home," I said.

Johnny glanced down. "Oh, it's early. Why don't we sit and have another. Talk a little bit more."

I knew better. Jackie, I told myself, it's time to go. You've had a nice evening; maybe you've found a friend. Don't spoil it.

"Johnny, I'd love to, but I really have to get home."

I could see disappointment cross his face. I suspected he had a different ending in mind. "If you have to," he said, with a tone of resignation. "You really look lovely tonight. Is that curl natural or do you do that?"

I had an unruly curl on my left side that had a tendency to slide over my eye. This was only the umpteenth time I had been asked that question.

"Why do you ask?"

"Well, it gives you a kind of mysterious quality, especially with your dark complexion and eyes. I thought maybe you did it on purpose. It can be rather disarming."

"Hate to shatter your illusions, but there's no sinister female plot. It's natural."

He blushed. "I had fun tonight. I'd like to do this again."

"Me too," I said.

It was only a five minute drive to my apartment. On the way I wondered if he was going to try to kiss me. We were both surprisingly quiet, as though we were mulling over the night, trying to gauge where we were. He didn't try to kiss me. He was a perfect gentleman, walked me to the door, thanked me for the company and left. I appreciated that.

All night long I'd been making my assessments: Is this really a nice guy, or is he capable of beating the shit out of me? He was very courteous, very soft-spoken, and very handsome. So why wasn't he married? "Why should I have to go through this every time?" I muttered, as I undressed and let my clothes fall to the floor.

It was a little over a week before the prosecutor, Randy Becker, convened a Grand Jury to consider an indictment for first-degree murder. The case was the talk of the town. Every night the local newspaper would have a front-page story, juicy little tidbits that someone in the police department or the prosecutor's office would provide. It appeared everyone knew about the diary and the letters. An enterprising reporter even talked to the director of the State Board of Psychologists and did a piece on license revocation. The Board had already set a date for a meeting to discuss Dr. Morgan's future.

Chris's world was crashing down around him with a vengeance. He had become a recluse. He even avoided me. The prosecutor invited him to testify in front of the Grand Jury. Of course, we declined. I could imagine the fun Randy would have taking Chris through his story. The Grand Jury took one full day, and the next morning's headline was just two words in bold print: "PREMEDITATED MURDER?"

Through this whole time, Jackie remained relatively quiet about Chris's case. She had filed her notice of appeal in Clint's rape case and had been doing research about a juror lying in *voir dire*.

I attended the pre-trial conference on the domestic abuse case Jackie had referred to me. I was starting to piece together her aversion to representing this particular kind of defendant. The guy was huge, obnoxious, and dumber than a fence post. After bowling and drinking beer all night, he came home about one in the morning and "wanted a little lovin'." His wife, who had to be to work at seven, preferred to sleep. He added, "I just had to bang her around a little bit to teach her a lesson." The people in the next apartment heard the screaming and called 911. The police took him to jail overnight. He didn't understand why anybody would have the right to stick his or her nose into his business. The judge and the prosecutor wanted him to undergo a chemical dependency evaluation and an anger assessment. His comment was: "Screw 'em." So we set the matter for trial.

When I got back to the office, Jackie was standing by Linda's desk. "Well, I just appeared with Mr. Cochrane," I said. "Interesting gentleman."

"That's putting it kindly," Jackie replied. "The guy belongs in a museum next to the Neanderthal man."

I grinned. "Well, he wouldn't take any deal, so the matter got set for trial. I don't suppose you wanna take him, huh?"

She shook her head, smiled. "Noah, I just have such a hard time with those guys. You know, if he came in and said, 'Hey, it was my fault, I need some help, I wanna work this out,' that would be one thing, but this guy firmly believes he has the right to come home drunk any time of the night and get laid."

I heard Linda gasp. That wasn't a term she was used to, nor what she expected coming from a woman.

"Judge Savano," I said, "has set Dr. Morgan's first appearance on the indictment for Monday morning. It'll be just a formality, but I was hoping to spend some time with Chris afterwards. He's been hiding out. Doesn't even return my calls. Elizabeth says he's working on his defense. Whatever that means. Do you want to be there?"

Jackie hesitated.

"I really think you should," I said.

"Okay," she sighed.

* * * * *

We were scheduled for court at 10:00 on Monday morning. Because I hadn't talked to him for close to a week, I made arrangements to drive. I told Chris I would come early for coffee so we could have a chance to talk over what I expected to happen.

Elizabeth invited me in. Chris was sitting in a little nook off the kitchen with a big mug of coffee in front of him. He had some papers out with a notebook and a pen. I could see he had been jotting notes.

"I've been going through the file, Noah . . ."

Elizabeth interrupted. "If you guys are going to be talking about this case, I'm going upstairs."

Chris gave her a wave of his left hand, his way of dismissing her.

"Are you planning on coming to court with us?" I asked.

"No," she said, as she turned and disappeared into the living room.

I could tell that things were not good in the Morgan residence.

"Have you two been fighting?" I asked.

Chris had been staring at his notes. He looked up. "It's so cold in here I could be living in an igloo," he said.

"Do you blame her?" I asked.

"Not really," he said. "She's too embarrassed about the whole episode to even go out. She's always been a very proud person and now . . ." He turned his face, his eyes misting.

"But I want to tell you, Noah, this girl's lying about the extent of what happened. She makes it sound like we were having sex every session—that wasn't true. It was only a short time before I told her it had to quit. That's when she went ballistic . . . In her diary she's embellished the hell out of what happened. I told you, she was a very disturbed person."

"That's even worse. How in the hell did you ever let this happen?"

"God, I've gone over it so many times, trying to remember the first time something stirred. She was a voluptuous young woman, and not as innocent and naive as she's portrayed. She'd gone through some terrible things in her life, though, being sexually abused by her dad for years. It's hard to imagine what she went through. Then the brutal rape by Clint. You know, her dad had put her through some terrible, terrible ordeals. As a result, she believed herself totally worthless. She said she had never had a sexual experience that hadn't been forced on her, and which hadn't ended with her in pain. We were working to get her beyond that, to deal with her sexual feelings in a healthy and rewarding way. I know it sounds terrible, Noah, but it really started quite innocently. Whether you believe it or not, there is some literature that would support therapy that involved changing her experience, having her experience normal sexual response . . . "

I interrupted, "If you think we can get a local jury to give that any credibility at all . . ."

"I know, I know," he said. "I wouldn't even bring it up, but between you and me, it's true. That's how it started. I was going to try and show her that sex didn't have to be bad and it didn't have to hurt. It started with her mimicking what her father did, making her lay on top of him and from what she remembered, he obviously had an erection and he would make her rub on him until he ejaculated. But with me, I didn't do that. The opposite happened. She started to rub her crotch against my thigh, and I could tell that she was experiencing something close to an orgasm."

The doctor got up from the table and walked into the kitchen to pour himself another cup of coffee. I knew the real reason was to break any eye contact with me. I assumed he was embarrassed about what he was going to tell me.

"Within the next couple sessions it got out of hand," the doctor continued. "She'd tease me, come on to me . . ."

"Hey," I interrupted, "don't pull that shit on me. You were the professional, the mature adult. She wasn't even out of college. Jesus Christ, Chris, she was your patient, there for your professional help, and you start dickin' her, violating every oath you took. You know damn well, if she was starting to turn you on, it was . . . it was time for you to refer her to somebody else. All the signals should've been there."

"They were, Noah. And everything you said is true. But the truth is . . . I didn't care. I never had sex with anybody but Elizabeth. And in the last ten years, very little of that. She was stirring emotions that I thought I had buried years ago. The first time she took her clothes off and I felt her body, it was like . . . forget it. No matter what I told myself intellectually, I wanted to experience everything I could with her."

"How long ago was this?" I asked.

"Shortly before Clint's trial. That night . . . well, I was just disgusted with myself. But then I thought of her going through the trial and all . . . she really needed support. So I met with her again, and then I had such mixed emotions. I think I was really falling in love with her, which, in turn, gave me greater feelings of guilt. When her demands and threats became overbearing, that's when I came to you."

"But I didn't tell ya to tell her that you were gonna marry her, for Christ sake."

He laughed. "More desperation. She wouldn't take no for an answer. I had to give her something."

"Who put you in touch with her in the first place? Who was paying your bill?"

"Bev from the Battered Women's Shelter referred her to me. The prosecutor's office had sent her over to talk to them. The County was footing the bill. I had to justify continued treatment on a weekly basis."

"Had she received any prior psychiatric or psychological help?" I asked.

"Quite a bit."

"Did you get any of those records?" I asked.

"I never had the time. One of the doctors in Minneapolis sent me a copy of the MMPI, a couple other tests. I thought the diagnosis sounded quite accurate. Sounded like she had a long history of counseling. I knew there had been a suicide attempt. She had this thing about cutting herself, self-inflicting wounds. She was on the edge, Noah; she needed some help. During our sessions she told me that she was feeling better, that I had gotten her along the path of healing better than anyone else. I believed her. It just all got outta hand."

He sat down across the table from me again, took a sip of his coffee. "See, it wasn't totally selfish," he said. "She was progressing and I . . . I every bit expected that when the trial was done, she'd go on her way, a healthier person. I didn't expect she would want to marry me. God, Noah, I'm old enough to be her father."

"That's the point, isn't it?" I replied.

"You know, Noah, I didn't murder Cheryl, but it really doesn't make a whole lot of difference, does it? Even if I can prove it, I'm going to live in prison the rest of my life. The only difference is going to be if there are real steel bars holding me in or self-imposed ones. I really made a mess, didn't I?"

The room went quiet. The only sound was voices from a morning talk show on the radio. Elizabeth had it playing louder than necessary, I suspected to drown out our voices.

"Noah," he finally said, "how are we going to prove I didn't do it?"

"Did you go over the autopsy report?" I asked.

"Yes," he said.

"Did you notice the doctor's comments regarding the estimated time of death?"

"He's saying eighteen to twenty-four hours."

"I know from talking to Detective Kropp that Randy Becker talked to her Monday morning. He says he talked to her about 9:15. The medical examiner's report on the contents of the stomach kind of supports that. He found toast, and the detective took a picture of a plate on the kitchen counter with crumbs. I don't know what her habits were, whether she ate lunch or not."

"She didn't," replied Chris.

"How do you know?"

"She was trying to lose weight. She considered herself fat and dumpy, which she wasn't. So she was just having toast and coffee for breakfast, maybe some orange juice, and then wouldn't eat again until late afternoon or early evening."

"So it would have to be sometime during the day. The doctor's giving us a twelve-hour window. Somewhere between 9:30 a.m. and 9:30 p.m. Can you account for your time?"

"I've already looked at that, Noah. I went through my appointment book. I had patients from ten until twelve and then nobody again until two. I've been trying to account for my time. I even asked my secretary. That was after our discussion, you know, and I remember hoping you were going to feel good enough to talk to her shortly, to put an end to the agony I was in. I had patients from two to five who are accounted for. I think I left about five-thirty. Elizabeth wasn't home, so I went out to eat. I went to Clancy's. I have a charge slip for that. I think I was there for an hour, and I think I went to the bookstore, browsed for a while. I was home around nine-thirty."

"Did you buy anything?" I asked.

"No."

"So you're unaccounted for from twelve to two and the evening hours."

"That's right," he replied.

"Do you recall what you were wearing that day?"

"My blue pin-striped suit, white shirt, my blue and white striped tie. I think that's it."

"Where are they now?" I asked.

"The suit's in the closet."

"The shirt?"

"I don't remember which one I had on."

"How about the tie?"

He thought for a second. "Actually, I think I threw that away. I think it got stained that night at Clancy's. I tried cleaning it when I got home. It just made it worse and I threw it away."

"Was Elizabeth here when you got home?"

"No, she was about an hour later."

"Did she see the tie?"

"I think I'd already tossed it by the time she got home."

"Has the suit been dry-cleaned since then?"

"I think so," he said. "You know, Detective Kropp was here after I was in custody. Elizabeth told me he had a search warrant. He looked through my closet. She said they were doing some kind of test, looking for bloodstains. They didn't find any. They took my shoes."

"I know," I said. "They sent them to some lab for testing. They're not back yet."

"With all the blood and everything, Noah, the way she was killed, wouldn't I have been covered with blood?"

"One would think so," I replied. I looked at the clock. It was time to get to the courthouse. "You know, Chris," I said, "there are going to be a lot of press people at the courthouse. Just be cordial, smile, and don't say anything."

"Don't worry," he said.

* * * * * *

An hour and a half later I found myself surrounded by microphones, repeatedly saying, "No comment." Chris stood stoically behind me. When we were finally able to push our way through the crowd, I drove Chris home and went to the office. I stopped at Jackie's office and asked her to come back for a moment. As she sat down across from my desk, I said, "Quite a zoo, wasn't it?"

"Do you think this is going to continue throughout the whole trial?" she asked.

"It will unless something more sensational comes up," I replied. "And I can't imagine what that would be."

"Maybe we can get into a nuclear war with the Soviet Union," she responded.

"I'm not sure even that would knock sex off the front page."

"It's going to get worse," she said. "One of the reporters this morning told me that he had been talking to Ron Crane, and he's ready to file his wrongful death complaint. Remember, I told you that Johnny Connors told me that their office had been hired to sue Dr. Morgan, but he wouldn't tell me who their client was. But the reporter let it slip. It's Cheryl's mother. She's been living in Boston. I've been going through the file in Clint's case to see if I can find out anything about her . . . There's nothing. There's not even a mention of her."

"I wonder how she came out of the woodwork." I replied. "Probably was the smell of money. I wouldn't doubt if Crane contacted her himself. He's a real ambulance chaser. We're going to have to watch that real close. I wouldn't put anything past him. By the way, how'd your date go?"

"It wasn't really a date. But to answer your question, it went fine. He can't figure out what I see in doing criminal defense work and I can't figure out what he sees in personal injury. Other than that, we got along fine."

"You might want to cultivate that relationship a little bit, Jackie. Doesn't hurt having somebody on the inside on their case."

"Noah!" she responded. "I can't believe you said that."

"Criminal defense attorneys need all the help they can get," I said.

"Well, don't count on me," she replied. "I couldn't live with myself if I did something like that."

"Like what?" I asked.

"Use my feminine charms for an unfair advantage."

"Don't give me that," I replied. "Women have been doing that since Eve."

She smiled. "We'll see."

I didn't tell Noah that Johnny Connors had been calling me almost every night. I knew I had Johnny hooked; I just wasn't sure that's what I wanted. Besides, I had other things to do. I found my research for Clint's appeal fascinating. There was very little law dealing with issues similar to what happened in Clint's case. From the cases I read, it was pretty clear the courts wouldn't grant a new trial just because one or more jurors had second thoughts or next-morning regrets about their verdict. So I had to convince the Appellate Court my case was different, that the corruption of the process took place during the *voir dire*, when Mr. Kaufman lied.

When I wanted to take a break from Clint's case, I would go through Dr. Morgan's file. I always seemed to come up with the same conclusion: he was guilty. Once he couldn't account for every minute the medical examiner had established for the time of death, and when Noah told me about the missing tie, it only reinforced my opinion. I didn't tell that to Noah, though; I could see how serious he was taking the matter. The case was wearing on him, and I didn't want to make it worse.

Weeks passed and Clint's case totally consumed me. The more I thought about it the more I convinced myself that he had not received a fair trial. My task was to sit down and write a brief that would convince the Court of Appeals. I found I wasn't quite the author I thought I was. I would sit at home at my desk for hours with blank sheets of paper in front of me, waiting for the muse to give me that one dramatic opening paragraph that would knock the justices off their seats. I would scribble something, read it out loud, and then laugh at how ridiculous it sounded. I was doing that when Johnny Connors called for the hundredth time. He invited me to dine with him on Friday night at the most expensive place in town. In a moment of weakness and despondency, I accepted his invitation. That was two days away. I must have been lonelier than I thought because I was really looking forward to seeing him.

I left work early on Friday, a little after three. Noah had taken the day off. I had no court appearance and the office was quiet. I parked in the lot by my apartment, and it was such a pretty day I decided to take a walk. There was a city park about five blocks from my apartment. I had been there once before in spring, and I thought I would see what the change in seasons brought.

For a Friday afternoon, the park was pretty quiet. I strolled through slowly, still trying to come up with that first line for Clint's brief. I was deep in thought when my self-defense mechanism kicked in, the hair on the back of my neck tingled, and I stopped for a second to listen. I could faintly hear the click of heels, male laughter. I turned around and two young guys were maybe half a block behind me, pushing and shoving each other, laughing. They were dressed in jeans and t-shirts. One had a cigarette hanging out of his mouth. They both looked like punkers. I tried to quicken my pace without seeming obvious, but I could tell from the click of their heels they were gaining on me. I nonchalantly looked around the park. It appeared we were the only ones there. I had no reason to be afraid. I told myself I was being irrational, they were just young guys walking through the park, but I could feel my body tense up. Their voices got louder but I wasn't hearing their words. My mind was racing, trying to come up with a plan. If they attacked me, what would I do? I thought about being grabbed, dragged into the bushes and raped, maybe even murdered. It wasn't that ridiculous. I knew things like that happened. Suddenly they were right behind me. I could hear their heels clicking off the cobblestone but there was no more talking or laughter. I wanted to scream and run but something was holding me back. Then I heard one of them say, "Beep, beep," and they passed me, one on each side. They kept going until they were a short distance ahead of me. Then one turned, smiled and said, "Nice ass." I blushed, slowed my step and inhaled deeply. By then we were at the end of the park. They took a right and I took a left back to my apartment. I felt silly, like I had overreacted.

Johnny picked me up exactly at seven. As we drove away from my apartment, I told him of my experience. He listened intently, as though it really bothered him that I had a scare. When I was done, he said, "You really have to be careful, Jackie. There are so many creeps around now."

"But it was a city park," I said. "Broad daylight."

"I know," he said, "but how many times have you heard of somebody being snatched up and sometimes they just disappear?"

"Women shouldn't have to live like that," I said.

"You're right," he said, "but until such things change, you have to use your head."

I don't know if it was because of my experience or the fact that I had ignored him for weeks, but Johnny was very solicitous the entire evening. On the other hand, it could have been the black silk dress I had on, which hung loose on my body, giving just a hint of what it hid. Unlike the discomfort I felt sitting across from Randy Becker as he appeared to leer at me, I found Johnny's glances flattering.

We sat there for a little more than two hours talking about everything. I had a couple glasses of Chablis with my lobster thermidor and I was feeling relaxed. Johnny had been drinking scotches with his tenderloin. When the waitress removed our plates, he ordered us each a Golden Cadillac. We sipped on the ice cream drinks as we continued to talk.

"What's happening with Dr. Morgan's case?" he asked.

Recalling Noah's suggestion to me, I responded, "You're not trying to get any secret information out of me, are you?"

"No, I'm just curious," he said. "It's been kind of quiet since the indictment."

"Somebody in your office must've called the press," I said, "because at our appearance after the indictment, one of the reporters told me that your secret client is Cheryl's mother."

He seemed surprised. "Who told you that?" he asked.

"I don't remember. One of the reporters at the court appearance. There were a lot of them. He asked me something about whether we knew Ron Crane was going to be suing our client for the dead girl's mother."

"That's surprising," he said. "I didn't think anybody was supposed to let that out yet."

"Why?" I asked.

"We just wanted to keep it quiet for the time being."

"Then it's true," I said.

He looked at me. "You are quick."

"Well, I don't understand why it's a big secret," I said. "Was she here or what?"

"I don't know. As I said, Crane's handling it. I'm just going to be doing the footwork. I'm sorry I even brought it up. Did I tell you that you look absolutely lovely tonight?"

"I don't believe so."

"Well, you do. You're probably the prettiest thing I've ever seen in my life."

"You have to come up with a better line than that."

He grinned as he reached across and gently brushed the curl from my eye. "You aren't going to give me a break, are you?"

"Johnny," I said, "I like you and I'd like to continue seeing you, but I'm not going to get into anything hot and heavy. I've got too many things going on, too many things to straighten out. So if you think I'm being standoffish, bit of a prude, it has nothing to do with you."

"I understand entirely," he said. "And thanks; I was starting to get worried."

"You don't have to."

"How'd you end up here?" Johnny asked.

"I was with the Public Defender's office in Rochester, but I wanted to get a little closer to home. Somebody mentioned to me that Noah might be looking for help. I came to town and watched him in a trial for a day. I was pretty impressed, so I decided to call him. Initially he was quite hesitant, and then several months later he called me. I think his doctor told him he had to slow down."

"So you're closer to where?"

"Fargo," I said.

"That where your folks live?"

"My mother's dead."

"I'm sorry to hear that," he said.

"It's been a long time. And my dad floats around the country."

"Who do ya wanna be closer to?"

"I was raised by my aunt Ruby. She and her husband Gene are like my folks. I've got two cousins, like brother and sister. So that's my family and I miss 'em, and I like to go there when I can. But with Clint's trial, and now this, it's been a while."

"Why'd you decide on law school?" he asked.

I couldn't help but grin at the question. It was something I had been asked quite often and something my law school girlfriends and I had discussed over many cups of coffee. My real answer was out of desperation—desperation for a little respect. I had graduated from college at the top of my class with a double major of American history and political science. After being on the job market for most of my senior year, the best offer I got was being a bartender at one of the restaurants, and I think the only reason I got that was because the owner knew my aunt. I found there wasn't a whole lot of demand for a history major and even less—which meant none—for a female history major. I couldn't even get a job teaching without additional education credits. But I had learned from experience that you didn't whine about it, particularly to men, especially fellow male students in law school. So I told Johnny what had become my routine.

"I was a *Perry Mason* fan when I was growing up. Watching the show Saturday night was a ritual around my aunt's house. She made a couple pizzas, we had a six-pack of pop, and we sat in front of the tube watching *Perry Mason*. She had all the novels by Earl Stanley Gardner. When I graduated, she kind of encouraged me to go to law school."

A little of that was true. We did watch *Perry Mason*. But in my senior year at college I was more interested in Picket's charge at Gettysburg than whether Mason beat prosecutor Hamilton Burger. It was a good story, though. "How about you?" I asked.

"My dad's in business; he deals with a lot of lawyers. Every time he'd get one of their bills, he'd say the same thing, 'Jesus, you gotta go to law school.' So I did. But he's a little disappointed in me. I didn't particularly like business law."

"What kind of business does he run?"

"Farm implements, down in Marshall, right in the middle of corn country. And he's in cash crops. He has a little more than three thousand acres that he has help farming. He's not hurtin'."

"So you're a farm boy?"

"He used to make me work in the summer. He got rid of the dairy herd when I was little so we never had any chores other than critters I accumulated."

"Like what?" I asked.

"I had a horse, a couple dogs, and a bunch of stray cats."

"A horse?" I said.

"Yeah, we had to put him down just two years ago, old age, cancer."

As we continued to talk, he reminisced about childhood memories, growing up in the country. Those years seemed to serve him well. He appeared to have a very gentle nature.

He smiled, reached across the table and covered my hand with his, squeezed it softly.

I looked at his hand and then looked across the table. His eyes were warm and soft. He gave me goose bumps. "Well, if you really want to be of some help," I said, "I've been struggling with trying to get Clint's brief going. I've got this mental block on how to start it."

The waitress came to the table to see if we needed our drinks freshened. Johnny looked at me. "You want another one?"

I looked at the waitress. "Is there any liquor in a Golden Cadillac?"

"Not much," she said.

"Then I'll take another," I replied.

"I'll have a White Russian," said Johnny.

When she left, he asked me to tell him what the case was all about. I summarized what had happened to my jury, the substance of my motion for a new trial. "I need an opening paragraph."

"For that?" he asked.

"Yeah," I said. "Something that sort of summarizes what my argument's going to be."

"Well, your argument's going to be that your client was denied the right to a fair trial by a jury of his peers," he said. "Your case was to be decided based on the evidence presented in court, not on what happened to one of the jurors or his family years ago. I would start out with some statement about how sacrosanct the right of a jury trial is and how that was compromised in this case. Go through the reasons we have a jury trial, the protections the forefathers were trying to preserve. You know, the star chamber in England and all that stuff."

I smiled at him. "By George, I think you've got it. I guess two heads are better than one."

89

"Well, sometimes," he said, "a person looks at something so long that you just go blank. That happened to me a lot in law school. I could look at a piece of paper for days and not come up with one word, and then all of a sudden, boom, it ran like diarrhea."

"That's an awful picture," I said.

"Yeah, I suppose I could've used a better simile," he said.

By then I was totally relaxed. I was even starting to wonder what it would feel like to cuddle up with him. But after my great speech of just moments before, I'm sure he would have wondered if I had any fortitude at all. So I let such thoughts pass.

I saw a different Johnny Connors that night, though, one more in-tune to my feelings. He never made an abrasive comment. On the way home in the car, he reached over and took my hand. "You have the hands of a pianist," he said. "Long thin fingers. Have you ever played piano?"

"My mother tried to get me into it when I was little, but I'm tone deaf. I don't know a B flat from a C sharp."

He laughed. "Sometimes I wish I could play an instrument, but you can't do everything."

When we reached my apartment, he walked me to the door. For a moment I thought about inviting him in, but I remembered my resolve. I could tell he wanted to kiss me, and without saying a word, I gave him a look that said it's okay. He leaned over, pressed his lips to mine and put his right hand on my shoulder. It stirred old urges. He pulled away. "Thanks for the evening, Jackie. I enjoyed myself."

"So did I," I said.

"Then let's do it again," he said. "Soon."

I nodded yes and went in.

I slipped out of my evening dress and got into a pair of shorts and a t-shirt. He had given me an idea. The adrenaline was flowing. I spread Clint's file out on the desk, took my yellow legal pad and started writing. By midnight, I had the first ten pages. I read it over. It was a little rough, needed some cleaning up, but I liked it. It seemed inspired.

"Well, whaddaya think, Brownie?  Give me some ideas."

It had been two weeks since our first appearance following the indictment. Shortly after the hearing, I had given the investigator, Brownie, a copy of the file and asked him to do his detective thing.

"Barring some miracle," he replied, "your guy's in trouble."

"I'm paying you for that?"

"You mean I'm actually going to get paid on this case?"

I let the comment pass.  Like me, Brownie did the work on a hope and promise he'd be paid.  Sometimes it didn't work out that way.  But he wasn't in it for the money.  He said it kept his mind sharp and gave him a chance to get out of an empty house.

"This is going to be one of your tougher cases, Noah.  I don't have to tell you what the jury's going to think of this guy.  He's got to have the greatest motive for murder I've ever seen.  I mean, she threatens to blab, he tells her he's going to leave his wife and they'll move to California, and a couple days later, she's dead."

"It's not as sinister as you think," I said.  "I told him to tell her that he would leave his wife."

"What?" he asked incredulously.

"He came to see me at the hospital and told me what was going on.  He said she threatened to tell Elizabeth.  I told him to just keep her happy until I could get out of the hospital and I would try to take care of it.  I didn't think he'd promise to marry her."

"Good old Noah," he said, "always trying to save someone's ass.  Does Kropp know that?"

"I haven't told him."

"Doesn't that make you a witness in this thing?"

"It may," I replied.

"You're not going to try this anyway, are you?"

"I'm going to have Jackie do it."

"You're kidding," he said. "Will Morgan stand for that?"

"She's ready, Brownie. She's as good as anybody he could find, and I can help her."

"Have you told her that?" he asked.

"Well, not quite in those words."

Brownie shook his head in disbelief. "We're sitting on a time bomb," he said.

"Well, then, help me. Where do we go with this?"

"Easy. We have to find somebody else with motive," he said.

"Who?"

"Somebody she knew," he said. "Let's assume it was somebody she knew. Did she have a boyfriend, or boyfriends? Was there somebody at school interested in her, stalking her? What about her family, maybe her old man?"

"He would have a motive," I said. "I mean—he'd sexually abused her for years. Now it was coming out. Maybe he was afraid he could still be prosecuted or maybe he was just pissed off at her for finally telling people."

"Does anybody know where he is?"

"That'll be your job," I said.

"What about the mother?"

"Ron Crane, over at Roberts & Crane, is going to start a civil suit against Chris. Jackie found out his client is the mother. Do you know anybody over there?" I asked.

"Well, I ran into, what's his name? Murphy, Tim Murphy, a few years back. Did a little work for him. I don't think he's gonna consider that he owes me any favors. But don't worry, Noah, I'll find out."

"I'm sure this will be set for trial within the next couple months, so do your thing and get back to me."

Just then Jackie appeared in the doorway. Brownie turned to her. "Noah, I didn't know you had an angel working here." Jackie walked in with a smile and slugged him on the shoulder.

"You haven't heard anything more about Cheryl's mother from your insider, have you?" I asked.

"Noah, even if I did, I wouldn't tell you. I'm not going to be a snitch."

Brownie sat there with a quizzical look on his face.

"She's seeing a young man who works at Crane's office. I told her she should snoop for us. She considers it improper. I don't know why. If the tables were turned, if Crane had somebody here . . ."

"Hey, maybe he does," I interrupted, looking at Jackie. "You don't suppose . . ."

"That's a terrible thought, Noah," she said. "Johnny was interested in me long before Dr. Morgan's case came along."

"I'm sorry," I said. "You're right. I'm becoming cynical in my old age."

Jackie handed me a stack of paper. "This is the draft of my brief in Clint's appeal. I was hoping you could read it over and see what you think."

I lifted it up. "Pretty hefty," I said. "Must've been a lot of work."

"Getting a new trial is important to me," she said. "I think I covered all the avenues."

Brownie got up. "Well, I've got my work cut out for me. I'll get back to you as soon as I can."

As he walked out the door, I told Jackie to have a seat. "I've been meaning to talk to you about Chris's case. I've put it off. I knew you were preoccupied with the brief and doing your other casework. I don't know when Judge Savano's going to set Chris's case for trial, but I suspect it'll be this fall sometime. I want you to be the lead trial attorney." I don't know what response I expected, but all she did was sink into the chair and stare at me.

"What're you thinking?" I asked.

"I'm too stunned to think of anything."

"I know you can do it, Jackie. I've watched you in court. You're good. And I'll be there to help you with all the technical stuff."

"This is murder, Noah. This is a man's life. If I screw it up, he goes to prison for the rest of his life."

"Weeks ago you thought that's where he belonged," I replied.

"I may still believe that," she said. "But I've given what you said a lot of thought. I was letting my personal feelings interfere with what I know to be my ethical obligations. I think if I hadn't just gone through Clint's case, spending all that time with Cheryl . . . then, the fact that Dr. Morgan took advantage of his professional relationship, all that affected me. So I know what our obligation is if we're going to represent him. I can set my personal feelings aside. I realize I have to set them aside. I'll do everything I can."

"I knew once you thought it over . . . and I didn't want to just drop it on you like this but I couldn't think of any other way. I haven't mentioned anything to Chris. I wanted to find out your reaction first. If you're willing to do it, I know I can talk Chris into agreeing."

"Well, I appreciate your confidence in me," she said, "but I'm not sure I'm ready for this. I think I need a few more cases under my belt before I'm willing to take on a murder trial."

"Believe me, Jackie, you're never going to feel comfortable about it. If you ever do, it's probably time to quit. There's no better way to get prepared for the kind of practice you want to do than just jump in with both feet. I did it almost forty years ago . . . I didn't have half your talent and I didn't have somebody like me to answer questions."

"I don't know," she said.

"You don't have to decide now," I replied. "Give it a couple days, let it sink in."

"I will, Noah," she said. "I'll give it serious thought."

After she left, I picked up her brief. Twenty minutes later I laid it down. It was good, really good. Excellent, in fact.

I stood in the kitchen stirring the wok filled with snow peas, sliced onions, mushrooms and fresh garlic. I loved the smell of fresh garlic in hot oil. The aroma filled the kitchen, but my mind wasn't on the cooking. It had been several days since Noah had sprung on me the idea that I try Dr. Morgan's murder case. What I found a little scary was that I really wanted to do it. A month earlier I would have considered a hanging by his gonads an appropriate result for what he had done to Cheryl, but Noah's words slowly eroded away that feeling. If I really wanted to be a criminal defense attorney, to do the big cases, I had to look at what my legal and ethical obligation was, which was to serve the interest of my client regardless how much of a scum bag I may consider him. More important, though, was Noah's unyielding conviction that Dr. Morgan was innocent. I believed I knew Noah well enough to know that, with his commitment to his profession, he wouldn't be saying that to me if he didn't really believe it.

Wrestling with what I should do, I decided to invite Johnny Connors over for a home-cooked meal and to pick his brain a little. I was going to find it interesting. I wondered what his reaction would be. I wanted him to be supportive, excited about it, because then I believed he considered me a real attorney. On the other hand, if he took the position that I shouldn't do it, or wondered why I would want to do it, it would create a problem for me.

Johnny was at the door at exactly seven o'clock. I like a punctual man. He was dressed casually, dark slacks with a powder blue polo shirt. He carried a brown paper bag, which he handed to me.

"I wasn't sure what you were going to have tonight so I got a white Zinfandel."

"That's nice of you," I said.

"It smells wonderful in here. What are we having?"

"Stir-fried shrimp. I put it on low. There are a couple ingredients I have to add yet, like the shrimp."

He followed me into the kitchen. I had put a lid over the top of the wok. I lifted it. He leaned over, took a whiff and went, "Mmmm." As I replaced the lid, he turned and gave me a peck on the cheek.

"Taking liberties?" I whispered, coquettishly.

"It's just such a domestic scene," he replied, "I was overwhelmed there for a moment."

"Make yourself useful," I replied. "Open the wine. The corkscrew's in the top drawer . . . there."

I watched him struggle with the cork. I didn't have an expensive type corkscrew, just one of those little cheapies that had a tendency to pull out of the cork when yanked. It was doing that to Johnny. By the time he was done, the cork was demolished, little pieces bobbing in the wine. He held it up to show me. We both laughed. "That happens to me all the time," I said. "I just pick the pieces out of my glass."

I put two wine glasses on the table. He filled them and we sat at opposite sides.

"What's new in your world?" he asked.

I was a little apprehensive about bringing up Noah's request that I be the doctor's lead attorney at trial. I had realized early on that lawyers, particularly young lawyers, had a way of competing with each other, especially when it came to handling what was considered serious cases. But I knew if there was any hope for Johnny and me, the relationship would have to be one where that kind of competition didn't exist. And if it was going to be a problem, I should find out right away.

"I had kind of a shocker this week," I said. "Noah wants me to be the trial attorney for Dr. Morgan."

Johnny was sipping his wine. He coughed, like he had let it go down the wrong tube. He took out his hankie and turned his face while he recovered his breath. I didn't know whether it was accidental or whether I had caught him that much by surprise.

He looked at me. "Are you going to do it?" he asked.

"I don't know. What do you think?"

He was quiet for a moment, having recovered enough to take another sip of his wine. He pursed his lips as he swallowed, never taking his gaze off me.

Finally he said, "Well, if you wanna be a criminal defense attorney, that's a great opportunity. If you're going to get your feet wet, this is as good a case as any. After all, your client is guiltier than hell. Nobody's going to expect that you'd get him off."

Even though the same thought had crossed my mind, his comment pissed me off. My smile disappeared. I think Johnny could sense that he said the wrong thing.

"Jackie," he said, "this probably isn't a good subject for us to be talking about. You know, I've had access to some of the police reports, Dr. Morgan's session notes; I've talked to Detective Kropp. Jackie, I'm just being honest. I mean, I think it's great Noah thinks enough about your abilities to believe you could handle the defense, but I think you have to be realistic—it's a loser."

Something happens to a defense attorney when somebody tells them they have a horseshit case. It makes them want to try even harder to prove everybody wrong. That was happening to me now. As we talked on, I could tell the more that Johnny summarized the evidence of Dr. Morgan's guilt, the more I tried to convince myself of his innocence. And then I did something inexcusable. "You know," I said, "Noah's known him for many years and he believes Dr. Morgan simply isn't capable of murder . . . not in a million years."

I wanted to take it back as soon as the words left my lips. I knew it was a violation of a confidence. It was said in haste, though, in a tone like, I know something you don't.

Johnny reached over and poured a little more wine in my glass. "Jackie," he said, "I sense I'm getting myself in trouble again. I think it's great that Noah asked you to do that. If I were you, I guess I'd be in a panic. It's a hell of a responsibility. If you're asking for my opinion, based on what I've heard of your abilities, I think you can do it. I think you should take it."

I had been so engrossed in our conversation that I wasn't paying much attention to my meal simmering on the stove. I stood up, picked up my glass of wine, took a big gulp and walked back to the kitchen counter. I lifted the lid. I had left the heat too high; everything had shriveled. I laughed. "I think I ruined this," I said.

Johnny walked over, put his arm around my back, and gently squeezed me toward him. "Looks fine to me," he said.

I turned toward him, our faces met. I tilted my head slightly and he took the invitation to kiss me heavy on the lips.

Within moments I pulled away. "Maybe we shouldn't talk about the law," I said.

"I'm game if you're game," he said. "I get enough of it during the day. I don't have to talk about it at night."

"Fine," I said, "let's form a pact," and we shook hands.

The meal was not as bad as I thought it was going to be. Johnny was graceful enough to say it was great. Despite our earlier resolve, though, we found our conversation somehow led to the law and the practice of law. We started comparing our law schools, how we ended up here, the judges we appeared in front of, and other lawyers. The evening flew by. It was almost midnight when we stood in front of my apartment door. Johnny was trying to get a commitment from me on when we could go out again. There was really nothing preventing me from seeing him every night. I was just reluctant to rush into anything. As we stood and talked, he put his hands on my hips, pulled me to him and we kissed a long, soft kiss. As our lips clung together, he moved his hands up my back, paused at the strap of my bra. I wondered, for a moment, about his intentions. Then his hands were on my shoulders pulling me tight.

Finally I broke for air. "Wow," I said, "that could get us in trouble."

Johnny smiled and started to move forward again. I turned my head. "I think we should save it for another night," I said as I pulled from his arms. I could see the disappointment cross his face. "You'll survive," I said.

"I know," he replied, a devilish grin on his face. "I'm in no hurry."

He said he would call me the next day to set up a time for Friday night. As I closed the door behind him, I felt a rush of heat cross my body. There was no doubt about it; Johnny was starting to get to me.

"Chris, you don't have many options. If you don't want to leave your case here, fine, find somebody else. But if you want my help, Jackie's going to be the trial attorney."

I could see a little panic on his face. He turned to the side, stared at a picture on the wall. Without turning back to look at me, he said, "Noah, I can't believe you're doing this to me."

"Don't pull that shit on me, Chris," I said. "You're the one who was poking a neurotic patient. If you'd kept it in your pants, you wouldn't be in this situation."

He shook his head in disgust. "You're free to leave any time you want to," I said. "But I'll tell you this— I can't believe you're going to find another attorney who knows you're innocent."

His head snapped at me.

"You heard right! I know you're innocent," I said. "I don't have any doubt. Whether I can prove it or not, though, is another matter. But think of it, Chris. With anybody else you're going to start with one big deficit—he's going to believe you're guiltier than shit. Moreover, I'm the best attorney around. I can tell ya this. With my knowledge and Jackie's skills, you're going to get the best goddamn defense your money can buy. Now, if you're still pissed at me, here's your file. You can go anywhere you want."

His face lightened up a little. "Noah, you have to understand, this is my life."

"You don't have to tell me that."

"I mean, I'm probably ruined professionally," he continued. "Elizabeth, if she has any sense, will probably kick me out. All I need to be is tagged as a murderer and I can go jump off the nearest bridge."

"We don't need any whining," I said. "You're in this mess. What we need is some help in figuring out what the hell happened. I've got Brownie working on it, checking into her background, whether there are any boyfriends out there angry enough to do something like this. What about her dad?"

Chris sighed deeply. "From everything she told me, he must have been a real bastard, abusive as hell. She said the last time she saw him was a little more than two years ago. She said she visited him to confront him. Apparently there was some talk in therapy that that might do her some good. She told me he denied everything. They ended up screaming at each other and she left. The next day was one of the first times she attempted suicide. She took an overdose of pills, and she ended up at the County Medical Center. Everybody viewed it as one of those suicide attempts that is really a cry for help."

"So he's in Minneapolis?" I asked.

"That's where he was the last time she talked to him."

"What does he do?"

"I never really asked her and she never volunteered."

"Did she ever talk about her mother?"

"No," he said. "And that was rather strange . . ."

"In what way?" I asked.

He continued to stare. "I'm trying to remember the first time I brought it up. I asked her about her relationship with her mother. She said she was dead. That's what her dad wanted, anyway."

"Can't be dead," I said. "She's starting a lawsuit."

"She admitted later that she made that up. When I asked her why, she said it was wishful thinking. I tried to delve into her relationship with her mother several times after that. She was strangely quiet about it. No amount of prodding on my part would get her to say anything. I assumed it was over the sexual abuse by her father. I think she blamed her mother for not being more of a guardian. I think she suspected her mother knew about the incest and was doing nothing about it."

The intercom rang and Linda told me she was sending Jackie in. She walked into the office rather cautiously. She'd already told me she was eager to be the trial attorney and she knew I was talking to Dr. Morgan. I suspected she was concerned whether Chris was going to give her any credibility.

Chris immediately sprang to his feet, reached out his hand, a smile on his face. "Jackie," he said, "Noah and I have been talking about the trial. He's told me of his plans. He has complete confidence in you. That's good enough for me."

Her eyes widened and she blushed. His comments obviously caught her by surprise.

"Sit down," I said. "We were just talking about Cheryl. You probably know her as well as anybody."

"Not quite," she responded.

This time it was Chris's turn to blush. I gave Jackie a dirty look. She turned away. There was an uneasy quiet for a moment. "Anyway," I said, "I've got Brownie doing some digging on the father. Have you heard anything more about the mother?"

"No," she said, firmly.

"I think we have to find out what's in her background. Why she ended up the way she did. There has to be someone else with a motive."

"Unless, indeed, it was just a random murder," said Chris. "The murderer's *modus operandi* is consistent with a serial murder. I mean there might just be some psycho out there who saw her on the street, in the mall, at school. Who knows? Found out where she lived or followed her home. She was quite gullible. Somebody she met at a bar. She might've invited him over."

"Chris, you're not making this any easier," I said. "If we have to try and find a serial murderer, a needle in a haystack, we'd have to rely on the cops for that. No way. I'm not saying that's not a possibility, but we have to start closer to home. And if everything ends up at a dead end, then we're forced to go on a fishing expedition."

"What do you think, Jackie?" Chris asked.

She puffed up in her chair. She appeared pleased that the doctor had asked her opinion. "I've been running possibilities through my mind," she said. "I even considered Clint. I crossed him off. As far as whom I'd like to talk to, the father's number one on my list. I think he has a motive. The question is whether he had an opportunity. Brownie has to find out if he has an alibi. The mother, she was in Boston. That isn't going to help us. Besides, from everything I've read, a man murdered her."

"What makes you say that?" Chris asked.

"The rage, the mutilation, the removal of her breasts. That's a demonstration of power. Whoever he was, he wanted to totally humiliate her as a female. He wanted to destroy what she was. How about in her sessions with you, Doctor, did she ever give you any indication of who she might be seeing?"

"I don't think she was seeing anybody. I think if she was, she would've told me. After we became intimate, I'm sure she wasn't."

"Well, Chris," said Noah. "We're going to have to start spending some of your money."

He laughed. "You mean the little I've got left."

"There's a forensic pathologist in Madison. I want to send him the autopsy and police reports, see what help, if any, he can give us on the estimated time of death. That may become important. Also, I think Jackie has something there. This guy's been called in on a couple serial murder cases. If the crime scene gives any indications of being something like that, I think he'll be able to tell us. As you said, it could've been a guy driving through, could've been looking for a small town to stop in, the right kind of girl to follow home. Who knows? Look at Bundy. Sometimes it was just happenstance."

"Maybe you're right," he said. "We do have to cover everything."

"Jackie," I said, "why don't you put together a package of the information we should send to Dr. Culligan. In the meantime, Chris, I know you've been digging through files. Do you have all the notes you took of your sessions?"

"Actually," he said, "all I did was summarize. Sometimes rather tersely. You can imagine a lot of the stuff that happened I didn't want to record." He managed to crack a smile. He had made a joke at his own expense. That was the most levity I had seen from him for a long time.

"Well, think about it, Chris. Go over all of those sessions. Try and recall anything she may have said that could help us. I mean, we're scratching here. In the meantime, Jackie and I will keep working on it from this end."

With that, Chris stood up. We followed suit. He shook my hand and he shook Jackie's hand. "Thanks for sticking with me," he said. "There's got to be an answer, because I didn't do it."

We said our farewells and he left. Jackie and I took our seats. "He's so sincere," said Jackie.

"He is," I said. "After forty years of doing this, Jackie, I have a sixth sense for the truth. My mind works like a polygraph. I look for little things in a person, a twitch, a blinking of the eyes, a glance away. Something that gives him away, and suddenly he knows that I know he's lying. It comes with experience. Chris has got all the symptoms of somebody who did an awful stupid thing, he's embarrassed as hell, but when he says he didn't murder her, he's telling the truth."

"It's starting to look a little daunting," Jackie said. "I don't know where to start."

"We start with Dr. Culligan. What's happening on Clint's case?" I asked.

"I'm waiting for the prosecutor's brief so I can put in a reply. Then I assume they'll set it for oral argument and we'll see what happens." She coughed out a laugh. "Clint sent me a little scribbled note. He said the jail inmates were right. He's got these two big guys staring at him like they're in love. I'm sure it's his imagination."

"Let's hope," I replied.

It was the dog days of summer, late August, and I was sitting in my office reading Randy Becker's Appellate Brief in Clint's case.  He had taken a very straightforward position.  The jurors had made a decision in the jury room; they were polled in the courtroom.  Nobody told the judge they wanted to change their mind.  If they had any lingering doubts—too bad.  If they felt any pressure from the foreman, they could have mentioned it to the judge when they were polled.  He argued that if the court opened the door to jurors second guessing their decision, hours or days later, it would lead to chaos in the court system. Deep down I guess I knew the Appellate Court was going to buy that argument.

When I finished, I put the brief back in the file, feeling a little discouraged. Linda buzzed me to say Brownie was on the phone.  He had been keeping us apprised of his investigation, nothing earth shaking.  The last time we talked, he was still trying to locate Cheryl's father.

I picked up the phone.  "Hello, Brownie."

"I found him," he said, "and he's one mean son-of-a-bitch."

"Where?" I asked.

"He's still in Minneapolis.  If you've got time, I'll run in."

"Noah's at home," I said, "he took a couple days off to spend with Maggie. I'll call him and see what he wants to do.  Where are you?  I'll call you back."

"I'm at Jimmy's Bar."

"This time of the morning?" I asked.

"Just coffee."

He gave me the number and we hung up.  I called Noah at home; he told me to bring Brownie out to his house.  I called Brownie back and we made arrangements to meet there in a half an hour.

Noah lived in the older part of town.  His home had been built in the early 1900's.  It was a two-story, tan and brown brick, with lots of nooks and crannies.

From the front it didn't look like much, but there was a vine-covered arbor that stretched along the entire side of the house, and once you reached the back it opened into a garden paradise. The back yard was enclosed in a vine-covered wood fence, the vines starting to show the colors of fall, speckled with red leaves. In one corner stood a big birdbath, surrounded by bird feeders hanging from iron poles and wood posts. In the other corner was a flower garden splashed in color. In the middle of the yard was a cobblestone patio with a brick fireplace. The scene was a kaleidoscope of color, muted by the leaves of three humongous trees that formed an umbrella over the entire backyard.

Noah and Maggie were lounging on the patio. He was reading the morning paper; she was knitting. As Brownie and I walked out of the arbor, he waved us over. It was about 10:30 in the morning and already hot. The morning dew still clung to the grass as we walked across the lawn. I could tell that by afternoon, the humidity would be worse than the heat. Noah wore shorts and a t-shirt. Maggie was in a loose-fitting blue and yellow summer dress. They both smiled broadly as we took a seat. For a moment I tried to imagine they were Johnny and me forty years from now. I wondered if we would look that happy.

There was small talk. Maggie asked us if we'd like a cup of coffee, she had just made a fresh pot. We both said we would. As she left, I asked Noah, "Who takes care of all this?"

"I'd like to say I do, but I'd be lying," he said. "I do some of the maintenance but all the gardening is Maggie's—she loves it. I do manage to fill the bird feeders, though."

"Are those vines going to turn red like that, like those leaves?"

"Yeah, in about the middle of September the entire arbor and fence will be bright red. That's Virginia Creeper."

"I don't know how you come to the office," I said. "I'd have a hard time leaving this."

"You get used to it," Noah replied.

Maggie came with a tray, a pot of coffee and three cups. She poured us all a cup.

"Aren't you going to have one?" Noah asked.

"No, if you guys are going to be talking business, I've got things to do. Weed that flower garden back there." She pointed to the corner.

"What are those bright red flowers?" I asked.

"Gladiolas," she said.

"And the kind of pink ones that stand above everything?"

"Purple cone flowers," she replied.

"The contrast is really pretty," I said.

Maggie turned around, went to the back of the house and then passed us pushing a wheelbarrow. She went to the far side of the yard, got on her hands and knees and started pulling little weeds out from between the flowers.

"That's what she loves to do," said Noah. He turned to Brownie. "You look like a cat that swallowed a canary. I assume that means you got something for us."

"Well, Noah, you need a suspect and I think her old man makes a great suspect. It wasn't hard finding his house, but he just never showed up. It was like he was in hiding. He's living in an older home a block off Lake Street that's been turned into several apartments. It was almost a week before he actually showed up. I'll tell ya, I was getting pretty tired just sitting there. I think I'd read maybe a half a dozen books. One of the neighbors told me what he looked like. A big guy, sandy gray hair. I was just about to leave last night when this pick-up truck parked across the street. The guy gets out meeting the description. He's probably six-three, two hundred and fifty pounds. None of it's fat, either. I approached him, told him who I was, what I wanted to talk to him about. He said, 'Get the fuck out of the way.' Sorry, Jackie."

"I've heard it before," I said.

"Anyway," Brownie continued, "it went downhill from there. He just kept walking and I kept pressing him. To make a long story short, as he got to the porch he said he hadn't seen Cheryl for years, her mother even longer. He was tired of cops; he wanted nothing to do with any of it. As far as he was concerned, he said, they were just a couple sickos."

"What the hell would he mean by that?" asked Noah.

"I have no idea," replied Brownie. "He slammed the door and I wasn't about to push him any further. I don't have disability insurance, Noah. I could just see myself lying on the sidewalk looking up, all my teeth gone. I'm not giving up on him but I'm gonna handle him with kid gloves."

Noah looked at me. "Whaddaya think, Jackie?" he asked.

I thought for a moment. "Big guy, bad temper, a lot of *animus*. If he had any idea what Cheryl was saying about him, he could be our man."

We talked about it for a while. Brownie said he would wait a couple days and then go back to see if he could get him to open up. I told him if he wanted me to go along, I'd be glad to do so. Maybe he would talk to me. Brownie said he would just as soon try again by himself. If that didn't work, we'd try something different.

As we talked, Noah would glance over at Maggie in the flower garden.

"Isn't that a picture?" he said. "She's as pretty as the flowers."

"Prettier," said Brownie.

"Yeah, you're right," Noah said.

"You're lucky, Noah," Brownie said. "I miss Jeannie, a lot."

Brownie looked at me. "My wife. She died of breast cancer about five years ago. That's why I'm so cantankerous."

"I'm sorry to hear that," I said. "For some reason I just pictured you as a con-firmed bachelor."

Noah broke in. "No, Jeannie was good for him. He only became obnoxious after she passed away."

"Do you blame me?" Brownie asked.

"Not really," said Noah.

Brownie and I had driven in separate cars. He said he was going to stay and visit with Noah for a while. He found it too relaxing to leave. I, on the other hand, had to get back to work. I said my goodbyes, went over and hugged Maggie and left.

\* \* \* \* \*

When I got back to the office, Linda handed me a package that had come in the late mail. It was wrapped in plain brown paper, addressed to me, and marked "Personal and Confidential." It had no return address. I couldn't imagine what it was. I took it back to my office and sliced the packing tape holding it together with scissors. I unfolded it to find a manila envelope with a clasp. I opened the flap and inside was a stack papers about an inch and a half thick. I pulled the whole pack out, set it on the desk and put the envelope aside. I glanced quickly at the first page. I could tell it was some kind of medical report and it had Cheryl Moore's name on it. I started leafing through. It was page after page of medical records dating back almost five years, long before she saw Dr. Morgan. There were reports by psychologists, psychiatrists, and results of psychological exams, an MMPI, medical records from admission and discharge to different hospitals. I was flying through the pages. I saw the words "suicide" and "suicidal" several times. When I got to the bottom of the pile, the last record was from the Medical Center in Minneapolis discharging her from the hospital against medical advice. It was dated six months before she identified Clint as her rapist.

I stacked the pages neatly on my desk and leaned back. The adrenalin was pumping. I could feel my heart pounding. I had such mixed emotions. Who would have sent these to me and for what purpose? Do I have a right to rummage through this young woman's nightmare? Do I need to know as much about her as I would learn in these pages? How would it affect my representation of Dr. Morgan? I sat there pondering all of the possibilities, almost afraid to start reading that first page.

An hour later, I turned the last page, dumbfounded and on the verge of tears. I had placed a piece of paper as a marker about a third of the way through the file. I opened to that spot and started to read again. It was a report by a Dr. Springer, a psychiatrist in the emergency care unit of the Minneapolis Medical Center. It summarized his sessions with her and I read it all again, word-for-word. She told the doctor of the incest by her father, that it started before puberty, and as she started to develop, she claimed her father would say things like, "Why are you getting those bumps on your chest? You don't deserve breasts. I should cut those off." She told the doctor that he had a straight razor and he would place it next to her bare breast and threaten to slice it off. She said a couple times he pressed so hard that he actually cut her skin and she bled. He would make her stand there naked while he would stare at her, then he would make her lay on the bed, spread her legs and again put the razor by her vulva and tell her that she was a useless whore, that he should cut it out. Then he would swirl his hand with the razor, make a whoosh sound, like he had cut out her vagina. She told the doctor that he would make her perform fellatio and sometimes just before he was going to ejaculate, he would pull it out of her mouth and cum all over her chest and then wipe it across her chest and say, "That's all you are, a useless whore."

I read the pages over-and-over. I didn't remember exactly word-for-word what Cheryl had testified to in Clint's trial, what she said he was supposed to have done to her in the car, but I knew, that in substance, the words here were identical. I looked at the date again. The first time she related this in any treatment session she was sixteen, years before Clint was supposed to have raped her. What were the chances that Clint, in the backseat of the car, would have used the same words as her father? Astronomical, I thought. One in a zillion. Never happen.

As I went through the file again, she had told this same version to other doctors in other settings. I leaned back in my chair and mumbled, "Jesus Christ, she lied. She wanted to get even for what her dad did so she picked some poor slob walking on Main Street. He's even the same height and weight as her old man." A real rage came over me. "What a terrible miscarriage," I muttered.

These records were available. The prosecutor should have known about them. Somebody should have known. If anybody had seen her history, they would have known she was lying. I found Clint's file and got out her statement. Prior to trial, I had highlighted everything of importance. I flew through the pages. There it was, in the statement to the detective, her words were almost identical to what she told Dr. Springer years earlier. Then I saw in her statement where she had told the detective, "Then he took the razor and ran it across my stomach, twice. I didn't know how bad he had cut me until I got back to my apartment. He had cut me bad, I bled all over." The prosecutor even introduced photographs showing the scars, claiming they were taken just days before the trial. I looked at all the summaries of the medical discharge reports from the hospital following the date she claimed Clint had done this to her. Every admission included a physical exam and not one report mentioned any scars on her chest or abdomen. I couldn't believe it. It appeared she'd even mutilated herself to convince everybody she was telling the truth about Clint.

I leaned back in my chair and exhaled deeply. A strange sense of calm came over me. I knew I had something here, something that would get Clint a new trial if not an outright dismissal of the charges. I was concerned, however, about what Dr. Morgan knew of all this. Had she told him what she claimed her father had done? If he sat through her testimony, he would have known that she was up there repeating the same lines. I couldn't imagine that he would have let that happen.

I reached for the phone and called Johnny's office. He was on the line in a matter of seconds.

"Did you send me a package?" I asked.

He was quiet for a moment. "You mean like roses or candy, something like that?"

"No, I mean a big brown package with documents?"

"What kind of documents?"

"Johnny," I said, "just tell me. Did you send this file?"

"What kind of file are you talking about?" he asked.

I knew it had come from him. Who else? This would have all been discoverable material in the civil lawsuit. It had obviously taken somebody weeks to put it all together. Probably somebody in his office. He knew what it would do for my case with Clint. But it was also clear that he was never going to admit that he had sent it.

"Are you still there?" he asked.

"Are we still on for tonight?" I asked.

"Yeah. I'll be there about seven."

Maggie invited Brownie to stay for lunch. The three of us ate and chatted at the table in the muted shade cast by fluttering leaves of big burr oaks. There were three, strategically placed many years ago, that now provided an umbrella for the entire backyard. Maggie kept threatening to cut one down so that more sun would reach her flowers. I told her it would be like cutting off your arm, you'd miss it every day. In the fall, the acorns would carpet the ground and I could spend hours watching the squirrels collect and hide them all over, or the chipmunks packing them in their cheeks and scurrying off. After the leaves had all fallen, I'd sit in the lounge chair under a full moon, lean back and just follow all of the gnarled branches, from the trunk of the tree to the tiny tips, some of them stretching thirty feet or more. It appeared there was no rhyme or reason to how they grew but I knew every little twist and turn was a reach for the sun.

It was a little after one when Brownie got up, said he was going to go fishing and invited me along. I looked at Maggie.

"Go ahead," she said, "but wear a hat."

"Brownie," I said, "I'm just too comfortable here to leave."

I had taken off a couple days to spend at home and I knew I would feel guilty sitting in a fishing boat, probably drinking beer, chewing on a cigar.

Brownie had barely left the yard when the phone rang. Maggie ran in and then called out the window. "Noah, it's Jackie, she sounds upset."

I should have known better than to think I could spend a relaxing afternoon at home. I could tell from the quaver in Jackie's voice that something drastic had happened. I didn't want to get dressed up to go to the office, so she volunteered to come back to my house.

As I put down the receiver, Maggie said, "Boy, at first I didn't recognize her voice. What's wrong, you think?"

"I have no idea, sounds like another crisis."

"Are you sure this is good for you, Noah? I mean, I don't want you back in the hospital, or worse."

"I feel great," I said. "I haven't had any palpitations or shortness of breath or anything for a long time. I'll be all right."

Maggie busied herself in the kitchen while I went out and sat in my favorite lawn chair. I wasn't quite as confident about my condition as I let on. There were times I would get tightness in my chest, a tingling in my left arm, and I wondered if I was on the verge of having the big one. But I had resolved, the day I left the hospital, that I wasn't going to baby myself. Other than my change of diet, I was going to do just as I did before, and if it meant falling over dead, well, so be it. I knew people who hid from life with the hope that they would live longer. It never made sense to me.

I heard Jackie's car tires squeal as she turned the corner and then the brakes squeak as she came to a halt in front of the house. The car door slammed and within seconds she burst through the arbor, like a whirlwind. She was holding a big envelope. Jackie not being one for hysterics, I knew something had to be seriously wrong.

Before I even had a chance to stand up, she was in the chair next to me, with the folder on the glass table. She flipped it open to a marker.

"You're not going to believe this," she said. "I'll bet in all your years of practice, you've never seen anything like this. You're not going to believe it. Read this."

She handed me a copy of the complaint in Clint's case. I had read it before; it outlined the allegations Cheryl had made about what happened the night she was raped. When I put it down, she handed me another sheet. She said, "Now read this."

At first I thought it had to be a copy of a police report recounting Cheryl's statement to them. Then I looked at the heading, the date, and the signature below, Dr. Springer.

I looked at the sheet, then at the complaint, and then back at the sheet. "What the hell is this?" I asked.

"That . . . that is a medical report by a psychiatrist relating what Cheryl told him about her father's sexual abuse. You'll notice the date; it's a couple years before Clint's raping her was supposed to have taken place. I ask you, what are the chances of Clint using the same words as her father?"

I thought for a moment. "Too improbable to even calculate," I said. "Where'd you get this?"

"I have no idea. It was there when I got back this morning. It's postmarked from town. There's no return address. It was mailed yesterday, August 26th. The only thing I can think is, it's a part of the civil case. Ron Crane, or somebody in his office, got these reports and knew what it would do for my case."

"Johnny?" I asked.

"I called him. He acted like he didn't know what I was talking about, but I wouldn't expect any different. It had to be him."

"Not so quick," I said. "Let's think this out. What would the attorney for Chris's insurance company benefit by getting this to you?"

Neither of us said anything. Jackie reached down and started flipping through the pages. "These are all of her medical reports. You wouldn't believe the crap in there. She was one sick girl. And Noah, the most bizarre part is nobody knew if anything she said was the truth. One doctor thought she could be making it all up just to get attention. What do you think this does to Clint's case?"

"They've got to dump it," I said. "But I just wonder if Randy Becker was aware of any of this."

"I've been wondering the same thing, Noah. If he was and he didn't tell me and he put on the charade of a trial, it should mean his license."

"I can't believe he'd do that, Jackie. Why?"

"Just to get Clint!"

"No, I would suspect, knowing Randy and how lazy he is, he didn't bother digging into her background. If nobody plopped it on his lap and said, 'here, look at this,' he wouldn't go out of his way to find anything. I'm sure for him this was just an easy case, a chance for a little publicity."

"How 'bout Dr. Morgan?" Jackie asked.

"That's been going through my mind," I said.

"Noah, if he knew about this, he allowed her to get on the stand and perjure herself and send an innocent man to prison. Is that somebody we want to defend?"

"I don't think he knew, Jackie. I asked him what records he'd obtained from her past treatment. He said there was nothing important, just some test results. But the quickest way for us to know is to ask him. Now."

Jackie and I went into the kitchen. Maggie took one look at me and got that concerned look on her face.

"It's no big deal," I said. "Jackie and I have to talk to Chris."

Maggie looked at Jackie. "He's not supposed to be getting stressed, you know."

"Maggie, it's not her fault," I said. "And I'm fine."

By then I had dialed Chris's number. He answered. I told him we would be over in five minutes. I kissed Maggie on the cheek and we left.

\* \* \* \* \*

"I wasn't aware of this history, Noah. These are all new. You've seen what I had; it was in her file, reports from one doctor, her MMPI."

"She was lying in Clint's case, wasn't she?" Jackie asked.

Chris paged through the documents without responding. "If I had known any of this," he said, "I certainly would've told the prosecutor."

Jackie persisted. "Was she lying in Clint's case?"

"I can't tell you for sure, Jackie. There are really two issues: she may well have been raped by Clint. Based on my sessions with her, I think she was. Because of what her dad did to her in the past, and because she was never able to get justice for it, she might've just used these experiences to embellish her testimony, to let people know what she went through. The second issue, though, is one of credibility. If you're asking me, would this destroy her credibility, I'd have to say it does, because I agree, there's no way one could ever explain how Clint could use the same threats as her father."

"Did you ever talk to Becker?" Jackie asked.

"Sure I did, a number of times."

"Did you ever get any sense that he knew any of this? I mean, did he ever quiz you about her background?"

"He never seemed concerned about that," Chris said. "All I was there for was to make sure he had a witness who wouldn't fall apart on the stand. I never sensed he felt sorry for her, had any empathy. I think to him this was just a way to get another notch on his gun. He prides himself in portraying this image as a hard-nosed prosecutor. I've worked with him on some of the battered woman cases—he's not very accommodating. Sometimes he's willing to throw the baby out with the bath water. He'd rather get the conviction than try and save the marriage. What does this do to my case, Noah?"

"To be honest, Chris, I don't know. With that history, and the fact that she's now in court testifying, telling the world not what Clint did to her, but what her dad did to her, certainly makes her dad a likely suspect."

Jackie interjected. "There were a few blurbs in the newspaper; he might've seen a story about her testimony. Might've been a real shocker for him."

"You're right," I said. "You're right. He hasn't seen her for years; he might've been complacent, thinking it was all in the past, nobody would ever find out. Then, all of a sudden, there it is, right in the newspaper. She's not saying he did it but he's got to know she's one step closer to telling."

I looked at Chris. "Brownie's located him, you know. He lives in Minneapolis. He says he's big and mean."

"Think about it," Jackie said. "Think about all the possibilities. She might've done this on purpose, to let her father know that someday she was going to tell, that she was going to name him."

I looked at Chris. "Could that have been her motive?" I asked.

"It could've been," he said. "There are all kinds of possibilities. I was just thinking, though, I should've seen some of this."

"Whaddaya mean?" I asked.

Chris peered away, deep in thought. I glanced at Jackie. I could tell she was steaming. There was no way she was going to buy his conclusion that Clint raped Cheryl. I was about to say something just to break the ice when Chris turned his head back toward us.

He said, "I was just thinking, she obviously spent a lot of time planning and scheming . . ."

Chris stopped in mid sentence; it appeared he had caught the meaning of Jackie's stare, his mind now torn between two thoughts.

"Let's assume for a minute, Jackie, that you're right, that Cheryl wanted to get even with her father and to do that she wanted to go public. But she also knew she could never attribute those terrible deeds to him; that would be too dangerous. So she decides to conjure up this rape as a way of going public . . ."

"And she picks some innocent guy out of a crowd," interjected Jackie.

"Assume that as well," continued Chris. "Can you imagine what kind of planning she would have to do? How devious she would have to be to pull this off . . . with a bunch of professionals, nonetheless?"

"But maybe you had lost your professional perspective," shot Jackie. "Maybe that was the purpose of the seduction."

"Then you're giving her more credit than I ever could," he replied.

"But are you a good judge of that?" she asked. "You'd like to believe that there was some sort of manly magnetism which caused her to lift her skirt and not some neurotic scheme to get even with her dad."

Sensing this could get ugly, I said, "Guys, this isn't getting us anywhere. Chris, you started out by saying you should have seen something. What should you have seen?"

"I don't know," he replied, frustrated. "Maybe Jackie's right, maybe I just got suckered in. Maybe everything was made up . . . but there still has to be a motive."

"Why would she go through all that trouble to get even with her father?" Jackie asked.

"Maybe you're right," he replied, now flustered. "Are there copies of these that I can go over?"

"Not right now," I said, "but we'll get you copies as soon as we can. There might be something that can help us in your case." I turned to Jackie. "Are you going to show these to Randy today?"

"I was so angry after I read them that I wanted to march right over there. But then I thought about the source of the documents. If Johnny's the source, once people know I have them, he may get in trouble. Who knows? I want to talk to him again before I do anything."

"You better do it quick," I said.

"I'm meeting with him tonight," she replied.

Johnny planned on coming over as soon as he could get off of work. He thought maybe about six or so. The apartment I lived in had a cookout area in the back, a couple of gas grills and picnic tables. They were very seldom used. I had discovered once I moved in that I was in kind of the geriatric section of town. Most of the tenants in the building were older than Noah, and the few times I had a chance to talk to any of my neighbors it always ended up with my getting a rundown of their latest maladies. Because of the effort necessary to make it from the apartments to the cookout area, it was usually empty. Johnny had agreed to pick up some steaks on his way over and I was to prepare everything else.

After leaving Dr. Morgan's house, Noah and I had a chance to talk as I drove him home. We had barely left the curb and I could tell he was a little upset with me.

"You have to quit sparring with Chris," he said. "He knows he did a terrible thing; you can tell he's crushed, you don't have to keep rubbing it in every chance you get."

"Noah, he just won't give me a break on Clint's case. There is no way in hell he raped that girl. For the doctor to even suggest that based on his discussions with Cheryl it really happened, well, that's just crap."

"Don't you think you've lost a little bit of your objectivity in this whole thing?" he asked.

"Maybe, but I'm not trying to cover up my sins."

"He's not either. There's no place left for him to hide. Maybe you should try and let him keep the little self-respect he's got left. Remember, you two have to work together."

I let out a deep sigh. "You're right," I said. "I'll work on it."

"I'm sure you will," he said.

He also told me to be very careful about how I approached Johnny regarding the documents. If he were the source, Noah didn't believe Crane would have given him permission to release them to our office. If the documents hadn't come from Crane's office, then he suspected that the only other source would have been the law office representing Chris's insurance carrier, but then he wondered what their motive would have been. His last words were that I should not pressure Johnny. I assured him that I would be the epitome of tact.

* * * * *

Johnny arrived a little after six with two New York strip steaks and a bottle of Merlot. My part of the meal was steamed asparagus and baked potatoes. He had a sullen look and was unusually quiet. He followed me into the kitchen and placed his package on the counter. As he turned, I gave him a peck on the cheek. He put his hands on my shoulders and smiled. "Thanks, I needed that," he said, as he drew me toward him in a powerful hug. As we broke apart I could see in his eyes that he was mulling something over. I didn't feel I should broach the subject of the mysteriously appearing medical records. I believed if he was the benefactor and he felt he could say something, he would.

We put everything on a tray and went to the patio area. I was right: no one else was out. The apartments were built in a U shape and every apartment had a balcony overlooking the garden area where the gas grills were located. The only sound was the hum of air-conditioning units and an occasional sliding glass door opening, one of the occupants coming out onto the balcony to see what was going on and then disappearing behind closed drapes.

Johnny started the grill, closed the lid, and we each took a glass of wine and sat in a lawn chair. I watched him as he took a big sip and washed it through his mouth, as if to get rid of a bad taste, and swallowed.

As his eyes followed the U shape of the balconies, he said, "I lived in a unit just like this in law school, on the third floor. It was a little noisier than this, though. It was all students and at this time of night they'd all be sitting on their balcony getting blasted."

"I think everybody here is probably done eating by five and in bed by seven,"

I said. "I don't think I've ever seen anybody out on their balcony for more than a few minutes."

"Every time I see a setup like this, I think about *Rear Window*. Did you ever see that movie?"

"No," I replied.

"It's a Hitchcock movie. Jimmy Stewart has some accident and he's in a wheelchair, spends his day on the balcony watching what's going on in the apartments across the garden. He thinks Raymond Burr has murdered his wife, cut her up and buried her in the backyard."

"That sounds terrible," I said.

"No, it's a great movie. When I was in law school, I got myself a cheap pair of binoculars and a lot of times I'd sit on my balcony after dark watching what was going on."

"You were a window peeper?" I said.

"It's not the same. Window peepers sneak around, trespass. I was on my own balcony. If they wanted their privacy all they had to do was close the drapes like your neighbors here. I never saw much anyway. One night I did see some guy taking his wife's clothes off, but they disappeared before he got her down to nothing."

"Didn't you feel like a voyeur?" I asked. "I mean, doing that?"

"Not really," he said.

"Remind me to keep the drapes closed."

"Oh, I wouldn't do it now, Jackie. That was a long time ago."

"Yeah, but you never know what eyes may be spying on us."

"Why? You have something in mind?" he asked.

I left the comment unanswered. "I think the grill's ready," I said.

It was such a beautiful evening we decided to eat on the patio rather than in the apartment. I went up and got the rest of the meal while Johnny barbequed the steaks. Unlike other evenings we had spent together, the conversation stayed away from our jobs and legal matters. Still, the topic of Cheryl's file was always on my mind.

We finished the bottle of wine at just about dusk. Throughout the evening I could see drapes opening and occupants peering down at these two young interlopers. They would stare for a few moments and then disappear again. Maybe they were hoping for something racy to happen. Soon the mosquitoes were swarming. We tried to survive the onslaught, to wait until dark when they subsided a little, but after swatting ourselves for a few minutes we gave up, gathered the dishes and went in.

The evening air had been warm. I had turned the apartment air conditioner on when I came home and as we opened the door there was a blast of cold air, sending a shiver over my body, giving me goose bumps. I placed the dishes on the counter and I felt Johnny's arms come around my waist and pull me tightly to his body. He felt warm and inviting. Then he kissed the nape of my neck and I trembled.

"Are the drapes closed?" I asked.

I sensed his head turning and he laughed. "No, they aren't."

His grip eased slightly and I took the opportunity to turn, peck him on the lips and break from the embrace.

"We don't want to cause any heart attacks," I said as I walked over and pulled the cord closing the drapes. I knew I was going to disappoint Johnny but I really didn't have anything more than a kiss in mind.

As I turned from the window he was opening the refrigerator. "Do you have anything else to drink?" he asked.

"I'm afraid not," I said. "I normally don't keep anything on hand."

He gave me a disappointed look. I knew I couldn't put it off any longer. "Johnny," I said, "we have to talk. I know you've been doing all of the grunt work on the lawsuit against Dr. Morgan, so you can't convince me you're not aware of Cheryl's medical treatment file."

I walked to the table where I had a briefcase, opened it up, took the sheaf of papers out and dropped them on the table with a thud for effect, saying, "These are going to become public real soon. I intend to confront Randy Becker tomorrow morning. But I wanted to talk to you first."

At that point I was going to ask him to tell me the truth, whether he was the anonymous sender, but I noticed a subtle change in his expression, a message unsaid that read, "Don't ask me." Instead of the question intended, I changed course. "Is there any reason why I can't give a copy of these to the prosecutor right away?" I asked.

"I suspect that the motive behind whoever sent these to you would've been to help you in Clint's case. You're right. I know what's in there, I've read them and it seems to me your guy got railroaded. I don't know why Cheryl would've done it, and I don't think it makes any difference as far as our case against Dr. Morgan, but now that you have them, I think you should use them for whatever purpose you believe necessary."

Based on his demeanor and his words, I was sure he was the source, but it had to remain our secret. I pondered the implications for a moment. Johnny sat across the table tapping his fingers, giving me time to digest what had occurred. Finally I said, "I hope the person who was kind enough to do this doesn't get in trouble."

"It's not something you need to worry about," he said.

It appeared at that point that we both decided enough had been said and we each mentally set the subject aside. I also noticed that our conversation had taken the edge off any romantic notions he may have had. We talked for a while and the evening ended with a warm embrace, a kiss, and a date to go to the movies.

I don't think Johnny really understood what the documents meant to me. I had been struggling with Clint's case for a long time. I had truly believed him when he told me he was innocent. Because of that, I never listened to those who told me his case was a hopeless task. It was because of that belief that I willingly, though not graciously, withstood the sarcasm and the jibes from Judge Savano and the prosecutor. Even though I had filed the appeal, I had pretty much resigned myself to the idea nothing would change, and because of that, Clint was going to spend the next twenty years in prison for a crime he hadn't committed. I believed it was my fault, my failure as his trial attorney. Now I felt some redemption and that in this case the system failed. So it was with considerable eagerness that I anticipated my meeting with the prosecutor the next morning.

I spent a very fitful night. It was even worse than the night before I made my closing argument in Clint's case. I kept imagining my meeting with Becker in the morning, going over my opening salvo time after time. His attitude and condescending manner had, to say the least, pissed me off and I was going to get even in one fell swoop. Noah had told me things like this happen so seldom in the course of a career that I had to savor the moment. I intended to do just that.

It was with some anxiety, though, that I sat in Randy Becker's office the next morning. I had called a little after eight and his secretary told me he was in a meeting with Detective Kropp. I told her that it was important that I talk to him and I would come over and wait.

Minutes later I sat in his outer office reading the morning paper. I could overhear Randy and Kropp talking. I couldn't hear the substance of the conversation but I could hear Kropp mention Dr. Morgan's name. Becker's secretary noticed me straining to hear and got up and closed the door. I pretended I didn't notice. I'd finished the local and national news pages when Detective Kropp came out of the office, saw me sitting there and immediately traversed the room and extended his hand.

His demeanor seemed different for some reason; his reaction to me a little over solicitous and it struck a cord of suspicion. I said, "Good morning," with a guarded smile.

"How's Noah doing?" he asked.

"He seems to be doing fine," I replied. "I know Maggie's a little concerned about him but he keeps telling me not to worry. You know how he is."

"I'm afraid I do," he replied. "We're kind of contemporaries; it's hard to keep an old dog down."

He grinned and his teeth looked unnaturally white against his leathery tan complexion. "Well, I have to get to work. He's all yours," he said, motioning to Randy's door. "He said I should send you in."

A nervous twitch went through my body. I had been waiting for this moment ever since I left Noah's yesterday. I could feel my mouth drying out and my hands trembling slightly as I took my briefcase from the bookstand and started to his door.

Randy was sitting behind his desk, a cup of coffee in his hand, a smile on his face. He was dressed casually: a light tan shirt, the top buttons open to expose the first tuft of chest hair. For some reason, his appearance was disarming. I wanted him clothed in the garb of a prosecutor when I dressed him down.

He offered me a cup of coffee, which I declined. I took the chair and for a moment tried to recall how I had rehearsed my opening line. Mentally straining for a clue that wouldn't come, I hesitated long enough that it started to get embarrassing.

Finally he said, "Well, Jackie, what's so important that you had to run over so early in the morning?"

I had the file on my lap and I tapped it a couple of times. By then I remembered how I was going to proceed. I started with a little white lie. "We received some discovery in Dr. Morgan's civil suit relating to Cheryl Moore's prior psychological treatment, records of treatment *before* the alleged incident with Clint."

"Let's not start with that kind of garbage," he interrupted. "Alleged, my ass. Your client's been tried and found guilty; it's no longer allegations, it's proven facts."

Keep your cool Jackie, I thought. "Well some of the documents that we've had a chance to review would seem to indicate that she was suffering some pretty severe psychological problems, and the doctors believed that those problems related primarily to allegations she made about sexual abuse at the hands of her father. Allegations that are surprisingly similar to statements she made in my client's case. Those started me thinking, Mr. Becker, about what you might've known about her prior treatment and the prior allegations."

He gazed at me for a moment, a cold icy stare. "You don't have to be formal with me," he said, "Randy will do. As far as your question, I don't have to tell you squat. But if it makes you feel any better, I don't have the slightest idea what you're talking about."

"It's very simple, Mr. Becker. I have reason to believe, based on what I've been able to review about her prior psychological history, that Ms. Moore lied to the jury, that she in fact made the whole Clint rape episode up and I want to know . . ."

"Hold it! Hold it!" he interrupted. "I know what you want to know, you want to know if I hid anything from you. And the short answer is no! I gave you everything the rules of evidence require me to give, nothing more, nothing less."

"So you're telling me that you were not aware that she had any prior psychological problems, that she had made allegations that she had been brutally and repeatedly raped by her father, that . . ."

"I'm not saying that at all. I'm saying I gave you exactly what I believe the rules required me to give you."

"So does your file include any information about her prior attempts at suicide?"

He looked away and gave no response.

I pressed on. "Does your file include any information about the numerous times she told treating psychiatrists or psychologists that her father had sexually abused her as a child; that, in fact, she said her father threatened to cut her breasts off with a straight razor?"

He turned back to say something, but I went on. "Does your file include any information about the medical treatment she received after Clint was supposed to have cut her with a knife, treatment that notes there were no cuts visible on her body? Where'd you get those phony pictures?"

"Jackie," he said, "I think it's time for me to get back to work, time for you to get out of here. I don't know what you're fishing for, but do it on your own time."

This wasn't going at all the way I had intended. For some reason I had thought I was going to be able to back him into a corner, caught and embarrassed, he would be putty in my hands, begging to know what he could do to correct this terrible miscarriage of justice. We would go up and see Judge Savano and in no time Clint would be back on the street—a free man. It wasn't going to work that way, though, and I knew why. I was right in the first place—Randy knew all along about Cheryl's past and he knew if any of this came out it would put quite a dent in his career.

I stood up, put the briefcase under my arm, tapped it a couple of times and said, "You know, Mr. Becker, I believe you were a knowing participant in a very serious breach of ethics and prosecutorial misconduct and I intend to prove it."

"Well, you go right ahead," he said, contemptuously. "But until you do, get out of my office."

I turned and quickly walked out, slamming the door behind me. His secretary jumped at the noise. She gave me a strange look as I rushed out. As soon as I got out of the courthouse, I found the first quiet place where I could sit and let what had happened sink in. Where had I gone wrong? My first reaction was to blame myself.

I was in my office with Brownie, having a cup of coffee and waiting for Jackie to get back from the prosecutor's office. Brownie was going to give us a briefing of his latest encounter with Cheryl's dad. I told him he may as well wait until Jackie got back so he didn't have to repeat himself. I told Linda to send her back as soon as she returned.

Brownie was telling me about the great time I missed by not going fishing with him. He had filled a bucket with three-quarter pound crappies and all the neighbors had come over for an evening fish fry. He had just finished his story when I heard Linda telling Jackie we were waiting for her.

I heard an uncharacteristic stomping down the hall. I looked at Brownie and raised my eyebrows. She burst through the door, the file under her arm, her face flushed.

"You were wrong," she said defiantly. "Becker knew all about this stuff and he purposely didn't disclose it."

Somewhat amazed, I asked, "He told you that?"

"Not in so many words. It was what he didn't say and the look on his face."

"So, he didn't admit it?" I asked.

"No. It's hard to explain; you had to be there. He had these records before Clint's trial; I'd stake my life on it. He's not going to do anything—he's going to continue covering it up. I think I should go to the judge."

"Jackie," I said, "if it was any other judge I'd agree, but you have two problems: First, all you have is a suspicion that Becker covered something up. Secondly, Judge Savano isn't going to listen to you."

"He's got to!" she said. "At least he has to look into it."

"No way," I interjected, "there's a history there. Randy's old man was on the Judicial Selection Committee. That's the only reason Savano's on the bench. Their friendship goes back a long way. Randy's dad had to call in a lot of chips to get Savano on the bench; he won't do anything to embarrass Randy."

Jackie stared incredulously at me across the desk. She shook her head to display her disgust and then said, "One of my law school professors talked about the 'good ol' boy' system. This must be what he meant."

Brownie, who had been unusually quiet, entered the conversation. "Jackie, it isn't all that bad. If everybody you're dealing with is honorable, the 'good ol' boy' system is a way of getting things done a lot quicker. Savano's just a little bit more indebted than most."

"I can't believe this. I just can't believe this. To any reasonable person, once they read her record, they'd say turn Clint loose. That's what should happen and you're telling me it won't."

"That's not what I'm saying at all, Jackie," I replied. "What I am saying is there are no shortcuts. You're going to have to bring Randy out into the open kicking and screaming. You have to lay it all out so neither he nor Savano have any wiggle room. Then, if Savano remains an impediment, we can talk to the chief judge."

"What do I have to do then?" she asked, grudgingly.

"Well, what exactly did Randy say?" I asked.

She gave me a five-minute summary of her discussion with the prosecutor. "Let's assume that you're right, Jackie, and I think you are, that he did have these records prior to Clint's trial, the only argument he would have for nondisclosure would be that they were privileged documents, you know, doctor-patient. I suppose he could argue that the records relate to her prior sexual experiences, the law's starting to get more protective of a complainant's background. So you can't get in, for example, the fact that she may have been promiscuous to support a defense of consent."

"I appreciate all that," said Jackie, "but this goes beyond that. This evidence is really exculpatory. I think under any scenario, it had to be disclosed. Even if it didn't have to be legally disclosed, I think ethically he had an obligation to, at the least, tell me about it."

"I don't know, Jackie, sometimes the law and ethics lead in different directions."

"There was never any indication anywhere in the entire file of Clint's case that she had received any prior psychological counseling or treatment. Nothing."

"Are you sure?"

"Noah, I took Clint's file home last night. I looked over every page thinking maybe Randy slipped something in and I simply missed it. There's nothing there."

"See, if you'd had any notice at all, you could've had the court do an in-chambers inspection of her records to determine whether there was anything in there that may be relevant to his defense. Those records would've been open for review by the appellate court. Where does the appeal stand?"

"It's set for oral argument October 14th."

"You're going to have to file another motion for post conviction relief with nondisclosure the only issue. Along with the motion papers I would send Randy Becker a demand for disclosure of all Cheryl's medical records he had prior to Clint's trial. It's important that you make it clear that it has to be prior to Clint's trial, because I'm sure he's gotten some of this stuff as a result of the murder charge against Chris."

Jackie looked pretty discouraged. "Welcome to the practice of law, Jackie," I said. "One thing you're going to find, there's no one out there who wants to give a criminal a break. Maybe that's the way it should be. If you can't live with that, you're going to have to find another occupation."

"I don't have to live with it, Noah. What they're going to find is that if they want to make my life miserable, I can be just as big a bitch as the next person."

Brownie choked on his coffee and let out a grunt. He slapped his knee. "I think they're in for a pissing contest, Noah," he said.

Jackie grinned. "You bet," she said.

"Let's go onto our next crisis," I said. "Brownie, where're we at?"

"Well, Mr. Moore, Benjamin, isn't going to help us one bit. I got a little help from a friend of mine at the Hennepin County Sheriff's Office. He did a record check, comes back clean as a whistle, not even a speeding ticket. He's a longshoreman, works on the barges on the Mississippi, has for over twenty-five years. Born and raised in South St. Paul. The few neighbors that were willing to talk to me say he's a quiet man, stays to himself. They've never noticed anything out of the ordinary. He isn't dragging women home. He goes out and hangs one on once in a while, one of the local dives that has exotic dancers . . ."

"Should've figured," interjected Jackie.

"Can't hold that against him, Jackie. I've done that myself a few times," Brownie said. Then he looked at me, "Only since Jeannie died."

I nodded my head and grinned.

"Anyway," Brownie continued, "after I gathered all this information I waited for him one night to get home, knocked on the door. He came out on the porch. The first thing he said was, 'You don't understand the English language, huh? I told you to get your ass out of here. I'm sorry she's dead. If your doctor's responsible, I hope they fry his ass.'

"'You know she's made allegations that you sexually abused her,' I said. 'For many years, when she was a child.' I could see the anger cross his face. I glanced down and he was making a fist. I was picturing myself flying backwards through the screen. 'Listen, Mister,' he said, 'I'm only gonna tell you this once, that's all bullshit! Whatever troubles she had were not of my making. The last time I saw her I told her she needed help, more than I could give her. I told her that until she got help, I didn't want her around. She left. They called me from the hospital, told me she took an overdose. You know what I told 'em? I told 'em it was bullshit. She had pulled that crap for years about how she was gonna do herself in. If she was serious, she would've been dead long ago.'

"I asked him about her mother, he said she was a fuckin' tramp and he got rid of her a long time ago. That was pretty much the end of it, guys. After that he said, 'Get off my porch and don't bother me again or I'll kick your ass from here to Lake Street.' And I think he meant it. I know damn well he could do it."

"That would be quite a spectacle to watch," I said.

"Well, you're not gonna get a chance 'cause I'm not going back. I'll tell ya something, I don't think he's our man."

"He has to be," I said. "No one else makes any sense."

"Dr. Morgan," Jackie mumbled.

"You're never going to convince me of that," I said.

"Noah," said Brownie, "we've known each other a long time. I respect your judgment but I think you're wrong on this one."

"I'm not," I said. "I'd stake my life on it."

128

"I hope not," muttered Jackie.

"You've been awful quiet," I said to her.

"I'm still recovering from one disaster, I haven't quite moved onto the next."

"Well, for the time being, you do your thing in Clint's case; let this one up to me. I'll talk to Detective Kropp. I'm sure they've checked into the old man. He'll be honest with me."

\* \* \* \* \*

I called Detective Kropp and told him I would buy lunch. I told him I wanted to pick his brain a little bit. Any other cop would've probably told me to kiss-off, but Kropp and I had a long relationship built on mutual respect. I met him a little after twelve at one of the hamburger joints. It really wasn't on my diet, but I figured I'd be all right if I ordered it well done. Kropp didn't have the same concerns. He ordered a cheeseburger with fried onions and a bottle of beer.

"How ya been, Noah?" he asked after the waitress took our order.

"I've been better," I said.

"I'm surprised you took Dr. Morgan's case."

"It's going to be a role reversal," I said. "This time I'm going to do the footwork, Jackie's going to do the trial."

"Really?" he said. "You think he's that guilty that you're willing to throw him to a novice? That's unlike you, Noah. I would've expected that if you couldn't handle the case you'd refer it to somebody with some experience handling murder cases."

"You've got a short memory," I said. "Remember the Kramer case?"

Instant recognition covered his face.

Over thirty-five years ago, when I'd been in practice for only a few years, a young man, in his early twenties, Tommy Kramer, was indicted for first-degree murder of his four-year-old daughter. The prosecution based its case on the testimony of one of the local physicians who swore that the injury that caused the death, brain trauma, could not have occurred accidentally, that it had to be intentionally inflicted. Kropp was a rookie investigator on the case. He was pretty

129

much convinced that Kramer was lying when he said the child fell down the steps. I obtained an expert opinion from a pediatrician in Minneapolis who testified that in his opinion, the injuries were consistent with such a fall. On his testimony, we were able to create a reasonable doubt. The jury found Kramer not guilty. In the hall afterwards Kropp came up and shook my hand, complimented me on a good job but then added, "Justice wasn't done." I told him he was wrong, justice was done; it's just that sometimes justice as determined by a jury doesn't have anything to do with the truth. He told me years later that that comment stuck in his mind. He said I was right, that in the legal system, justice is what the jury says it is, which doesn't necessarily have to correspond with the truth of what really happened.

"Everybody has to start somewhere," I said, "and Jackie's better than that young attorney who took Tommy Kramer to trial."

"But that case was about a reasonable doubt," he said. "This one isn't. In this case there's no doubt who murdered Cheryl."

"You really believe that?" I asked.

"You bet," he said.

"I'm curious," I said. "What've you been able to find out about her background? About treatment she may have received prior to talking to Chris?"

"Well, you've seen everything I have," he replied.

"All we received are the files from Dr. Morgan's office. Were you involved in Clint's case?"

"Nah, that was Henry."

"Have you seen the files from that case?"

"No, I haven't. Why?"

"I was just curious to see whether there was anything more in there on her treatment."

"I can certainly look," he said. "If there's anything relevant to this case, I'll let you know."

"Well, Morgan's notes indicate that she told him that she was sexually abused by her father and I understand there's some records to indicate that she's told other treating doctors the same thing. I noticed there's nothing in the reports about you guys talking to the old man. Have you?"

"Several times. It's all been dictated, it just hasn't been typed. You'll get everything. He denies the sexual abuse, claims it's all a figment of her sick imagination. Said he hasn't seen her for a couple years and after their last meeting he had no interest in seeing her. I asked him if he'd do a polygraph test, he said he would. I may still do that if I think it's necessary. I even dug through the divorce file. There are no allegations of any sexual abuse in there. The mother got custody but she turned her over to the aunt. I understood the mother wanted to move out of town and Cheryl didn't wanna leave. I asked Mr. Moore why, he said I should talk to the old lady."

"Do you consider him a suspect at all?" I asked.

"No way. I don't need any suspects, Noah; I know who did it, your client."

"Does Mr. Moore have an alibi for the day she was murdered?"

"Actually, Noah, he doesn't. He said he had the day off and he spent it at home. He said there isn't anybody who can account for his time, but it doesn't make any difference to me because I'm not gonna pursue it."

"But you know Chris; he couldn't have mutilated that young lady. No way in hell."

"I think he did, Noah, and I have an expert who agrees with me. The whole scene bothered me the first time I saw it. It looked contrived, like it was set up to lead us to believe that her murder was some sort of sadistic sexual ritual, committed by a sexually deviant psychopath. And to be honest, that was my first inclination until I found her notebooks and discovered her relationship with the doc. She had kept copies of all the letters she had written to Chris, along with his letters to her. Then it all kind of made some sense. Who better than a psychologist to stage a scene to make you believe it was done by some sexual deviant? I sent the file to an expert in D.C. who agrees. The scene is all too neat; as I said, staged to be what it was meant to portray. No, Noah, accept the fact your client murdered her. He might not have gone over there with that intention, but something happened to make him mad enough to do it. I suspect she was gonna tell somebody. I suspect she told him that if he didn't follow through on his promise to marry her, she'd blow the whistle on him. I suspect that at that point he got her into the bedroom, got her undressed, probably with the expectation of sex, and then he slit her throat. She was murdered right there on the bed. That gives us the premeditation, Noah. We know from the medical examiner's reports that the wound was such that she would've been dead in just seconds. All the other stab wounds are post-mortem. The heart had stopped pumping by the time they were inflicted. This, I guess, is some little consolation. Being spread-eagled, turning her head to the side in some grotesque fashion; that was done to make us believe that it was some psychopath. So, Noah, I know you've pulled off a few miracles in your time but this isn't gonna be one of 'em."

I had known Kropp long enough to know that he believed everything he said. He was so convincing he even had me second-guessing myself; maybe Chris *was* conning me. It was hard for me to believe that I could misjudge so badly.

"You know her mother's bringing a wrongful death civil suit against Chris, right?"

"Yeah, Ron Crane's been in touch with us. I'm not gonna go out of my way to help him. I'll give 'em what I absolutely have to. I don't understand how she's entitled to a dime."

"Well, there's an insurance company involved," I said. "Smell of money, you know. Have you talked to her? Cheryl's mother?"

"Yeah, first by phone, then when she was here to talk to Crane. Attractive lady, a widow. Her name's O'Malley now. Her second husband drowned. She said she had very little contact with Cheryl, mainly by phone. Said she asked Cheryl to move to Boston but she wouldn't."

"Did you ask her about the allegations Cheryl made about her ex-husband, the sexual abuse?"

"She said she never suspected anything. She didn't know it was going on. She said she left him because of physical abuse, his drinking."

By then the waitress had brought our meals. Now I was discouraged that I had even called him. Maybe it was time for me to rethink everything.

We talked about other matters as we finished our meals. Kropp told me he had been meaning to call Brownie to go fishing. I sort of urged him to do that, thinking maybe that after he and Brownie had a few beers, Brownie might be able to pry something more out of him.

# 21

"Noah, here's my motion," I said as I dropped it on his desk.

He paged through it quickly. "That's all you should need," he said. "Make sure you serve it along with your request for production of documents so he has to give you everything in the file."

"What do you think is going to happen?" I asked.

"Too early to say," he replied.

"Noah, if there's any justice in this world . . ." I could tell Noah was about to say something and then thought better of it. His stare seemed to go right through me. Then it was like he changed gears.

"I had lunch with Detective Kropp yesterday," he said. "He doesn't consider Cheryl's dad a suspect at all. As far as he's concerned, they have the guilty party. I did learn, though, that he's never seen Cheryl's medical reports. All he's ever seen is what's in Chris's file. He said he's going to check with the detective who handled Clint's case, what they might have had. After talking to him, my first inclination was to go right over to Chris's house and confront him—telling him he's been bullshittin' us. But now that I've had a chance to sit and think about it, I just know Kropp is wrong. Jackie, there's something we're missing. The only thing Kropp said that has me thinking is that they don't believe that this was any sort of random slaying, some sexual pervert who gets his kicks out of raping and murdering young girls. It sounds like the fact that there was no sign of sexual assault, at least no semen . . . they have some expert from D.C. who's telling them that although it was set up to look that way, there are certain things that tell him the scene was staged."

"He told you all this?" I asked.

"I assume we'll get all this in discovery yet to be given to us, but he gave me his own twist on it, which I wouldn't get from the written page. That's one

133

advantage of the 'good ol' boy' system. He doesn't consider me the enemy, just a professional doing a job like he is. Even though her old man may not have been the bad guy in this, Jackie, he still has to be the key. I mean, girls don't grow up to be that mixed up without something very sick happening in their background. If it wasn't her dad, maybe it was some other relative . . . some neighbor."

He sighed deeply, sinking into his chair. The lines on his face belied the casual demeanor he tried to display. He closed his eyes, slipped deep into thought. The silence made me uncomfortable. I didn't know if he was in pain or what. Finally I stood up and his eyes snapped open.

"I'm going to go file my motion right now," I said. "The sooner the better. I don't want Becker to think he's going to get away with anything."

Noah nodded. "Are you okay?" I asked.

"Fine," he said. "I get this way when things don't seem right. I'll tell ya, Jackie, I'm missing something and it's starting to bug me."

"Let me get this filed, then we'll agonize together," I said.

He smiled. "We'll do that."

* * * * *

I served a copy of my motion on the prosecutor's secretary, signed the Affidavit of Service and filed the original with the Clerk of Court.

Johnny and I had planned on meeting for lunch at noon, a half an hour away. With a little free time I decided to spend some time in the law library researching the issue of discovery. Noah was right—everything was in kind of a flux. Women's rights advocates had been successful; a woman's prior sexual history would be closed to the defense in rape cases except in special circumstances. As a result of the changes, the courts were struggling with concepts of privilege and relevancy and the defendant's right of confrontation. That was Clint's case precisely. Had we known Cheryl's history, we could have indeed confronted her with it. The medical record would have, I believe, destroyed her credibility. Clint's right to a fair trial had to override any considerations the law may have for her right to privacy.

I met Johnny at Joyce's Café for lunch. He was already there in a back booth when

I arrived.  I could tell immediately something was wrong by his concerned look.

"God, you look like you've seen a ghost," I said.

"Worse than that," he said.  "Ron Crane called me into his office just twenty minutes ago; he wanted to know about our relationship.  After I told him we were friends, he asked whether I had slipped you anything from our wrongful death file."

"Oh my God, Johnny. What did you tell him?"

"I told him I had no idea what he was talking about.  That seemed to satisfy him, but it was obvious to me he had talked to somebody.  Who knows you have those documents?"

I told him about my meeting with Randy Becker and the motion I had just filed.

"Yeah, that explains it all," he said.  "I've heard that Crane and Becker are big buddies, went to law school together.  Ron helped run his campaign when he ran for county prosecutor.  I bet Becker called him as soon as he read your motion."

"Are you in trouble?" I asked.

"For what?" he asked, a coy look on his face.  "I haven't done anything, right?"

"Not as far as I'm concerned," I said.

"Those documents will all be a matter of public record at some point which, unfortunately for your client, could be a couple years away," he said. "Also, there could've been a settlement with the parties agreeing to keep everything confidential.  Who knows, Crane might've done that for Becker.  I suppose the worst that could happen is I'd lose my job.  Maybe then I'd come and work with you."

"But you said you wanna make money.  You're never going to make money doing what I do."

"You never can tell," he said.  "We could form a team, be as famous as F. Lee Baily, somebody like that.  Demand big retainers, you know."

"You are a dreamer," I replied.  "You aren't going to do that in this area.  You have to be in the big cities for that."

"Well, then, money isn't everything," he replied.

I was really starting to like this guy.

\* \* \* \* \*

There's this famous quote: "The wheels of justice grind slowly." Now I understood what it meant. August slipped into September. The hearing on my motion in Clint's case had been set for September twentieth and then for some unknown reason, and without my permission, was canceled, a new date to be set by Judge Savano. Dr. Morgan's trial was set for the first week in November. We had received all of the discovery, including the report of the expert the State had hired, an expert whose *curriculum vitae* made him look like the "who's who" in crime scene reconstruction. Interestingly enough, the documents didn't include any of Cheryl's medical records. When Noah called him to ask why, Becker claimed that there was nothing in the medical records of any relevance to Dr. Morgan's murder defense.

The thirty days for Randy Becker to respond to my own demand for documents in Clint's case came and went without a reply. When I would see him in the courthouse and ask him where they were, he'd shrug his shoulders with no response. When I called his office, he wouldn't take the call. I talked to Noah and he said I should file a motion to hold him in contempt of court for failure to follow the rules—which I did. I also filed all of the documents with the Appellate Court asking for a stay of the oral argument until discovery had been completed. A week before the oral argument was set, the court granted the continuance.

A day after receiving the notice from the Appellate Court, I got a call. "Ms. Geroux," the officious voice said, "my name's Steve Gordon. I'm with the Attorney General's office in the Appellate Division. I'm calling regarding the matter of *State of Minnesota v. Clint Sadowski*. We received a copy of the Appellate Court's Notice of Continuance. I really would like to spend some time talking to you about this case. I'm hoping we can reach some resolution."

I gulped hard. "What kind of resolution?" I asked.

I had no idea what he was talking about and I had no idea how he got involved in Clint's case. The words Attorney General's office, however, were enough to grab all my attention, and the term "resolution" enough to keep my interest.

He replied, "Something that would be beneficial to your client."

"In that case, where and when?"

We set up an appointment for the following morning. He was even willing to drive the seventy miles to my office. I was flabbergasted; this was totally outside of any experience I'd had, anything I'd expected.

Noah was in court with Cochrane, the wife abuser, so I didn't get a chance to talk to him until late in the afternoon. I was sitting in my office ruminating over the significance of the call when I heard Johnny's voice. He asked Linda if I was in and she buzzed me. I was a little surprised because he hadn't said anything about coming to see me.

As soon as he walked in the door, I knew something was wrong.

"You'll never guess what happened," he said.

Before I had a chance to guess, he said, "We got fired."

"You mean *you* got fired?" I asked.

"No, *we* got fired. Cheryl's mother, she fired our firm. She's bringing in some big shot lawyer from Boston, said she didn't want to stay with some little podunk outfit that couldn't handle the case properly anyway. When I found out I thought Ron was going to be so pissed that he would fire me, but he hasn't said anything . . . yet."

"Why would he fire you now?" I asked.

"I don't know," he replied. "Maybe as a favor to Becker."

"Something's going on here that we don't understand," I said.

I told him about my call and meeting with the Assistant Attorney General's.

"You're right, Jackie," he said. "There's a whole lot of crap going on here that you and I know nothing about. Did he tell you what he wants to do?"

"He just said it would be beneficial to my client."

"You can bet it will be beneficial to more than just your client," he said. "Somebody's gonna cover Becker's ass."

"Do you really think so?" I asked.

"What are you willing to bet?" he asked, with a devious smile.

"Not that," I said.

"Too bad," he replied. "I think you'd enjoy it."

"You'll find out in time."

Johnny and I had become very comfortable with each other. We'd been into some heavy kissing but nothing more.  One time in his car he tried to feel me up and I slapped his hand—good-naturedly.  He took it as his answer and never took the liberty again.

\* \* \* \* \*

"What do you think happened to Mr. Cochrane?" Noah asked me when he returned late that afternoon.

"He was pilloried," I replied with a grin.

"There were a few women in the courtroom who would've voted for that, but even Judge Savano has progressed beyond that.  No, I told him he didn't have much choice but to plead guilty.  He didn't like it but he could see the handwriting on the wall.  So he did with a thirty-day jail cap.  The judge gave him all thirty days.  His wife filed for divorce.  She was there with somebody from the Battered Women's Shelter.  She outlined a long history of being abused. Savano saw a chance to make some points with all the women in the courtroom, *ergo* the maximum sentence.  Mr. Cochrane was rather upset with me.  He wanted to know what he had paid us for.  I told him for the pleasure of our company."

"Good for you," I said.  "You never get paid enough to represent creeps like that.  I've got even more interesting news, though."

I told him about my call from the Attorney General's office.  "Johnny was here a few minutes ago.  He said Cheryl's mother had fired their office, hired some big shot firm out of Boston.  He thinks somehow it's all tied together, that somebody's trying to save Becker's butt.  Do you think that's true?"

"Well, it's unusual for the Attorney General's office to call.  It's even more unusual for them to suggest it's in your client's best interest to meet.  It is just before Randy's contempt hearing, maybe somebody asked the Attorney General intervene.  We'll just have to wait and see."

\* \* \* \* \*

I went to work the next morning wearing the most businesslike outfit I owned: a navy blue suit, a white blouse, and medium-high heels to give myself a little more stature. Mr. Gordon showed up at exactly 10:00. I heard him give Linda my name in his deep voice. I immediately went out to greet him. I had tried to picture what he would look like from our short discussion on the phone. I couldn't have been more wrong. He was tall, probably six-four or more, thin, athletic build, broad shoulders, narrow hips. I guessed him to be in his fifties. Very handsome, gray hair, distinguished looking. He carried himself with an air of confidence. He greeted me with a smile.

"Ms. Geroux," he said, "so glad to meet you. I've heard such good things about you."

Just what I had expected—a little bit of the con in him. He handed me his card. He was the chief of the entire Appellate Division. Without fully comprehending what it meant, I knew this guy was pretty important within the hierarchy of the Attorney General's office. I felt butterflies in my stomach. I had this presage that he was here for one purpose, to sweet-talk me into something. I thought about Johnny's comment: "You can bet it will be beneficial for more than just your client." I wondered how he knew.

I invited him back to my office. I had already made arrangements with Noah that if I needed his help, I would discreetly summon him. He suggested I handle it by myself, show the guy who's boss. I started out intending to do that, now I had some doubts.

He took a seat. I offered him a cup of coffee, which he waved off without comment.

"I want to make this as easy as possible, Ms. Geroux," he started. "I've had a chance to review the entire file in your defendant's case. I've read your motion papers and I've had a chance to review the psychological file of Ms. Moore."

"I don't understand," I interjected. "How did your office get involved in a motion in front of the trial court?"

"We provide support to all the prosecutors in the state."

"So Mr. Becker asked for your help?"

"I didn't say that," he replied. "Let's just say our office was asked for help."

"Somebody from this county?" I asked.

"Ms. Geroux, before you go into your cross-examination, why don't you hear me out?"

I could tell he was a man not used to being interrupted by one he considered his underling.

"I think there's a way of resolving your client's case without having the matter go to the Court of Appeals and without the necessity of having to argue the motion to find Mr. Becker in contempt. Let me put it this way, Ms. Geroux, your client's not going to get a new trial on appeal, it simply won't happen. Now whether any judge will reopen the matter based on what you contend is newly discovered evidence, even that is problematic. However, some of us who have looked at this file believe that in the interest of justice, your client should be let out of prison. What I am proposing is this: we will do a stipulation of facts putting forth the entire psychiatric history of Ms. Moore. That stipulation will be signed by you, as defense attorney, and by me as attorney for the state. It will then be presented to the judge as part of your motion for post-conviction relief. The judge will make findings that, while the newly discovered evidence does not rise to the level needed to reverse the conviction and grant your client a new trial, given all the circumstances, it would seem that in the interest of justice, your client should be released from prison. Basically, Ms. Geroux, the judge will re-sentence him to time served and your client can be released."

I sat there, stunned, my mouth agape, my mind spinning. How did they ever come up with this? I gazed across my desk at him.

"I know what you're thinking, Ms. Geroux," he said. "Don't go there. This is the best deal your client's going to get."

"And Becker never has to admit to a thing," I said.

"Like what?" he asked.

"Mr. Gordon, you're obviously not dumb or naive, everything I know tells me that Becker had those reports before he tried Clint's case. He knew if he released any of her records to me her credibility would be zero—so he hid the records from us. I think people should know the truth."

"For what purpose, Ms. Geroux?"

"People like that shouldn't be in a position of authority."

"Who's to make that decision, you? He was duly elected as County Prosecutor."

"Yeah! And if the people knew what he pulled, he wouldn't get re-elected."

"Well, that's not going to happen," he replied. "The only condition to this little agreement is that it stays between us."

"What do you mean, between us?"

"Just that," he said. "The stipulation will be marked confidential; the file will be marked confidential. Neither will be open for anyone's perusal except by court order."

"Who's ever going to approve this agreement?" I asked.

"It's already been approved."

"You mean you've already discussed this with a judge?"

"Let's just say it's been approved."

I leaned back in my chair, shaking my head in disgust.

He ignored me. "There is some urgency to this, Ms. Geroux. I suggest you discuss it with your client and let me know by the end of the week."

"Let me see if I've got it right," I said. "We're going to put together a stipulation outlining Cheryl Moore's entire psychiatric history."

He nodded in agreement.

"That stipulation will be submitted to whom? Savano?"

He nodded.

"And based on that stipulation, the judge is going to say what? That the interest of justice requires that Clint be released immediately?"

He nodded again, a curl meant to be the start of a smile etching the corner of his mouth.

"How long have you been an attorney, Mr. Gordon?" I asked.

The smile never surfaced. "This spring it'll be thirty years."

"Do you believe that this is in the interest of justice?"

His gaze turned sardonic. "I believe it is in your client's best interest. You should be pleased with yourself, Ms. Geroux. After all, you saved him more than twenty years in prison; he would have rotted there."

There are times in your life when you'd give your right arm to come up with a good retort and this was one of them, but for the life of me, I couldn't think of a thing to say.

I stood and he followed suit, reaching his hand across the desk. "It's been my pleasure," he said.

We shook hands, and as he walked out he said, "I expect to hear from you by Friday."

I dropped back into my chair trying to mentally reconstruct what had just happened. My major in college was history. The word *blitzkrieg* came to mind. In one swift blow, the power brokers had backed me into the corner and now stood waiting for me to put up the white flag. Instead of Becker having to answer for his manipulation of the truth, his malfeasance would be hidden from public view by a judicial stamp that simply said "CONFIDENTIAL".

I gathered up enough energy to go into Noah's office. He was sitting behind his desk, wide-eyed as I came in.

"Somebody brought in the big guns," he said. "He's the Attorney General's right-hand man. There's some talk he'll be appointed to the next opening on the Supreme Court."

I took a chair without saying anything.

"Well don't keep me waiting, Jackie. If they sent him, this has got to be good."

"It is," I replied. I laid the whole thing out for him with no editorial comments. When I was done, Noah got this strange smile on his face. He sat there quietly gazing at me.

"Savano has to be behind this whole thing," he sighed. "But I'm just trying to figure out where the connections would be. Becker wouldn't have called in the Attorney General's; he'd have too much explaining to do. He's too gutless for that. If I had to guess, when Savano saw the motion papers, he probably called Becker up to his chambers. Becker had to admit that he'd had the documents. At that point, I suspect Savano would've been really pissed. But on the other hand, he couldn't throw Becker to the dogs either. So he must have some connections in the Attorney General's office and they came up with this plan to put everything quietly to bed."

"Noah, how can they do that?" I asked. "Becker's not supposed to be talking to the judge *ex parte*, without me there. And the judge isn't supposed to be making any commitments to these guys as to how he'll dispose of my motion. He told me this was already approved by the judge. The whole thing stinks to high heaven."

"You're right," Noah said. "But what are your options? The first thing you have to do is talk to Clint. It's his case. They have this all thought out, Jackie. There's no way Clint's going to say don't take the deal, and they know that."

"But it's not like they're going to reverse the conviction," I said. "It's not like he's going to be not guilty. He'll still be a convicted rapist."

"Jackie, if you wanna go through with your motion and appeal, it could take another year or two. You're going to have to tell Clint that. You'll have to tell him that if he wants to continue fighting, he could be sitting in prison for at least another two years . . . if not longer. On the other hand, if he takes the deal, he could be out in a matter of weeks. Whaddaya think he's going to say?"

I didn't have to answer. I knew what Clint would say. He'd say, "Get me out of here!" "Noah, have you ever seen anything like this?"

"Well, things don't always work the way they should. The system isn't perfect. As long as you've got human beings responsible for operating it, you're going to have the Randy Beckers of this world and the Judge Savanos to save their butts. At least there are people like you who are trying to keep the system honest. You'll find there are very few big victories, though. You measure your career by little wins at a time."

\* \* \* \* \*

The next afternoon I found myself standing in the alcove of the state prison filling out a professional visitor's form. I handed it through the bar and the guard hollered, "Open her up."

I heard an electric hum and the gate opened slowly to the side. I walked in and it closed behind me with a clang, the noise sending a shiver down my spine.

"I have to search that," the guard said, motioning to my briefcase. I handed it to him and he emptied the contents on a table. "Walk through that, please," he said, pointing to the metal detector.

I went through with no beeps. He handed me my briefcase and waved through the Plexiglas to a guard sitting at a big board of lights. The steel bars opened. "Straight ahead is visiting," he said. "They'll bring him right down."

I walked down the long corridor. It appeared to be all administrative offices.

At the end it opened into a large room with tables and chairs, vending machines along one side. It must have been visiting hours because half the tables were occupied. It appeared most were couples. I noticed a few inmates trying to sneak a feel under the table. Everybody seemed to gawk at me as I walked in. I stood there, momentarily confused as to where I was, what was supposed to happen. Then, from the far side, I saw a guard bringing Clint in. When he saw me, he burst into a smile and walked briskly across the room.

From twenty feet away he hollered, "Jackie, boy am I glad to see ya." And he walked right up and hugged me so hard that I lost my breath.

The guard had followed him, tapped him on the shoulder. "None of that," he said.

"Oh, George, it ain't nothin' like that. This isn't my girlfriend, this is my lawyer."

"Miss," the guard said, "if you want some privacy, you can take that table back there," and he pointed toward the corner.

"Come on," said Clint. Then he took my hand and pulled me toward the table. We took a seat across from each other and he said, "Ya wanna pop?"

"No, I'm fine."

"Ya care if I get one?" he asked.

"No, go ahead."

"See, we don't get pop unless we get a visitor."

"You need money?" I asked.

"No, I got change."

He got up and shuffled toward the pop machine. He looked quite comical in his prisoner garb. Unlike the jail, they had a size that fit him but even then he was more stoop shouldered than I remembered and his slippers seemed too big so he shuffled his feet to keep from losing them.

He got his can of pop and turned when one of the other prisoners hollered from a table, "Hey Clint, who's the puss?"

Clint showed him a fist. The guy laughed and hollered, "Oh, I'm scared! You wuss, you wouldn't hurt a fly."

I thought of the comment as Clint walked back. That was my opinion as well: he couldn't hurt anybody. A gentle giant. As he sat down, he took a big gulp of his Mountain Dew.

"Am I gonna get outta here?" he asked. "I gotta get outta here, Miss Geroux. Everything they told me about this place is true. There's some bad people in here. You know what happened the other night? They brought this young guy in for burglary. Three big dudes caught him in the hall and gang-banged 'em."

"Where were the guards?" I asked.

"They look the other way."

"Doesn't anything happen to them for that?" I asked.

"Like what? They just don't care."

"Have you been okay?" I asked.

"The only thing that's saving my ass, excuse me Miss Geroux, is my size, but that don't mean they haven't threatened. I gotta get outta here."

It took me twenty minutes to explain to him the offer made in his case. I had to go over it several times, answering questions that had nothing to do with where we found ourselves. Clint was totally confused. In the end, the only thing he understood was that if we agreed to the proposal, he could be out in a matter of weeks.

"That's the bottom line, Clint," I said. "You get out but you keep a record as a rapist."

"But I didn't do it. You know I didn't do it."

"And we may be able to actually prove that, but that's going to take a lot longer."

"Then just get me outta here.

"Are you sure?"

"Look," he said, "I'm not gonna run for president or nothin'. With what I do, nobody's gonna care if I got a record. Just get me outta here."

Noah was right. A person should be happy with little victories. Clint thought I was the greatest lawyer in the world. I was sure he would tell everybody about this great mouthpiece he had who saved him from a life in prison. And except for a few people, that's all anybody would ever know. Where it appeared I beat the system, the truth is, it was a corruption of the system that landed him in prison in the first place.

"Chris," I said, "we're at a standstill. If your case went to the jury right now, I would suspect it would take them about two hours to find you guilty. Dr. Culligan, the forensic pathologist, got back to me last week. He said there was nothing in the medical examiner's report that he could argue with. The only question would be the time of her death and he's saying there's nothing in the evidence that would narrow that down any better than what the medical examiner estimated."

"What about that crime scene guy they have?" Chris asked.

"I found an ex-FBI agent in Kansas City who's willing to take a look at the report and get back to me. He said it would be next week sometime."

"They won't let that guy, that Lance Carter, testify anyway, will they?"

"His testimony has been admitted as an expert in some pretty high profile cases," I said. "Savano will consider his opinion the last nail in your coffin. He'll let it in."

"But it's garbage," he said.

"I don't know, Chris. It seems to make some sense to me."

My comment seemed to take all of the air out of Chris. He sat there, a dejected look on his face. "I'm not saying you're the one who staged it. I'm simply agreeing that there may be some basis to suggest certain things don't look right. The point is, Chris, somebody staged it; somebody wanted to divert any suspicion from himself. So it seems to me it still comes down to somebody who knew her, somebody she would have invited into her apartment, maybe even into her bedroom. But who? We're at a dead end. It wasn't you. It wasn't her dad. We haven't been able to find any boyfriends. We're stuck."

Chris had not moved. He sat in a trance.

"And the one with the biggest motive in the world is you," I continued.

He turned toward me and gave me a piercing gaze.

"Chris, I'm just getting you used to it. That's what Becker's going to tell the jury.  And when he does, you can't be giving him the finger or anything, you just have to sit there and take it with this innocent, 'who me?' look on your face."

"We've got to do something before that, Noah.  I've been around the court system long enough to know I don't stand a chance in that courtroom.  I could resurrect Clarence Darrow, it wouldn't make a damn bit of difference."

"Unfortunately, you're right," I said.  "Now the real reason why I brought you here this morning.  I got a call from Kevin Young.  You know Cheryl's mother hired G. Gordon Pettiman to handle the wrongful death case.  Pettiman wants to take your deposition."

"Before the trial?" he asked.  "Do I have to do it?"

"No, you don't.  That's the point.  As long as the criminal charges are pending, you have the right to remain silent, to take the Fifth Amendment.  But if you do that, everybody is going to think you're guilty."

"Then I'll testify.  I don't have anything to hide."

"I agree.  The only problem with a deposition is Becker will know exactly what you're going to say.  So if we have anything we can surprise the jury with in your testimony, he'll know it and be prepared for it."

"What am I going to do?" he asked.

"I can try and postpone it until after the trial, tell them we're too busy.  But if he wants to be a prick about it, he could attempt to force it to happen."

The room was quiet while we both pondered the alternatives.  Finally Chris said, "You know, I've had my deposition taken before and I think I handled it pretty well.  It might be a good dress rehearsal for the trial.  We don't have any surprises.  I only have one version to give—the truth," and he paused, "and the truth shall set me free," he grinned.  "In my dreams."

"You're right," I said.  "That's better than taking the fifth.  That has all kinds of awful implications.  Jurors always agree that they won't use the defendant's right to remain silent, to not testify, against him.  But that's bullshit.  They wanna know; if the guy's innocent—why doesn't he get up and tell us?"

Chris and I talked for a while and agreed on some dates for his deposition.  When he left, I asked Linda if Jackie was back yet.  She wasn't.

Jackie had spent the last week going over the final details of the stipulation in Clint's case.  Now, with Cheryl's history of treatment set out in black and white, summarized in chronological order, it was even more obvious that she, as psychologists like to say, transferred her experiences with her father to Clint and he was in fact just some poor slob she picked out of the crowd. Maybe because he might have reminded her of her dad—in size, if nothing else.

The stipulation was presented to the judge for his approval. Clint's release was a *fait accompli;* the final requirement was the judge's seal of approval. That was scheduled for this morning at nine. It was close to noon when Jackie finally came into my office, flustered.

"That bastard didn't even show up."

"Who?"

"Becker! He sent one of his underlings. He couldn't even face me. Then Savano makes us wait until he's got the whole damn morning calendar done. He justifies it by saying this was supposed to be a secret proceeding. Secret proceeding, Noah! Think about it, there isn't supposed to be any such thing as a secret proceeding."

"I think what he meant, Jackie, is confidential."

"Confidential, secret, same damn thing," she said.

"And Clint?" I asked.

"Oh, he's as happy as a lark. As soon as the judge said, 'Take him back to the jail, give him his civilian duds and release him,' he danced out of the courtroom. The most pathetic thing is, Noah, he doesn't understand any of this. All he knows is he was in prison and now he's free. This was just another bad episode in a life filled with bad episodes. For him, I'm sure they all seem to run together. The fact that he's going to be tagged a rapist doesn't even dawn on him. In fact, in his circle, it might even give him some stature."

"If there's any consolation, Jackie, we're always going to know the truth, and Becker's going to know you know the truth. He has to live with it, and I think that's always going to put him at a disadvantage in his dealings with you."

"I don't think that's true, Noah. I suspect this isn't the first predicament he's been able to slime out of. It's probably only going to make him bolder."

"Well, the best thing you can do, Jackie, is to close the file and get on with it. I had Chris in this morning. They want to take his deposition in the civil case and we've decided we'll use it as sort of a dress rehearsal for the trial. The truth is, though, his testimony isn't going to get him an acquittal, no matter how sincere and credible he comes across. You know, this is a first for me, I've never had a case before where I knew my client was innocent and there was absolutely nothing I could do to prove it. Whoever set this up did one hell of a job."

"Have you heard back from Brownie?" she asked.

"He's at a dead end," I replied.

"Has he tried to contact Cheryl's dad again?"

"No," I replied.

Silence settled in. I could see her mind working. "Don't get any crazy ideas," I said.

"Well, her dad's our only chance. As you said, something's not right and there has to be somebody who knows why. It's got to be him."

"Well, don't you try and talk to him," I said.

"I won't," she replied.

As she got up to leave, I asked her, "By the way, did Savano have anything to say to you afterwards?"

"No, he didn't. But if looks could kill, I would've been dead."

"Yeah, I suppose a man like that doesn't have a whole lot of chips stored up. You might've made him empty his till. He won't forget you for that."

"Well, he can be assured I won't forget him."

"It's nice to keep that edge, Jackie, but you have to remember, you're first duty is always to your client. Sometimes you have to swallow your pride to get what you want."

* * * * *

One of those lulls set in that seems to happen before every major trial. The office takes in fewer cases because you know you're going to be tied up for a long time. Typically you've done everything you can to prepare for trial. You start to fine tune things and wait for the big day. The only difference this time was weeks before the murder trial was scheduled to start, Mr. G. Gordon Pettiman was going to take Chris's deposition.

149

Jackie and I had brought Chris into the office and put him through a dry run. Chris was right; he made a very good witness. No matter how hard we tried, we couldn't get him flustered. And he stuck to the only theme we had: Yes, I had sex with Cheryl Moore; yes, it was wrong, maybe even criminal; yes, she threatened to go public if I didn't marry her; but I didn't murder her.

However, I knew from experience that it was going to be a little tougher with G. Gordon. I had done some digging into his reputation. I found he was a mediocre student and a mediocre lawyer until he hit his little niche in the legal profession: suing the church for the sexual escapades of the clergy. Many of the settlements had been into the seven figure area. In one of the dioceses, where the parish priest had been abusing the little altar boys, the church paid twelve million to settle. G. Gordon was riding the crest of a wave and he knew it. At first I couldn't figure out why he would take what for him was a penny ante lawsuit against Dr. Morgan, whose insurance coverage was a measly half-a-million. But I was to learn at one of the impromptu bar meetings at one of my favorite pubs, where I was relegated to drinking soda, that Mr. Pettiman had figured out a bigger target. Actually, there was a little poetic justice in it. Since Dr. Morgan had basically been retained by the county at the request of the prosecutor, Randy Becker, G. Gordon was going to argue the theory of *respondat superior*—that the employer should be responsible for the acts of its agent. If that theory survived, the deep pockets of the county would be available for payment. Now things seemed to be making a little bit more sense. I was sure that wasn't an avenue that Ron Crane would have pursued. He had way too many friends in county government, his office the recipient of too much county largesse, to risk suing the hand that fed him.

But none of this was making it any easier for Dr. Morgan or his attorneys. The prosecutor couldn't offer him a plea bargain and, even if Becker did, we couldn't accept it. Even if Chris's insurance company wanted to offer the policy limits to settle, at this point I knew G. Gordon wouldn't accept it because he was after the real deep pockets.

G. Gordon Pettiman lived up to my expectations. Rather than use my office, which is rather cramped, we scheduled the deposition in one of the smaller courtrooms available for that purpose. We were set for 10:00 on a Tuesday morning.

Chris, Jackie and I were there early, nervously walking the halls. I didn't see this as a make or break situation for Chris's murder trial but I knew there was always the possibility of some *faux pas* from which we could never recover. Things were bleak enough without something more going wrong, and I kept trying to impress Chris with the notion: just answer the questions, don't volunteer anything and don't get into a pissing contest with him. He agreed and told me not to worry.

I was watching the entryway when a small entourage appeared. Four people entered the courthouse door. In the center, in a black cashmere overcoat, looking like an ad from *G.Q.*, was G. Gordon. He was about five-six or five-seven, in his middle fifties, with a full head of silver-gray hair. Even though there was a brisk north wind, not a strand was out of place. His features were small and his face tan. I imagined him spending his summers on his yacht in Boston Harbor. I assumed he took some perverse pleasure in knowing that some of the good clergy weren't taking their annual pilgrimage to Rome at his expense. Not having put any money in the collection box for many years myself, I wondered how many Sunday parishioners realized that the contents of the envelope they dropped in the woven basket was going to pay for G. Gordon's yacht. Poor St. Benedict must be rolling over in his grave.

Though we were standing in the hall directly in front of the designated court-room talking to Kevin Young, the entourage seemed to ignore us while a young woman helped G. Gordon remove his coat to reveal his Armani three- piece pin-striped blue suit, white silk shirt, and dark blue tie clipped with a diamond tie clasp. Only when he was good and ready did he turn, approach the three of us and stick out his hand.

"I'm G. Gordon Pettiman," he said. I noticed the glint of a diamond stud cufflink.

"I'm Noah Schepers," I said, shaking his hand. "This is my assistant, Jackie Geroux."

He shook her hand and winked.

"And this is Dr. Christopher Morgan."

He moved from Jackie to Chris, but Chris would have no part of it, he simply nodded with a grunt. G. Gordon looked at his bare hand extended and appeared a little embarrassed as he brought it back to his side. All the pleasantries, or lack of them, over, we settled into a long agonizing day.  It started slowly.  G. Gordon took Chris through his entire education, training, background, his experience prior to coming to town, and his experience here right up to the first day he met Cheryl Moore.

"It's my understanding," he said, "that you do some counseling for the Battered Women's Shelter.  Is that correct?"

"Yes, it is."

"And I believe some of that is volunteer service, correct?"

"Yes, it is."

"And as a result of your volunteer services, do you ever get any referrals to provide counseling on a fee basis?"

"That happens rarely," Chris responded.

"But it does happen, correct?"

"Yes, it does."

"And, in fact, that's how you got involved in the treatment of Ms. Moore. She was referred to you by somebody at the Battered Women's Shelter, correct?"

"Yes, she was."

"And we have the notes and minutes of your meetings here with Ms. Moore, Doctor.  You've had a chance to look those over. Do they appear to be all here?"

"Yes, they do."

"And included in those is a memo that you wrote directed to the County Social Service Office.  It appears to me to be a summary of the services provided and a request to continue based on the patient's continued needs.  Is that correct?"

"Yes, it is."

"So the county was paying for your services?"

"Yes."

"Because Ms. Moore did not have insurance to cover your services?"

"That's correct."

"And it would be fair to say that it was your understanding, was it not, Dr. Morgan, that the reason you were involved was to help Ms. Moore get through the trauma of being the complaining witness in the matter of *State of Minnesota v. Clint Sadowski.*"

"It started out like that, yes."

"Well, it didn't just start out like that, Dr. Morgan. That was your responsibility throughout the course of the entire treatment."

"The focus changed after a while," Chris said.

"I understand that," he said, "and we'll get to that. But up until the time of the trial and through her testimony, at least as far as the County Attorney, Randy Becker, was concerned, your sole purpose for treating Ms. Moore was to make sure that she made it through the trial. Yes or no?"

"Yes."

"And those were the services you were being paid for. Yes or no?"

"Yes."

I could see the anger and resentment building up in Chris. It wasn't just the questions, it was G. Gordon's entire demeanor, a persona I assumed he had spent years in perfecting, one meant to place the cross-examinee ill at ease and on the verge of losing his cool at any moment.

"It's almost 1:00," I said. "Maybe this would be a good time to take a lunch break."

"I usually don't eat lunch," he said. "I have a flight out of Minneapolis tonight, so my preference is to keep going."

"Well, I'm sorry," I said, "but I have blood sugar problems, and if I don't eat I can be in trouble. We'll only take a half an hour."

G. Gordon looked at his assistants, gave us a shrug and told the court reporter we'd go off the record.

\* \* \* \* \*

The three of us sat at a coffee shop across the street from the courthouse. I was too uptight to eat. I got a cup of the strongest coffee they made.

"I didn't know you were diabetic," Chris said with a grin.

"I could tell he was getting you angry. I wanted a chance to talk and let you cool down before you continued."

"He's just such an arrogant bastard," said Chris.

"But you have to admit, he's pretty smooth," said Jackie.

"What I'm finding interesting," I said, "is he's probably discovering most of this stuff as we're going along. You notice he has a notebook he keeps referring to and it's not his handwriting. I've seen him make notes in the margins, so somebody has done all this work for him and he's kind of picking it up as he goes, by the seat of his pants."

"You think so?" asked Jackie.

"I know so," I said. "What it tells me is you're just a little blip on his radar, Chris. You're probably one of a hundred lawsuits he's got going. Everybody else keeps doing all the work and handing him the ammo, he just fires the gun. I've seen a lot of G. Gordons over the years," I said.

"And I'm not going to worry about him," said Chris.

"I'm willing to bet," I said, "after today the county's going to be brought in as a new defendant, and we'll have one more attorney to deal with. What you have to do, Chris, is just keep your cool."

"I understand," he said.

And he did—for most of the afternoon. It was painful, even for me, to have to sit and watch Chris go through every detail of the relationship with Cheryl. An intelligent, grown man making a total fool of himself for sex. Even if I gave Chris the benefit of the doubt that at some point in the relationship he had real feelings for Cheryl, it didn't make it less painful. Throughout the entire afternoon, Chris handled himself with dignity, never once trying to cast the blame for what happened anywhere but squarely on his shoulders. When G. Gordon finally asked him point blankly, "Did you murder Cheryl Moore?" Chris looked him squarely in the eyes and very quietly and sincerely said, "No."

Just when I thought we should be at the end, G. Gordon had beaten every issue to death, he brought up Cheryl's entry in the diary.

"Dr. Morgan," he said, "you've had an opportunity to read the entries in Ms. Moore's diary, correct?"

"Yes, I have."

"I want to go to a particular entry toward the end of the diary. By all indications it was written shortly before she was murdered. Here it is," he said, and he shoved the diary, or a copy of it, across the table. "Why don't you read that quickly?"

Chris glanced at the diary and looked up. "I know what it says."

"Yes, Dr. Morgan, it says that you were at her apartment that day. You told her that you had decided you were going to divorce your wife, marry her and move to California. Isn't that correct?"

"Yes, it is."

"But you didn't have any intention of following through on that, did you, Dr. Morgan?"

Chris looked at me.

"Don't look to your attorney for an answer," he said. "You had no intention of following through with that, did you?"

"You don't understand why I told her that," Chris said.

"Well, maybe you can enlighten us."

Again Chris looked at me. It dawned on me at that moment that I had been sloppy in my preparation of Chris for this deposition. We had gone through everything several times, except my advice to him. For some reason, it just never occurred to me that G. Gordon would make an issue out of that one entry in the diary. If we had one thing that Randy Becker didn't know, that was it—that I had given Chris instructions to keep Cheryl happy and quiet until I had a chance to talk to her, until I was released from the hospital.

"Dr. Morgan, I'm waiting," he said.

Chris was still looking at me. I nodded.

"I did that on the advice of my attorney."

I could see the realization cross G. Gordon's face, the satisfaction that came from uncovering something new, unexpected.

He glanced at me, a gaze of amusement at my expense. "That's interesting, Dr. Morgan, maybe we should explore that a little bit. Are you telling me that your attorney told you to tell Ms. Moore that you intended to marry her? Before you answer that, let me ask you this, what attorney are you referring to?"

"Noah."

"You mean Noah Schepers, your attorney who's here, present during this deposition?"

"Yes."

"And now let's go to the next question. Did Noah Schepers tell you to tell her that?"

"No, he didn't."

"Well, what did he tell you?"

Chris seemed defeated. "You have to understand," he said, "I told her our relationship had to end, but she wouldn't take that for an answer. I went to Noah and asked him for his help. He was in the hospital; he had just suffered a heart attack. There was no one else I could turn to. I hated to do it but I had to. He told me I had to do something to keep her appeased until he got out and could help me. That's why I gave her that line."

"And it was a line, wasn't it?" he asked.

"You mean did I intend to marry her and move to California? The answer is no, I did not."

"So what you're saying, Dr. Morgan, is, you lied to her?"

Morgan shook his head.

"You lied to her to get time. It doesn't do any good to shake your head, Dr. Morgan; the court reporter can't get that. You're shaking your head no, but you've already admitted that you lied."

"It wasn't a lie," Chris said, "I just needed some time."

"Well, it wasn't the truth, was it?"

I interrupted. "I think this is getting a little argumentative. Chris you don't have to answer that."

"Listen, Mr. Schepers," he said, "I have a right to get to the truth here."

"And I have a right to stop you from badgering my client. I'm saying move on."

"I can understand why you'd be taking that position," he replied.

I wanted to stand up and deck him, but I was too old to start a new career. Becker would've probably even made me sit a few days in jail. I swallowed the comment and told him to just keep going.

Now he seemed to have Chris against the ropes. I knew this was exactly what Becker was going to do. Once the evidence came out that Chris's promise was simply meant to appease her, anybody right out of law school could have made the next logical jump.

For us the deposition was meant to be a dress rehearsal. Instead, we were dressed down. When it was over, I felt like the emperor with everybody in the room too embarrassed to tell me I was standing there bare-assed naked.

As I drove home that evening, I had a hard time getting Chris's deposition out of my mind. We were dead in the water. I was going to try my first murder case and what Johnny had said kept ringing in my ears: "After all, the guy's guiltier than sin. Nobody expects you to get him off." I wasn't going to accept that. I couldn't accept that.

I could tell Noah was down after the deposition. As we walked back to the office, not a word passed between us. So I didn't have to worry about it all night, I asked him just before I left whether his instructions to Chris to appease Cheryl and Chris's subsequent promise created any problems as far as us representing him. Noah was very noncommittal. He said he didn't think so. He wasn't going to raise it anyway. But the prospect that, after all of this, we may have to walk away from the defense bothered me.

When I got home, I called Johnny. I had promised I would give him my impressions of G. Gordon Pettiman, but there was more to it than that; I wanted company. This case seemed to be crashing down around me and the last thing I wanted to do was give Randy Becker the slightest satisfaction.

Johnny was a welcome sight. He wore Levi's and a University of Michigan sweatshirt. The air had turned cool and there was a fall mist. His face was damp, his hair curly. He looked good enough to kiss, and I did, right on the lips.

"Thank you," he said, as I pulled away. "Can I take this to mean any change in your attitude?"

"About what?" I said.

"About us," he said. "About, you know?"

I punched him on the shoulder. "Men!" I said. "You only have one thing on your mind."

"That's not true," he said. "I have several things and they all involve your anatomy."

"Well get your mind on something else, 'cause it's not going to happen tonight."

"You'd be amazed at my patience," he said.

"I already am. Do you want to hear about Mr. Hot Shot or not?"

"Sure, I do," he replied.

I started to give him a summary of the deposition and he sat there with a silly grin on his face.

"You're not listening to a word of this, are you?"

"Yes, I am," he said, "and at the same time I'm wondering how I ever got so lucky."

"You haven't gotten lucky yet, but pay attention. It's pretty clear that they're going after the county. It's just as well you guys are out of it."

"You know, I don't think that's something that Crane even thought about."

"Well, G. Gordon may be getting us out of it, too."

I told him about Noah's instructions.

"That's interesting," he said. "I wonder if the fact that Noah may be a potential witness could disqualify you from trying the case."

"That's what's been bothering me. When it first came up months ago, I didn't pay a whole lot attention and then today, G. Gordon made such a big deal out of it. Now I'm concerned, and I can tell Noah is too."

We both sighed. His penetrating gaze changed to a sly grin.

"What?" I asked.

"Do you wanna go neck?"

"Oh, I thought you had something important. I have more important things on my mind than sins of the flesh."

"What's more important than that?"

"Finding a way to save Dr. Morgan's butt."

"Way too serious for me," he said.

"I am serious," I replied. "I know I asked you this before, but what was Cheryl's mother really like?"

"Very attractive," he said, "and I think pretty bright."

"What'd she look like?"

"Blonde, blue eyes, pretty face, nice shape for her age which is what, forty-two, forty-three, maybe younger."

"Quite a bit younger than Cheryl's dad then."

"How old is he?"

"Brownie said he was in his mid fifties."

"A few years difference," he replied. "She dressed very nicely, lots of class, great perfume. I never paid a whole lot of attention to perfume until that night I took you to the movie. She smelled good, too."

"You said you thought she was bright, so you didn't spend all of your time assessing her feminine qualities?"

"Most, but not all."

"Well, what made you think she was bright?"

"Very articulate, expressed herself very well. You know, just struck me as an educated person."

"How did she ever get hooked up with Cheryl's dad, then? From what Brownie says, he's big, mean, and vulgar. He's been a longshoreman all his life, working on the river."

"How old was Cheryl?"

"Twenty-one," I said.

"Well, that makes her mother probably twenty when she got knocked up, maybe even a little younger."

"Knocked up," I said. "I expected better . . ."

"Alright, she could've been probably twenty when she got pregnant. It might've been one of those situations where she just wanted to get out of her house. Cheryl's dad comes along, mature, strong bull type, has a job. It's a way for her to escape. She gets married, has a baby. Or maybe the other way around, she was with him ten, eleven years, finds out he's an abuser. She finds out he's not only a wife batterer, he's sexually abusing their daughter, doing awful things to her. She files for divorce and moves to Boston. I mean she didn't have to be dumb when she married him. She could've been a smart girl who saw very few alternatives. She moves out to Boston, has the looks and moxy to get ahead. At least she's aware that if somebody murders her daughter, somebody who has a few bucks, she might be able to reap some monetary benefits."

"Johnny," I said, "are you making this all up or did you find this out from her?"

"A little of both," he said. "It was important that we find out about her re-lationship with Cheryl."

"If Cheryl was so important," I said, "how come she left her with the aunt?"

"We asked her that. She said it was very simple. She couldn't stay anywhere near her ex and Cheryl didn't want to move to Boston . . . aunt seemed like a good alternative. She said they kept in touch a lot. Cheryl called often. Mom sent her money. I think most of that can be verified."

"What'd she say about the sexual abuse of Cheryl?"

"Surprisingly very little. She said when she found out she confronted Cheryl and she admitted it. She got her out of there right away. She said she would've never had the nerve to confront her husband, he would've beaten her bloody."

"My God," I said, "what kind of person does it take to do what her dad did? And then her mother? Once she finds out, she abandons her. How do you think Cheryl felt?"

"Cheryl was what, eleven, twelve years old? It would make sense that she said she wanted to live with an aunt. You know, Jackie, kids like things that are fa-miliar. Maybe she had her friends, her school. Lord knows she had enough to cope with without thinking of a whole new town, school and all the things that go with that. It makes sense to me, I guess."

"I'd like to talk to Carol," I said. "I was surprised she wasn't at the deposition. Noah said it wasn't required that she be there. I was looking forward to seeing her."

"She's rather memorable," he said. "Remember the other day I was talking about Hitchcock's *Rear Window*? Jimmy Stewart's girlfriend was Grace Kelly. She looks a lot like Grace Kelly."

"You know, now that you mention that," I said, "I see a little of Grace Kelly in Cheryl, too. Cheryl was a very attractive girl. How do you think she got such a bad impression of herself? It's obvious she had no feeling of any self-worth. She considered herself fat and dumpy, homely, which she wasn't. I can imagine the first time Dr. Morgan got close to her . . ." I didn't finish the thought.

"Well, you know how some men are," Johnny said.

"Yeah, right, tell me about some men."

"Hey, don't look at me," he said. "I've been a perfect gentleman."

"I don't know if I would say perfect."

I gave him a come-hither look and he leaned across the table and kissed me on the forehead.

"You're going to be a nervous wreck before you're done with this," he said.

"Johnny," I said, trying to use my best seductive voice, "you can help me."

"How?"

"I want to go talk to Cheryl's dad and I need somebody to go along."

"You out of your mind?" he asked.

"Why?"

"What good is that going to do you?"

"Every time Noah and I talk this over, it always comes back to the same thing: Benjamin Moore holds the key to this case. Think about it, Johnny, Chris didn't do it, her dad didn't do it, and at least the police don't consider him a suspect. It wasn't some stranger in the night— it was somebody she knew. The police obviously aren't looking anymore and Brownie hasn't been able to find anybody who can tie her to any guy around here. She wasn't dating. She had a few girlfriends but they only saw her at school. So there's somebody from her past, something happened."

"You want me to accompany you to talk to a sexual pervert who did unspeakable things to his daughter in hopes that he will help you find her killer? You know how ridiculous that sounds?"

"Not to me it doesn't. I think that summarizes it pretty well."

\* \* \* \* \*

The next morning I telephoned Brownie and started asking him some questions about Benjamin Moore, trying to stay discreet enough so I didn't telegraph my intentions. I already knew where he lived, where he worked. What I needed to know was some of his hangouts, where we might be able to approach him on his own turf. Maybe buy him a drink, show him we're just two hard-working attorneys trying to make a living, hoping that he would ignore the fact that I was representing the alleged murderer of his daughter. Brownie seemed a little suspicious but he gave me everything I needed. Now I just had to muster the courage to follow through.

Johnny and I planned on driving to Minneapolis to talk to Mr. Moore on a Friday night. I thought because he didn't have to work the next day, we could catch Mr. Moore in one of his haunts in a good mood. Late Friday afternoon I called his place of employment, whoever answered said he couldn't take personal calls. I asked him if he could tell me when Benjamin got off and he told me 5:00 p.m. I also asked him if Benjamin had to work on Saturday and he said no. I called Johnny and we decided that tonight was the night.

Brownie had given us the names of three bars where Ben liked to hang out. One that was close to his job, the other two close to home.

The drive took a little over an hour and on the way we tried to devise a plan, some way to approach him where we wouldn't end up getting our heads knocked off. There was a giddy nervousness in the car. We both knew we were out of our element.

"Maybe we can be the new Nick and Nora Charles," Johnny said.

"Who are they?" I asked.

"Didn't you ever watch the *Thin Man* movies?" he asked.

"Is that all you do is watch movies?" I asked.

"I like the old classics. Anyway, Nick and Nora Charles were detectives, always involved in solving murder mysteries."

"I've got a career, thank you," I said. "All I want to do is survive the night."

"Why would this guy be dangerous for us?" he asked. "He's not a suspect. Cheryl's dead. Nobody could ever prosecute him for the sexual abuse; he shouldn't have a worry in the world."

"You read Brownie's reports," I said.

"Yeah."

"Well, he's got a bad attitude."

"You know why he's got a bad attitude?" asked Johnny. "Because his mother named him after paint. Can you imagine how much teasing he must've taken in school?"

"I never even thought of that," I replied.

"Well, it's something to think about."

The conversation continued with no particular direction. We rambled on with nervous chatter because we didn't know what to expect.

I had never spent much time in what were considered the seedier parts of the Twin Cities. My time had been spent on the University campus, Dinky Town, and the West Bank. Once in a great while some classmates and I would explore beyond that, but never any place considered dangerous.

Our first choice was a bar near the wharf called Mick's. We had to weave our way through the warehouse district, down to the shore of the Mississippi. After a few wrong turns, we found it, an old two-story brick building in a respectable state of disrepair for its location, with a neon Budweiser sign blinking through a window fogged over on the inside from years of grime. The only identification was a sign hanging on a steel post over the front door, in which the neon "M" flickered on and off, changing the name back and forth from "Mick's" to "ick's."

We found a parking place across the street and I noticed Johnny's hands were gripped tightly to the steering wheel. I reached over and grasped his right hand. "We don't have to do this, you know," I said.

"Hey, I'm okay," he said. "It's in the interests of justice, right?"

"I hope so," I replied.

Ick's was a fitting appellation for the place. When we opened the door, there was a rush of foul smells: stale smoke, burped beer, overrun toilets, whatever. Johnny led me through the door, holding my hand. I reached over with my other and grabbed his elbow.

"I don't think we should be here," I said.

"It's too late now," he replied. "Come on."

It was about 6:30 and the place was packed. There wasn't a spare table. There was a little room at the edge of the bar and Johnny motioned to squeeze in, which we did. Actually, it turned out to be a good spot to watch the crowd. This was a workingman's bar and from the looks of it there were a few working girls too. Johnny and I stood at the edge of the bar. I didn't know about him, but I felt totally out of place. The bartender was slowly working his way in our direction. He was surprisingly neat and clean for the surroundings. I guess I had expected some big grease ball. He was dressed in jeans and a denim shirt, a stained apron strapped around his waist. He was clean-shaven, a nice face, not

163

handsome but nice, with long washed out blonde hair. I thought I saw a little reticence in his eyes when he saw us, as if he was trying to decide whether we were old enough to drink.

"What'll ya have?" he asked.

Johnny looked at me. "Beer?"

"Sure," I replied.

"Two Buds," Johnny said.

The bartender looked at me again. I thought he was going to ask me for an I.D. but must have changed his mind. He went to the cooler, put two bottles of Budweiser on the bar and said, "Four bucks."

Johnny gave him a five and said, "Keep it."

"Thanks. You new to the neighborhood?" he asked.

I didn't imagine it would do us a whole lot of good to play games with him so I simply said, "We're looking for Benjamin Moore, we heard he might be here tonight. Do you know him?"

"Oh sure," he said. "Yeah, he's around here somewhere. I saw 'em just a little while ago. You aren't Cheryl?"

The question shook me. I was dumbstruck for a moment.

"I just thought maybe you were his daughter. He talks about her all the time. If I see 'em, I'll tell 'em you're looking for 'em."

By then somebody was hollering for him on the other side of the bar. "Hey Cliff, ya gonna spend your whole night over there?"

As he turned and walked away, I looked at Johnny. "How bizarre is that?" I said.

"What?" he asked.

"He's talked to him about his daughter, Cheryl, but he didn't tell him that she'd been murdered."

"You're right," he replied. "That is bizarre."

"From what Brownie said, it sounded like he didn't want to have anything to do with her," I replied. "Why would he be talking about her to the bartender?"

"I don't know," said Johnny. "What are we looking for anyway?"

"Brownie says you can't miss him."

I ran through the description he had put in the report. Johnny quickly glanced around the bar. "I don't see anybody like that. Maybe he's already taken off."

I slowly perused the tables. Smoke rolled through the place, my eyes were already burning. I took a couple swallows of beer and I almost gagged. It wasn't my favorite drink. I didn't see anybody who looked like Benjamin Moore.

Johnny said, "That's not him, is it?"

He motioned with his head toward the end of the bar. The bartender was talking to a man leaning over the bar who was looking our way.

"I don't think so. No, that's not him."

"Maybe he just wants to know what the hell a couple college kids are doing in here," Johnny said.

A couple more moments went by and I said, "We might as well get out of here."

Johnny had finished his beer. "Aren't you going to drink that?" he asked.

"No, I don't like beer."

"Then why didn't you tell me?"

"I didn't think this place would carry a good glass of Chablis."

"Well, I'll finish yours and we'll go."

He had just put the bottle to his lips when a deep voice behind him said, "I hear you're looking for me."

Johnny coughed up his beer and I turned and froze. Benjamin Moore was even bigger and more ominous looking than Brownie's description. His face was big, dark brown from his years on the river, skin tight against the bones. His presence loomed over us. Stammering for words, I finally said, "Mr. Moore?"

"Who are you and whaddaya want?" he asked.

"I'm an attorney from St. Cloud," I said. "Jackie Geroux. I have to talk to you about your daughter."

The air seemed to go out of him. "Won't you bloodsuckers leave me alone?" he said.

"It isn't like that," I said.

"Like what? In the last two months, I've had nothing but cops, attorneys, investigators and insurance men wanting to talk to me about Cheryl. When she needed help, not a goddamn soul was there. Now that she's dead, you all wanna pick at her bones."

"I'm really very sorry, Mr. Moore, but Cheryl was a very sad and desperate person. I'm just trying to figure out what happened."

He looked at Johnny. At that point I realized he hadn't been introduced. "Oh, I'm sorry; this is my friend, Johnny Connors. He's also a lawyer."

"Should've figured," he said.

"Really, Mr. Moore," Johnny said, "we really don't want to make this difficult. All we want to do is get to the bottom of what happened to Cheryl."

"The cops know what happened; at least they told me they know what happened. This slug Morgan murdered her, slit her throat, and mutilated her like the goddamn pervert he is."

"We don't believe that's what happened, though," I said.

"That's what you're paid for, right?" he snapped.

"I can understand why you'd believe that," I said, "but . . ."

"But nothing," he interrupted.

He looked like he was going to turn and I reached out and grabbed his arm. It was like a rock, as though he could use it to sledgehammer you into the ground. My touch made him pause for a moment.

"Mr. Moore," I said, "there's absolutely no reason for you to believe me or for you to give me the time of day. Did you ever have a situation where you believed you were right but you couldn't convince anybody? You know, not just a hunch, but in your gut you know you're right? Well, I work for a man who believes that of Dr. Morgan, that he didn't murder your daughter, and the more I work with him and the more I work with Dr. Morgan, the more I believe he's right. The police certainly have enough to convict Dr. Morgan of Cheryl's murder. But if they do, the real killer's going to go free and I'm sure you don't want that to happen."

His body seemed to ease up. He put his other hand over mine, squeezed it gently. "I can't be of any help anyway," he said, with a hint of regret. "Everybody who listened to her believes I'm a child molester."

The gruffness of his face seemed to disappear; suddenly his thoughts appeared distant.

"All we'd like to do is talk to you for a few minutes," Johnny said. "How 'bout another beer?"

"I have a booth over in the corner," he said. "Why don't you join me?"

"What'll you have?" Johnny asked.

"Jack Daniels water."

Johnny ordered us another round. This time he got me a glass of wine. We went to the back corner of the room. There was another man sitting in the booth.

"Hey, Roy, I need a little space for a few minutes. Why don't you get lost," Ben said.

Without hesitating, Roy slid out of the booth, grabbed his beer and left.

Johnny and I sat on one side, Mr. Moore on the other. Mr. Moore picked up the glass of Jack Daniels, held it in both hands for a couple seconds. "Tennessee gold," he said and took a big swallow.

He set the glass down and put his elbows on the booth. "You know," he said, "I never touched that girl. As far as I was concerned, she was everything."

It was said in a very gentle way for such a big man.

"You know what she told people about you?" I asked.

"The cops have beaten that to death," he said. "All I told 'em is, just get out of my life, I don't even want to talk about it."

"Did you deny it?" I asked.

"Of course! It's pure bullshit. That's the end of it, Miss—I don't even remember your name."

"Jackie," I said. "Jackie Geroux."

"That's the end of it, Miss Jackie Geroux. It never happened! I'm sick of talking about it. That's it, period!"

He slammed down the rest of the Jack Daniels. Johnny got up, "I'll get you another," and he walked to the bar.

"Quite a place, isn't it?" he said. "You can get anything you want here. See that tall dude over there? He's got any dope you want. See that chunky redhead over there? Twenty bucks, she'll do anything you ask. This isn't where you belong, Miss Geroux."

"Believe me," I said, "I wouldn't be here unless it was absolutely necessary. We need help. We have to find somebody with the motive to kill your daughter."

Johnny put another drink in front of him and sat down. Ben took it, drank half the glass in one swallow, and said, "I've been coming in here for a little over ten years, ever since the divorce. Before that, I had little interest in bars, this kinda bullshit. Now I find that these are some of the best friends a man can have. There's no fraud here, everybody is what they are. Whatcha see is whatcha get. Cheryl's mother wasn't like that. She wanted to be something more than the wife of a longshoreman. She had uppity ideas."

"I met her," Johnny said.

"You did?" he asked, incredulously.

"Yes. She had contacted our law office about suing Dr. Morgan in civil court for damages in Cheryl's death."

That's a fuckin' joke, too," he said. "Why should she get any money? She didn't pay that much attention to her in the last ten years. How'd she look?"

"Very nice," Johnny said.

"Yeah, I heard that," he said. "First year she's out in Boston she meets some rich dude. Son-of-a-bitch ends up drowning a couple years ago, out in the ocean somewhere. Never did get the whole story. She hasn't had to bust her ass since. Even with a few extra bucks, she couldn't take any time out to do anything special for Cheryl."

"When was the last time you saw your ex-wife?" I asked.

"The day we walked out of the courthouse."

"How come Cheryl lived with her aunt?" I asked.

"I knew the court wouldn't give me custody of her. She didn't want to go with her mother. At the time it seemed the right choice. I didn't know that her teenage cousin was going to be poking her."

"You heard that too?" I said.

"Yeah. The cops asked me about it. I'm not sure that happened either. The kid denies it. I went over there one day, cornered him, he said he never touched her. Knowin' Cheryl, what I knew, I believed him."

I wanted to ask him what he knew but I didn't want to push him. He appeared to be getting relaxed. It seemed to me that he had been looking for someone to talk to who he didn't consider threatening. Maybe he wanted somebody to finally hear his side.  If that was the case, I was going to give him that opportunity.  There was no sense rushing him.

"When was the last time you talked to Cheryl?" I asked.

"Couple years ago.  Right here, in fact.   She met me after work one night.  We came over here.  It was a lot quieter than this.  This is the Friday night crowd.  She wanted me to get ahold of her mother for her.  There were things she wanted to get straightened out.  I told her she had to talk to somebody else, maybe her aunt.  She didn't understand why I wouldn't help her.  Now looking back at it, I wish I would've.  But you have to understand, I hate her mother with such a passion."  He shook his head and finished the drink.

Johnny quickly leaned in.  "I'll get you another.  Jackie, how 'bout you?"

"No, I'm fine," I said.

I stared at Ben's face.  I could tell his mind was lost somewhere in the past, probably conjuring up an image of his ex, or Cheryl.  He didn't look like he wished to have his thoughts interrupted so I sat there quietly waiting for Johnny to return. There was a constant din in the bar, laughing, shouting, swearing, coughing.  Every so often, somebody would put money in the jukebox and some twangy country western song would mingle with the clatter.  It was hard to keep focused.  I reflected on what had been said so far.  What had happened between Cheryl and her mother, I wondered.

My mind was drifting when a voice said, "Hey, Ben, who's the chick?"

He seemed to snap out of a trance, smiled and said, "She's my lawyer."

"Yeah, right," the guy said as he passed by.

Johnny slid in next to me and put another drink in front of Ben.

Ben glanced at him.  "Whaddaya trying to do, get me drunk?  Forget it, you don't have enough money."

Johnny smiled.  Ben smiled back.  "You guys think you're pretty clever, don't you?"

"Why?" I asked.

"You're not fooling me."

"We're not trying to," I said.  "We're just trying to find out what happened to Cheryl."

"Talk to her mother," he said.

"We intend to, but we have to know the right questions."

"Have you seen the pictures of Cheryl's body?" he asked.

"Yeah," I said.

"I didn't want to see 'em. They called me to identify her body. I couldn't do it. Her aunt went. She told me about the pictures. Then she accused me of doing it. She hasn't talked to me since. All she said was, 'How could you do that to your daughter?' I didn't, you know, I really didn't."

He picked up the glass of Jack Daniels, held it up as a priest would a chalice. "Sometimes this is the only thing that stops the pain," he said. He took another swallow.

"How'd Cheryl end up so mixed up?" I asked.

He peered straight at me, his eyes filled with pain. "Because we made her that way. First her mother and then me." He paused for a moment. "Her mother, Carol, was a very sexy woman; I mean—she liked screwin'. I was ten years older, a bachelor, when we met. On our first date she's all over me. I think she got knocked up already that first night we did it. Of course I was going to do the honorable thing. We found a preacher and got married. If she was going to have a baby, she was going to have it close enough to nine months so she didn't have to answer to her mother. Her mother was a puritanical bitch. She told me stories about her. Just unbelievable. Her mother saw her kiss a neighbor boy when she was like eleven or twelve. She dragged her home, stripped her down, told her she was evil; she beat her and washed her mouth out with soap. She couldn't talk about boys. Through all of high school, she didn't get a date. She told me she couldn't wait to be eighteen and get away." He looked at me. "Maybe you can tell me, what's it like to be a young girl coming into you know . . . your thing? Urges and all that. And you think it's all evil. If you have a bad thought, you're going to hell?"

It was a rhetorical question. He was spilling his heart, not because he wanted to reveal anything to us, but for some reason, he chose this moment for a catharsis. His eyes were transfixed on the booth behind us, gazing somewhere between Johnny and me.

"That's how she lived, and when she got away, she went wild. I wasn't the first; somebody else had broken her in. I regretted that. I often imagined what that would've been like. She was pretty experienced by the time she got to me but I didn't give a shit. I mean, look at me. She was a beautiful girl; I wasn't going to do any better than that." He took the last of his drink. "Here, Johnny-jump-up, do your job."

I could tell Johnny was a little perturbed. I didn't know if it was because he would miss part of the story, which now had us both mesmerized, or if he felt like a waiter.

Ben must have noticed. "I'll wait for you," he said.

"Seems like a nice guy," he continued, as Johnny made his way to the bar. "That's what Cheryl needed. She needed somebody to help her out. Not the freaks she hung with."

"Did you ever meet any of her friends?" I asked.

"After the divorce, for a while, until she was about sixteen or so, then she didn't want to see me anymore."

"Why?"

"'Cause I was starting to tell her she was wasting her life. She kept talking about her mother. I told her to forget her, she was long gone."

When Johnny came back and handed Ben his drink, Ben thanked him and took another swallow. "Anyway, where was I? Oh yeah, marriage. Then Cheryl came along, taking care of a baby got old real fast for Carol. She hated motherhood. She hated it enough that she even wanted her mother to come and stay with us for a while. I said absolutely not. Not after the horror stories she had told me. Life got pretty miserable. She didn't go running around or anything, she knew I wouldn't stand for that. But she just bitched and moaned a lot. And it stayed that way until Cheryl got to be around seven or so and then they seemed to get friendly, like a real mother and daughter. At first I was really happy, but then it seemed to get a little weird. You know, Cheryl always wantin' to sit on her lap at night, they would cuddle up. God, they'd take showers together. And when I'd say something, she'd say she wanted to make sure that Cheryl got all the soap out of her hair, shit like that. But from what I could see, that's as far as it went. I never caught Carol doing anything. Then when Cheryl got a little older, things started to change for the worse . . . and I could see it. They would scream at each other. Get into violent arguments. Her mother would call her a pig. One night she called her a little whore. That was about as much as I could take. Carol and I got into a fight, I mean a real screaming match. I didn't hit her or nothing, but I had her up against a wall, I could've broken her fuckin' neck. Then Cheryl started pounding on me, trying to protect her mother. After that, it was just miserable at home. I couldn't do nothin' right. We stopped talkin'. Shortly after that, she filed for divorce. Cheryl told me she wouldn't stay with me. We got our divorce. No big deal, I didn't have anything anyway. The few trinkets I had, I said, here. Told Carol to get her ass out and I never wanted to see her again. But to be honest with you, I still loved her. I was hoping that Cheryl being here might bring her back. From almost the very beginning, from moving in with her aunt, Cheryl was having problems. I knew she was seeing a shrink, threatening suicide. Like I said, I never heard of any of this screwin' by the nephew until after this shit all came up.

"They had Cheryl in one of those treatment centers. I went to one of the first sessions. The shrink wanted me there. You know what they do? The first thing Cheryl confronts me with is how I could've been so mean to her mother. It was all my fault that she left us and she said she hated me for it. Can you believe it? The doctor says, "Hey, now we're getting somewhere. Let's talk this out'. You know what I told 'em?"

He looked at me, expecting an answer. I shrugged. "I told 'em to kiss it and I got up and walked out. My fault, my ass. I found out what really happened two years later when Cheryl met me after work one night. She'd been in to see one of those blood suckin' shrinks again. She said she had to straighten things out. She does. She tells me the most God-awful things; things I had suspicions of but never dared believed were true. All this time people thinkin' that I am the one who sexually molested her . . ."

He took another swallow of his drink. He looked at Johnny, then at me, his eyes wide, sparkling. "It was her mother! If you can fuckin' believe it. Started with her when she was like seven, before she showed any signs of being a woman. Would lick her down there. Can you believe it? Would suck the girl between her legs. How goddamn sick is that?"

I sat there, stunned, my heart in arrest. There was never any doubt in my mind that he was telling the truth. This wasn't something he'd made up. This

172

was the nightmare he lived and had kept inside of himself and now, decided Johnny and I should hear it, probably the first time ever told.

He finished his drink again.   Johnny was going to get another.  Ben said, "Don't bother.  You've spent enough.  The real kicker was that she told me that she promised her mother if anybody ever found out, ever asked any questions about anything sexual going on, she should tell 'em that I was the one who did it, not her.   And she said she swore to her mother that she would do that.  All that shit about cutting off her breasts and cutting her down there, her mother said that.  Her mother was mad because she was becoming a woman.  She wanted her little girl back.  When I heard it all, I was mad, really pissed.  She came for my help and I felt so sick about it, all I told her was to get the hell out, I never wanted to see her again.  She ended up in the hospital.  When they called the next day, I wouldn't even go over.  I called her mother and said if I ever saw her again, I'd take her fuckin' head off.  She called me a pig and hung up."

I leaned back in the booth, my shoulders tight against the wood planks, inhaled deeply to catch my breath.  This was not at all what I'd expected.  My emotions for Cheryl had already been on a roller coaster ride and now I had to contend with a whole new revelation.

Ben fixed his eyes on mine, a penetrating stare.  "It's true," he said, barely audible over the din.

"Why do you think she chose that moment to tell you?" I asked.

His gaze softened.  "It was the nightmares," he said.  "She told me she was having terrible nightmares involving her mother. She said she'd wake up in the middle of the night sweatin', gasping for air . . . her dream was . . . her mother was trying to suffocate her."

"What did she want you to do?" I asked.

"She wanted me to talk to her mother, to get to the bottom of things . . . she wanted the dreams to stop," he said, his voice mournful, full of loss and regret.

"Did it seem like she had told someone else, outside the family, about her mother and herself?"

"Oh, no!  She'd been seeing the shrinks for years but she wouldn't give up her mom.  No way."

"Why not?" I asked.

He took a moment to answer, then he gave me one of those penetrating stares again and asked, "Would you talk about that?"

I took a moment to think about it, shuttered at the prospect, and I couldn't come up with a reply. "I read your statement to the police. Why didn't you tell Detective Kropp about any of this?"

Without a second of hesitation, he replied, "I want my little girl to rest in peace."

"And what if her mother killed her?" I said. "Wouldn't you want the cops to get her?"

"Look," he said, "you guys are being paid to try and get this creep off . . ."

I could tell immediately by the tone of his voice and the force of his words that his attitude was changing, and he was about to become combative. "I just mean," I quickly interjected, "that our client may be innocent."

"Then you do what you have to but don't look at me for any help," he replied, brusquely.

I let the air settle for a moment and then quickly changed the subject. We talked for a while but I could tell his mood had changed for good—now we were interlopers. His attention left our table. He started to acknowledge people in the bar, waved, made comments. It was time to leave.

* * * * *

Fifteen minutes later Johnny and I were back on the main highway to St. Cloud. I went over everything in my mind making sure that as soon as I got back I could dictate it almost word for word. Mr. Moore told me he would not repeat any of this to Detective Kropp, nor would he testify at Dr. Morgan's trial. There was no doubt in my mind that this was a man who was in pain, suffering self-recrimination about things done or undone. He must have felt obligated to at least tell somebody his version of the truth and I was that person. For whatever purpose, he had confided in Johnny and me; now with that accomplished, he wanted to put it all behind him and get on with his life.

It was a little before midnight and there was very little traffic on the highway. I was in a trance as I stared at the darkness beyond the beam of the headlights,

my mind befuddled by combating thoughts. I had always felt that things had been difficult for me, and, compared to some of my friends in law school, they had been. But compared to what Cheryl went through, my life had been idyllic.
 The theme, "once a victim always a victim," kept interrupting my thoughts. This young woman was never going to get out of that cycle. Maybe it was her one effort to do so that resulted in her death. Maybe in desperation, she finally confronted her mother. I had absolutely no doubt Benjamin Moore was telling the truth.

We were almost halfway back to the city before either of us spoke.

"Do you believe him?" I asked.

"Absolutely," he replied without hesitation.

"No doubts? No feeling he was trying to con us because . . ."

"Nope! That man has agonized over this, Jackie. I'm surprised he's not suicidal. He really blames himself for her death."

"Cheryl had to be really miserable toward the end," I said. "That's probably why she glommed onto Dr. Morgan. The thought of getting out of here, starting a new life . . . but that was all a pipe dream—that's all she had were pipe dreams. I can see how she would've been threatening to the doctor. Once he tried to destroy the dreams by telling her it was over . . ."

We were both quiet again. The only sound was the pounding of the tires off the pavement.

I broke the silence. "I was angry at my mother for abandoning me, and it wasn't even her fault. But I wanted a life like the other girls, with a mother and father, a home. And before I could really understand it all, I blamed her, like it was something she really had control over. Then I think about Cheryl and her childhood. I try to imagine what that must have been like, to have a relationship where you cuddle and hug with your mother, a closeness, a physical closeness that you think is perfectly normal because you don't know otherwise. Then to suffer your mother's rejection, actual threats of violence to your body and then she up and leaves. Then you slowly start to realize, as you grow older, that it wasn't a normal relationship at all, but really something quite perverse and sick. You were used as a sexual toy by the one person who was there to nurture you." I turned to Johnny. "That would have a tendency to really fuck you up, huh?"

175

He took my comment in stride. Without taking his eyes off the road he said, "Sure would." Then, after a few moments of silence, he asked, "What did you know about your mother? What did your aunt tell you?"

"That she was a beautiful woman, that she was looking forward to having a baby, that she would've been a great mother. Things you'd expect her to say."

"When was the last time you talked to your dad?" he asked.

"When I had him on the phone asking him why he wasn't going to show up for my graduation from law school."

"You mean he didn't show up?"

"Nope. He was in contract negotiations. He said a big important deal. Said he was sorry. Sent me a card with a check for five thousand dollars. That's what he always did when he disappointed me, sent me money."

"When was the last time you saw him?" he asked.

"Probably five years ago or so."

"That's really sad," he replied.

"Tell me about it," I said.

It was a warm, sunny morning and Brownie and I were on the lake, fishing from his boat. I had just hooked into a huge walleye. Every time I got the fish near the boat and I would try to net it, it would turn, diving into the deep water, the reel spinning in my hand. Out of nowhere I heard Maggie's voice hollering my name. I looked to the shore, but she wasn't there. Then she had me by the shoulder, shaking me, saying, "Noah, Jackie's on the phone."

As I opened my eyes, my first thought was that now I was never going to know whether I caught that fish. I looked at my clock; it was 7:02. I thought for a moment. It's Saturday. What could have happened now?

As I got out of bed, I felt a pain in my hip. It stayed with me as I hobbled into the other room for the phone. Every time this happened, I swore I was going to get another phone extension next to the bed, but as soon as I left the house it never crossed my mind again.

"It's Saturday morning, Jackie," I said, "and Brownie and I were fishing."

I thought the line would knock her off guard but she paid no heed. She started with what was by now a familiar line:

"Noah, you're not going to believe this. You're never going to believe it."

Before I had a chance to ask what I wasn't going to believe, she continued, excitedly, "I talked to Cheryl's dad last night, Benjamin Moore . . ."

"You did what?"

"I talked to Mr. Moore."

"Are you out of your mind?" I asked. "After what Brownie told us?"

"Johnny went along."

"Oh, that's different," I replied sarcastically.

"No, he isn't like Brownie said at all. I mean he is big and mean looking, but he isn't. You know what I mean?" I had no idea what she meant. Moreover, I was upset. She could have jeopardized her safety; she could have jeopardized the case. It was not something I wanted her to do without even speaking to me about it.

The line went quiet for a moment. Finally she asked, "Are you mad?"

"I'm not mad, Jackie, I'm just a little upset. It's not something you should have done without talking to me first."

"You'll feel different when you find out what he said. I've been up most of the night writing it all out before I forgot it. Johnny was there—he's my witness. Can you come to the office?"

It was evident she was going to be a nervous wreck until she got the chance to tell me everything. But I didn't relish the idea of getting dressed and driving to the office, so I invited her to my house. She said she'd be there in ten minutes. I told her to make it twenty.

I went into the bathroom to clean up. As I looked in the mirror, I wondered who that old man staring back at me was. I put my hands on the sink, leaned forward, my mind adrift. That's exactly what I would've done forty years ago, I thought. If you need something for your case, don't rely on anybody else—get it yourself. That was, I believed, the difference between being just a lawyer and being a good lawyer. I recalled the times that I believed it truly made a difference.

I turned on the faucet, splashed cool water on my face and shook out the cobwebs in my brain as I dabbed with the towel. I ran my comb under the faucet and tried to straighten out the few unruly hairs. I concluded I looked terrible and no amount of preening was going to make a difference. I slipped on my Levi's, stepped into my slippers and grabbed my plaid shirt on my way out of the bedroom. The aroma of freshly brewed coffee filled the house. Maggie was sitting at the kitchen table sipping her coffee. She had the radio on behind her, listening to the morning news. As I walked in, she reached around and turned it off. I poured myself a cup of coffee and sat across from her. I looked at her face. She had aged way more gracefully than I. The wrinkles were barely noticeable and there was a mature beauty to her face. She caught my gaze, smiled and said, "What?"

"I was just thinking how pretty you are."

Her smile continued. "No, I won't make you bacon and eggs," she said.

"You always think I have an ulterior motive," I replied.

"Normally you do," she said.

"Well, this time I was just complimenting my wife."

"Yeah, right," she said. "What did Jackie want?"

"You'll find out soon enough, she's on her way over. I can't believe her. She and her boyfriend, Johnny Connors, somehow located Cheryl's dad, the accused sex abuser. The one Brownie called big, ugly and mean. They talked to him last night. She claims they have new information. She's all excited again."

"Whaddaya think it's about?" she asked.

"Well, we'll just have to wait and see," I replied.

Within moments, Jackie showed up. Maggie let her in and poured her a cup of coffee as she sat down across from me.

"You're going to love this, Noah. You always said something stunk about this case—I think we found out what it is. Cheryl wasn't sexually abused by her dad," she paused for effect. "It was her mother!"

"Oh my God," said Maggie.

"What're you talking about?" I asked.

She went through the whole evening, referring to her notes here and there, while Maggie and I sat listening in amazement. When she was done, we were all quiet.

"Well?" Jackie looked from me to Maggie and then back to me, waiting for some response. Maggie broke the silence. "You think it could be true, Noah?"

My mind had been flying through the years of cases I had handled involving allegations of sexual abuse of children, and I recalled only one where the defendant was a woman, and that involved a mother having sexual relations with her son. She had taught him the art of intercourse at the age of fourteen because, she explained, she didn't feel capable of having sex with another man after his father had left them.

"I don't know," I said, shaking my head to clear it. "After all, we only have his word."

"No, Noah," Jackie said, "it all makes sense. Johnny and I talked about it on the way back. If you had seen the pain on this guy's face when he finally broke down and told us, he wasn't making this up. He loved that little girl and then her mother corrupted her. I could sense the tremendous betrayal he felt . . . and the anger, he's still not over the anger. He lost his little girl, his little princess. And not to some disease or accident, or even some pervert outside the family, things he could understand, her own mother corrupted her for her own pleasure. There's a whole neurosis here that I don't understand."

"My God," said Maggie, "this is starting to sound like a Greek tragedy."

"The point is," said Jackie, "what if Cheryl told her mother she was going public. Cheryl felt betrayed by her father; she tried to get even. And, for some reason, in her own mind, that didn't work, and now she was going to go after the real source of her problems, her mother. And if she told her mother and her mother had to shut her up . . ."

I pondered the thought. "It's certainly a possibility," I said. "But how would he ever prove that? Nobody's ever going to believe him. The only record that exists is Cheryl telling everybody he's the perpetrator. Cheryl's dead and her mother . . . well, her mother can simply deny it and we can't prove otherwise."

"But it gives us someone else with a motive, Noah. We needed someone else to look at. She's it."

"You're right," I said. "I wonder if Chris is up. I think we should talk to him. He's the expert."

I called his house, Elizabeth answered. She said that Chris had taken to jogging to get rid of some of his pent-up emotions, and that he should be back shortly. I told her that Jackie and I were coming over.

During the drive I had Jackie tell me again everything that had happened during her meeting with Ben Moore.

"You're lucky you didn't get your head taken off," I said when she finished.

"I wouldn't have done it if Johnny hadn't agreed to come along. But it was pretty exciting, Noah. It got Johnny thinking, he said he's never had this much fun doing personal injury work."

"Fun!" I said. "What was fun?"

"Well, you can't imagine how high I was when we walked out of Mick's place. The whole evening was an adrenaline rush. I don't think I've come down yet."

That a girl, I thought to myself, you're hooked.

We stood on the steps to Chris's house pounding on the door. Nobody answered. I noticed Elizabeth's car was gone. Chris's Volvo was parked in the driveway.

"Maybe they didn't want to see us," Jackie said, grinning.

Then I heard the door unlock and Chris opened it. He looked terrible. He was still in his jogging outfit; a big V of sweat soaked the front from his neck down to his belly button. His hair was damp and matted to his head. He looked surprised to see us.

"I didn't expect any company," he said.

"Didn't Elizabeth tell you we were coming?" I asked.

"No, she wasn't home when I got back from jogging."

"Well, I called just a short time ago . . ." I said.

"She doesn't want to have anything to do with this anymore," Chris interrupted. "As soon as she gets some of her stuff cleaned up, she intends to move out. I can't blame her."

He invited us in, saying he just needed a minute to go and change.

The house was an old Victorian two-story built either to accommodate a big family or just to be ostentatious. Jackie and I sat in an ornate living room with twelve-foot ceilings with aged oak paneling and a large octagon window overlooking the garden. We sat in overstuffed chairs that I knew were antique, because the entire house was filled with antiques. Elizabeth was an antique hound. Many times she would spend the entire weekend driving through southeastern Minnesota, visiting every antique store along the way to find prizes that would be the envy of the neighborhood. Searching for antiques had become, I thought, the leisure time for the rich and bored.

I could hear the shower running. Within minutes, Chris was back in clean clothes, his hair combed tightly to his head, curling at the edges on the back of his neck.

I looked at Jackie. "Well, it's your show. You might as well tell him," I said.

She started fidgeting with the notepad on her lap, appearing nervous. She looked at me and then at Chris. She started. "I talked to Cheryl's dad last night."

I was watching for Chris's reaction. I could see the surprise cross his face.

"He was belligerent at first but I told him that it was really important that he talk to us. I had Johnny Connors along. For some reason, after awhile, he just kind of softened up and he told us one hell of a tale."

Chris's expression widened, the surprise deepened as he listened to Jackie recount the night's events.

"At the end," Jackie continued, "I pressed him as hard as I could. He never flinched. He stuck to his statement. All of those terrible things that were done and said to Cheryl were perpetrated by her mother."

The word "mother" seemed to echo off the polished oak of the ceiling. The room went dead quiet. We both stared at Chris, waiting for his reaction. The only sound was the swinging of the pendulum of a large grandfather clock against the far wall.

His head dropped, his eyes closed. Finally, he looked up and said, "I should've seen it. Sexual abuse by a mother isn't common but it isn't unheard of either. There haven't been a lot of studies done on it, mainly because I believe there are some psychologists who deal with issues of sexual abuse of children who simply believe it doesn't happen, that mothers aren't capable of doing that to their daughters. I've never had a case myself but from the little literature I've read, I guess there were some telltale signs. The few times she said anything about her mother she would talk about her in such childish and endearing terms, like she had been a little playmate of hers. It is my understanding that sometimes that's what the sexual abuse amounts to, the caressing, touching to promote stimulation. Sometimes it goes further than that. That's what happened here. Maybe as a sexless child, Cheryl was unthreatening, but then as she reached puberty, her breasts developing, her sexual organs more pronounced, her mother considered her a threat. That's the reason for the threats of mutilation, removing her breasts, her vagina. Nobody would want her. Then, just when she needs help the most, somebody to step in and protect her, the parents are divorced and from Cheryl's perspective, she's abandoned . . . totally abandoned. But her love is still for her mother despite the betrayal, her mother is still the nurturing parent and she can't betray her mother, she wouldn't. Except for the threats of mutilation, her recollection would be of a warm, caring and sensuous relationship. She may have even repressed the fact that her mother was the source of those threats, the sexual abuse."

"Whaddaya mean?" Jackie asked.

"Freudian psychologists believe that when people, especially children, suffer a traumatic experience, such as sexual abuse, the mind can repress it, close it out like it never happened. Then, sometimes years later, something in their life will trigger a recollection and it can all come back, sometimes in a flood of anguish. I had a young lady in treatment a while back who claimed to be recalling episodes of sexual abuse as a child by her brother."

"So you give some credibility to what he's saying?" I asked.

"I have to," Chris said. "It may even be why Cheryl initially told me her mother was dead, to protect her to the very end."

"It all makes me want to cry," said Jackie.

"What does this mean for my case?" asked Chris.

"I have to admit," I said, "my head is swimming with the possibilities. It could mean nothing. We're going on the statement of one guy, and he's an alleged sexual abuser. Until we can give them some reasons to the contrary, Kropp and Becker aren't going to give him any credibility whatsoever. On the other end of the spectrum, she could be the murderer. We have to give the cops some reason to look at her, something more than we already have." I glanced at Jackie. "You know Cheryl's file backwards and forwards. Is there anything in there at all that would help us as far as the mother is concerned?"

"I looked through it again this morning when I couldn't sleep. Nothing."

"Well, I've been thinking," I said. "We have one tool available that you normally wouldn't have in a criminal case, she's the plaintiff in the lawsuit against you, and we can take her deposition. You're entitled to be there, Chris. We can ask her all those questions, confront her directly: 'Did you ever place a straight edge razor against your daughter's breast and threaten to cut it off?' It will be interesting to see her reaction."

"Do you think you can tell if she's lying?" asked Jackie.

"Unless she's really good, I know I can," I replied.

"I can't wait," said Jackie. "I want to get her."

\* \* \* \* \*

That afternoon I called Kevin Young, the defense attorney representing Chris's insurance carrier. I explained to him where we believed our investigation was leading, and told him he should set up Carol O'Malley's deposition as quickly as possible.

"Holy balls," he responded. "If she really did that, takes a lot of guts for her to now turn around and sue, claiming she misses her little sweetheart. You pull this one off, Noah, I'll come over and kiss your ass."

Kevin was always prone to comments like that. I think it had something to do with being a defense attorney for insurance companies.

"That won't be necessary," I replied. "You can just talk your company into paying part of Chris's attorney's fees."

"You get us out of this thing with O'Malley, you can bet your ass I will. I'm going to call the prick, Pettiman, right now and tell him we want to set her deposition for next week and we wanna do it here. I'll call you back."

I looked at Jackie who had been taking in the conversation from the other side of my desk.

"He's going to try and get her here for a deposition next week," I said.

She beamed.

"I hate to put a pin in your balloon," I said, "but this could all be nothing, you know."

"I don't think so," she said. "Like you, I'm starting to get gut feelings and I've got one right now. She's our culprit . . . I can just feel it."

"Now don't you do anything crazy without talking to me. I'm still upset over what you guys did. This time I'm willing to forgive and forget, but don't push your luck."

I gave her a fixed stare. "This is a dangerous world, Jackie. You're too pretty, too nice and have too much of a future to end up in a back alley somewhere. Use your head."

"I will," she said, as she reached across the desk and tapped my hand.

I went about my other business. Because I had been around for so long, in addition to my criminal practice I had a lot of friends who were asking me to help them with estate plans. It seems that when people get my age, they start to worry about what they're going to do with the little wealth they've accumulated. Everybody wants to make sure Uncle Sam doesn't get the little nest egg they've set aside for Junior. I always advise them not to worry about Junior, to just go out and spend it and have fun while they still could. But that never sat very well with most of them. So I busied myself putting together some simple wills.

It was late afternoon when Kevin called me back. "They're stonewalling us, Noah. First G. Gordon Pettiman said he didn't think it should be any problem. Then he talked to her, called me back and said she's busy next week. So I've been on the line with him a half-a-dozen times. Every time I come up with a suggestion, she's got something else going on. I even told him we'd fly out there to do it."

"But we don't have a whole lot of time, Kevin. Chris's criminal trial is set up in five weeks. I want to pin her down on some stuff with some time left to do some investigation. Isn't there something we can do to push it?"

"I can file a motion with the judge to compel her to submit to deposition."

"Savano will know exactly what we're doing," I said. "Is it possible to get it in front of somebody else?"

"I can certainly try. Judge Mueller's going to be here for civil calendar next term. I can call his clerk to see if he's willing to hear it."

"Do that," I said.

"It'll probably be tomorrow before I hear," Kevin said.

"That's fine, just let me know."

As I left that afternoon, I told Jackie what had happened.

"She can't squirm out of it, can she?" she asked.

"Not if I can help it," I replied.

Kevin called me the next morning just as I was leaving for lunch. "I talked to Judge Mueller. I told him there was some urgency, that we had to continue with discovery or we would never get it done in time, and the first thing we needed was her deposition. He had his clerk set up a telephone conference. Judge Mueller told G. Gordon he understood how things were done in Boston but we like to keep things simple here. So if we want to set up a deposition, it has to be done in a reasonable time. So Pettiman has to get back to me with dates when she'll be available within the next three weeks. And, Noah, if need be, we may have to fly to Boston."

"I hate planes," I said.

"Maybe I can get the insurance company to pay for first class," he replied.

"Won't do me any good," I replied, "I can't drink anyway."

I met Jackie at the front desk and told her about Kevin's call.

"Yes!" she said, giving me a high five. "Now we're getting somewhere."

Our exuberance, unfortunately, was rather short-lived. I had barely sat down at my desk the next morning, reached for my first cup of coffee, when Kevin was on the phone.

"Noah," he said, "we just got snookered. She's going to dismiss her lawsuit."

"What?" I hollered.

"You heard me; she's going to dismiss her lawsuit. Pettiman says she's way too distraught over the death of her daughter and how it happened to go through a deposition now. When I pressed him, he said they're going to simply dismiss. They'll start it later, after she's had a chance to recover."

"That slippery . . . I was wondering how she was going to get out of this. She must be guiltier than I thought."

"That I don't know, Noah, but she pulled the rug out from under you."

"Do you have any information on her at all?" I asked.

"Very little. Just what the insurance company was able to get off the state records. She's actually been doing pretty well, you know."

"Can you send what you've got over?"

"Sure," he replied.

"Let me know when you get the dismissal in. We're going to have to get to her somehow, though."

"Good luck," he said as he hung up.

I leaned back in my chair, my mind wandering aimlessly among all of the possibilities. Out of all the things I had anticipated, this was not one of them. Kevin was right: we'd been snookered. Best laid plans.

I heard Jackie come in. As she walked by, I waved her into my office. "This time it's my turn, you're not going to believe this. I got a call from Kevin this morning; Mrs. O'Malley's dismissing her lawsuit."

Jackie had worn a warm smile up to then, now her face went blank. "How can she do that?" she asked.

"Well, it's her case; she can do whatever she wants to."

"Isn't it over then?"

"No, she can restart it anytime within the statute of limitations."

"So, she did it for one reason, so she didn't have to answer our questions."

"Sure looks like that to me," I said.

"Can't we get to her some way?" Jackie asked.

"We can send an investigator out to talk to her but she doesn't have to talk to him, she can tell him to go to hell, which I'm sure she would."

"It doesn't seem fair, Noah. But it tells me one thing—she's hiding something. But what? How are we going to find out?"

Jackie," I said, "you've come a long way from believing Chris is guilty, don't give up now."

"I'm not going to give up," she said. "If I have to I'll go camp on her doorstep until she talks to me."

"We don't have that much time, Jackie. I'm going to send Brownie out there right away. Kevin says he can get in touch with the insurance company, they have a local investigator who'll help us."

"Why don't you talk to Kropp?" she asked.

"No, I thought of that. First, he's not going to believe us, but more importantly, if he starts digging, he could spook her. Brownie can be discreet. Kropp would be like telegraphing our suspicions."

Brownie wasn't looking forward to going to Boston; he liked flying even less than I did. He said the seats were too close together and he felt cramped. I told him there was plenty of room between the seats if you didn't have a big potbelly. His comment was, "That's very funny coming from a stick man."

And he was right. On my new diet, I was starting to look awfully skinny. I was starting to feel better, though, so I took it as a compliment.

The next morning I drove Brownie to the airport. On the drive, a little over an hour, I kept impressing on him how important this trip could be. I brought him up to date on everything that had happened, all of our suspicions, our conclusion that she was the murderer. We had to find something to flush her out.

On the way back, by myself, I wondered if I had put too much pressure on him. I always believed that if anybody was going to go by a heart attack, it would be Brownie.

When I arrived back in town, I went straight to Chris's house to bring him up to date. He was home alone again. He said Elizabeth spent as little time with him as possible. He told me he had researched sexual abuse of girls by their mothers. He'd only found one published paper. He told me his recollections were right, many times the sexual abuse didn't involve penetration but rather fondling and caressing, sometimes using the child as a means of masturbation. Cheryl's dad talked about how much she and her mother cuddled. He believed that was a pretty good indication that something more was happening.

"You want to know something rather bizarre?" he asked. "There was a conference in California of psychologists and social workers dealing with sexual abuse. One of the presenters gave a case study of a young client she had that had been sexually abused by her mother. The report I read said that a noted psychologist stood up, told the presenter that she didn't believe her, and that she'd never heard of a mother sexually abusing her daughter. She didn't believe a woman was capable of doing that. That kind of thinking gives you a pretty good idea, Noah, of why there's very little information out there. It also tells me one more important thing as far as my case is concerned—the bias of that psychologist is pretty prevalent. It's going to be pretty tough to convince a local jury that a mother could do that."

He was only partly right, though. Anytime your case dealt with issues of sexual abuse of children, incest, the defense had to be especially diligent when picking the jury. The whole subject was taboo, not just whether a mother could sexually abuse a daughter. As a result, you could never rely on what a prospective juror may tell you during *voir dire*, no one was going to readily admit they know anything about such goings on.

But from forty years of practice, I knew that sexual abuse of children had always been with us. One of my earliest cases was a father who, in the term he preferred to use, "broke-in" all of his daughters. By the time they got him to court, he was sixty-six. The only reason the abuse came out was because one of his granddaughters told her mother that he had been touching *her.* Her mother, who was thirty-eight at the time, had never told anybody about what her father had done to her. She had five sisters but she thought she had been the only victim. After her daughter had told her that grandpa had put his hand down there, she called her sisters to warn them. Each one told her what had happened to them as a child, all six daughters had been sexually violated by their father without knowing that their siblings were also victims.

At the time, incest wasn't considered a criminal offense; it was handled in juvenile court as a family matter. I was appointed to represent the father. At trial, all six daughters paraded before their father, took the stand, looked him in the eye and told him what his abuse had done to them. The mother took the stand and, to the shock and dismay of everyone in the courtroom, testified that she didn't know what everybody was making such a big deal about, her father had done it to her and her sisters, that's just the way it was. She knew what was going on and though she didn't condone it, it didn't concern her. I could hear the daughters sobbing behind me as she matter-a-factly told the judge she wanted her husband back home.

There wasn't much the court could do. The judge ordered that he could have no contact with any minor children, especially his granddaughters. He was put into counseling, his wife as well. The court order would remain in effect until the counselor felt it was safe to reunite the family.

I had many cases that ended like that until the abused daughters finally pushed lawmakers into making incest a crime. Then the pendulum swung the other way and prosecutors prosecuted with a vengeance. Fathers were sent to prison; many deserved it, but others were taken away in handcuffs while their daughters, the abused, bawled in open court, pleading with the judge to let their daddy come home. The whole thing became an ugly mess. One could only hope that with time, the crime would no longer exist; there wouldn't be any more perverts who would do that to a child. As I thought about it that day, at Chris's house, I knew that hadn't happened yet.

"Jackie and I have been talking about the trial, Chris," I said. "We'll have to be very careful in picking the jury. We're going to have to look at background, family, and attitude. All the sympathy's going to lie with Cheryl. Becker's going to try and make you out to be an unscrupulous opportunist, seducing this sick girl with promises of marriage. Chris, you can't imagine how many times I've lain awake in bed at night, the nightmare of this trial going through my head. When I finally manage to fall asleep, I have this recurring dream. We're standing in the courtroom, waiting for the jury to come back with a verdict, the door opens, they all walk in with big smiles on their face, hollering 'He's guilty! He's guilty!'"

"That's funny, Noah, I have the same dream."

We both managed a good laugh. That's what it had come down to for both of us, waiting for the inevitable to happen, and we were going to put Jackie out front for cannon fodder.

"Jackie," Noah said, "I've been going over a list of questions I think you have to ask the prospective jurors in *voir dire*. You can't let any ringers on there like happened in Clint's case."

"I've been doing some research on that since this all happened," I replied. "The experts say that statistically twenty-five percent of all girls are sexually abused by somebody in their family. Twenty-five percent, Noah. One out of four. That means out of twelve prospective women jurors, the odds are four of them are likely to have been sexually abused."

"I would suspect the ratio's probably higher in this area," Noah replied.

"In Clint's case, out of sixteen potential women jurors, only one indicated that she'd had any experience with sexual abuse. That was with her daughter and a neighbor boy. 'Course casting blame on the neighbor boy could've been made up. Too embarrassed to admit it was in the family."

"I guess that's the point," Noah said. "You can't necessarily rely on what they tell you, you're going to have to look to body language, innuendo, anything that might give you some indication that they're covering something up. I don't think you want anybody with a lot of daughters; the potential there is just too great. Anybody who's had a daughter sexually abused isn't going to think twice about hanging Chris."

"Noah," I said, "I've been thinking. Why don't we just subpoena Cheryl's mother? I mean, I've already put her as a witness on my list. That was funny, actually. Becker called me and wanted to know what she was going to say; I told him I didn't have the slightest idea. Then he asked me, 'Why'd you even bother putting her on the list then?' and I replied, 'Just to piss you off.' He hung up on me. Can you believe it?"

"The problem with calling her, Jackie, is we don't have anything to go on. Once you ask her a question and she answers it, you're stuck with her answer unless you have something to prove she's lying. Think about it. If she's done everything we think she has, this is one clever lady. Nobody's even looking at her."

"She can't be that clever, we're looking at her," I replied.

"Only out of desperation," Noah said.

I had to admit he was right. If we'd had any other reasonable explanation, I would never have talked to Cheryl's dad and we wouldn't be looking at her either.

"I think you did the right thing by putting her name on the witness list, but that doesn't mean we have to call her. The first thing you have to do is file a motion before Judge Savano asking him to issue a certificate to the court in the county in which she lives that will require her to appear here to testify. For that, we'll have to convince him that she's a material witness. We're not there yet, but we have to get started. At least this way we can keep Becker form screaming about surprises."

Well, I'll keep working on this stuff," I said, "but it's getting a little bleak. I hope we hear from Brownie soon."

* * * * *

"You have a very interesting lady here," Brownie said. "And she was the beneficiary of a rather fortuitous event."

We sat in the bar at the Minneapolis-St. Paul International Airport. Noah and I had driven the eighty miles to pick him up following his return on a red eye special, both of us too anxious to let it wait until morning. Noah told me during the drive that Brownie's messages had been too intriguing to wait.

The airport was quiet, the bar quieter. We sat by ourselves at a table in front of a wall of glass, watching the planes taxi on the runways. The only sound was Johnny Carson on the Late Show in the background and the roar of jet engines as a 747 lumbered down the runway struggling to break from the tug of the earth.

"She's a social climber," said Brownie. "Kind of the sweetheart of the artsy crowd. From what I can piece together, she moved to Boston in '72, finished some schooling and then went to work in a real estate office owned by a guy named John O'Malley. He was doing pretty well before she went to work for him, but he got involved in some commercial transactions in the late '70's that turned his business around. He made some big bucks on a commercial waterfront development. My source for most of my information is a lady who worked for him. Let's see."

He flipped through the pages of his notebook. "Lori Driscoll," he said. "She worked for him twenty years or so. It was quite obvious she didn't think much of Carol, considered her kind of a tramp. This O'Malley, he's about fifteen years senior to Carol, single, not particularly handsome, I saw his picture. Kind of shy, I guess. Before long, Lori said, he's head over heels in love with Carol. She said Carol was quite a looker. In her opinion, Carol seduced him. She said he didn't stand a chance. Claims she smiled a lot and wiggled her butt around the office. It went from work to play and a couple years after she's there, they get married. From everything I can find out, sounds like they had a pretty good relationship . . . for a while, at least."

Brownie paused for a moment. I looked to the side and saw a Northwest Airline 747, the nose rising from the ground, the back tires skimming the tarmac, clouds of black smoke twirling from the engines to spiral upward into the cold air.

When I looked back, Brownie had a puzzled expression on his face. "You think there's any possibility, you know, based on this lady's background, that she may be, you know, a switch hitter?"

"What would make you ask that?" asked Noah.

"This Lori said that she thought there may be some possibility of that. Just a hunch she had. She said it appeared that things started to fall apart between Carol and O'Malley toward '78 or so. She said one time she heard them, in the course of an argument—they didn't know she was standing outside the door— she heard O'Malley telling Carol he didn't want her bringing this woman around the house anymore, people were talkin'. Lori said she'd seen them at the office together and they seemed a little too friendly. O'Malley was concerned that if people found out about the relationship it would hurt the business. So it sounds like he's concerned about Carol's lady guest and her reputation."

"Maybe it was a *ménage a trois*," said Noah. "Does Lori think O'Malley was into anything kinky?"

"I didn't get that impression," said Brownie. "Anyway, at that point, Lori says the relationship between Carol and O'Malley seemed rocky. There wasn't the kissy huggy crap that had been going on in the office before. Carol was still working in the office but Lori said O'Malley seemed distant. Then he became concerned about the finances, put a little tighter clamp on Carol's spending.

"Then fortune steps in. In the late summer of '78, O'Malley takes his sailboat out for a moonlight cruise. At least that's what Carol tells the cops. Nobody ever sees him again. I had a chance to review the police reports. According to everybody, it wasn't unusual for him to take his sailboat out when he wanted some quiet time alone to think. Carol's statement to the police is that she didn't get worried until probably noon or so the next day when she hadn't heard anything. The harbor patrol found the boat anchored out by an island. He wasn't on it. They never found the body. Figured he ended up fish food. I guess there's some pretty strong currents through the bay that could've carried his body out."

"No evidence of foul play on the boat?" Noah asked.

"No. What kind of clinched it, I guess, is he had a bad heart, Noah. He'd had a heart attack several years before that. They were recommending by-pass surgery but he considered it too risky. They had a coroner's inquest. The conclusion was that he probably had a heart attack, fell off the boat and floated away. When it was all over, though, she ended up being a millionaire."

"You're kidding," said Noah.

"No, he had no other relatives. No family. She got it all. I went through the probate file—his net worth was close to six million. Most of it in real estate. Lori said within a year Carol had closed down the office, cashed out everything she could, and has pretty much been living a life of leisure. She's gotten herself onto a couple charitable committees, some of the Arts council things, slowly working her way up the social ladder. As far as Lori knows, the money's all invested in pretty solid things where she doesn't have to worry about where her next buck is coming from."

I sat there listening to Brownie, stupefied. If she had all of this money, why wasn't she helping her daughter? Why would her ex, Ben, not know any of this? More to the point, if she was so well off, why would she sue Dr. Morgan for money damages?

"Was she ever a suspect in her husband's death?" I asked.

"I talked to the detective who worked the case," Brownie said. "Another nice Irish guy, O'Bannon. I'll tell you exactly what he said—he said whenever you have an attractive woman marrying an ugly cuss who's fifteen years her senior, and then the guy dies in suspicious circumstances, and this pretty woman inherits all of his money, you have to wonder. But she had an alibi. She'd been to one of her meetings earlier in the evening and then left with another lady who told the police they had dinner together and she was with Carol until almost midnight. There was no record of anybody leaving the marina in a small boat. They suspect someone could've gotten out there, did something to O'Malley, and gotten back. O'Bannon said he checked every marina up and down the bay, nobody saw anybody that looked like her. He said he gave up, had to move on to other cases. Said it was probably just what it looked to be, O'Malley's time had come. So she's been pretty much living the life of luxury."

"Does she have an alibi for the day that Cheryl was murdered?" Noah asked.

"I don't know," said Brownie, "because I don't think anybody's asked her. The investigator and I checked with Logan. Within twenty-four hours before the time frame for Cheryl's murder, there were eleven different flights that left from Logan and ended up in Minneapolis-St. Paul, directly or after some other stop over. It took some effort, but we got a copy of the rosters. Her name doesn't appear. That doesn't mean she may not have been on the flight or maybe even left before that. But I don't know how we're going to be able to get it."

We were all silent after that, all of us lost in our own thoughts. The bartender came around the bar and indicated last call. Noah and I shook our heads no. Brownie ordered another beer. We all kind of snapped out of the daze when the bartender clunked Brownie's beer bottle on the table, reached for a five-dollar bill and said, "Thanks."

Brownie looked at us. "Five bucks for a bottle of beer. What's this world coming to?"

Noah smiled. Brownie took a big swallow of his beer as I weighed the impact of my next statement. "I'll go out to Boston and talk to her," I said.

"You'll do no such thing," Noah said. "Whaddaya think this is, make believe? This lady could be a murderer . . ."

Brownie interrupted. "Jackie, if that's true, this lady's a manipulator with no conscience. If you appear to be a threat, who knows what she'd do."

"Don't even think of it," said Noah.

"Then what're we going to do?" I asked. "Let Dr. Morgan go to prison for something he didn't do?"

Brownie said, "O'Bannon said he'll keep looking. If he can come up with anything, he'll let us know."

The bartender turned off the lights to give us a hint that he wanted to close. Brownie gulped down the rest of his beer. While we walked out of the terminal to the short-term parking lot, no one said a word. We were back on the highway headed toward home when Brownie said, "Well, if anybody cares, I had some great seafood. O'Bannon took me to a place one night that had a seafood special, scallops, clams and shrimp, all you could eat for only $39.00 per person. I charged it to the insurance company."

"I'm sure I'll hear about that," said Noah.

"Oh yeah," Brownie said, "just about forgot. I found out why G. Gordon uses the G. His real name is Gervace. Gervace Gordon Pettiman."

"I like Gervace," I said.

"Apparently he doesn't," replied Brownie.

I stared out the window for a while. Brownie and Noah were both quiet.

"Can't I at least call her?" I asked to break the monotony.

"I don't know," said Noah. "I've been thinking, trying to figure out at this point what we can do. We've got her as a witness on the witness list for Chris's trial, but we don't have the slightest idea what she's going to say. We have to have some basis to call her as a witness. If we tell the judge our theory that she's a suspect for the murder, he's going to require that we show some foundation, some credible evidence that would point to her as a suspect. Without that foundation, he probably won't even honor our motion to get her here, much less let us put her on the stand."

"What if Cheryl's dad would be willing to testify?" I asked. "What if he would be willing to tell the jury that Cheryl told him that her mother was the one who sexually abused her?"

"Even if he would be willing to do it," Noah replied, "it would be a question of whether the judge would even let it in—it's hearsay—and then as we talked about before, Becker would destroy his credibility."

Noah leaned over, switched the car radio on and tuned to Minnesota Public Radio. We were all too tired and depressed to think about the case any longer. My head bobbed as I tried to keep myself awake.

* * * * *

For the next couple days, between Noah and me, Carol O'Malley became a subject that just wasn't discussed. We both knew something had to be done, but what? I had to defer to his knowledge and experience. If it had been up to me, I would have been on the next plane, pounding on her door, demanding answers. Deep down, though, I knew that wasn't the way to handle it. I concluded that when Noah had it figured out, he would let me know.

Two days later Noah called me into his office. He motioned for me to have a seat as he slid some documents across his desk. The heading read "Northwestern Bell".

"Cheryl Moore's telephone bills," he said. "The morning after we brought Brownie back, I called Kropp and asked him if he had ever looked at her telephone bills. I asked him if there were ever any long distance calls to Boston. He said he knew there were because when he looked at the bills, he was looking to see if there were any numbers for people who might be possible suspects. When he found out that the number in Boston was Cheryl's mother and he had talked to her, he just put them away. But look at the number of calls in the last month and then two days before she dies, they talk for fifty-nine minutes. Kropp's going to try and get the telephone bills for the last year, see if there's any pattern. But I'm curious, why should she be calling her all of a sudden? So often? Then that long conversation just before she's murdered?"

I sat there looking at the dates and the times trying to imagine the substance of the conversations.

"I think you should call Mrs. O'Malley," Noah said. "You have a soft, non-threatening voice. Woman-to-woman, maybe she'll talk to you. It worked on her ex."

I let the undertone of the comment pass.

"I'll give it a try. How do you think I should approach her?" I asked.

"Be up front. Tell her you're the defense attorney for Dr. Morgan. You understand the grief she's gone through, how she must feel. And then turn to Mr. Moore, his denial of the sexual abuse. Don't say anything about the fact that he accused her. Just see what her reaction is. It's worth a try."

I closed my eyes for a few moments, running through the scenario in my mind. I picked up the phone, looked at the long distance number on the telephone bill and dialed. I could feel my pulse quicken, my mouth go dry. It rang seven, eight times and I was about to hang up with a sense of relief when the receiver was lifted and a pleasant voice said, "Hello."

"Is this Mrs. O'Malley?"

"Yes, it is."

"I'm sorry to disturb you, but my name is Jackie Geroux. I'm an attorney in St. Cloud, Minnesota. I represent Dr. Morgan in the trial that starts in two weeks. I believe . . ."

She interrupted. "I know who you are, Ms. Geroux, and I have nothing to say to you."

"Please! Please!" I said. "Give me a moment."

"I don't know why I should."

"It's about your ex-husband," I said.

The line went quiet. "That slime?" she finally said. "What's he up to now?"

"You know that Cheryl told the doctors that he had sexually abused her while the two of you were still married?"

"I know that," she said. "I told it to the cops. I hadn't known it was happening at the time, but Cheryl told me years later. I told her to go to the police, turn him in. She didn't want to."

I glanced at Noah, motioned with my hand to have him give me a notepad. He slid it across his desk. I nodded at him as I started to take notes. I had obviously hit upon a subject that she had no reluctance to talk about.

"You think that if I'd have had any knowledge that it was going on that I wouldn't have stopped it? I probably would've shot the bastard myself. It never dawned on me that poor Cheryl was going through such horror."

"When did you first find out?" I asked.

"Several years ago, after her suicide attempt. She called me from the hospital. I wanted to come right back, turn the bastard in, but I had my own problems. I had just lost my husband."

"Oh, I'm sorry to hear that," I said.

"It was an accident," she replied. "I had things I had to clean up. I felt terrible about not coming to Minnesota to help Cheryl. If I had, this would have never happened."

"What?" I asked.

"Her murder."

"What makes you think that?"

"I would've brought her back with me. I really feel terrible. After all she had been through, when she most needed me . . ." Her voice drifted off.

"When was the last time you talked to her?" I asked.

"I'm sorry to say, we didn't talk enough. She called me several times during her trial, the rape trial—that must have been terrible for her, too. Being a mother, it's just hard to imagine all that happening to your daughter. I told her I'd come to Minnesota but she said she had help—your doctor. We know what kind of help he was."

"Did she ever talk about Dr. Morgan?" I asked.

"Just that she was seeing him. She thought he was being a great help. He was being a big help, all right."

"No particulars?"

"No."

"I understand you've dropped your lawsuit against Dr. Morgan. Why?"

"My attorney told me I don't have to talk about that," she snapped.

Wrong question, Jackie, I thought, don't lose her now. "Well, I can understand how it would be difficult for you as her mother to go through this terrible ordeal, I don't mean to make it worse," I said. "I apologize."

The line went quiet for a moment. "When I heard of her murder, the first thought that crossed my mind was Ben. Then the detective told me about the letters and the diary. That was quite a shock."

"Did Cheryl ever tell you what happened when she was raped? What her rapist actually did to her?"

Another silence. "No, she didn't and it wasn't something I was about to bring up."

"So you never heard any details?"

"No."

"Do you remember the last time you may have talked to Cheryl?"

"I don't remember. I know she called the night before she was scheduled to testify, kind of in a panic. I could tell she was petrified."

"What gave you that feeling?"

"Listen, Miss, she was my daughter. I didn't need any particular insight. I could tell."

Anger was swelling in her voice again. I knew I needed to back off a little.

"Did you talk to her after the jury came back and found the rapist guilty?"

"I don't think so," she said. "Listen, I have to go. I've been talking way longer than I intended. You do what you have to do, but I told the cops I thought it was my ex. I think he was afraid and that's why he killed her. But they don't buy that, so it's out of my hands. Good bye."

I listened to the dead air for a few moments and then hung up. Noah stared at me eagerly.

"What a bizarre situation, Noah. She's lying about her contacts with Cheryl. You heard me ask her specifically about telephone calls after the trial. Her answer was she didn't remember. Who would Cheryl have been talking to if not her? Stranger still, she told the police it was Cheryl's dad who murdered her. She still believes that. Why would she then sue Dr. Morgan? I don't know, Noah, maybe the whole family's nuts."

Noah sat there quietly, the wheels turning. After several moments, he said, "Diversion. All she's trying to do is divert attention from herself. As crazy as it sounds, let's consider it for a moment, Jackie. If Cheryl's dad's telling us the truth, that Carol is the sick one in the family, sexually abusing her daughter, maybe at some point Cheryl finally told her mother she could no longer keep it a secret. Cheryl could've come to that conclusion at any time; or maybe she wanted something from her mother, something she couldn't get unless she threatened. Carol O'Malley is now a Boston socialite, hob-knobbing with the rich and famous, a multimillionaire, and all of that's at risk if Cheryl goes public. Imagine the headlines: 'Millionaire Socialite Accused of Sexually Abusing Daughter'."

"That's quite a scenario, Noah," I said.

"Just hear me out," he replied. "She knows things may be collapsing all around her, she has to do something. Maybe Cheryl even told her that she was going to run away with Dr. Morgan, move to California and get married. Cheryl would eventually tell Morgan. Who knows what was going through Carol's head. From what we know, the only thing that Carol actually knew is that Cheryl had accused her dad in all those therapy sessions. If something happened to Cheryl, who would be the obvious suspect?"

"Ben," I said.

"You're right," he replied.

"That's what she told me, Noah. She told me she thinks the police are wrong, that Ben is the real murderer. That's what she told the detective. I'm sure she meant Kropp."

"Can you imagine her surprise when she finds out they charged Dr. Morgan?"

"Exactly, Noah," I replied. "She said she had no idea about the diary or letters."

"So she's in a panic, has to do something quickly. Somehow she gets to Minnesota without being seen. Not that difficult. Cheryl let's her in. Her mother murders her and stages the sexual scene by mutilating the body to correspond with what Cheryl said her dad threatened to do. Then she's gone, believing that she would be the last one anyone would suspect. When she learns of Chris, that he's indicted, she sues him to continue to divert any attention from her." Noah leaned back in his chair, his eyes lifted toward the ceiling.

It all made sense to me. Moreover, there was just something in my conversation with her that disturbed me. I couldn't put my finger on it. I couldn't articulate why, but her comments sounded rehearsed.

Noah's eyes slowly reached mine. "The problem is, Jackie, how do we flush her out?"

"How about the fact that she lied about the phone calls? We have that."

"To you!" he said. "Do you want to be a witness? That's the problem with you talking to her. If you want to impeach her with anything she said to you, you end up becoming a witness."

"Maybe I should've taped it," I said.

"We can try again but I have a suspicion that's the last she's going to talk to you. This is no dumb lady. I'm just trying to figure out what she thought she had to gain by telling you those things. I think it's time I talked to Detective Kropp. I think we have enough now to pique his interest."

It was early morning and I was sitting across the table from Detective Kropp at Sally's Café, each of us sipping a cup of coffee. For the last twenty minutes, I had been outlining all of my suspicions regarding Carol O'Malley. To say he was skeptical would be quite an understatement. Every time I came up with a new twist, he would roll his eyes and give me that you-expect-me-to-believe-that look.

"Noah," he said when I was done, "if this was coming from anybody but you, I'd laugh. But let me get this straight. You believe Cheryl's mother flew out here to murder her daughter to cover her own ass?"

"It makes sense, Bob," I said.

"When I talked to the old man, why didn't he tell me that his ex was the pervert in the family?"

"Who knows? Maybe he doesn't like cops. Maybe he just didn't want to get involved. Maybe now that Jackie's softened him up, he's willing to talk."

I took a sip of my coffee and gave him time to mull it over. I could see his mind working. Nobody loved a good mystery better than Kropp. If he left with even an inkling that I may be right, I suspected that he'd be on it by the end of the day.

The café was filled with the blue-collar crowd. There was a constant din of small talk covered by laughter, the clinking of dishes. I continued sipping my coffee, giving Kropp all the time he needed.

Finally he said, "If nobody saw her here, how are we ever gonna prove it? If we can't trace any tickets . . ."

"How about car rental?" I spurted. "We haven't been able to look into that because we don't have the resources. But to get from Minneapolis to here she would've had to have a car."

"I can check into it," said Bob. "But it's going to take some time."

203

"Well, the trial starts in two weeks," I replied. "I've already talked to Savano about getting it postponed. He said no way. He said if we don't get it done now, it gets moved to between Thanksgiving and Christmas. He doesn't want to sit in a two to three week murder trial during the holidays, nor does he want any jurors put through that. As far as he's concerned, it stays put. So if there's anything you can do to help, we need it quick."

Bob gave me a strange look. "Help? I'm not even sure why I'm talking to you. It isn't my job to help you. As far as how I view the evidence, we've got our murderer."

"Then why did you even listen to me?" I said.

"There's always that one in a million possibility that I could be wrong. I don't like anybody thinking they can get away with murder."

\* \* \* \* \*

I had planted the seed in Detective Kropp's mind, now I just had to sit back and see what happened. I knew from experience that the prosecutor, Randy Becker, would laugh me out of his office if I tried to lay any of this on him. He had been unusually quiet since Clint's matter. I suspected he was spending every waking hour preparing to send Dr. Morgan to the big house. The conviction of Dr. Morgan would be his crowning achievement, redemption for his screw-up, and maybe even lead to bigger and better things. He would be ready for this trial, his file memorized, everything outlined, nothing left to chance. I knew our next move was going to rock his boat.

Jackie and I sat in the law library struggling over the right words to use, our task was to file with the court our response to the prosecutor's *Motion in Limine*. When we filed our motion before Judge Savano to request that Carol O'Mally's county of residence issue a subpoena requiring her to appear as a witness at the trial, Becker filed the motion asking the judge to preclude us from calling her as a witness. The purpose of the motion is to bring issues before the court that you intend to raise in the course of the trial and to ask the court to rule on those issues before trial, so you knew how far you could go, and, if need be, the judge could set guidelines as far as how the evidence could actually be presented. The only way Jackie could call Carol O'Malley as a witness, and ask her the kind of questions she had to ask, was if we could create a reasonable foundation for the court to agree that she may be a suspect in the death of her daughter.

"I'm not sure what we're trying to do here," said Jackie.

"We're trying to construct a basis on which to argue that Cheryl's mother had the motive and the opportunity to murder her daughter," I said. "The judge won't let us put her on the stand and just start firing questions at her. Our only reason to offer any testimony about another suspect is to create a reasonable doubt in the mind of the jury. Before he can allow us to do that, the judge has to agree that there's some foundation to allow it in. Becker wants the judge to rule on that now, that there is no basis to call her other than to confuse the jury, and for that reason he should deny the subpoena."

"I'm starting to get butterflies, Noah. I think by the time the trial starts, I'm going to be a nervous wreck."

I thought she needed some positive reinforcement. I said, "That's good. That means you're ready. Have you ever listened to an interview with some jock before a big game? Like a professional football player, he's as ready as he's every going to be—fine-tuned. But before the big game, like the Super Bowl, he's got butterflies. Once the game starts, all gone. I used to have butterflies before every big trial too. Once the opening salvo sounded, I'd be fine. You'll be too, just wait and see."

"That's an interesting observation, Noah, but I'll have to take your word on it. I never watch football," she replied.

I gave her a look of disbelief.

We each had a stack of Case Law Reporters in front of us, with markers on the page where the case we were interested in reading started. It was probably twenty minutes later or so that Linda buzzed me to say Detective Kropp was on the phone. I gave Jackie a thumbs up as I walked to the bookcase and picked up the phone.

"Detective Kropp," I said, "thanks for calling. Good news?" I stared at the wall, listening. "I can be over in a couple minutes," I said. "Do you mind if Jackie comes along? Okay, we'll be over. Thanks." "Kropp wants to talk to us. Sounds like we're making some headway. He's waiting for us at the Law

Enforcement Center."

Within minutes Jackie and I sat in one of the conference rooms while one of the deputies tried to locate Detective Kropp.

We waited. Jackie asked, "He didn't give you any indication of what he found out, did he?"

"No, just that he talked to Benjamin Moore. Apparently he was a little bit more cooperative."

I glanced around the room. Pretty bleak. Concrete blocks painted a high gloss tan, no windows, in one corner a bookcase with training manuals. My eyes settled on Jackie who had fixed her stare on me. The lights of the fluorescent bulbs shadowed the contrast of her black hair, the errant curl that now drooped over her left eye, and the olive sheen of her skin. Although only seconds passed, her stare seemed to have a touch of concern.

"How have you been feeling?" she asked.

"Great," I replied. "Since I've been on my new diet, I've been sleeping pretty well. I haven't had any angina for quite a while. I do miss my pipe, though."

Just then we heard a voice holler, "Hey, Bob, they're in there."

I heard the clicking of his boots on the tile floor and he strolled into the room. We exchanged hellos and he sat down.

"I had another visit with Benjamin Moore," he said. "Quite interesting. I found him to be an entirely different person from the last time we talked. He told me he liked you, Jackie. He said if you had the guts to come to Mick's place on a Friday night, even with your boyfriend, it told him something."

"That she's crazy," I said.

Kropp managed a little laugh; Jackie managed a grin.

"Anyway," continued Kropp, "that's the only reason he talked to you. He told me the same story, though, that Cheryl's mother sexually abused her. I asked him if that was true, why he kept quiet for all these years. He said to protect Cheryl more than anything. As strange as that sounds, to him it made sense. I asked him why he didn't tell me the first time I talked to him, after Cheryl's murder. He said he was too angry to want to talk to me about anything. He was blaming himself. If he had done something earlier, maybe it would've been different. Anyway, I got a whole different version of what life was like in the

206

Moore household years ago."

"So you believe him?" I asked.

"I don't know. He seemed sincere . . . but so did Mrs. O'Malley when I talked to her. Even if I believe him, though, Noah, I can't take any of this to Becker, I need something more. You know exactly what he'll say."

"How about the car rental?" I asked.

"I've got somebody working on that. Nothing yet. But I did talk to Detective O'Bannon from Boston homicide. He doesn't see how she could have been involved in her husband's death, but he had to admit that it worked out pretty well for her. So it's all got me thinking, Noah. I have to admit that I was a little disturbed after my meeting with Mrs. O'Malley when she was here after Cheryl's murder. She acted a little, I don't know, different for somebody who just had a daughter brutally murdered. I couldn't put my finger on it at the time."

"That's the same way I felt after I talked to her on the phone," Jackie said. "There's something in her attitude, in the way she talks that makes you wonder."

"That's right," Kropp said. "So that's where we're at. Nothing to help Dr. Morgan at this point but I'll keep working on it."

"Do you intend to talk to her again?" I asked.

"I would, but only if I get something more."

We were both quiet on the way back to the office. As we reached the front door, I said, "I don't have anything on my calendar the rest of the day, I'm just going to go home and sit. Sometimes I think better when I get away from the office."

I went in, told Linda I'd be out for the afternoon and waved at Jackie as I walked out the door.

I went to my office and called Johnny to see if he'd have time for lunch and to do a little brainstorming. Now that his office was no longer representing Mrs. O'Malley, I felt comfortable keeping Johnny current with what was happening in Dr. Morgan's case. One evening, in fact, I practiced my opening statement in front of him. It was a little difficult at first because he sat there smiling.

"You aren't making this any easier," I said. The jurors won't be sitting there with big grins on their face."

"I think the guys will," he said.

"Well, I know what's on your mind," I replied, "and forget it. Besides, I'll be dressed a little bit more businesslike in the courtroom."

"I hope so," he replied.

Now I walked into the O.K. Café and saw him at the designated spot. In the short time we had been dating, we'd become very relaxed with each other. The little testiness I felt after our first date was gone. I never felt any competition. He listened while I told him what I was doing; I listened while he told me what he was doing. We could both offer suggestions without getting, as lawyers like to call it, argumentative.

I told him about the motion we had been working on and our meeting with Detective Kropp. Johnny was unusually quiet as I went through everything. He listened intently but didn't respond.

"You're not being much help," I said.

He nodded.

"Anyway," I continued, "we have this motion hearing set for next week to see how far Judge Savano will let us go. I'm hoping that Detective Kropp will find something between now and then that will help. If I can get her on the stand, maybe, with a little luck, I can get her to say something." He nodded again, a distracted look on his face.

"What is wrong with you anyway?" I asked.

"I have a confession to make," he said.

I gazed at him and I could tell he felt uneasy under my stare. He looked away for a moment and then back at me.

"You know, Jackie," he said, "it was really a dumb thing to do. I'm really sorry . . ."

"What're you talking about?" I asked finally, in frustration.

He looked away and then back again. "I didn't send you those medical records . . . you know . . . Cheryl's medical report." And he stopped to let it sink in.

"What are you talking about?" I asked again.

"The medical records you received. The ones you called me about right away."

"Yeah," I said.

"I didn't send those to you."

My mind raced back to our conversations. "Why did you let me believe that you did?" I asked.

"It was stupid, Jackie. It seemed to me that I had started off on the wrong foot. I could tell from your reaction that day in the café that they meant quite a bit to your case." He shrugged his shoulders. "You assumed I had sent them so I just let you believe that. I'm sorry."

I sank back in my chair. We were both quiet. I raised my head and glanced at Johnny. He was really suffering, his face was flushed, his eyes had misted over, not in tears but in anxiety. "You're never going to be much of a trial attorney if you can't put on a better poker face than that," I said.

He managed to grin. "I didn't lie to you, Jackie, I'd never lie to you. I just took credit for something I didn't do."

I analyzed it. He was right. I had assumed he was the benefactor and that to protect his job he couldn't tell me the truth. Inadvertently, I had staged the entire scenario. My inclination was to somehow use this to my advantage with Johnny, but he already looked like a beaten pup. More importantly, as I thought about it, was the question of who had really sent the records to me. And why had they sent them?

"Who had access to the file?" I asked.

Johnny thought for a moment.  "Realistically, everybody in the office.  As a practical matter, though, it would've been me, Ron and Ron's secretary . . ."

"The insurance company's attorney had a copy as well, right?"

"I believe so," he replied.

"Did Carol O'Malley have access to the file?" I asked.

"She never asked me, but that doesn't mean anything."

"Well, Noah talked to Kevin Young," I replied.  "Kevin said they didn't come from his office.  In fact, on the day I got the reports, he hadn't even read them yet.  Who actually put all of these reports together?  Who gathered the information?"

"Kay in our office," he replied.

"How did she know who to contact?"

"Cheryl's mother told her."

"How would Cheryl's mother know?" I asked.

We stared at each other, our minds working.

"There could have only been one source," he said.  "Cheryl!"

"That's what I'm thinking," I replied.  "Carol O'Malley knows all along what Cheryl's telling the doctors, the threats of mutilation made by her father, except Carol knows that Cheryl's lying to the doctors, she probably even told Cheryl to lie, to tell 'em it was her dad.  She stages the murder scene to make it look like Ben carried out those threats, and then she has to make sure that what Cheryl told the therapists becomes public knowledge, part of the case."

"Carol O'Malley sent you those reports," he said.

"She had to.  Who else?" I replied.

"How do we prove it?" he asked.

"There has to be some record of how she got them copied. . . I wonder if she left her fingerprints on them."

"You think there'd still be traceable prints on those documents?  How many people have handled them?"

"I'm not thinking about the documents, Johnny.  They came in a manila envelope wrapped in brown wrapping paper.  Because of the way they mysteriously appeared, I kept both.  They're in a drawer at the office.  She's been so careful about everything, what if she got sloppy and left her prints all over them?"

"But what does that prove?" asked Johnny.  "That may only prove that she mailed the documents to you."

"But think about it, Johnny. Why would she do that? There's only one reason."

The waitress interrupted our train of thought with our lunch. As we ate we continued talking, nothing new, just rehashing the different possibilities. I told him I wasn't upset with him. I understood his motivation. His silence in the long run might've even proved beneficial.

I called Noah as soon as I got back to the office. He said he would call Detective Kropp immediately. An hour later, Kropp was in my office. I showed him the manila envelope and wrapper I had kept in a bottom drawer of my desk. He picked them up with tongs and placed them in a clear plastic bag.

"I don't imagine her prints are gonna be on record. If any clear prints can be lifted, we'll send them to the FBI immediately. But if they don't have a match, we're gonna have to try and get her prints somewhere. I'll let you know."

He hesitated for a moment as if he had something on his mind but then thought better of it. He turned to leave.

"You're starting to believe us, aren't you?" I asked.

"I'll tell you what, Jackie, when I first walked into that bedroom and I saw her body like that, it was terrible, one of the worse scenes I've ever been at. And even for an old veteran like me, I wanted to heave. Just the sight of it, that somebody could do something like that, made me ill. But more than that, it made me angry. I vowed to myself I'd get the sick bastard who did it. I'll be honest with you, my first thought was that it had to be sexually motivated but as I studied the scene, I started second guessing myself. If somebody had done it in a fit of anger or rage, if there'd been a struggle, there'd be signs of it. There was none of that. It was like she'd been lying in bed and somebody just quietly cut her throat, and then moved the parts of her body around to conform to some sort of notion of what a scene should look like."

His expression grew thoughtful, as though he was attempting to recall precisely the thought process of his investigation. I could tell that this was something he had spent a lot of time analyzing. This was an experienced detective's mind at work and I could also tell from his expression that something was bothering him.

"At the time," he continued, "before I found the diary and letters, the mutilation made no sense to me. I had read accounts of murder cases where the sexual organs were removed, according to expert's—*defeminization*. But I had never seen it. Of course, I had no idea of Cheryl's history. I hadn't been involved with Clint's trial, and I had never seen any of her medical records. After reading Cheryl's diary and Dr. Morgan's letters, discovering their sexual encounters, my first thought was that Dr. Morgan had staged the mutilation to throw us off track, to make it look like the random act of some sexual pervert. Later, after Dr. Morgan was indicted, once I had a chance to read Cheryl's entire medical history, my first thought was whether her father could have done it. Had he carried out the threats that Cheryl claimed he made when she was a child? But after talking to him, I didn't think so.

"As far as Dr. Morgan, to my knowledge, he wasn't privy to those records while he was treating Cheryl, but he certainly heard her testimony in Clint's trial. That might have given him the idea."

His eyes leveled on me. "The only thing I know for sure, Jackie, is that this was not the act of a stranger, some roaming sexual pervert. And it isn't just the fact that the pathologist found no semen. These perverts don't always have to get off that way . . . No, this was done by somebody she knew, somebody she trusted, and it was done with the purpose of casting suspicion on Benjamin Moore. Dr. Morgan may have known more than we think. She could have certainly confided in him . . ."

"But she didn't," I interrupted.

"You only have his word for that," he replied. "If he did know, that would explain why he left her body the way he did."

"So in your mind," I said, "there are only three possibilities: Dr. Morgan, Benjamin Moore, or her mother."

"I don't think it was Mr. Moore. If he was aware of what Cheryl was saying about him to her therapists, for him to kill her and then mutilate her like that . . . well, he might as well have left us his calling card. He doesn't strike me as that dumb.

"Once you guys started raising the prospect of her mother, though, then if what Benjamin Moore told you is true, she might be a suspect. But we have to put her here, in town, on that date, and right now we have nothing to support that."

I asked, "Do you know for sure whether Benjamin Moore was aware that Cheryl told anyone about him, the alleged threats he made, before Cheryl was murdered?"

"I don't. When I talked to him after the disclosure of her records, he was so angry he wouldn't talk to me. By then we'd already indicted Morgan, so I didn't press it."

"When Johnny and I talked to him, he told us about the threats and mutilation, so he knew then."

"Well, it'll be important to find out what he knew and when. As I said, if he knew, why would he leave us such an obvious signature?"

"That should also rule out any stranger," I said.

"I never believed it was a stranger. From the beginning it was Dr. Morgan. I strayed from that for just a moment when I found out about the father. Now, no thanks to Noah, I'm willing to look further, I'll look at the mother."

"How're we ever going to get to Carol O'Malley?" I asked.

"Keep doing what we're doing, piecing it together."

He smiled and was about to leave again when I asked, "Have you told Becker about your doubts?"

He reeled around. "No, I haven't and I don't intend to, not until I have something nailed down. I know what he did in your case, Jackie. If I had been the investigator on that case, that would've never happened. The detective who worked it assumed Becker had let you know about her records and he chalked it up to your inexperience that you never brought them up at trial. He's learned a lesson. Becker . . . well, I don't think Becker will ever learn. Right now he's happy with the case he's got. We'll let him think he's got it sewn up. I'll be talking to you."

He took another couple steps and stopped. "By the way," he said, "have you ever been printed?"

"No. Why?"

"Depending on what we find on here, if we find prints, we're going to have to have everyone who touched these envelopes printed for comparison."

"Linda will really appreciate that," I replied.

"I'll break the news on the way out."

"Your Honor, this has to be one of the most blatant, undisguised efforts to get inadmissible testimony before a jury that I, in my experience, have ever seen any attorney have the gall to proffer. What Miss Geroux wants this court to do is unconscionable. She wants you to allow her to bring the murdered girl's mother, Carol O'Malley, before the jury to portray her as the perpetrator of this horrific act. She wants this court to do that on her bare assertion that if given the chance, she can somehow produce some evidence, like a magician pulling a fact out of a hat, that could point to Mrs. O'Malley having some motive to murder her own daughter. And on what basis is she asking the court to do this? On the most tenuous offer I've ever seen: hearsay! Not just hearsay, double hearsay; on her affidavit that Cheryl's father, Benjamin Moore, told her that Carol O'Malley sexually abused Cheryl as a child.

"Can you imagine that, Your Honor? I know she has all of Cheryl Moore's medical records, and the court is aware, as well as I am, that in every statement this poor victim made in the course of her treatment, treatment made necessary because of the degrading and disgusting things she suffered at the hands of her father, she names her father as the perpetrator. Then this poor young lady is murdered and every piece of evidence we have, Your Honor, points to Dr. Christopher Morgan as the murderer. The defense has been able to come up with nothing, not one shred of credible evidence, which would point to anyone else. Now, in desperation, they have to try and smear this poor dead girl's mother. It is nothing more than that, Your Honor, a tactic proffered in desperation."

We were in court on Thursday morning, just days before the trial was scheduled to start, and Becker had argued his Motion *in Limine* requesting the judge to deny our request for a subpoena to bring Carol O'Malley here as a defense witness. For the nervous wreck she was when we walked to the courthouse, Jackie had made a very credible argument. We had both expected the prosecutor's harangue, but he was more pompous than I ever remembered him in the past. Even though I was not going to get to respond, I could feel the little tingles emerge at the end of each nerve as he rambled on.

"Your Honor," he continued, "this is just a boldfaced attempt to circumvent the rules of evidence. It's an affront to our intelligence and I hope the court gives it the consideration it's entitled to—none! Thank you, Your Honor."

He sat down with a smug look on his face. The judge looked at Jackie. "Do you want to add anything, Miss Geroux?"

"Yes, Your Honor," she said as she stood. "I'm not saying, Your Honor, that we have established a sufficient basis for the court to give us a definitive ruling as to whether we can call Mrs. O'Malley or not. The main reason for my motion at this time was to put the State and Your Honor on notice that our investigation is continuing. We did not want the prosecutor to be in a position of arguing surprise or that somehow he was prejudiced by our actions. We have put him on notice that we intend to call Mrs. O'Malley. We are simply asking the court to issue a request to her county of residence to serve her with a subpoena so that *she is* on notice. And I can assure the court that by the time we are ready to call her, we'll have sufficient evidence on which this court can allow us to proceed."

What a bluff, I thought. She's raising the stakes with no idea whether she's ever going to be able to cover her bet. But she was doing what I would have done—making them think. And if in the end we can't deliver, it's not really going to make any difference anyway. If we can't somehow tie this murder to Carol O'Malley, once the prosecutor finishes his case, Chris might as well pack his bags.

"Well, I have to tell you, Miss Geroux," Judge Savano said, "I have to agree with the prosecutor. It seems to me that at this point, based on what you're telling me, there's little basis on which I can allow you to call Mrs. O'Malley, other than try to confuse the jury. As far as anybody knows, she was fifteen hundred miles away when this crime was committed. Unless you have something more to put her in the vicinity, and something more than the hearsay you're relying on, I'm going to have to grant the state's motion. However, I'll tell you what I'm willing to do. I'll issue the request to the district court in Boston to prepare and serve Mrs. O'Mally with a subpoena to appear here for trial. I will reserve, for now, a final decision on the state's argument as to whether she actually gets on the stand. You may be spending a lot of money for no purpose. I just want to let you know that."

That was pretty much what Jackie and I had expected, but we had accomplished our purpose. Now we had to hope that Detective Kropp or Brownie would come up with something before the state closed its case. Otherwise, we had one witness, Dr. Christopher Morgan, and he'd be mincemeat by the time Becker finished his cross-examination.

The one thing I thought we may have some control over is whether we could get Benjamin Moore to actually agree to come to court to testify. I tried to imagine what sort of consternation it would cause Carol O'Malley to know that he was willing to get on the stand and name her as the pervert. Up to that point, and mainly at the insistence of Jackie to not cause him any more anxiety, we had not listed him as a potential witness.

When we got back to the office, I asked Jackie to call him to see if he would at least meet with us. She said she'd try that evening and let me know. She called me back about nine and indicated he was reluctant, especially if Detective Kropp was going to come along. She said that after she had done some pleading, he had finally agreed to meet but made it clear that we shouldn't expect him to change his mind. She had set up the meeting for Saturday morning at his house.

The next day I talked to Kropp and we agreed to meet Saturday morning at Sally's Café. The plan was that Jackie and I could leave our cars there and ride with him. I was about to hang up when he said, "Becker called me yesterday after your court appearance. He was clucking like a peacock, said that Savano dumped all over Jackie. He asked me if I knew what you guys were trying to pull."

"What'd you tell him?" I asked.

"Not a damn thing. You think I'm gonna let him screw this up? But I'll tell ya, your young lady's in for some shellacking if it's up to him. I heard a little bit about this Clint thing, only because some deputy had to drive him from the prison to here. I know he got popped loose. I mean, Becker's attitude has always been . . . well, he's always been a dink, but his attitude about Jackie is worse than that. He's headhunting. He expects to see that pretty face of hers as a trophy on his wall when this is all done."

"He's just pissed because Jackie made him eat crow for what he did in Clint's case," I replied.

"I don't know why he thinks that getting the conviction is the most important thing in the world," Kropp said. "It's just the way he's always been, and he just doesn't give a shit as to how he gets there."

We were both quiet for a moment. "Well," he continued, "I'm not going to tell him anything about what we're doing. Besides, it's all just a hunch."

"It's more than a hunch," I replied.

"It may be to you, Noah, but I'm stuck with the case I've got. Becker's never going to listen to me, so if I can't come up with anything concrete I'm not gonna tell him anything at all."

\* \* \* \* \*

Dawn broke on Saturday morning to reveal a frosty wonderland, everything coated with thick, sparkling luminous flakes. I sat with my first cup of coffee by the window overlooking my backyard, watching the first cardinals land on the feeder in the shadows of early day. I watched as the eastern sky went from pink to rose to a flaming red, with the first rays of the sun filtering through the leafless branches, bouncing off the crystals of frost to send shimmers that cast an iridescent red to my birds. I sat there mesmerized, my senses overloaded, when Maggie said, "You're going to be late."

I looked at the clock. It was ten to eight. I had ten minutes to make it to Sally's Café.

The beauty of the morning, the brightness of everything outlined in white against an azure sky, seemed to affect all of us. We each took our turn commenting on the scenery, but as we progressed east, toward Minneapolis, we watched as the warmth of the sun caused the frost to flutter to earth and return the roadside to the drab tans and grays of early winter. The change led to silence until we neared our destination, when Kropp asked, "What do ya think he's going to be willing to do, Jackie?"

"I honestly don't know," she replied. "I've been trying to figure him out and

I can't. The night Johnny and I talked to him, it was like he was a big puppy dog, a big St. Bernard who had been kicked around by somebody and now crawled up to you and just wanted to be your friend. Maybe it was the booze, I don't know, but he said on the phone he would never repeat in court any of what he told us. I asked him why; he said he had his reasons. Who was I to push him? I don't know what's motivating him. It was obvious to me that he was madly in love with Carol and truly crushed by the divorce. He told us that he was glad that Cheryl had stayed here because he thought that might bring Carol back. Then I tried to imagine what it must have been like when Cheryl finally told him the truth. The two people he really loved . . . one corrupted the other. I think he realized that Cheryl was beyond help, at least in his mind. That's why he sent her away."

"But Cheryl was playing a dangerous game," said Kropp. "It looks to me like she was trying to use one parent against the other and it wasn't working. That's probably why she latched on to Dr. Morgan. She thought he was her ticket out of her misery. That whole California thing must've looked pretty good."

"I've said it before," said Jackie, "this whole thing makes me sick. I can't imagine the kind of person it takes to do something like that, to sexually abuse your daughter, then to brutally murder her and mutilate the body. This whole sexual perversion thing is incomprehensible to me!"

"You might as well get used to it," Kropp said. "If you're going to stay practicing criminal law, you'll see a lot of it. Remember Curtis, Noah?"

"How could I forget?" I replied.

"That was another sick bastard," said Kropp.

Jackie looked at me, obviously waiting for the story.

"What was that? Two, three years ago?" I asked.

"About that," Kropp said.

"It was about this time of year," I started, "after a high school football game. This fourteen-year-old girl was walking home; within a half a block of her house, she was abducted at knife point. The guy took her to the cemetery where he proceeded to do some of the worst things I've ever heard of—at least up 'til Clint's case. He raped her both vaginally and anally, made her perform fellatio and then the sick bastard peed in a cup and made her drink it. After that, he makes her get dressed, tells her not to tell anybody and then drops her off at her front door.  The girl was in shock.  She could've never identified him in a million years."

"How'd they catch him?" Jackie asked.

"There had been a similar incident in Rochester, almost identical M.O., including the urine, a couple months earlier.  A guy named Curtis, Steve Curtis.  He was out on bail on that charge waiting trial.  The St. Cloud police picked him up.  He had a prior record of sex offenses.  He was the prime suspect, but he had an alibi for that evening, he was out to eat at a local restaurant in Rochester with his mother and her new fiancée.  The cops couldn't break the mother down; she swore that they were out for dinner.  Her fiancée confirmed it.  The records of the restaurant showed that they did have a reservation for three.  So I gave the prosecutor notice of my alibi defense."

"I checked into it," said Bob, "it all panned out.  We were about to turn the guy loose when I started going through some of the records we had taken in the search of his apartment.  It showed a cash withdrawal from an automatic teller one mile from the crime scene at quarter to twelve.  We got the videotape from the drive-up ATM.  Sure as shit, there's his face as big as sin making a cash withdrawal ten minutes after he dropped this girl off."

"I confronted him," I said "He was so shocked that he had done anything that stupid, he told me to get him to court, he wanted to confess and get it over with.  That was one of Becker's big cases.  I still remember that smug look he had on his face when he came into the courtroom and tossed a copy of that videotape on the table.  He said something like, 'Take a gander at the kind of scum you're representing.'  I asked him what was on it, he said, 'Your client's mug at the First American Bank the night he's supposed to be dining with mother dearest'."

"His mother lied for him?" asked Jackie.

"When I told her what was happening, she said she and her fiancée must have had the wrong night.  Prior to sentencing I got some of the psychological reports in his case.  All of the doctors were pretty convinced that all of his victims were intended to be his mother; it appeared she was a domineering bitch.  But he still loved her.  That's why he was so solicitous of his victims after putting them through such degradation, when he'd drop them off at their house . . . he wouldn't want to make his mother walk."

"What happened to him?" Jackie asked.

"He went to prison for a long, long time. He'll probably be there another twenty years or so," I replied.

"So, Jackie," said Kropp, "you may as well get used to it. There are some real psychos in this world you're going to have to deal with."

"I'll never forget that sentencing," I said. "The victim, this little fourteen-year-old girl, pretty as could be, showed up with her mother. She gave Becker a statement to read. It was probably one of the most gracious things I'd ever heard. This little girl said she held no animosity, that she felt sorry for him that he was going to spend so much of his life in prison. She wanted him to know that she was going to pray for him and that she forgave him. Becker actually broke down at the end. I just about did, too. When it was all over, I turned to the back of the courtroom, this little girl was sobbing in her mother's arms. Curtis took it rather stoically. He told me it didn't matter, he was going to be free in a couple months—he was going to commit suicide."

"That's what he told the jailers driving him to prison, too," said Kropp. "I've followed up on it. Last time I checked was probably a year ago. He was still there. He probably found himself a playmate."

"What a terrible thought," Jackie replied. "Clint says that goes on all the time. Can't they stop it?"

"They don't want to," said Kropp. "It keeps the inmates happy and peaceful."

I glanced at Jackie. Her face was all scrunched up. She held her arms across her stomach again. I quickly changed the subject.

"Speaking of Clint," I said, "have you heard from him at all?"

She paused for a second. "Yeah, he called me several weeks ago, told me he got his job back, maintenance at this shop. He told me he's telling everybody who needs a lawyer to give me a call. I told him I appreciate it, but that was okay, he didn't owe me anything. Luckily, nobody's called me on his referral."

"You're getting kind of jaded early, aren't you?" asked Bob.

"No, it's strictly financial. Noah, what do you think we made on him?"

"Five dollars an hour, if that," I replied.

We came off the interstate onto Lake Street. An air of apprehension filled the car while Bob found Ben Moore's house.

Moore came to the door dressed casually, jeans and a plaid shirt. His hair was wet and combed to the back, as if he'd just come out of the shower. This was the first time I had seen him and I understood Brownie's concern. In both height and weight, he towered over me. I would've been but a passing thought if I had gotten in his way. But I could see the subtle smile cross his face as he took Jackie's hand and gently shook it. I glanced around the living room as we sat down. It was an older two-story home. The room was small, sparsely furnished but everything was neat and clean. I could detect the hint of cigarette smoke and then I noticed an ashtray on a coffee table with one crushed butt.

After we settled in, Ben Moore looked at Jackie. "I told you over the phone that I don't want to be a witness at the trial. I've done some checking and I don't have to. A lawyer told me the worst that could happen is you could make me sit in jail for a while. That doesn't even bother me."

Jackie told him about the motion hearing, our argument before Judge Savano. "We have to come up with something more before the judge will let us put Carol on the stand," she said.

"Mr. Moore," Kropp chimed in, "to everybody concerned with the state's case, including me, Dr. Morgan looks guilty. If that's not the case, if you have any reason to believe otherwise, we need your help."

A hint of anger crossed Ben's face. "You guys just don't understand, do you? This is all for you. I could give a shit what happens to Dr. Morgan. I mean, he's screwing my daughter. A guy old enough to be her old man. If it was up to me, I'd cut his balls off and feed 'em to my dog. But as far as I'm concerned, Cheryl's dead and whether you convict Morgan or her mother, or whoever, it isn't gonna bring her back. I was needed several years ago and . . . my pride interfered. Now I just wanna get on with my life. And I'll tell ya something: I don't wanna face her mother in any courtroom. I don't wanna see her."

I looked at Jackie; she was staring at Mr. Moore. "I understand that, Mr. Moore," she said. "Maybe you could be of a little help without having to come to court. You told me the last time we talked that you never saw the pictures of your daughter's body after the murder . . ."

"I didn't want to," he snapped.

"I understand that," she said. "But you were aware, even before her death, that she had told some treating therapist that you had sexually abused her as a child."

"She told me that. She told me that at Mick's that night. I told you."

"I know," Jackie said. "I know that. What I'm trying to ask you and it's painful for me to even ask, when did you become aware that Cheryl had said that *you* had threatened to cut her breasts off, you know . . . and other things?"

Mr. Moore froze, as though he was considering whether to answer my question or throw us out. I could see the heat in his eyes linger on my face, as if he was angry that he had to dredge up those awful thoughts again.

"What I told ya, Miss Geroux, is what Cheryl told me, what her mother threatened to do to her. That included all the ugly details, right down to pokin' her with a knife, cuttin' things off."

Jackie looked at Kropp, arched her eyebrows. Mr. Moore must have considered it some signal.

"Now I'd appreciate it if you'd get outta here. This is it for me. No more!"

"I respect your wishes, Mr. Moore," said Kropp, "but I would like to know that if we come up with something definite about your ex's involvement with the death of your daughter, that we could come back and talk to you."

"I don't think that's going to happen," he replied, his voice softening. "I don't think she was involved in Cheryl's death."

"Why do you believe that?" I asked.

"She did some monstrous things, but I don't think she could've done that."

\* \* \* \* \*

We left Mr. Moore's pretty disappointed. As we pulled back onto Lake Street, toward the interstate, Jackie said, "I know what his problem is."

"What?" I asked.

"He's still in love with Carol."

"After all that?" I asked.

"From everything I've heard," said Jackie, "she's a very attractive woman and

I would suspect she was quite a knockout when Mr. Moore met her for the first time years ago. When we talked the last time and Johnny told him that he had met her, the first thing Ben asked was, 'How'd she look?' When Johnny said, 'Very good,' he said, "Yeah, I heard that.' Then he went on to tell us, in some detail, what their love life was like. He believes that she was way too pretty for him . . . now what's he got? Spend some time in Mick's, see who hangs out in there. I'm sure he looks around there and compares it to what he had. He's probably never been able to forget her. Maybe he's clinging to the hope that if he keeps his mouth shut, if Carol knows that he helped her, that for some reason she'll come back."

"We accomplished one thing," said Kropp. "At least we confirmed that he was aware of the threats of mutilation . . ."

"It was quite obvious he got a little upset with me, wasn't it?" asked Jackie.

"I was a little surprised at the question," I said. "It seemed to have an accusatory tone."

Kropp said, "No, Noah, I just wanted to make sure of when he became aware of those threats. As I told Jackie, it would be pretty dumb of him to murder Cheryl and mutilate the body that way, to duplicate the threats, if he, in fact, had been the source of the threats."

"So, it was part of your process of elimination," I said.

"Too much of a coincidence, Noah," he said.

"So we're down to one," Jackie said.

"Yeah, but which one?" Kropp replied.

When I was in law school, there were several times when some friends and I went to the courthouse to sit through parts of high profile criminal cases. I remember watching the lawyers come in, very businesslike, opening their briefcases, laying out the files, appearing to be very at ease, like this was just another day at the office. I often wondered if their cool was for real or just my perception.

As Noah and I walked from the office to the courthouse for the first day of trial in the *State of Minnesota v. Christopher Morgan*, I knew that I had never prepared for anything so well in my life. There were times in law school that I had crammed for a test until I thought I'd fried my brains, but this surpassed any of that. And despite every conscious effort I made to lower the level of my anxiety, it simply didn't work. I was strung tight like a rubber band, hoping I didn't snap.

It must have been obvious to Noah. When he first saw me that morning, he took my hands, clasped them together, and wrapped his hands around mine. "Jackie," he said, "you're going to do fine. It isn't going to do anybody any good if you pop a blood vessel at this point."

It was enough to bring a half smile to my face.

"I'll be right there with you," he said. "See, I'm even going to bring my yellow pad. Any thoughts that come to me, anything I think you should cover, I'll write 'em down. But I want to tell you, this is your case, Jackie. I'm only there as a legal advisor. I'm not going to interfere with your tactics, second-guess your questions. I have absolute confidence in your ability to handle this. So does Chris. So we'll be fine. Believe me."

And I wanted to believe him. Nobody could have prepared me better for this trial. For the months we worked on it, he was there as a guiding hand, not with a sledgehammer but a velvet glove. For not having any children, I wondered how he understood the young so well.

So I was prepared, but that didn't make it any easier. Ever since I left Becker's office that day after the confrontation over Cheryl's records, I wanted to drive him into the ground, embarrass him to the point he wouldn't show his face. Unfortunately for me, Dr. Morgan's case wasn't a good vehicle for me to fulfill such ambitions.

There was a cold breeze out of the northwest stinging my eyes as Noah and I walked up the courthouse steps. The trial folder had gotten so thick we had put it in two separate folders and we each carried one. I could feel my eyes tearing from the wind as he reached for the door handle. He pulled open the big brass door to let me go first and we entered the courthouse. The ground floor was packed with people, perspective jurors waiting to get counted and seated in the jury waiting room. The nervous chatter ceased and they parted to let us by as we made our way to the elevator. The door was open and the elevator vacant, Noah and I quickly walked in. He gave me a kind of a fatherly grin as he pushed the button for the third floor.

"I'd dab my eyes a little," he said, "it looks like you've been crying."

"The wind," I said.

"I know," he said, "but we wouldn't want to give Becker the wrong impression."

When the elevator door opened on the third floor, we stepped into chaos. The hallway was filled with reporters and television crews. Camera flashes were going off everywhere. Reporters were trying to get Noah to say something, but they ignored me. Noah pushed his way through and I followed.

I had anticipated a rather solemn entrance, which seemed to have heightened my anxiety. Now, with the commotion, it had more of a carnival atmosphere and for some strange reason, I started to feel at ease. Maybe I pictured myself just another clown at the circus.

But that was short-lived. Within moments I opened the door to the courtroom and the gravity of the task I was about to assume came home with a thud. The prosecutor was at the counsel table, trial notebooks stacked neatly in front of him. He wore a dark blue suit with a white shirt and navy blue tie. Dr. Morgan was sitting in the first row of the spectator session, which had been reserved for the jury pool, looking lost. The edges of his mouth cracked slightly as he saw Noah and me enter through the door. The court clerk sat at her post to the right of the judge, shuffling through the cards of perspective jurors. Other than the noise of her flipping the edges, there was not a sound.

The courtroom, with its high ceilings and sterile polished oak and marble atmosphere, was intended by its designers to cast a pall of seriousness on all that transpired there. And there was nothing more serious to come before the court than a case of a person charged with murder. As I stood there, the impact of it all closing in on me, I wanted to vomit. Then I felt a gentle hand on my elbow, a slight tug, and Noah guided me to our table. Noah motioned to Chris to join us at the counsel table. Becker looked up and said something in a grunt, Noah acknowledged him with a nod. I didn't. With trembling fingers, I went about the task of taking the files out of the briefcase and setting everything neatly in front of me. That task accomplished, I reached for the water pitcher to pour myself a glass of water, knowing I would have a parched throat in no time. Noah noticed my trembling fingers and interceded. Before I had a chance to reach across the table, he had snatched up the pitcher and a glass. "Might as well get us a drink," he said, setting a full glass in front of me. We then took our seats and quietly waited for the judge. I had learned during Clint's trial that Judge Savano was a stickler for starting on time, exactly 9:00 a.m. You could set your watch by it.

My arms were in front of me on the counsel table and I stared at the face of my watch and counted the seconds as the dial ticked away. At exactly five seconds to nine, Frank, the Court Reporter, strolled through the chamber's door. Directly behind him was Glen, a retired Deputy Sheriff acting as bailiff, followed closely by Judge Savano. The bailiff grabbed his gavel on the sidebar and rapped three times. "All rise. Hearyee, hearyee, hearyee," he hollered. "The District Court is now in session, Judge Peter Savano presiding."

The judge whisked by him on the way to the dais. There was a commotion as everybody stood. As the judge settled into his high back leather chair, he motioned with his hand that we could sit. Within moments, the courtroom went silent.

"Good morning, ladies and gentlemen," he said. "Are we ready to proceed?"
Becker jumped to his feet. "The state's prepared, your Honor."
"Miss Geroux?"

226

I stood, slowly. "The defense is ready to proceed, Your Honor."

"Fine, then we'll call the jury panel in and I'll tell them what this is all about."

Again, quiet settled in as the bailiff motioned to the back to bring in the jury panel.

This is it, I thought. All of the months of preparation, the anxiety of the last several days, so we would be here in this venue where Dr. Christopher Morgan was to be judged by a jury of his peers. The procedure was as old as our history, the system tested in millions of cases from rural county seats to the boroughs of New York City. Time and experience, though, hadn't made the process infallible—as evidenced by this case. I knew they had the wrong defendant and I wondered how it would play out.

Jury selection was long and painful. By Wednesday morning, after two full days of *voir dire*, we had three jurors. The fifteen or so excused jurors to that point fell into two categories: The first, because of all of the pre-trial publicity, some admitted right up front that they believed Dr. Morgan was guilty and it would take some rather substantial evidence by the defense to convince them otherwise—the judge excused them for cause; in the second group, those a little bit more insidious, it was obvious from their answers to the questions that they considered Dr. Morgan guilty but they wanted to be on this jury so badly, they tried to hide it. A lady named Grace Johnson, called by the clerk for *voir dire* late Tuesday afternoon, was a typical example. She was a matronly type, in her late forties, dressed rather casually, her hair, starting to turn gray, neatly pulled back in a bun. She admitted she had read all of the newspapers articles regarding the murder and the forthcoming trial. She initially believed Dr. Morgan was guilty, but now, being here, she thought she could wait until she heard all of the evidence to make that decision.

I asked her, "Do you want to be on this jury?"

She smiled. "Oh, yes."

"Why?" I asked.

"Oh, I think it would be exciting."

Noah, Dr. Morgan and I had worked out a code where we would rate the jurors from one to five, one being the worst and five being the best as far as the defense was concerned. At the end of her *voir dire*, I looked at the yellow pads in front of them—they both had number one circled circled. I removed the juror with a pre-emptorary challenge. I could see the disappointment on her face when Judge Savano told her she was excused. She had thought she'd answered all the questions right. From the look of disdain as she passed our counsel table, though, I knew we had made the right decision.

In our discussion, Noah had said that we had to be careful of jurors who were trying to hide their true feelings. We had to acknowledge to ourselves up front that the majority of people called would have knowledge about the case and would have formed an opinion of his guilt. Some would be honest about that, others would hide it in the hope that they would get on the jury and hang the bastard.

"You never know if you're making the right decision," he said. "It's all in your gut. First impressions, though, are normally the right impressions."

So we struggled until about 2:00 on Friday afternoon when Judge Savano took a recess and called us into chambers. He motioned for us to take seats around the conference table and he sat there quietly, shaking his head for a few moments.

"You know, Miss Geroux, I think you're taking way too much time with these jurors. Even when you have a good one, you just keep pushing and pushing. You aren't going to get a perfect jury, you know."

"Your Honor," I said, "we told you this was going to happen when we made our motion for a change of venue. Everybody in this county has heard about this case and it appears that everybody thinks Dr. Morgan is guilty."

"Listen," he said, "we could've moved this out of the county, to one of the metropolitan areas, spent all kinds of the state's money, and it wouldn't have made any difference. Isn't that right, Noah?"

"We'll never know," Noah replied.

"Well, I agree with you, Judge," said the prosecutor. "There were a number of jurors she could've kept on, nice honest people who told her that they would be open, fair and impartial. No reason to remove them. Look at me, I haven't struck one yet."

I glanced sideways at Becker. It was getting to the point that every time I looked at him, heard his voice, my blood pressure rose.

228

"Well, I've had enough," Judge Savano said. "We've got six jurors. I've got things to do. We'll start again Monday morning at 9:00." Then he turned his gaze on me. "And you, you sharpen your pencil. If you're going to continue beating everything to death, I'm going to take over *voir dire* or I'll make Noah do it."

"No, you won't, Your Honor," Noah said. "Jackie's the trial lawyer here. She has every right to have asked the questions she has. You start interfering with the fair selection of the jury, Judge, and you're giving us an issue for appeal. I'm sure Mr. Becker believes he's going to convict Dr. Morgan." Noah looked at Becker. "I don't imagine you'd like to try this case all over again because of a judicial error in jury selection."

"That's never going to happen and you know it," said Judge Savano. "I'm telling you, I'm not going to waste another week picking a jury."

With that he slammed his notebook shut, stood up, walked to the coat tree and took off his black robe. The conference was over.

Noah, Dr. Morgan, and I went into a private room while the rest of the court personnel closed up and left. I walked to the far end of the room, stood looking out the window over the courtyard watching the jurors talk and laugh as they made their way down the steps to the parking lot. After a week in a small room together, it was now like they were big buddies, old friends. I noticed it every morning when I walked past the jury assembly room—the chatter was getting louder. Dr. Morgan came up behind me and put his hand on my shoulder. "I think you're doing a great job, Jackie, don't let him get you off track."

I turned my head to look at him and smiled. "Thanks," I said.

"Well, he's right, Jackie," echoed Noah. "You just stick to your guns, push him as far as you can, maybe he will screw up the record."

"Oh, good," said Chris, "you mean I'd have to go through this all over again?"

We all joined in a little nervous laughter.

As the week had progressed, I started to feel more and more at ease. The morning trembles had disappeared by Wednesday. By Friday, I was actually feeling a little cocky. While my questioning of the jurors had been stiff and formal the first day, by Friday I was in an easy pace, connecting with them both verbally and emotionally. The six jurors we had kept on the panel were people I felt I had connected with and would truly listen to the evidence and consider the law in making a decision. That's all we could ask for.

* * * * *

"I snuck in to see you this morning," Johnny said. "You were really doing a good job."

"When?" I asked.

"About 9:30 or so."

"How'd you ever get in?"

"The bailiff let me in when one of the jurors was leaving and another one was coming in. I had to stand against the back wall. He wouldn't let me come back in after the morning recess."

"Why didn't you come up and say something?" I asked.

"You were talking to Noah and the doctor, I didn't want to interfere. I liked how you were handling the questioning."

I thought for a moment, nine-thirty, that was the second juror called this morning.

"When that teacher from St. Joe, that redhead, was called . . . what was her name again?"

"Wilson. Donna Wilson," I said.

"You're lucky you didn't end up with her," he said.

"Yeah, and you want to know the interesting thing about it? She started out answering the questions so well, Dr. Morgan slid a note across. It said, 'Accept her, no more questions'. For a moment I was going to do it, and then it bothered me."

"Well, you were lucky she was honest," he said.

"I was. I was going to rate her really high until that last question. I never expected that. Just a simple question, 'As you sit there, do you believe that Dr. Morgan is guilty?' And she looked at me and in a very matter-of-fact voice, said 'Yes, I do'. Afterwards, Dr. Morgan said he was totally misled by her previous answers. That's the frightening part of jury selection, if I hadn't asked her that last question, she'd probably be sitting on that panel. That jerk Becker is so convinced of his case, he's asked very few questions and hasn't struck one juror."

"Yeah, you can tell he's enjoying himself," Johnny said.

It was Friday evening. After hashing over the week's events with Noah and Chris for a half an hour or so, I felt totally beat and I told them I was going home. I got home a little after four. As soon as I walked into my apartment, I felt cold, I had the shivers, and I couldn't warm up. I think the nervous energy I had been running on all week sucked all the heat out of my body. I drew a bath, the water as hot as I could stand, and I soaked for the longest time. As I sat in the hot water, the steam rising to fill the bathroom like a warm fog, I thought about every juror I had questioned that week, from Monday morning until the recess today. I relived all of the highlights and lowlights of the *voir dire*. When I got out of the bath, I crawled into bed, piled as many covers as I could over me and fell into a deep sleep until the phone rang.

It was dark out, my head was thick, and I was disoriented. The red letters on my clock said 8:04. I reached over and picked up the phone and I was happy to hear Johnny's voice. After we talked for a while, I told him the state I was in and he said it sounded like I needed a little tender loving care. He was going to pick up a pizza and a bottle of wine and he would be over.

I put my head back on the pillow and pulled the covers up around me. I drifted in and out of consciousness. I knew I should be getting up but this was as good as I had felt for a long time. I laid there in the fetal position, my hands tucked between my legs. I imagined Johnny lying next to me, his strong arms pulling me toward him, our warm bodies touching. My hands went up my thighs and I felt a warmth. My body shuddered and my mind floated into a fantasy where Johnny and I were making love. My breathing became heavy and I felt my body shake at my own pleasure.

I was still in that state of euphoria as I sat across the table from Johnny watching the changing expression on his face as he tried to figure out what was going on with me. When he arrived with a pizza in one hand, a bottle of Chianti in the other, I greeted him with a kiss. I must have been a sight, dressed in pajamas, wrapped in a quilt, my face flushed, and my body warm. My gaze remained fixed on him as he talked, while I sipped my wine and nibbled on a piece of pepperoni pizza. He was excited about an argument he had made before the court in another county that afternoon and he was sure, based on the comments of the judge, that he had won. I wasn't paying much attention to the substance, though, because my mind was wondering whether this was the night. I suspected, based on Johnny's stare, that I was sending signals, body language saying, "Why don't you stop talking and come over here."

He stopped in mid-sentence. "You haven't heard a word I've said, have you?"

I blinked my eyes a couple times to bring me back from my pleasant thoughts. "Yes, I have," I said coyly. "But I'm just wondering why you don't come over here and kiss me."

He smiled widely and his eyes sparkled as he got up from his chair and came around the table. I leaned my head back, he put his lips softly on mine and I felt the tip of his tongue probing. I parted my lips slightly and his tongue slid in. His left hand slipped under the quilt onto my breast while a flood of emotions crossed my brain. I raised my right hand and put it on his chest and pushed gently. He broke the kiss, raised his head, his eyes burning. I rose from the chair and let the quilt drop. I could feel my flesh turn warmer as his eyes explored my body. I reached down and took my glass of wine, brought it to my lips and filled my mouth. I placed the glass on the table and I leaned into Johnny with the cool wine still on my lips and it warmed as we kissed.

I let my lips slide off of his. "I hope you don't have anywhere to go tonight," I said.

His eyelids narrowed. "A team of wild horses couldn't drag me away."

I took his hand and led him into the bedroom.

* * * * *

It seemed strange waking up with a man in bed next to me. I could hear him breathing. The room was in the half-light of dawn; the drapes had been pulled tight. I wondered what my neighbors would think when they noticed his car still in the parking lot.

There I go again, I thought, worrying about what other people think. But it had already started—doubts. As soon as I opened my eyes, I had that nagging feeling that I may have made a mistake. The night had been wonderful. Johnny was a good lover. But now, having gotten what he was after, would he change? I didn't want to go through another deteriorating relationship. I couldn't. I'd rather spend the rest of my life celibate than feel the pain of rejection, the anguish of a self-doubt that I had experienced in the past. For that reason, I had been very cautious in my relationship with Johnny, I couldn't imagine he would turn on me, but then again . . .

I heard him move, his arm wrapped over me and he tugged to pull me close to him. "I love you," he whispered.

I was going to tell him, "I love you, too." But I hesitated, and then the thought left. I was in love with him, though. I realized that as I watched him from across the table last night. When the words would finally leap from my brain to the tip of my tongue, however, I'd bite my lip, swallow them back, afraid to make the commitment the words promised.

We lay there quietly as the sun rose and the room brightened. Physically, I was as content as I had been in a long time; emotionally, I was anxious. I remained in that semiconscious state, thinking about Johnny and me, never once thinking about the trial.

The ringing of the phone shook me out of my contentment. I gently slipped out of Johnny's grasp and walked to the living room. It was Noah.

"What're you up too?" he asked.

"Oh, nothing," I replied. "Just recuperating from the last week."

"Well, Brownie's got some interesting information for us. He said he'd meet us at the office at ten. Can you be there?"

"What is it?" I asked.

"It's worth the trip," he said.

"I'll be there."

* * * * *

When I got to the office, Brownie and Noah were both sitting in the waiting room sipping big cups of coffee from a coffee shop.

"I brought one for you," said Brownie, as he pointed to the corner table.

I walked across the waiting room, picked up the paper cup, and removed the plastic cover as the steam and the smell of strong, fresh coffee hovered in my nostrils. I took the chair next to the table, sat and sipped my coffee while the two of them seemed to watch my every movement.

Settled in, I looked at Brownie. "Well?" I asked.

"I've got Carol O'Malley in town on the day of the murder," he said.

"How?" I cried.

"We'd hit a dead end on all the car rentals, limos. I was at the airport, just about ready to give up, when I saw this little guy carrying a couple bags and wearing a jacket that said, 'Executive Express'. That's the only thing I hadn't checked into."

"What's that?" I asked.

"It started just a short time ago," he said. "It's a van, an eight or a ten-person van, that picks up people at the Holiday Inn on the west side, drives them to the airport. They can leave their car at the motel and don't have to go through the expense of parking. They run regular routes between here and the airport. They only have two drivers. The guy I talked to said he didn't have any records with him but passengers had to fill out a short form with name, address, that type of thing. The company doesn't spend any time trying to verify it. They just need a name and address. I had this picture of Carol that I picked up in Boston from one of the real estate ads when she was still selling. I showed it to him."

Brownie paused to take a sip of coffee. "This is where it gets good," he continued. "The driver looked at the picture for the longest time. Then he said, 'It's the eyes. This lady had the sexiest eyes I've ever seen. Those are the eyes, but she wasn't blonde . . . she had long black hair.'"

"A wig?" I asked.

"That was my thought," Brownie replied. "But first I thought he was pulling my leg. You know, how do you recognize somebody from the eyes? But he said it was a noon run to the airport, she was in the seat right behind him. He said he watched her during the whole trip, in the rearview mirror, that face and eyes. He said she was a turn on, he was even getting a boner . . ."

By now Brownie and Noah were both laughing.

"You're puttin' me on," Noah said.

"No! I couldn't believe it when he told me that. Think I'd make that up?"

"How old is this guy?" I asked.

"I don't know. Maybe seventy-five, somewhere around there."

"And he's gettin' turned on by this lady's eyes?" I asked.

"Yeah, but there's more. He said she had a really sexy Boston accent. See, there were two guys on the trip. He said they were trying to hit on her. She was teasing them, leading 'em on a little . . . he's positive it was the lady in the picture, Carol O'Malley. So we checked the passenger list at the home office, she was registered as a Judy Severson, hometown of Cloister, Massachusetts, on the van leaving town at twelve noon the day Cheryl's murdered. I talked to the two male passengers, two salesmen from town. They agreed she was quite memorable, that the picture looked like her, but they couldn't be sure. They said she disappeared right after they hit the airport, never saw her again."

"So she was here," said Noah.

"I'd be willing to bet my life on it," said Brownie. "I talked to Kropp, told him everything. So he and I went back and had the airport police go through the plane manifests but we couldn't find a similar name."

"But airlines are required to get some sort of identification, aren't they?" I asked.

"Yeah," replied Brownie, "but that's no big deal. She could've fudged something."

"Maybe she even has a fake I.D.," said Noah. "Who knows?"

I had been listening carefully while trying to decide if this information was any help at all. It seemed quite weak.

"You know," I said, "I can hear Becker screaming, 'Judge, now she wants you to allow her to bring Carol O'Malley in to testify based on the statements of some horny old fart who thought she had sexy eyes.'"

"I'm not sure you should call him a horny old fart," said Brownie, a grin widening on his face. "I'm a horny old fart and I don't wanna be put in the same class as this guy. This guy was a *really* old horny old fart."

"Yeah," said Noah, "that's the second time you called somebody an old fart. I'm not sure I like that phrase either."

"Okay," I replied. "How about elderly gentleman who just happens to be horny?"

They looked at each other, grinned and nodded. "That's better," said Brownie.

"So, how reliable is this elderly gentleman going to be?" I asked.

Brownie replied, "Well, there are two things. First, he's convinced if we put black hair on this picture of O'Malley, that that's the lady he drove to the airport; second, he had plenty of time to listen to her, he said he's been around long enough to recognize a Bostonian accent when he hears one."

"But she isn't from Boston," I said. "She's only been there ten years or so. Besides, I talked to her on the phone, I didn't notice any accent."

"I think it's a cultural thing," said Noah. "If you live in Boston, particularly in the upper social circles, you have to sound like a Bostonian. As soon as she heard your voice, she probably reverted back to good Minnesotan."

"That's true, Jackie. Especially if you're trying to be upper crust Irish," said Brownie.

I think they were trying to have a little fun at my expense.

"Jackie," Brownie explained. "You have to understand, you only get little tiny breaks at a time. This is more than we had. Kropp's going to go through all the forensic stuff. Now that we have another suspect, he wants to see if there's anything that was missed the first time around. Have you ever heard of the theory of transfer and exchange?"

Before I had a chance to answer, he continued, "Well, the theory is that at every crime scene, there's this transfer and exchange of things from the people that were there to the scene, or vice-versa; you know, bits of stuff which are carried away from, or deposited at, the crime scene. Like fibers from the shoes, hair, something from the clothes, little things that are picked up by the crime scene specialist that may help put somebody at the scene. Kropp said he would go over everything again this afternoon."

* * * * *

We talked for a while and the meeting broke with the understanding that if either one heard from Kropp before Monday morning, I'd be called. I'd left Johnny at the apartment and I expected he'd be gone by the time I got back. I don't think he wanted to leave. I think he expected to be spending the day with me and possibly renewing the activities from the previous night. But I had told him a little white lie: that I expected to be at the office the rest of the day. Now I was feeling a little guilty about that. My first thought this morning was whether Johnny had used me. Now after reflection, I was wondering whether I'd used Johnny—after all, I seduced him. We had a good relationship without the sex, which would have come in time, but maybe by rushing it, I had jeopardized what we had.

I knew I was overanalyzing everything again. I should just learn to accept things the way they are, the way they happen. But not me. I wasn't happy unless I mentally beat everything to death. I knew it was my own insecurity. Whenever anybody tried to get close to me, I immediately became suspect of his or her motives. No matter how hard I tried to overcome what I perceived to be a flaw, at times my guard went down and I slipped back into my old ways.

I was right. When I got back to my apartment, Johnny was gone. I had a sense of melancholy as I loitered around the empty apartment trying to think of what I should do to keep myself busy. I opened my trial folders, started paging through, reviewing the list of prospective jurors who may still be called. What a difference a week makes, I thought. The Saturday before, I had spent the entire day glued to the pages. Today everything was just a mess of words. Before long, my arms were on the table, my head cradled in them and I drifted off.

The phone jogged me out of my sleep. I awoke to the ring, my neck stiff, and my head sore. It was Johnny; he wanted to talk about us. I told him I had a splitting headache, we'd have to save it for another day. He asked me if I was mad.

"About what?" I asked.

"You know, about what happened last night."

"What happened last night was because I wanted it to happen. Why should I be mad at you?"

"You just seemed, I don't know, upset this morning."

"There are just too many things happening, Johnny. That's all. This trial is wearing me down."

"Is there anything I can help you with?" he asked.

"I appreciate the offer, but I have to do this myself."

"I love you," he said.

Once again I couldn't force myself to say it. I let the phone slip from my ear and placed it on the receiver. I mumbled to myself, "You can be a real bitch at times, you know?"

"Mmm, that smells good," I said. But it was said in jest and Maggie knew it. For years on Sunday mornings we'd had a sausage and egg brunch as we traded sections of the paper, relaxing with a pot of coffee. Now I'd been relegated to powdered eggs, I'm not even sure what was in them, and meatless sausage that no matter how long it cooked, would never turn brown. It came out of the pan with a kind of blah mud puddle gray look. I could have real coffee, though, so typically Maggie made it a little stronger than usual to cover the taste of everything else.

We'd finished half of the pot of coffee and most of the Sunday paper when she said, "I'm worried about Elizabeth, she won't return my calls. The last time I talked to her she said she was pretty convinced Chris had done it."

My head snapped up from the paper. "What?" I asked.

"I didn't say anything," she replied, "because I didn't want to interfere with your trial, but she thinks Chris murdered Cheryl."

"Well, he didn't," I replied.

"How are you going to prove that?" she said.

"Well, we're working on it."

"I don't know," she said, shaking her head.

It wasn't unusual for Maggie and me to talk about my cases—at least a sanitized version of what happened. Maggie followed my career with a rather distant pride. I could tell she admired me for the work I did because, like garbage collectors, I served a useful societal purpose. And she even celebrated with me a couple of times when I got not guilty verdicts in high profile cases. However, I always had the feeling that if she knew what my defendant was really like—compared to what was in the press, or what ended up before the jury, or what I actually told her—she'd have a different impression of my work.

This case was different, though, she knew the defendant as well as I did. I had not told her much about Carol O'Malley but I thought this was the appropriate time. When I finished, we sat there for a few moments in silence. I could see the wheels turning in her head.

Finally she said, "You better hope you have more than that, otherwise I have to agree with Becker, that's pretty flimsy."

Maggie had always been an excellent sounding board for me. Lawyers typically have a lot of faults, but the one that could be the most deadly to a career is when they start to believe their own rhetoric. Often in the past, when I thought I was ready for trial, I would lay my whole case out to Maggie and she would proceed to pick it apart and at times leave it in shreds. The problem was that I looked at the case as a lawyer; she looked at it as a lay person—from the perspective of a juror. If I was going to sway a jury, I had to answer her questions first. So now she was just being honest with me and I knew it. We couldn't create a reasonable doubt in Chris's case with the little we had—even assuming the judge let it in.

Maggie could tell she had me thinking. "You wanted my opinion," she said.

"I know," I replied. "Unfortunately I know."

After a few minutes of silence, Maggie asked, "Does Jackie ever talk about her childhood, you know, about growing up?"

"Not really," I said. "I did meet her aunt and uncle, the two who raised her. They stopped in the office one day on their way to Minneapolis. Nice people. I could tell Jackie was really glad to see 'em. But she doesn't volunteer much."

"Does she ever mention her father?" she asked.

"A couple of times she's made kind of snide comments about him, only enough to let me know she doesn't think much of him."

"I wonder how he could have left her behind," Maggie said. "How hard we tried to have children. Can you imagine if you were her father, leaving her behind? Some people who have children just don't deserve them."

"That's always been true, Maggie," I said. "You don't have to pass any kind of parenting test to have children. The other day I came out of the courthouse, it was probably about ten in the morning. This family was leaving the bar across the street. Big guy, long stringy hair and a black leather jacket, skinny little blonde with him, three of the cutest kids walking in front of them. The boy,

240

maybe five, six years old, was crying. The guy kept kicking him in the butt with his engineer boot, yelling, 'shut up!' I figure if I live long enough, that kid will end up being one of my clients."

"You should've said something," said Maggie.

I smiled at her. "Thirty years ago I would have. Now, I'd just as soon stay away from anybody leaving a bar at ten in the morning. Especially when they're big and ugly like he was."

She sighed deeply. "The world's going to pot," she said.

"Not all of it," I replied, "just a good share of it."

The only thing she managed to do was spoil the rest of my day. It wasn't her fault. I had put my hopes on Brownie or Detective Kropp coming up with something more. I was pleased with what they had, but it took Maggie to put it into perspective. I poured myself the last cup of coffee and went to my recliner where I did my best thinking. On the way I grabbed my favorite pipe, chewing on the stem and remembering what it was like sometimes spurred the mental process. But no matter how many times I turned it all over in my head, it always came out the same—we needed something more.

I leaned back in my recliner, chewed on my pipe and thought. There was a time when I would have been out scratching around for clues rather than just lounging away the afternoon. The day went by without me hearing from anybody. Between yawning and chewing on a stale pipe, Maggie said I was driving her nuts. I finally turned on the television and watched the end of the football game. As dark settled in, I decided to call Brownie. He had not heard from Kropp. My call to Kropp's home went unanswered, so I tried Jackie. She was in the process of making herself a salad. She was going to do a little work on the file and then try to get to sleep early.

* * * * *

My experience had been that by the second week of jury selection, all of the prospective jurors looked a little better. A person gets so tired of asking the same questions over and over that just the sheer boredom of it leads you to want to finally accept anybody on the panel. Jackie apparently didn't feel the same way.

Out of eight prospective jurors called on Monday, she had accepted two. So now we had a total of eight. Despite Judge Savano's admonitions from Friday, he pretty much kept his nose out of the process. I watched him closely. I could see his frustration but he knew if the jury's going to convict, why screw up the process and give the defendant something to argue on appeal? Besides, why should he care? He was getting paid the same whether he was doodling, as he did most of the time, or actually doing something constructive.

When Jackie, Chris, and I walked out of the courtroom at the end of the day, the bailiff handed me a note from Detective Kropp. "When you get back to the office, give me a call, we have to talk."

I knew he wouldn't want Chris there, so I told him we would call if we got anything new. Chris had become rather stoic about the whole process; he said little, smiled even less. His world had collapsed around him and he had accepted his fate.

Brownie was at the office when we got there. Kropp had called him also, but he had no idea what Kropp may have found.

"I walked over to the courthouse earlier this afternoon," he said. "Christ, I couldn't even get in, there was a full house. I talked to the bailiff; he said you're doing a good job, Jackie."

She blushed but remained silent.

How odd, I thought. Here's a young woman with enough cool to try a first degree murder case, but when she gets compliments from the old guard it makes her blush. She went back into her office and Brownie and I sat in the lobby waiting for Kropp.

When she was out of hearing range, Brownie said, "She's a very interesting gal. Don't you wish you were thirty years younger?"

"I'm not sure either one of us could handle her, Brownie," I said. "They grow 'em different now-a-days. Can't imagine she'd be happy staying home and taking care of the kids."

Brownie and I chatted for a while wondering what Kropp had found.

"How many jurors you got?" Brownie asked.

"Eight. She's really doing a nice job of jury selection. I can tell the ones we have like her. That can be very important. Sometimes jurors are willing to overlook some of the transgressions of the defendant if they like the defense attorney."

"That's wishful thinking," said Brownie. "Based on the case the state's going to present, right now those jurors would all have to be madly in love with her to let him walk."

I saw Kropp's car turn the corner. I walked back and got Jackie. She was sitting in her office leaning back in her chair, her hands behind her head, her eyes closed. "Meditating?" I asked.

Her lids opened slowly. The edges of her mouth turned up for a slight grin.

"Kropp's here," I said.

Without saying a word, she got up and followed me down the hall.

Kropp's movements were animated as he rushed into the waiting room, a file in his hand. I could tell he thought he had something good.

"Well, we're waiting," I said.

"The reason I didn't get back to you guys yesterday is I had to wait until the Post Office opened this morning. After I left you on Friday, Brownie, I started to think. If your van driver was right, and that was Carol O'Malley that he drove back to the airport at noon the day Cheryl was murdered, she had to get here from the airport somehow. We struck out everywhere else and then it dawned on me, why wouldn't Cheryl have picked her up at the airport?"

"Duh!" said Brownie. "That's so obvious; I can't believe I didn't think of it."

"That's why it took me so long," replied Kropp. "There'd been a hold placed on her mail, so this morning I went to the Post Office and recovered her bank statements and MasterCard statements . . . The night before she was murdered, she filled up her car at the Rogers' Amoco, two-thirds of the way to the airport."

"Sure as shit!" said Brownie. "Her mother's coming to visit her, why wouldn't she go pick her up?"

"It's starting to make some sense," said Jackie. "Detective Kropp, if you look at her telephone records . . ."

"I know," he said. "There are a number of calls a week before she was murdered . . ."

"I think the last one was two or three days before . . ." Jackie interrupted.

"Two days," said Kropp. "And the last one was pretty long."

"So there are a number of possibilities," Jackie said. "She could've been telling her mother that she couldn't keep it a secret anymore, that she had to tell some-body about the sexual abuse, what her mother did to her. Or she could've been telling her about Dr. Morgan, that she was going to run away to California with him. Can you imagine what would have been going through her mind if she sus-pected that was true? Here, her daughter, the one who held a deep dark secret of what her mother was really like, was going to marry a psychologist who coun-sels women who've been sexually abused. Either way she's got to be in a panic."

"That's certainly a possibility," said Kropp.

"So she arranges to fly out incognito," Brownie said. "Cheryl picks her up at the airport, she spends the night with Cheryl. Not able to persuade her other-wise, her only alternative is to kill her."

"She was probably there when Becker called Cheryl that Monday morning to see if she wanted to be at Clint's sentencing," said Jackie.

Brownie nodded and continued. "So if she murders her at that point, she's got to believe that the only allegations of sexual abuse people are aware of are those Cheryl told about her dad. So she makes it look like Cheryl's dad had car-ried out the threats by removing her breasts."

"It's as plausible a scenario as Dr. Morgan doing it," I said. "But we still have a lot of problems. Our scenario rests on some pretty good conjecture but it's based on rather flimsy evidence. We have the statement of Benjamin Moore, but he certainly has a reason to lie—although none of us believe he is. We know Cheryl drove to Minneapolis the night before she was murdered, but that could be for any reason. We have a possible eyewitness of Carol O'Malley by the van driver, but any good attorney could make that look ridiculous. So it looks like everybody in this room may be convinced that she's the murderer, but that Dr. Morgan's going to be convicted."

"What about the telephone calls?" asked Jackie.

"She could make up a million excuses about those," I replied.

Brownie asked, "Bob, how about the forensic stuff? Were you able to find anything in that apartment that would put her mother there?"

"Nothing so far," he replied. "You know they vacuumed and scraped up everything, there's all kinds of little plastic bags of dust, hair, dirt, carpet fiber. There's a number of different strands of hair, but other than those we could tie to Dr. Morgan and Cheryl . . ."

"No long black hair?" I asked.

"Nope."

"I don't imagine she would've worn the wig in the apartment," said Jackie. "How about blonde hair, like in the picture?"

"There's some, but like I said, we'd have to have something from Mrs. O'Malley to compare it with, we don't have that . . . yet. But even if we get a sample from her, all they're going to be able to tell us is that it's microscopically similar. That's not foolproof. The FBI is doing some research on DNA, but nothing that's going to help us here. And there are all kinds of hair. There's cat hair, somebody in that apartment had a cat at one time. You know hair doesn't decay so some of that hair's probably been there for years."

We all sat there quietly, mulling everything over.

"Well, I'm gonna call O'Bannon in Boston," said Brownie. "He's got a picture of Carol O'Malley, the same one I have. I think he should hit the airport again, start showing it to ticket agents, flight attendants, see if he can come up with an identification."

"What's chilling about this whole scenario," Kropp said, "is if we're right, Carol O'Malley already knew, or had a pretty strong suspicion, when she left Boston that she was going to have to murder her daughter. That's the only reason she would've had to cover her tracks. I would say that's a pretty good argument for premeditated murder."

"So would I," I replied.

I found myself in a rather unique predicament. In my entire career, I'd never had a case where I absolutely, positively knew that my client was innocent. I had plenty of cases where the defendant claimed innocence, where we were able to create a reasonable doubt for an acquittal, but I never really knew if my defendant was innocent.

As we sat and plotted our moves, it was obvious to me that we all had the same thought: This lady's going to get away with murder. There was a sense of desperation in the suggestions being made. For example, Brownie thought we should just fly out to Boston and confront her, as if he could beat her into a confession. That may have worked thirty years ago when he was a young deputy,

it wouldn't work now and it certainly wouldn't work on Carol O'Malley. I suspect she would have said something like, "Kiss my ass," as she slammed the door
in his face.

So the meeting broke up with everybody agreeing on certain tasks. Brownie
would contact the Boston detective; Kropp would review his file one more time
(since he had to do that anyway, he was going to be one of Becker's first witnesses); I would talk to Chris again to see if there was anything we were missing;
Jackie was going to keep her mind on the trial.

The days really started to wear on me. Every morning I walked into the court-room and there sat the prosecutor paging through his trial notebook. He'd glance up as I made my way to the counsel table, then he'd get that smug smile and say, "Good morning, Counselor." I wanted to just walk over and bop him. Instead I played his game; I smiled back and mumbled, "Good morning."

Judge Savano, though, actually became more tolerant; at least he let me do my questioning of the jurors without giving me icy stares. Everything became quite routine: we started every morning promptly at nine, a juror was called in, and he or she would take the stand and be sworn in. I would question first, then the prosecutor, and then the juror would either be accepted or dismissed.

By early Friday afternoon we finally had our jury, twelve of Dr. Morgan's peers, consisting of nine women and three men on the regular panel and two men as alternates. By the time the twelfth juror was picked late Thursday after-noon, overall I was pleased with our jury. There were only two jurors who claimed they had no knowledge of the case, and both were from farm commu-nities on the far edge of the county. One was a housewife, the other a widow, who both claimed they had never read the local paper and very seldom watched television. Rather, they spent their time working or with their children. I liked them both.

I talked to Johnny every night by phone—a couple of times for over an hour. I could tell he wanted to come over. There were subtle hints in the course of our conversation, but he never asked and I never offered. I remained in my ambiva-lent state: glad that we had been so close but worried about our long-term prospects.

When not in court, I spent my time agonizing over what I should do for an opening statement. I knew from my experience with Clint's trial that Randy Becker was going to give such a detailed outline of his case to the jury that when he was done, they were going to wonder why we were wasting their time. I suspect their consensus would be to take the doctor out and shoot him, so I had to give the jury something, some argument so they would keep an open mind. But unfortunately, at that point, I couldn't tell them anything about Carol O'Malley, or even hint that we had another suspect. It would be devastating to Dr. Morgan's case to suggest to the jury that there may be another killer and then not produce one piece of evidence to back it up. So I had to pick my words carefully. I had to touch their conscience, their sworn statement to me in *voir dire* that they would be fair and impartial, that they'd wait until they heard all of the evidence before they made a decision.

I had spent many hours running everything through my mind, but with time it kept changing. I was trying to put the finishing touches on it that Friday evening when Johnny called. I'd told him the night before that if we got done with jury selection on Friday, I would consider going to a movie just to get my mind off the trial. So as soon as he called, I agreed, changed clothes and waited for him.

With a few minutes to think about matters other than the trial, I realized everything in my life was in conflict. Even my date with Johnny, I assumed, would result in conflict, with him trying to get me to bed and me trying to gracefully prevent it. Not that I was worried that he would get physical or anything like that, I just thought I knew what he would have on his mind and assumed he would ply his best manly skills to accomplish it. I, on the other hand, was in no mood to make love. I wanted a nice quiet evening of congenial conversation between two friends who sensed and abided by each other's boundaries.

To my surprise, that's exactly the kind of evening I had. I waited for Johnny in the entryway and as he drove up, I ran out. He came around and opened the passenger's door for me. As we slipped on our seatbelts, he leaned over and gave me a peck on the cheek.

"I missed you," he said.

"I missed you too," I replied.

At the movie we held hands and I felt like a teenager. After the movie we went to a restaurant on the outskirts of town. The waitress found us a table overlooking the Mississippi River, with a view of the water that bubbled and sparkled by the light of the moon after its rush over the dam. I ordered wine and he ordered a scotch and we sipped as we told each other about our week.

"You don't have to answer this," I said, "but I'm curious, did you consider Carol O'Malley sexy?"

"Where did that come from?" he asked.

"I wanna know. Did you consider her eyes sexy?"

"Compared to whom, you?"

"No, silly. When you looked at her face, did you think she had sexy eyes?"

"Honestly, yeah. I considered her sexy all over. She exuded sensuality. I don't think I necessarily attributed that to her eyes . . . although, now that you mention it, they did have a way of dancing about like she was sizing you up. That may not be fair, but she did have a sexy accent. I love the Boston accent."

I had never told Johnny about the van driver from Executive Express. As I listened to him, watching his expression change as he recalled the meeting with Carol, I could see where she may well have had that effect on the old geezer. Johnny certainly seemed to have a very clear recollection.

"But she isn't from Boston," I said, recalling my phone conversation.

"Ron asked her about that. She said she purposely worked on the accent when she started selling real estate in her husband's office. She said people wanted to deal with one of the locals, not a foreigner from Minnesota. But she said every once in a while somebody would catch a Midwest term and would confront her; she'd have to confess she was from Minnesota. She said the most obvious one was when she replied 'You bet'. She stopped using that. Why are you asking me?"

"No particular reason," I responded. "We're still listing her as a witness and I was just curious what she was like."

"Well, I just considered her quite foxy. I'd be careful on how I handled her."

"Foxy, huh?" I replied. "Is that a Midwest term too? Is that foxy like sexy or foxy like smart?"

"Both," he replied.

I was starting to dislike this woman more each time her name came up.

"Isn't she still a suspect?" he asked.

"As far as we're concerned, she is, but we just haven't been able to pin anything more down.  We can't go on with just what Ben told us."

"I wish I could be of more help," he said.  "They've got me locked away doing some briefs on insurance coverage.  We have a case where this young guy moved back home, was living with his folks when he got into an auto accident.  The question is whether his folks' insurance helps cover the claim of the other driver.  The insurance company's denied coverage."

"That doesn't sound real exciting," I said.

"It isn't.  I have to read all these appellate court cases where they're trying to define insurable risk and exclusions.  It's like being with Alice in Wonderland."

I turned to look out the window.  In the beam of light from the mill across the river, I could see a flock of ducks bobbing in the water.  With the strong current, they would swim upstream then dive underwater to pop back up fifty, sixty yards down stream.  They had big white patches on their cheeks but other than that they were just black shadows on shimmering water.

"Do you know anything about ducks?" I asked.

"I used to hunt years ago."

"What are those?"

"They're called golden eye.  They summer way up north; they're just here until it gets colder.  They're diving ducks, and they're feeding."

"This looks like an interesting spot," I said.  "I'd like to come back here in the daytime."

"I was here last year in spring, sitting right here.  A hen mallard had a whole fistful of babies.  There had to be nine or ten little ducklings following her in the water.  I was watching them kind of struggling.  One was trailing way behind.  Suddenly out of the water this big mouth shot, it was just a second, boom, the last duckling was gone.  It was either a big northern or a muskie.  The hen squawked and they all scattered to shore."

"How awful," I said.

"Well, the fish have to live too."

"They can eat other fish.  They don't have to go after little ducks."

This was just the kind of evening I had been looking forward to, what I needed to rebuild my psyche.  We sat there for another hour exchanging stories.  He had grown up in the country and had an affinity for nature.  I, in contrast, had grown up in an apartment in a neighborhood where the most excitement we could have in the summer was playing tin can alley in the shadows of the corner street light. I liked his stories about farm life and the country.

He drove me home and we sat in the car for a while. I didn't know whether he hoped I would ask him up or not. He never brought it up.

"I suppose you're going to be busy all weekend," he said.

"Yeah, I have to put together something for an opening statement and practice in front of the mirror."

"You can practice in front of me if you want," he said. "I'd be a good listener."

"I know you would . . . but not tonight."

"It was just a suggestion," he replied. "If you change your mind, let me know."

With that he leaned over and kissed me on the cheek. I turned my face toward him; he pulled away and then kissed me on the lips.

"I love you," he whispered as he pulled away.

I tried to give him a warm, affectionate smile. I followed it with, "Thank you for the evening. I really enjoyed myself. Give me a call this weekend. I'll want to talk."

He promised me he would. As I slid out of the car, I told him he didn't have to bother walking me to the door.

To be honest, there were a number of times over the weekend that I wanted to call him and invite him over. By Saturday noon, I realized that everything I could possibly do had been done—most of it overdone. I just wanted the hours to fly by. I wanted it to be Monday morning. I alternated between reading, sleeping and watching television. I found that my mind actually shut down Saturday afternoon about four. From that point on, no matter how hard I tried to focus on the files in front of me, it didn't work.

I took that as some sort of mental signal that I should give it a rest. So Sunday was spent lounging around the apartment watching the Sunday morning talk shows, an old movie in the afternoon and *Sixty Minutes* in the evening. The hour before bed I spent talking to Johnny.

Monday morning I was at the office before sunup. I was running things through my head when I heard Linda come in and start the coffee. A little while later I heard Noah's voice.  Within minutes there was a knock on my door.  I told him to come in.  He had a big cup of steaming coffee in his hand that he put on my desk.

"A little caffeine to get you going," he said.

"I'm not sure I need anything," I said.  "I just wanna get started; this waiting is driving me nuts."

"I have a few calls to make," he replied.  "Unless there's something you wanna talk to me about?"

"I'm going to take your advice, Noah.  I've decided to make a short opening statement right after Becker's done."

"Well, good," he said.  "I think that's the right decision.  I assume you know exactly what you're going to say."

"If I don't know by now, I'm never going to," I replied.

"Then just let me know when you're ready to go," he replied.

\* \* \* \* \*

I knew immediately there was something different about Becker when I walked into the courtroom a little later.  He smiled, but it was a tense smile, as if his cheeks were going to crack from the pressure.  I knew he felt the stress.  This was his big morning, his task to make that jury absolutely despise my client.

Dr. Morgan was sitting at the counsel table.  Noah and I sat next to him.  He'd stopped smiling or even acknowledging us sometime in the middle of last week.  Noah told me not to let it bother me and I didn't.  I had more important things on my mind than making Dr. Morgan happy and comfortable during the course of his trial.  I sat there, facing straight ahead, tapping my notebook.

From the first morning, Noah had taken the responsibility to make sure that we each had a glass of water.  He was doing that now, as the bailiff rapped the gavel on the side bench and hollered, "All rise!"

Noah startled, his hand slipped and the Styrofoam cup of water landed on the table, teetered precariously for a moment but stayed upright.  Noah actually blushed.  I hadn't seen him blush since I saw his tush in the hospital.

Judge Savano seemed to miss it because, as Noah was wiping the little that

spilled on the table, he looked at Becker and then at me. "Are we ready to proceed, counsel?"

We both indicated we were.

The judge turned to the bailiff, "Bring in the jury."

The bailiff went out the side door and within moments we heard the shuffling
of feet, the commotion of the jury walking up the steps and down the hall to the
courtroom. Since jurors had been picked individually, and *voir dire* had gone
over a period of two weeks, it was like seeing some of them for the first time. I
had forgotten what some of the early selection had even looked like. I could tell
as they passed in front of the counsel table that they were a little anxious. A
couple of the women jurors smiled as they saw me and then quickly must have
thought better of it. As their eyes hit Becker, the smiles faded. Once all were
seated, my eyes panned the jury box. I started to recall the *voir dire* of each juror,
the answers they'd given, why I had decided to leave them on the jury. Some
made eye contact with me, some with Becker, but most of them were looking at
the judge for some direction.

The judge smiled broadly. "Good morning," he said.

They acknowledged him with different greetings.

"Ladies and gentlemen of the jury, we're about to start the case of *State of
Minnesota v. Christopher Morgan*. As you are aware, you've been read the indictment; Dr. Morgan has been indicted by a Stearns County Grand Jury of murder
in the first degree. Murder in the first degree means that it was premeditated and
intentional. At this time, I'm going to give you some instructions—some legal
principles that apply in this case—and I want you to keep them in mind as the
trial progresses. You will be given instructions at the end of the trial as well as a
copy to take along with you into the jury room for deliberations. I'm giving the
instructions to you now to simply give you a little framework to apply as you
hear the evidence."

He smiled again, opened his book, and started. For the next ten minutes, the
judge went through all of the preliminary instructions, telling the jury that the
fact that a Grand Jury had returned an indictment was not to be considered any
evidence against the defendant, the fact that he was presumed innocent and the
state had the burden to prove him guilty beyond a reasonable doubt to the sat-

isfaction of each juror, that the procedure called for the state to present its case first and then the defendant had an opportunity to present his witnesses. Because of that, the jurors should keep an open mind until they'd had a chance to hear all of the testimony. He closed his notebook, glanced at the jury again, and smiled. "I'm sure you all intend to do that. At this point, the prosecutor has a right to give you his opening statement. Mr. Becker."

The prosecutor stood by the counsel table, perused the notebook in front of him for a few moments, closed it with a noticeable thud and walked to the front of the table to face the jury.

"Good morning ladies and gentlemen," he started. "It's been some time since some of you have been in here; I want to welcome you back and thank all of you for your services. I now have an opportunity to give you what we call an opening statement. The opening statement is nothing more than an opportunity for me to discuss with you what I expect the evidence will be, what the state intends to prove. What you will learn, ladies and gentlemen of the jury, is that this defendant, Dr. Christopher Morgan, held a position of trust and respect in this community. You will find that he holds a Ph.D. in psychology and he's licensed in that profession by the State of Minnesota, that he's maintained a practice here in our town for more than twenty years, that he's highly respected and considered a man of tremendous talent.

"There was another member of your town, a young lady, Cheryl Moore, the victim in this case, a student at the University, who filed a complaint against a man for a vicious rape. That case was set for trial and she needed someone to help her, to counsel her through those terrible months to prepare her for her day in court. Because of his reputation, because of the trust people placed in him, Miss Moore was referred to the defendant for professional help. That's how she came to be his patient."

Becker turned casually toward the counsel table, took a glass of water and sipped from it. He appeared deep in thought. He replaced the cup on the table and took one more step closer to the jury box.

"She was referred to Dr. Morgan's office because of his known skill with dealing with young women in her situation. What you will learn, ladies and gentlemen, is that he used that skill to take advantage of her, to exploit her for his own sexual purposes. Even though Cheryl Moore will not be here to testify, she'll be here telling you what happened. See, we have this little book—her diary. What she did, in the pages of this diary, is she documented, she memorialized, every session she had with Dr. Morgan. The diary will be introduced into evidence. You'll have it with you to take back in the jury room. What that diary's going to tell us, in Cheryl Moore's own words, is that over a period of months the sessions with Dr. Morgan went from therapy to sexual exploitation, to the point where she was lying naked on a blanket on the floor of his office having intercourse with him."

The last words were said with such force that they reverberated in the silence of the courtroom, and there were audible gasps from some of the jurors. I didn't bother looking up. I was pretending to take notes of his opening statement. What I was really trying to do was pretend I wasn't there.

"What you'll learn, ladies and gentlemen, is that this young woman's last entry in her diary tells how the good doctor was at her apartment just days before she was murdered. She wrote that he told her she should be patient, he was going to leave his wife and they would move to California. Within days of making that entry, she was dead . . . brutally murdered, her body mutilated, stabbed repeatedly, her throat cut ear to ear . . . her breasts severed from her body, removed . . . never to be located."

The prosecutor stepped back and paused in his statement, letting the impact of what he had just said settle on everyone. Up to that point, the jurors had never been told the extent of the mutilation of her body. Now I looked up at the jury panel, not one of the jurors was looking at Dr. Morgan. Every one of them had their eyes glued on Randy Becker, making sure they didn't have to make eye contact with anybody sitting at the defense table. This is exactly what I had expected.

"How are we going to prove to you that Dr. Morgan was the killer? I can tell you at the outset that Dr. Morgan hasn't denied any of the sexual impropriety. In fact, he gave a deposition in which he admitted everything. He even admitted that he told her he was going to marry her and that they'd move to California. But he told the lawyers taking that deposition that this was a lie . . . he had no intention of doing so. Why do you suppose he had to admit the sexual exploits? Because you'll find that he knew he could never deny them and get away with it. One of our first witnesses is going to be Detective Robert Kropp. He was the chief investigator on this file. He will tell you that he's the one who discovered Cheryl Moore's diary, hidden in her closet, and along with the diary there were letters written by Dr. Morgan to Miss Moore. Letters that he admits he wrote. Letters that confirm the sexual encounters. Letters in which he tells Cheryl Moore that he loves her and nothing will ever separate the two, that even if his wife was to find out, he wouldn't stop seeing her.

"Detective Kropp will also tell you that the forensic unit lifted numerous fingerprints from the apartment and Dr. Morgan's prints were found in the bedroom—in fact, on the bedpost. In the closet they found a white dress shirt, telltale lipstick on the collar and the initials C.M. embroidered on the pocket. You'll learn that he doesn't deny he left it there."

Becker reached back and grabbed a glass of water again, took another sip, reached for his notebook and opened it by a tab. He turned the pages quickly, put it back on the table and again faced the jury.

"Every crime, ladies and gentlemen of the jury, has to have a motive, and every defendant has to have had an opportunity to commit that crime. The medical examiner is going to testify that the exact time of death cannot be pinpointed, but in his opinion it was within a twelve-hour period on Monday from approximately nine o'clock in the morning until nine o'clock that night. We will be introducing Dr. Morgan's calendar for that day and you will find that there's a number of blocks of hours unaccounted for. He had the opportunity. As far as motive, it's right there on that last page of the diary . . . it's in his deposition, he had no intention of marrying that young lady. After having his way with her, he wanted out but she wasn't going to let him go . . . promises had been made. What would it do to his reputation in this town, to a doctor of psychology, if she went public and everyone knew what the good doctor had done?"

He gave it another moment to let the rhetorical question sink in. "He would've faced ruin. You'll see the pictures. Exactly what that young cop and Detective Kropp saw that morning when people called because they were worried about her not showing up for school. You're probably going to ask yourself: Why would he have mutilated her that way? Anger? Rage? Both possibilities. We will explain that through another witness, Lance Carter, a noted criminologist, an expert in crime scene investigation and reconstruction. He's going to give you his opinion as to why the scene was left the way it was. Who better to create a scene to make it look like the act of some madman then a man trained in the workings of a deviant mind?"

By now I had given up the charade of pretending I was taking notes. I leaned on the counsel table and stared at the jury panel. Every so often one of the jurors could feel my gaze and would slowly turn their eyes to me and then quickly move back to Becker. He went on for another fifteen minutes or so, summarizing, repeating. There were times I was going to stand and object where I thought he was getting off the purpose of an opening statement, becoming argumentative, embellishing what the evidence was actually going to be. But I didn't. I let him ramble on because my whole defense was built around one proposition: That when the cops discovered Dr. Morgan's diary in Cheryl's closet, he became their only suspect, they never looked any further. Detective Kropp admitted as much. So I listened, looking for a little opening here and there.

"Ladies and gentlemen, I apologize for going on a little longer than I had expected but I thought it was important for you to have a good grasp at what we believe happened here . . . what we intend to prove happened here. So that when the final word is spoken in this courtroom and you go into that room over there to deliberate, you can confidently tell each other: Mr. Becker told us what he was going to prove, and he certainly did . . . we believe the defendant's guilty. Thank you."

Judge Savano looked at me. "Miss Geroux," he said.

There was a moment there when I doubted my sanity. My concern was why anyone would voluntarily put themselves through this. It was something I had thought about more and more in the last couple of days. Here I stood, about to make an opening statement in a murder case, in which, when I started, I believed my client was guilty; now I knew he wasn't and the burden was on me to convince the owners of the eyes staring at me of his innocence. The thought shot tingles to every nerve ending in my body.

I stood frozen, my eyes scanning the expressionless faces of the jurors that I read to say: Don't expect much sympathy out of us.

I cleared my throat and began. "Ladies and gentlemen of the jury, I too wish to thank you for the time and patience you have shown. Although you have all assumed this task as your civic duty, I think you already see that it's not going to be an easy task. After all, you've heard we're dealing with the ugly side of life. The prosecutor has already told you of all of the terrible things you will learn. And as hard as it may be for you to believe at this time that you'll hear anything good in this trial, anything with any redeeming value, I can tell you that you will. Because there's a whole different side to Dr. Christopher Morgan; one of tremendous compassion, a willingness to help people in need; a portrait of a professional that will stand in stark contrast to what the prosecutor wants you to believe about this honorable man.

"After listening to the prosecutor tell you what the state expects to prove, I'm sure some of you are wondering why you may even be here—it sounds so open and shut—isn't this defendant just going to waste our time? But doing your civic duty and making sure that justice is done is never a waste of time. What you have learned already, what the judge has told you, is that simply because a Grand Jury has returned an indictment charging Dr. Morgan with first degree murder, that indictment doesn't mean a thing . . . that's simply the procedure used to get us here. As the judge told you, once Dr. Morgan stood in front of him in this very courtroom and said, "not guilty," all the rights we believe are so fundamental to our freedom settled like a mantle over Dr. Morgan, guaranteeing that he would never be found guilty of this terrible offense unless each and every one of you believed, beyond a reasonable doubt, and to a moral certainty, that he's the one who perpetrated such a dastardly act.

"You will recall, I'm sure, that in *voir dire*, when the prosecutor and I got to talk to you before you were selected as jurors, I asked each and every one of you if you could keep an open mind in this matter until you heard all of the evidence, until we've had a chance to make our closing arguments and you've had a chance to hear the final legal instructions from the judge, until you've had a chance to sit and talk to your fellow jurors. You all indicated you would. And now, as we are about to introduce evidence in this case, I'm asking you to keep that promise.

"What you'll find in this case, ladies and gentlemen, is that everything the prosecutor told you he expects to prove is true . . . with the exception of one very important thing: Dr. Morgan did not murder Cheryl Moore! What this case is all about is not only what the detectives did, but also what they didn't do. I believe the evidence will show that once the government discovered Cheryl Moore's diary and Dr. Morgan's letters, everyone concluded that he had to be the guilty party, the one who killed her. What you will discover in the course of the trial is that, once the police arrived at that conclusion, as far as they were concerned, the case was closed. Over! It could be no one else! So why waste time looking?

"To be fair and up-front with you, I'll admit that if the police missed something, if they left gaps in the case, we have to fill those gaps. We have to give you something to rely on to reach a different conclusion. All I'm asking at this time is that you give us an opportunity to do so. I believe if you do so, being the fair and open minded people you are, when we are all done, when you go back to that jury room to decide, I believe you will have a reasonable doubt and you will find Dr. Morgan not guilty."

As her last words settled softly in the courtroom, I had goose bumps. I had made what I thought were some reasonably good opening statements, but I don't think I would have changed one word in Jackie's. She had given, I believed, the only opening statement that would preserve any credibility whatsoever with the jury. She played to their fairness, their conscience, to their sense of duty. I couldn't imagine anybody having done better.

Before Jackie got back to the counsel table, Judge Savano was on his feet. "Well, ladies and gentlemen, this seems like a good time to take our morning recess."

There was a noticeable easing of tension in the courtroom as people started to stand. I could hear murmuring from the back, the press and spectators scoring the opening statements of the prosecution and the defense. I stood up just as Jackie reached the table. I took her hand. It was warm and clammy and I could almost feel the tension leave.

"Excellent. Absolutely excellent," I said.

She looked at me, her eyes glazed over and she smiled and softly said, "Thank you."

I looked toward the jury box and as the last woman juror stepped from the box she caught our exchange and her face softened.

Once the jury was out, Chris reached over and squeezed Jackie's arm. "Thank you," he said. "I think I just recovered a little of my self respect."

"I hope it continues," she replied.

By then the courtroom was nearly empty. The three of us stood there in silence, the realization settling in that as the prosecutor slowly laid out his case, there'd be very few opportunities for moments like this.

If a criminal defense attorney can come up with any advantage he may have in the trial process, it's the period following the opening statements, when he gets to ease up a little bit while the prosecutor has to proceed with his case. It always seemed to me it was easier to be in a position to sit back and take pot shots at the prosecutor's case than have to come right out of the chute presenting your evidence.

Randy Becker had the mentality and the patience to be a prosecutor. A man of infinite detail, it had always appeared to me that he loved the challenge associated with setting out the state's case in the most painstaking minutia, often to the point where the jurors' eyes clouded over from the tedium of his presentation. That's exactly what happened today. He had managed to go through the testimony of the first officer to arrive at Cheryl Moore's apartment rather quickly. Next he called Detective Kropp for just a few minutes to establish that he was the second officer at the scene and supervised the collection of forensic evidence. But when he got to Dr. Redman, the medical examiner, he took him through his autopsy in such a fastidious fashion that I wanted to stand up and scream, "Would you just move on!" I had learned from experience, though, that even that wouldn't have made any difference with Becker. He was a man enamored with himself and any attempt at criticism of him, or his methods, would have been sloughed off by him as mere jealousy.

From the defense point of view, there wasn't much we had to do. I had learned long ago that you kept faith with the jury by only asking questions that you needed answered, and not trying to baffle them with your brilliance by conducting a lengthy cross-examination, the only purpose of which is an attempt to convince everybody that you're earning your fee. That was particularly true today.

In a series of pre-trial meetings the parties had reached an agreement as to how many, and the content, of the medical examiner's photos of Cheryl Moore's body would be allowed. From Becker's point of view, he wanted to get in every graphic detail he could. We, of course, wanted the photos sanitized. Judge Savano, as judges are prone to do, tried to steer a middle course. But even with the worst slides removed, it was still very difficult and painful to look at the pictures of her mutilated body, to listen to the detail as Dr. Redman explained to the jury every muscle, artery, vein and nerve severed by a razor sharp knife.

Jackie, although I'm sure she knew this all by heart, was taking copious notes, her right hand flying across the page.

When Becker finished up with Dr. Redman, he thanked the doctor and turned to Jackie. "Your witness," he said.

Judge Savano said, "Miss Geroux, if you're going to take any time with this witness, we can have him come back tomorrow morning. It's nearing 4:30 and I would like to let the jury go. It's been a long day."

Jackie stood. "Your Honor, with your permission, I only have a few questions and I believe I can get through them quickly."

"Go ahead," he replied.

"Dr. Redman, in your autopsy report, you indicate that you did a sexual assault protocol."

"Yes, we did," he said.

"And that is standard procedure with any type of case where you have a female decedent who died as a result of unnatural causes?"

"That's true."

"Doctor, in response to questions by the prosecutor, you gave us your experience with the number of autopsies you've actually performed. How many have you performed in a situation similar to this, where the body has been badly mutilated?"

"Luckily, ma'am, this is a first for me. I've been involved in a number of autopsies, probably ten or so, where the victim has been sexually assaulted and murdered, but never with the type of mutilation I saw here."

"And in those prior cases, Doctor, the sexual assault kit was also completed as part of the protocol?"

"It certainly was."

"And to your recollection, Doctor, in each of those cases, did the sexual assault protocol develop that the victim had been raped?"

"All but one."

"So if your memory serves you well, Doctor, if you had ten cases similar to this, you're saying in nine cases it was apparent that the victim had been raped. Is that a fair statement?"

"Yes, it is."

"And in each of those nine cases of rape, Doctor, the evidence that supported the rape was the fact that there was semen and other physical indications of sexual intercourse. Is that correct?"

"Yes, it is."

"And in the one case there was no indication of intercourse?"

"She had been attacked vaginally with a broom handle," he said.

"In this case, Doctor, can you tell this jury whether Ms. Moore had intercourse at, or shortly before, what you believe to be the time of death?"

"No, I can't."

"And that's because the sexual assault protocol found no evidence of intercourse and no detection of any semen anywhere on her body or at the crime scene."

"That's correct, counsel."

"Thank you, Doctor, I have nothing further."

* * * * *

"You have to admit, Chris, I wasn't wrong, was I?"

"So far it doesn't appear so," he said.

"I can't think of anybody who would've put in a better first day than that. Even me."

"Come on, Noah," he said. "Don't try to con me anymore than you already have."

"No, I mean it," I said. "The advantage you have with her is, from watching that jury panel, she can keep most of those women jurors, if not on her side, at least willing to hear what she has to say. And as far as I'm concerned, the only way she could have screwed that up at all is to piss 'em off by playing them for fools, or be condescending, something like that. And she's not. She's letting the jury see that she agrees with everybody that this is serious business. Trust me, she's doing well."

"I know she is," Chris replied, "but this is only day one. Becker's just getting warmed up."

After saying goodbye to Jackie, Chris and I had decided we should end the day with at least one drink. Because we didn't want to run into anybody we might know and have to waste time explaining to them how the trial was going, we crossed the bridge to the east side and went to a little bar frequented by an entirely different clientele. The first drink went down way too easily and now we were sipping our second, hashing over the day's events.

Despite Jackie's first day's performance, Chris maintained the sullen attitude he had shown all along. That's the difference between dealing with a defendant who's bright and one whose elevator doesn't leave the first floor: Chris knew, as he had said many times, that he didn't have much of a chance. He told me that Elizabeth had finally confided in him that, for appearance sake only, she would stick with him until the trial was over and then would be filing for a divorce. While listening to him and finishing my drink, I concluded that he wasn't a whole lot of fun to be with and as soon as my drink was finished, I told him I would see him in the morning.

\* \* \* \* \*

It was quite obvious to me, as we sat around the counsel table the next morning, that the little glow we had the night before, sparked by Jackie's performance, had tarnished overnight. I didn't see much joy on Chris or Jackie's face. Becker seemed particularly anal this morning, grubbing through his trial notebooks oblivious to everyone around him.

As normal, Judge Savano started precisely at nine. He acknowledged the jury with a smile and a good morning then turned to the prosecutor.

"Mr. Becker," he said, "your first witness."

"The State calls Detective Robert Kropp."

Bob, looking pretty spiffy, approached the clerk to be sworn in. I think the only time I ever saw him in a suit was at a funeral of a fellow officer or when he had to testify. Today he wore one that I had not seen before, gray tweed with a white shirt and a gray tie. The drabness of the color seemed to subdue his rosy complexion and gave him a much more serious looking demeanor.

Becker took him through all the background stuff, his years of service, his training, his commendations. At the point where he was almost losing the jury to an early morning siesta, he got to our case.

"Detective," he said, "directing your attention to Tuesday, July 14, 1986, were you on duty and did you receive a call that day involving a possible homicide?"

"Yes, I did."

"Do you remember about what time?"

"Yes, it's on the log.  It was exactly 10:02 a.m."

"Did you respond to that call?"

"Yes, I did."

"Where was it?"

"It was an apartment house at 284 17th Street."

"Why don't you tell the jury what you found when you got there?"

"Officer Richard Powers was there.  He advised me in the hallway that he had responded to a call because people were worried that this young lady had not shown up for school."

"What young lady?"

"Cheryl Moore."

"Go on, Detective."

"Anyway, he explained to me that the caretaker had opened the apartment for him and that he had found a body, a young woman.  I told him to stay at the door and not let anyone in, that the forensic unit was already on its way. The caretaker was there, he was sick to his stomach.  His face was as white as a sheet.  I told him he could go to his apartment.  We would call him when some of the other officers arrived and somebody would take his statement.

"I then proceeded into the apartment, went directly into the bedroom.  I'll be honest—I thought I was going to lose it for a moment.  It was like nothing I had ever seen before."

I would suspect that in total, from the time Kropp got to Cheryl Moore's apartment until he found the diary, he had probably spent about two hours. Becker managed to stretch Bob's telling of his investigation into over three hours. Through most of his testimony, Bob had maintained a quiet dignity even though I knew under that facade he was reaching boiling point.  Shortly before lunch he started putting his finger in his shirt collar and pulling on it.  I'm sure he wasn't even aware he was doing it, but to me it was sending signals that he was suffocating under Becker's monotone examination.  Always the professional, however, Bob had been careful to maintain eye contact with Becker and the jury and only once, that I recall, did he even glance at our counsel table.

When we came back from lunch, Bob was standing in the hallway outside the courtroom talking to the prosecutor. Becker was waving his arms, animated, as if he was trying to pump some fire into the stoic detective. I could see Kropp take it in stride. Like a duck in rain, it was all running off.

Within minutes, we were again situated at our stations in the courtroom and I heard Becker say to him, "You may as well get back on the stand."

Kropp walked up to the bench into the witness box, sat down and leaned back. For the first time he directed his gaze straight at me and his face said it all. He tugged at his collar again and then finally gave in, opened the top button, loosened his tie and during the process sunk even deeper into the upholstered chair.

Becker started with the diary. He held it in his hand as he stood in front of the counsel table in a relaxed pose, as though he didn't have a worry in the world and said, "After the scene had been cleared, the body removed, what did you do?"

"I made sure that the fingerprint people had dusted anything they felt could produce any prints. Then I started to do a more thorough exam of the apartment."

"Specifically, Detective, I want to ask you about this little diary I'm holding."

"Yes," said Kropp. "In the victim's bedroom closet, on the floor she had a box of shoes. On top of that were thrown some clothes, other items that looked like she hadn't used them for a while. I started separating some of the items, putting them aside when I located a little wooden box, like a treasure chest."

"We'll stop there for a second, Detective," Becker said. "Showing you what's been marked State's Exhibit Thirty-four, can you identify that for us, please?"

Becker handed him the diary. "Yes, this is one of the items that I found in the box."

"What does it appear to be?" asked Becker.

"It appears to be, and it is, a diary. See, it says, 'DIARY' right across the front."

"I'm aware of that, Detective, we have to let the jury know."

"The diary is exactly that," Kropp continued. "It starts at a time before Miss Moore was being treated by the defendant. Relevant to us here is the entry starting right about . . ."—and Kropp paged through the diary very gently as if he was afraid to disturb the pages—"the first entry starts right here."

"Why don't you read it to us?" asked Becker.

Jackie stood up. "Your Honor, I believe the diary should be offered and accepted before the witness starts to read from it, and I'm not sure the reading is really necessary, the document speaks for itself."

Savano looked at Becker. "I'm sorry, Your Honor," he said, "I'll offer Exhibit Thirty-four."

"Received," said the judge. "As far as the reading, I'll give him some leeway on that. I think it's helpful to the jury at this point, they should know what some of the entries contain."

"Thank you, Your Honor," said Becker, in a tone as if he had won a huge victory.

As Becker took the detective through the highlights—or lowlights, depending on your perspective—of Cheryl's diary, it appeared to me that Becker was getting off on the whole episode, like a voyeur, being privy to the most intimate details of a clandestine sexual encounter. A vicarious thrill.

But I could tell Becker was making points with the jury. We had expected that this would be the nadir for the defense team; human nature being what it is, I suspected there were some jurors who eagerly anticipated hearing the salacious side of the case. When the State has this kind of evidence, everything else in the trial up to the point of its introduction is like a promo, similar to a television station trying to hook you with little bits and pieces, so that once they run the story, it's to a captive audience.

Becker made sure that Detective Kropp read her last entry where Chris promised to take her away. After it was read, Becker then took him through each sentence as if it needed explaining to the jury. When he thought he had adequately explained the nuances of every word, he took the diary from Kropp and turned to Judge Savano. "Your Honor," he said, "I would like to publish this document for the jurors' inspection."

Jackie was immediately on her feet. "Your Honor, he's already indicated that the jury will have a copy of that diary when it comes time to deliberate. With the Court's indulgence, he's already gone over almost every relevant entry in there. I don't think it's necessary to now turn that diary over to the jury so that they can peruse it while I'm doing my cross-examination."

Before the judge got to say anything, Becker shrugged his shoulders and said, "Fine, if that's the way she wants to be," and walked to the bench to hand it to Judge Savano.

"Ladies and gentlemen, I have to agree with the defense. You will have access to this document, and now I think it's best that you give us your full attention. But, before you do that," he said, looking at the wall clock, "I think we'll take our afternoon recess."

The three of us stood without exchanging a word while the jury paraded out in front of us. Becker walked up to the witness stand to once again confront Detective Kropp, while the press and spectators chatted even louder and faster with the new revelations.

I motioned my counterparts out into the hall. Once away from everyone, I told Jackie, "You know, Jackie, Becker's got Bob so worn down, I'm not even sure you should cross-examine him this afternoon. I think he's a powder keg ready to explode."

"What is wrong with that guy?" asked Jackie. "God, he's got to beat everything to death."

"I think there are two things. He's so afraid of losing that he thinks he has to cover everything over and over and in every minor detail, so nobody could ever say if he had done this or if he had done that, the results would've been different. More importantly, though, I think he just loves to hear himself talk. He alienates the jury but he keeps winning and, truthfully, in most of the cases, he should."

"But it makes it pretty painful for the people who have to sit through it," said Chris.

Just as he said that, Kropp came out the back door of the courtroom. He saw us huddled in the corner and he walked over.

"Noah," he said, "we've talked about it before, but I think I could really get off with mental illness, an irresistible impulse, if I whacked that bastard."

We couldn't help but break into a laugh, so hard that I had to wipe the tears from my eyes.

"If you do," I said, "I'll defend you. Free!"

"Well, give me a call tonight," he said, "I want to talk to you. I better get going now before he sees me and thinks I'm in cahoots with the enemy."

As he walked away, Chris asked, "Isn't he going to get in trouble, I mean talking to you?"

"Why?" I asked.

"Well, he's on the other side."

"As far as he's concerned, there is no other side. We've talked about it many times; this is supposed to be a truth finding process. He's not sure yet that he's found the truth and it's important enough to him that, if necessary, he would join forces with the devil to get there."

"That's the way I understand it's supposed to be," said Jackie. "Not the devil part, but the rest of it."

I think Kropp's comment to me took a little edge off of his growing animosity toward Becker. At least he didn't seem quite as short with him as Becker took him through Chris's letters to Cheryl. After I had read the letters in my first review of the file, I had somehow convinced myself that they weren't that damaging, that they showed poor taste and even poorer judgment, but listening to the substance of them in court, after all the other testimony before that, gave me a whole different picture. One could conclude from Chris's choice of words, in light of what subsequently happened, that he indeed tried to portray himself as a sexual suitor rather than a therapist. And once he accomplished the object of his solicitation, a roll on the floor, he wanted to dump her. It was certainly reasonable for the jury to reach that conclusion.

The entire inquiry was particularly tough on Chris, who took to staring at the polished oak of the counsel table and drawing connected little circles on it with his index finger. Several times during Kropp's testimony I punched Chris on his thigh to get him to quit. He would only give me a confused look and I realized, like Kropp pulling on his shirt collar, it was being done unconsciously.

After Kropp summarized the last letter, I thought Becker would turn him over to Jackie for cross-examination. I was wrong.

"Detective, before we're finished today, there are a couple more things I want to go through with you." He had the stack of Dr. Morgan's letters in his hand and he looked at the jury. To me it appeared that he was going to again ask the Judge to allow him to hand the documents to the jury for their review. Then thinking better of it, he walked to the bench, dropped the letters in front of the judge and returned to the counsel table to pick up a transcript. He walked back to stand in front of Kropp.

"Detective, showing you what's been marked Exhibit Thirty-Nine, do you recognize that? Maybe you can read the cover page for the jury."

"It's a copy of a transcript. It says it's a deposition of Christopher Morgan. It's entitled, '*Carol O'Malley, Administrator of the Estate of Cheryl Moore, Decedent, Plaintiff v. Christopher Morgan, Defendant.*'"

"Have you reviewed this document?"

"Yes, I have."

"So you are familiar with its content?"

"Yes, I am."

"And you reviewed it as part of your investigative duties in this case?"

"Yes, I did."

"There are just a couple points I wish to discuss, Detective. First, who is G. Gordon Pettiman?"

He's the plaintiff's attorney for the estate."

"And he's conducting the deposition?"

"Yes, he is."

"At some point, in that document, does he ask the defendant about the last page, the last note in the decedent's diary?"

"Yes, he does."

"And again, to refresh the jurors' memory, that's specifically about what?"

"About the defendant leaving his wife and he and Cheryl moving to California."

"What did Mr. Pettiman ask the defendant?"

"He asked him whether that was the truth. Whether he really intended to do that."

"And what was the defendant's reply?"

"That no, he didn't."

"What did Mr. Pettiman ask him next?"

"Whether the defendant would admit that he lied."

"And what was the defendant's response?"

"That he did lie."

"When Mr. Pettiman asked the defendant about his sexual relationship with the victim, what did the defendant say?"

Kropp paused for a moment as if he was measuring his words, then he said, "Dr. Morgan admitted he had a sexual relationship with the victim."

Becker reached for the transcript, closed it with a rather dramatic gesture and placed it on Judge Savano's bench. He then glanced at the clock again and made it to his counsel table where he sat down. I could see him turning pages in his trial notebook making sure he had asked every question.

Suddenly he said, "Oh, yeah. Detective, you indicated fingerprints were taken at the scene. Defense counsel has been kind enough to agree that the results of the fingerprint tests can be introduced through you so we don't have to call the examiner. I believe that's part of the pre-trial record, Your Honor."

"Yes, it is," replied the judge.

"Okay then, Detective, why don't you just tell us what the results of the fingerprint testing showed."

"We were able to recover numerous sets of prints that were the victim's. We were also able to identify fingerprints that matched prints of the defendant."

"Where were those located?" Becker asked.

"Pretty much throughout the apartment."

"Were there any found in the bedroom?"

"Yes. On a closet door, on a chest of drawers and . . ." Kropp paused.

"How about the bed?" asked Becker.

"Yes. We found some on the brass bedpost at the foot of the bed."

"In addition to prints from the defendant and the victim, did you find other prints?"

"Yes, we did."

"And were you able to identify who they belonged to?"

"No, we weren't."

"And is there a reason for that?"

"The only way you can identify prints is if the FBI or the Bureau of Criminal Apprehension already has a set of matching prints on record. If a person's never been printed, and that's the majority of the population, you would have no prints to compare with the ones we took from the crime scene, as in this case."

"How many prints did you recover that you've not been able to identify?"

"I believe the expert's opinion is that there was an additional four unidentified sets of prints lifted."

Becker again started paging through his trial notebook, this time a little bit more frantically. The clock had just reached 4:30 and it appeared he wanted to get his direct examination of Kropp over before the judge recessed for the day. I had no clue why.

As we waited for Becker to do something, the judge broke the silence. "Mr. Becker, maybe we should resume this tomorrow morning."

"I think you're right," said Becker, "but I would have to ask defendant's counsel's indulgence again. The only matter I wish to cover with Detective Kropp was his final analysis of the scene that was preliminary, and, as a preface to my first witness tomorrow morning, Lance Carter. I didn't anticipate my direct would take all day so I have him set up first thing at nine. So if I could put Detective Kropp on first, as sort of a lead-in, and then put my expert on, and then defense counsel would have to wait until the expert was completed before she could cross-examine Detective Kropp."

"Do you have a problem with that, Miss Geroux?" asked the judge.

She stood, "No, Your Honor. Anything to accommodate the prosecution."

Judge Savano almost cracked a smile, not quite. I could see he wanted to but wouldn't give up his judicial demeanor.

"Thank you. Maybe Mr. Becker can do the same for you sometime."

I heard Jackie mumble, "Hardly," as she retook her chair.

"Then, ladies and gentlemen," the judge said, "we'll resume again tomorrow morning at 9:00. Remember, this has been a pretty full day. Don't discuss what you heard today with anybody. And for God's sake, don't read anything that those guys back there are going to print." He motioned to the reporters in the back as he finished.

The three of us stood in the hall again, discussing the day's events. Chris looked more forlorn than ever before. Jackie's spirits, though, were surprisingly high. I could tell that under that calm exterior emotions were bubbling. Several times while we talked I had to bite my tongue to refrain from spouting about trial strategy. I had promised Jackie that this would be her case, and I was not going to interfere. There was nothing that had happened to that very minute which would make me regret my promise. And from the comments she made, I knew we were pretty much on the same track. So, as diplomatically as I could, I let a few thoughts drop which she immediately grabbed onto and then embellished. So I went home feeling good.

\* \* \* \* \*

Lance Carter cut a pretty impressive figure. Probably six-two or so, hundred and eighty, hundred and ninety pounds, I could tell that under the three-piece navy blue suit there probably wasn't an ounce of fat. After Becker told the court that Carter was the State's next witness, he approached the clerk and stood as straight as a board and took the oath as someone comfortable with the whole court scene. In his late fifties, he still had a full head of wavy dark hair with a hint of gray at the temples. Some Hollywood director could well have scripted him into his part as an FBI agent—which is what he used to be. I had heard his name or read articles about him many times over the years, primarily because he helped solve some high profile serial murderer cases. He was one of the pioneers in criminalistics, the science of crime scene investigation and preservation of evidence, and comparing crime scenes to establish similarities.

When we started at 9:00, Becker first put Detective Kropp back on the stand to set the stage for Lance Carter. Kropp told the jury pretty much what he had already told me: that when he had a chance to really think, once in the quiet of Cheryl Moore's apartment, when all of the commotion ended and the technicians left, something about the whole scene bothered the detective in him. He told the jury how he went through the details of the scene in his head one more time and when he was done, formed an opinion, based on his experience, that everything had been staged to make it look like she was murdered and mutilated as part of an act of sexual perversion, an attempt to avert attention from the real motive. His testimony gave the jury a chance to see Detective Kropp at his best. I watched the jury as they listened to him explain his thought processes in detail that lead him to his opinions. When he was done, there could be no question that this was an experienced detective at work.

In a pre-trial motion we attempted to exclude the testimony of Lance Carter.

Our argument was that the jury didn't need his opinion because it was cumulative to what they'd already heard. But Becker wouldn't be denied his opportunity to call, in his words, "An agent of the FBI, a world-renowned expert in criminalistics, and an expert who can give the jury a professional opinion as to why this crime scene was a reproduction from a bad movie." Becker was always over impressed with credentials.

Even though the defense had stipulated to Carter being called as an expert without the necessity of going into his entire background, Becker spent probably twenty minutes taking him through his entire career, including the publication of his book co-authored with a retired New Orleans Detective called *Crime Scene Investigation*. I could see from the expression of the jurors, Becker was accomplishing his intended purpose. With his looks and personality, his demeanor on the stand, it was obvious the jurors liked him.

"Mr. Carter," Becker asked. "What documents have you been provided with in respect to this case?"

"I have reviewed all of the police officers' reports, including those prepared by the forensic unit. I was provided copies of all of the photographs of the crime scene and her autopsy, the preliminary and final autopsy reports."

"Is this the typical information you would be provided when called upon to render an opinion?"

"Yes, it is."

"Specifically, Mr. Carter, when you receive that documentation, what are you looking for?"

"Well, the job of the criminalist is to review all of the investigative reports, everything prepared by the forensic units, the autopsy, fingerprint analysis, everything generated by the investigative officers and experts. You examine all of the information with a view to looking for clues to the possible motive of the perpetrator. The preliminary questions are: What took place? Why did it occur? Who could have done it? When you're viewing a crime scene like this one, where on the surface it appears to have been sexually motivated, additional questions come up: Was it the result of a lovers' quarrel; or the result of interpersonal violence; or was the killing sexually motivated, a rape or a sodomy; or the work of a sexual psychopath with sadistic or impulsive implications? Those are some of the preliminary assessments."

"Can you tell us, Mr. Carter, what conclusions, if any, you formed after those preliminary assessments?"

"If you look at just what's obvious, the naked body, the provocative pose of her legs, spread, the fact that her breasts are missing, your first impression is that it was a lust murder, that it might have been the work of a sexual psychopath bent on relieving some sort of deviant sexual impulses. But upon closer examination, things are wrong with that scenario."

"Like what?" asked Becker.

"You start out with a premise," Carter said, "that either she was murdered by somebody she knew or by a stranger. If it was by a stranger, one of two things is possible: First, he either entered the apartment with rape or burglary on his mind. In the latter case, I have seen numerous cases over the years where the initial motive of entering a building was for the purpose of committing a burglary, and once inside, the burglar has found a woman there alone, defenseless, vulnerable, and took the opportunity to rape her. Then, because he can be identified, the scene turns deadly.

"But in that case you would expect telltale signs, signs of struggle, torn clothes, turned over furniture, anything to show that the victim struggled. The same would be true if the original motive of the intruder was to rape. For example, if she were being stalked by somebody who entered for the sole purpose of raping or sodomizing her, you would expect to see the same disarray in the apartment, something to indicate a struggle. In this case, there's nothing like that."

"In your opinion, what is significant about what you *do* find at the scene?"

"Let's look at the most obvious as far as I am concerned. The investigators found no indication that she had been wearing any clothes at the time of the attack. Her body's naked, there are no clothes on the bed, on the floor, anywhere in the apartment that are not placed where they are suppose to be. The only item of clothing found was a nightgown draped over a chair in her bedroom. There's no damage to the nightgown, no signs of blood, nothing to show that it had been removed violently. In my opinion, it was removed and placed there before the victim laid on the bed. Again, all of that simply supports what I said; there was no sign of any struggle.

"Then, look at the wounds. In the opinion of the pathologist, the first wound was the slicing of her throat. She died very quickly, massive bleeding as indicated in the photographs: It's apparent from the photos, the bloodstain patterns, that she never moved. All of the stab wounds, forty-seven separate stab wounds across her entire chest and abdomen are, in the opinion of the pathologist, post mortem. The removal of the breasts, post mortem. So the assailant slits her throat in one forceful slice of the knife and maybe even has to hold her there momentarily in her state of shock until she dies, and then proceeds to mutilate her body. So, on the surface it looks like a lust murder."

Carter sat in the witness box leaning slightly forward, his arms on the banister and his stare directly at the jurors. His voice was calm, matter of fact, and the jurors were glued to every word.

"The problem is rape was not a motive. Sexual gratification was not a motive. As the pathologist indicated in his report, there is no evidence of any sexual assault."

"Let me interrupt you, Mr. Carter," said Becker. "In the number of cases you have been involved with, is that unusual? I mean where you have all of the overt signs of, as you said, a lust murder, but no evidence at the scene to show that the aggressor attempted to satisfy that lust?"

"In my experience, never."

"So how does that affect your opinion in this case, Mr. Carter?"

"As I said in the beginning, my purpose in looking at all of the evidence is to try to determine a motive. Based on what I see, my opinion is that this was not a crime of sexual gratification. This was not a lust murder but one made to look like it. Whoever murdered this young lady was not a stranger to her; in fact, the murderer would have been familiar enough to have been invited into her bedroom, onto the bed. This homicide falls into the classification, in my opinion, of being interpersonal, with the motive having to do with the relationship between the assailant and the victim. The mutilation of the body was simply to cast suspicion somewhere else."

\* \* \* \* \*

"Pretty impressive," I said to Jackie, as we sat in the conference room during the morning recess.  Becker had finished with Carter, and Jackie would cross-examine him when court resumed.

"Well, I pretty much agreed with everything he had to say," Jackie replied. "Did you know you and Carter have something in common?"

"We're both handsome?" I replied.

"Well, that too, but he also has a bad heart."

I gave her a shocked look.

"Yeah, I did a little checking on him.  He's had three heart attacks.  His last one was two years ago. He's apparently waiting for a transplant."

"Who would suspect?" I said.

"Looks can be deceiving.  He's been told he has to get into the best shape he can before the transplant."

"Where'd you find all that out?" I asked.

"At the University Library.  One of the cop journals did a story on him."

"Well, then you better not give him a hard time.  All we need is to have him collapse in front of the jury because of some grueling cross-examination."

"You know I'm not going to give him a hard time," she replied.  "In fact, I think he can be helpful."

* * * * *

"Mr. Carter," Jackie started, "I just want to make sure I understand your testimony correctly.  It appears to me that in arriving at your opinion, you pretty much used a process of elimination.  In other words, eliminating possible suspects based on motive.  Is that a fair statement of your process?"

"I believe it is."

"In your opinion, the easiest suspect to eliminate would be the rapist, or burglar turned opportune rapist, correct?"

"I believe that's true in this case."

"And if the perpetrator had been, in fact, a sexual pervert who simply selected Ms. Moore randomly to carry out his sexual fantasies, based on your experience, you would expect the scene to be entirely different?"

"As I said, Miss Geroux, the lack of any indication that there was any struggle

277

or any sexual penetration of any kind, the lack of semen, weighed heavily on my mind against this being a crime perpetrated for sexual gratification."

Jackie had, in my mind, made a mistake. I know her question wasn't intended to be open-ended, but it sounded that way and Carter took the opportunity to expound on his answer far beyond what Jackie intended.

"You have to understand that I've been involved in hundreds of cases," he continued, "cases all over this country, the vast majority of them solved, and I've never seen a situation where the crime was committed by somebody we would term a sexual pervert with the scene of the crime left as it was here. I've also been involved in a number of cases where, in a moment of anger, a fit of rage, a husband or a boyfriend has murdered his wife or girlfriend, sometimes with his hands, sometimes with a weapon, and then tried to make it look like a burglary that turned to rape and murder or the act of a sexual pervert, and believe me, it's just not the same."

"I have no reason not to believe you, Mr. Carter," Jackie replied. "Believe me, I don't doubt your credibility, I just want to make sure that I understand precisely what you're telling us."

"Fine," he replied, rather defiantly.

"I guess we're in agreement when I say I'm a little surprised as well that, given the sexual overtones of the crime scene, there's no semen located anywhere."

"Then we have the same concerns, Ma'am."

Jackie paused for a moment letting the silence settle in. She had been looking at her notes and she raised her head slowly, gazing directly at Mr. Carter.

"What if the perpetrator was a woman?" she asked.

During the entire cross-examination, Mr. Carter had directed either his attention to Jackie when she asked the question or the jury when he answered. Now, with the question before him, he turned his head slightly toward the prosecutor's counsel table. I assumed their eyes met because Carter got an almost imperceptible grin. His eyes narrowed.

Before he could answer, Jackie followed up. "Wouldn't it be reasonable to conclude, Mr. Carter, that with the absence of semen, the perpetrator could have been a woman?"

"I can honestly tell you, Ma'am, that subject did come up. For various reasons, that possibility was rejected."

My instinct was telling me to lean over and tell Jackie to let him go. He had become the expert who was a loaded cannon. The examiner had no way of knowing what his answer was going to be. By the time I turned my head and opened my mouth, it was too late.

"Why is that, Mr. Carter?"

"First, we don't have a female suspect with a motive. Secondly, as you'll see in the police reports, Cheryl Moore only had a couple close female friends and they all had alibis. And finally, we're talking about my experience. In my experience with this type of homicide, I've never had a case where a woman has been the perpetrator."

"Would that opinion change, Mr. Carter, if, in fact, the victim had been threatened with sexual mutilation of the same nature she suffered by her . . ."

Becker was on his feet. "Your Honor, objection!?"

". . . by her mother."

"Your Honor!"

The gavel came down with a bang. "Both of you hold it!" Judge Savano hollered. "Neither one say a word." He turned to the jury. "Ladies and gentlemen of the jury, an issue has come up here that we have to discuss. I'm going to ask the lawyers to join me in my chambers. This might be a good time to take another recess."

He stood and uncharacteristically waited until the jury had all exited the courtroom. He looked back at Jackie. I expected him to scream, tear her head off, but he didn't. Instead, he motioned us toward his chambers.

We had barely taken our seats when Becker whined, "Your Honor, I can't believe she would do something like that. She knew she wasn't supposed to do that. I want her held in contempt of court."

Judge Savano was surprisingly calm. He looked at Jackie. "Young lady, would you mind telling me what you think you're doing?"

"Your Honor, the defense believes that there's a strong possibility that her mother's the real murderer. We know that her mother is the source of those threats . . ."

"You don't know anything of the kind," said Becker. "All you have is this deviant father who's trying to put the blame on everybody else." He turned toward the judge. "Your Honor, we've gone over all of this. You've already ruled on it."

The judge looked at Jackie and with a slight shrug of his shoulders he said, "He's right, Miss Geroux. As I told you before, if you can't come up with something more than mere hearsay, I can't let you go on some tangent and conduct a witch hunt. You can have all the suspicions you want, but in court you have to have proof. I'm not going to let you get into this line of questioning with this witness."

"But what if we develop something more before this trial is over, something that will convince you that we should have the right to bring Carol O'Malley in as a witness? Then this guy's gone, I can never ask him those questions."

"Believe me, counsel," Becker replied sarcastically, "if you get that far, I'll bring him back myself."

"There you go," said Judge Savano. "You can't get a better offer than that. So right now, that's it." The judge stood up and shook his finger at Jackie. "And don't try to bring it in through your cross-examination of Kropp either. You hear me?"

"Yes sir," she replied.

"Good," he said. "Let's take a little recess ourselves."

As Jackie and I walked back into the courtroom, I motioned her over to the corner, out of anyone's hearing. "Something's happening, Jackie," I said.

"What do you mean?" she replied.

"Savano should have been all over you like flies on manure. He absolutely hates it when attorneys try to get away with something like you did. I almost expected to see him have the deputy haul you off to the holding pen."

"Maybe he figures Becker's got it made. Why screw it up at this point?" she replied.

"I don't think so," I said. "There's something more."

\* \* \* \* \*

Jackie excused Mr. Carter and then asked for Detective Kropp to return to the stand.

As he walked to the witness box, I leaned over and whispered, "Remember, Jackie, don't push your luck."

She remained stone-faced.

"Good morning, Detective," Jackie started. "Thank you for coming back this morning."

"Well, I would have been here anyway," he replied.

"You sat through Mr. Carter's testimony, I assume?"

"Yes, I did."

"Sounds like he pretty much reached the same conclusion you did."

"Sounds like it."

"We won't cover that again," she said.

"Thank you," he replied.

"Detective, I'm interested in the fingerprints."

"Sure," he said.

"You were able to positively identify some prints from Miss Moore, is that correct?"

"Yes."

"And you were able to positively identify some prints from Dr. Morgan, is that correct?"

"Yes."

"And there remain some prints which you have not been able to identify, correct?"

"Yes."

"How does the government obtain a person's prints? For example, in this case, Miss Moore's?"

"Miss Moore was a complainant in a previous court matter. She filed a complaint alleging that she was raped. When the authorities made an arrest in that case, a possible perpetrator, they dusted his car for prints. That's where the rape was supposed to have taken place, and to do some comparisons, they took her prints . . ."

Jackie quickly interjected. "And as far as Dr. Morgan, he volunteered to be fingerprinted, isn't that correct?"

"Yes, it is."

"So we don't know who the other prints may belong to?"

"That's correct."

"Do we know if they are from a woman or a man?"

"No way of telling."

"If we wanted to get prints from other people to see if we could find a match, how could we obtain those prints?"

Becker stood. "Objection, Your Honor, irrelevant."

"Seems to be, but I'll let him answer it," said the judge.

"Really, one of three ways," Kropp said. "First, the person could voluntarily agree to give us his or her prints. Or second, if they were charged with a crime, we take the prints as a matter of procedure. And finally, by court order under probable cause to believe that the person is, or was, involved in a criminal offense."

"Thank you," Jackie said. "In addition to dusting for prints, the forensic unit collected other evidence at the scene, isn't that correct?"

"Yes, it is."

"Some of that evidence hasn't been introduced here, isn't that correct?"

"Yes."

"For example, in looking through the lab reports, there were quite a number of strands of hair found in the apartment?"

"That's right," he said.

"And under microscopic examination, the examiner has given us an opinion that some of those belonged to Cheryl Moore, correct?"

"That's correct."

"Some have been identified as belonging to a cat. To your knowledge, Miss Moore did not have a cat, did she?"

"We checked into that. She did not."

"Do you know if the prior tenant had a cat?"

"Not to the landlord's knowledge. It was a pet-free building."

"Does anybody know how the cat hair might have gotten into the apartment then?" she asked.

"A number of different ways. Cheryl may have brought it with her on some of her clothing. One of her guests may have brought it in. Or, one of the previous tenants may have had a cat without the landlord knowing."

"And I believe they found hair identified as microscopically similar to Dr. Morgan's hair."

"That's correct."

"And it's my understanding, Detective, that with the present state of science, there is no way to positively identify who a hair may have come from."

"That's correct."

"But it is true, is it not, that the qualified examiner can tell us that the samples are microscopically similar, and that the questionable hair and the known hair have come from the same source?"

"That's correct."

"So again, if we would want to try and find out who the unidentified hairs may have come from, we would have to obtain a hair sample from our suspect and then have it examined to see if it was microscopically similar?"

"That's correct."

"According to the reports, the technicians also vacuumed the entire apartment."

"Yes, they did."

"And it appears to me from the reports that there are some fibers, carpet fibers, that were found, that appeared to be brought in from another source."

"At least they don't match anything in her apartment," he replied.

"So in order for those to be of any help to us, we would have to find where they came from, or who may have dragged them in?"

"That's correct."

Jackie had developed a real cadence to her questions, a sort of rhythm, and it caught me by surprise when she stopped. I turned my head to look at her and I could see she was studying the page in front of her where she had something written out with big red X's on both sides. Kropp took the opportunity to shift his weight in the chair and take a sip of water.

"Detective Kropp, just a couple more questions," Jackie said. "First, would it be fair to say that once you discovered Cheryl Moore's diary and Dr. Morgan's letters, which led to Dr. Morgan's arrest that night, as far as law enforcement was concerned, you had your defendant, there was no need to look any further.

Is that a fair comment?"

That question was basically the substance of our defense. If we couldn't get Carol O'Malley in to testify and do something to her, the only argument Jackie could make would be that they made a snap decision and then didn't look any further. I knew the question had to be asked and Detective Kropp knew that the question had to be answered.

However, he didn't answer it the way I expected. I thought he would say, "Yes counsel, that's true." Instead he said, "No homicide investigation is ever complete until the guilty party pleads guilty or is convicted by a jury. And even then, even after a trial, if someone can convince us we made a mistake, we'll keep looking. The real question you should have asked, Miss Geroux, is after I discovered the diary and Dr. Morgan's letters, was our office actively pursuing another suspect? The answer to that question is no. Will we continue to look for other possibilities if circumstances warrant? The answer to that question is yes."

Jackie took the rebuff in the spirit it was given, with a pleasant, "Thank you, Detective, I have nothing further," as she closed her notebook.

Detective Kropp stood and was about to leave when Becker said, "Just a minute, Detective, I might have a question."

I assumed Detective Kropp's candor had caused Becker some concern. Finally he said, "Detective, I guess I'm just a little confused."

I could imagine Kropp wanting to say, "More than just a little."

"I don't understand. Are you telling this jury that you are now actively pursuing another suspect in the murder of Cheryl Moore?"

"No. But I think anybody who's familiar with police work knows that you're required to keep an open mind about things. That's all I'm saying."

I'm sure that made it as clear as mud for Becker. He finally showed a little common sense and left well enough alone.

"I have nothing further, Your Honor," he said.

The judge turned to the jury. "Ladies and gentlemen, it's getting toward the end of the day. We'll break a little early. I'm going to meet with the attorneys and find out how many witnesses we have left. So we'll recess for now. We'll see you bright and early in the morning.

"This is going a little faster than I thought it would," Judge Savano said as he removed his robe and hung it on a coat rack. Randy, what do you have left?"

"I'm basically done, Your Honor."

Jackie glanced at me, panic taking over her face. "Your Honor," she said, "I have a problem. The prosecution is going much faster than I expected, too. All my witnesses are subpoenaed for Monday."

"Well," he said, "get 'em here tomorrow."

"I'm not sure I can," she replied. "Most of them are character witnesses, professional people. They had to change schedules already to be here Monday. I can't believe they could do that on a couple hours notice. My other witness is Carol O'Malley. I have her subpoenaed for Monday as well."

"You're not going to drag her all the way out here just so she can sit in the hallway and go home," said Becker. "Judge, why don't you just tell her now to forget it?"

"Mr. Becker, I'll tell her what I please; this is my courtroom. I told her before that I would keep that final decision open. It's still open, but I'm not going to waste a whole day. You must have somebody."

"I was going to call Dr. Morgan, but I wanted to make him my last witness," Jackie said.

"Well, you don't have the luxury of doing that. Put him on tomorrow morning. See if you can get some of those character witnesses here. I assume he'll take up most of the day. I've been doing some research; I'll let you know tomorrow about Mrs. O'Malley."

I followed Jackie out to the courtroom, Chris behind me. I turned. "What do you think, Chris, you ready for tomorrow?"

He raised his eyebrows, inhaled deeply. "I really don't think it's going to make any difference. Why don't we just put me out of my misery, tell 'em we concede."

"Do you wanna spend the rest of your life in prison?" I asked.

"Right now it doesn't look like that bad of an alternative. Maybe I can write that book I've always wanted to."

"If you live that long," I said. "You know what they do to guys who murder and rape young women? There's a hierarchy in the joint, you'd be the lowest critter there."

Jackie said, "No, Doctor, I'm going to put you on in the morning. It might do us some good to start with you. You can recover some of the lost ground, and then we can hit them with our character witnesses on Monday. End on a high note."

Chris replied, "Yeah, until Becker asks every one of them if the fact that I was banging one of my patients on the office floor changes their opinion about me. And when they all say, 'No, that's all right, he's still an upstanding professional of the community,' the jury's going to buy that, right."

"Chris, we don't have any choice," I said. "If you don't cut this shit out, I'll do just that, I'll call Savano and tell him that you wanna throw in the flag."

"Well, I'm just being realistic."

"Why don't you go home, think about it. Jackie and I've got work to do."

A trial provides you with a roller coaster of emotions. Sitting in my apartment Thursday night preparing for Dr. Morgan's testimony, I figured I had pretty much experienced the gambit. Tonight I was on the low ebb. I was moping over my tuna sandwich when Johnny called.

"How's it going?" He asked.

"Terrible."

"Why?"

I explained to him that it appeared to me the judge was not going to let me bring in Carol O'Malley; that I was stuck with my denial by Dr. Morgan, with my character witnesses, all of which would never turn the tide.

We talked for close to an hour. He wanted to help, but every suggestion hit a dead end. I was stuck with what I had.

"How about the detective out in Boston?" he asked.

"Brownie says he's shown O'Malley's picture around the airport until he's blue in the face. Nobody recognizes her. Why would they? I mean millions of people go through there. We're all a faceless mob at an airport. These people all stand there, smile and say, 'Thanks for flying with us.' But they're not paying any attention to your face. They wanna get outta there, get home, get drunk, get laid, whatever."

"You're in a foul mood," he said. "Maybe I should come over and cheer you up."

"How about tomorrow night?" I replied.

"Is that an invitation?"

"Sure is."

"Oh boy," he said, like a little kid.

"Don't get your hopes up," I warned.

"Jackie," he said, "I'm not expecting anything. I just want to see you."

\* \* \* \* \*

Dr. Morgan probably turned out to be the best witness of the week. Despite the blues from the night before, or maybe in spite of them, he delivered his testimony with a kind of light spirit and sincerity that you wouldn't expect from a maniacal murderer. He was, he said, truly sorry for the lapse in his behavior, both as a person and as a doctor, he had no excuse for what he did. He admitted that he was a disgrace to his profession. There were times in his testimony when the pain he was enduring was so obvious, the humiliation so complete, that he fought back the tears, bit his lip, and swallowed back the bile to wince at the pain.

Even Becker's cross-examination couldn't hit its mark. Demonstrating viciousness in cross-examination has a tendency to produce results only when the witness returns viciousness, blow-for-blow. Dr. Morgan wouldn't do that. When Becker confronted him about the diary entry, he used almost the same approach as G. Gordon Pettiman.

"It's true, Doctor, isn't it," he asked in a harsh tone dripping with sarcasm, "that when you told this young lady that you were going to leave your wife, that was a lie, wasn't it?"

"Yes, it was."

"And when you told this young lady that you were going to marry her, that was a lie?"

"Yes it was."

"And when you told this young lady that you were going to take her to California, that was a lie?"

"Yes, it was."

"So you admit that you are willing to lie when it serves your purpose?"

"Regrettably, that's true."

"And now you're telling this jury that you're not a murderer. How do they know you're not lying to serve your purpose again?"

"Honestly, Mr. Becker, they don't."

The answer caught Becker by surprise. He seemed stunned for a second but recovered quickly. "That's right, isn't it Doctor, they don't know whether you're lying?"

"No, they don't."

"Just like Cheryl Moore didn't know you were lying. You used lies to lull her into a sense of security, to give yourself enough time to plan her murder, didn't you?"

"No, I didn't."

"I wouldn't expect you to say anything else, Doctor." The words oozed with disgust. "I have nothing further."

I looked at my watch; it was 2:30. I could arrange to have only one character witness there in the afternoon, a fellow psychologist, and he promised to make it by 3:00. I figured I could hold Judge Savano off.

As Dr. Morgan left the witness stand, I stood. "I have one more witness who promised to be here by three. If we could take a short recess."

"That's fine, counsel. I would like to talk to you for a few moments anyway."

I waited until Chris made it to the counsel table and I shook his hand. I was surprised how soft and supple it was, I felt none of the tension I expected.

"You did a great job, Doc," I said. "You gave me everything I could hope for."

"Well, you did a nice job prepping me," he said.

"What is this?" Noah asked. "A mutual admiration society?"

It was said with the purpose of providing a little comic relief, and it did.

The three of us made our way to the judge's chambers. Judge Savano was standing behind his desk, his hands on his hips, holding his robe out. He reminded me of Batman ready to spring on some evildoer. He was looking out the window on a bright, sunny November day, his body silhouetted against a late afternoon sun streaming through. It was the first time I noticed how big of a guy he really was.

We all stood behind the conference table leading to his desk. Without turning, he said, "Have a seat."

His voice was surprisingly mellow. Again, without turning, he said, "I'm going to let the defense call their witness, Carol O'Malley."

I could hear the air go out of Becker, but he recovered quickly and sat up in his chair. "Judge, I can't believe this. What could possibly have changed since she made her argument at the pre-trial conference? Nothing! They don't have anything more to go on than they did before. You're going to just let her go on her little fishing expedition hoping she catches something."

The judge wheeled around to face us. "I don't disagree with any of that, Randy. But I know things the jury doesn't. I know that poor girl's long psychological history. I know that *somebody* made threats to cut her breasts off . . . What do I have? I have a victim lying there with no breasts. It seems relevant to me to inquire as to who made the threats. Maybe Dr. Morgan knew all that and did a copycat, it certainly looks like it. The Grand Jury believed it. But I've got concerns, so I'm going to let Miss Geroux call her and I'll watch the questioning very closely and if it starts to get off track . . ."

"Judge, you can't do it," Becker said. "I'm not going to let you do it. I mean, the case law is pretty clear, unless they can lay some foundation, they shouldn't be allowed to call her as a witness. They haven't! We're going to screw this record up so badly that I'll end up having to try this case all over again. I can't let that happen. If I have to, I'll go to the Court of Appeals tomorrow morning, tell 'em what you're doing, ask to get your decision reversed."

I could tell from the change of expression on Judge Savano's face, Becker had pushed it too far. The conciliatory look he had been attempting to maintain was replaced by one of intense anger.

"I'll tell you what, Mr. Becker, you do exactly that," he snapped. "Here, I'll even be of some help. I believe I have the telephone number of the Chief Appellate Attorney with the Attorney General's office. I'm sure he would be happy to help you present your case to the Court of Appeals tomorrow morning. In fact, Mr. Becker," he continued, looking at his watch, "I'm sure a man of his position will still be at work. Why don't we give him a call right now? Here, I'll let you use my phone. Since it's my mistake, no sense using the County Attorney's budget to correct judicial error."

Becker didn't move. His face turned bright red. He got up and left without saying a word.

The judge looked at Noah, and then he looked at me. "You'd think screwing up one case in your lifetime would be enough. Jackie, is your witness here? Let's get the afternoon over with."

My character witness took all of fifteen minutes. In the context of a criminal case, character witnesses are limited to testifying about the defendant's reputation in the community for being an honest, truthful and upstanding community member. Because character relies on reputation, if the prosecution knows some dirt about the defendant that might affect the opinion of the witness about the defendant's character, the prosecutor has the right to cross-examine the witness about that dirt. It meant that Becker had the right to ask the witness whether the fact that Dr. Morgan had a sexual relationship with a patient, and the fact that he admitted that he lied to her, would change the opinion of the witness as to his character. Obviously, you only put witnesses on the stand who had already told you that it would not and that's why we chose Dr. Sufka. But after Becker got a chance to repeat the sexual liaison and the lie one more time, it seemed like a waste of effort on our part.

As the witness was dismissed, the judge turned to the jury. "It is my understanding that we only have one witness left for Monday. Based on that, there's a possibility that this case may be submitted to you for deliberation late Monday afternoon. If that is the case, you are going to be sequestered until a verdict is reached. So I would suggest that you all make arrangements to bring an overnight bag along or have somebody prepared to drop it off if necessary because you may not be going home."

I took the opportunity to watch the jurors' faces. My own assessment was that we had made a few points in the course of the week, but in my heart, I was sure it was not enough to get a not guilty verdict. Even Carol O'Malley was just a shot in the dark.

Chris disappeared quickly after the judge excused everybody. Noah and I walked to the office. He was surprisingly quiet. There was an early winter chill, a threat of snow. The air was damp and heavy. Linda asked us how things were going as we walked by her desk. We both kind of mumbled, "okay." She took it to mean that things weren't okay at all.

"Jackie, let's go to my office and talk for a few minutes," Noah suggested.

He sat in his leather chair, opened the top drawer, took out his favorite pipe and started chewing on it, pretending to inhale.

Finally, he said, "I know what happened and I'm willing to bet my life on it."

Without giving me a chance to answer, he continued. "I'm willing to bet any money that Kropp got to Judge Savano."

I sat up in my chair. "Like what?"

"Listen, Jackie, those guys go back a ways. I mean Savano used to prosecute; Kropp was the investigative officer. I wouldn't put it past either one of them to sit down and talk about this case."

"Without anybody else knowing about it?" I said.

"Nobody else is supposed to know about it because they aren't supposed to do it, just like Savano wasn't supposed to talk to Gordon Smith without you being there. Just like I trust Kropp, I'm sure Savano has the same opinion. Maybe there's something in this case, something in your argument that causes him some problems. So what does he do? He goes right to the horse's mouth and Kropp's going to tell him what he's been doing since our discussions. I told you a couple days ago there came a time when it seemed Savano's attitude had changed. He's not risking anything. He gives you a chance to take a shot at Carol O'Malley. If you fall on your face, it's not his fault. If Morgan gets found guilty . . . well. There's also the fact that he does know about Cheryl's background. All that crap that got brought up in Clint's motion, the stipulated findings, that's got to make him wonder."

"Yeah, and right on the heels of Clint's reversal. He has to wonder whether another innocent guy will be found guilty, especially since he's known Morgan for many years. Who knows, Chris did a good job today, maybe Savano believes him."

"Well, something happened," Noah said. "Now we just have to make the best of it. You know what you're going to ask her?"

"I have a pretty good idea."

By the time I got back to my apartment, I had a brain splitting, eye-popping headache. I took a couple extra-strength headache killers and stretched out on the couch. I had no idea what to expect Monday morning. I knew how I was going to approach Carol O'Malley, but my plan depended on how she was going to answer the questions.

The pain medication started to work and as my headache slowly disappeared, my eyes grew heavy and I fell asleep. I was still in a deep sleep when I heard pounding on the door and Johnny's voice. I tried to say something but the medication had dried my mouth out. I kind of rolled off the couch onto the floor and I used the arm of the couch as a brace to pull myself up. I think I had taken one too many pills.

Johnny's face flashed concern as soon as I opened the door. "You all right?" he asked.

"Yeah, I'm just recovering from a little headache."

"You look dazed."

"I feel dazed."

"Come on back and sit down."

He led me back to the couch. He sat down and I sat next to him, my head on his shoulder. He put his arm around me, tucked me close and within moments I was asleep again.

Through squinty eyes I managed to see the clock on the television. It read 9:30. I was disoriented and I could hear a rhythmic thumping that I came to realize was Johnny's heart. I lifted my eyes upward without moving my head. He was looking down at me.

"I'm sorry," I said. "How long has it been?"

"Just about three hours. I've had to pee since about an hour ago, but I didn't have the heart to wake you. So I'm going to get up now whether you mind or not."

"What a guy," I said, as he pulled his arm out from under my head and bee-lined for the bathroom. I got up and looked in the mirror. God, I looked terrible. My hair was wet and matted on one side from the sweat; my eyes had dark rings around them. My lips were dry and cracked.

I heard the bathroom door close and footsteps coming up behind me. Johnny put his arms around my waist, nestled me into him and kissed me on the nape of my neck. It sent goose bumps shooting over my body.

"I missed you," he said. "When is this trial going to be over?"

"Sooner than I anticipated," I replied. "Probably Monday."

He pulled way. "That fast? What happened?"

"There just hasn't been a lot of dispute over the evidence. It is what it is. Let's go eat and I'll tell you about it."

"Where do you wanna go?" he asked.

"How 'bout pizza?"

"That sounds good to me."

Fifteen minutes later we were ushered into a booth at Sammy's Pizza. We ordered margaritas and a fifteen-inch sausage and pepperoni pizza. I told Johnny what had happened in the course of the week, how Judge Savano had finally dumped on Becker and was going to let me put Carol O'Malley on the witness stand. I told him exactly how I intended to cross-examine her.

"You think it's going to work?" he asked.

"I don't know," I replied. "The real question is whether Judge Savano's going to give me that much leeway. I can imagine Becker will be jumping up and down, objecting to everything. Even if Noah's right about Savano's motives, unless it appears that I'm getting somewhere, he'll have to stop it."

"What happens if he does?"

I let out a deep sigh. "Then I have to be prepared to make a closing argument which . . ." I didn't finish the thought. I had already agonized too many times over the content of my closing argument. I still needed to put the finishing touches on it tomorrow, but as it stood, it would be relatively short.

Johnny said, "I have to call Ron tomorrow and tell him I'm going to sit through the trial on Monday. He's got me doing some paperwork that I'm sure I can promise I'll finish in the evening. I don't wanna miss this. If you pull it off, Jackie, well, you'll be the talk of the town."

"And if it doesn't work, Becker will make sure that I'm the laughing stock of the town."

"You spend way too much time worrying about him, Jackie."

"I know, but he's like a fungus, he just keeps spreading."

We left Sammy's and drove to an all night truck stop where we ordered a pot of decaf coffee and lemon meringue pie. The evening had been very good for me. It was not something I had intended when we left my apartment but my time with Johnny was like a dress rehearsal for Monday morning, it gave me a chance to solidify my thoughts—ideas that, before our conversation, had just been kind of rumbling through my brain. Now I was anxious for Monday morning to get here.

Johnny dropped me off close to midnight. He told me he would be in court on Monday and then would plan on staying with me while the jury was out. He figured I would need some company. In a moment of fantasizing, we even talked about what we'd do if the jury came back not guilty, we'd have a big party, take a couple days off to celebrate. I wasn't really planning on that possibility.

On Sunday I lounged, doing as little as possible. I picked up the Sunday paper, and the reporter covering the trial had written a summary of the testimony. It was actually pretty objective, and based on the article, the reader could even surmise that Dr. Morgan had a slight chance. The reporter must have been impressed with his testimony.

Later in the afternoon I called my aunt Ruby. With the preparation and the trial it had been several weeks since I had talked to her and I felt bad that I seemed to ignore her. We talked for an hour. I gave her a pretty good summary of the case and I could tell by her comments she was impressed that her little niece was this big shot attorney. If she only knew. But I wasn't about to burst her bubble. I promised her that when the trial was over, I would drive to Fargo and spend some time with them.

That evening I had to make just two calls. The first was to Noah, a sort of a last minute check to see if there was anything more he wanted to discuss or suggest. The next call was to Brownie. He was expecting it.

"Did you talk to him?" I asked.

"Yeah, I did."

"And?"

"He wouldn't commit."

"Did you tell him that the judge decided to let me put her on the stand?"

"Yes. How dumb do you think I am?"

"Sorry," I said.

"He doesn't want to see her, Jackie. Why don't you just subpoena him?"

"Even if I had time," I replied, "I'm not sure I would do that to him."

"Well, I told him what time we were starting. I even offered to pick him up. He said he'd think it over. So we just have to wait and see."

"Let's hope," I replied. "By the way, do you have the number for John O'Malley's secretary? What was her name again?"

295

"Just a second, let me get my notes."

I looked at the clock; it was 8:03 p.m. That would make it 9:03 in Boston. Not too late to call her.

"Here it is. Lori Driscoll. Her home number is 555-481-1515. Why do you want it?"

"I want to talk to her about some cats."

"What's that about?"

"You'll find out tomorrow. Thanks for your help, see ya in the morning."

* * * * *

On Monday morning I got to court early. I wanted to be there when Carol O'Malley made her appearance. When I came through the side door, some of the jurors were already in the hallway waiting for the bailiff to open the jury assembly room. Their acknowledgments were polite but I could tell they wanted as little eye contact with me as possible. From everything I had ever read or heard, that was not a good sign.

I took up a location at the end of the hall leading to the big courtroom, a spot where Carol O'Malley would have to pass. Some of the press and spectators started trickling in. The reporter who wrote the article for the Sunday paper saw me and stopped. I told him I couldn't talk to him now, I would be glad to give him some comments when it was all over. He seemed like a nice young man, probably right out of journalist school and hadn't picked up any obnoxious habits yet, so he said, "Thanks," and left.

Just as he left, two women turned the corner coming up the stairs, and I had a full view of them. I recognized on of them; she had been with G. Gordon Pettiman when he took Dr. Morgan's deposition. The other had to be Carol O'Malley. I saw it in the eyes immediately. What everybody said was true. She was a strikingly beautiful woman.

They reached the top of the stairs and walked by me like I wasn't even there. The companion approached one of the deputies in the hall and he pointed to the far side. They were looking for a restroom. They made their way back to the ladies room and I gave them a minute or so before I followed them in. Carol

O'Malley was standing by the sink looking into the mirror. Her companion was in the stall. O'Malley acknowledged me with a "Good morning".

"Good morning," I said. "A little crowded in here."

"We're just about done," she replied.

She took out a comb and ran it through her hair. She had shoulder length blonde hair, thick, highlighted. Her face was tan, not dark, but just kind of a healthy glow. Even in the mirror, her bright blue eyes seemed to dance. I don't think I'd ever seen that deep of a blue. There was nothing gaudy or flamboyant about her outfit, just a very pale blue business suit with a light blue blouse. From what I could see, she wore a wedding ring and no other jewelry. When she finished combing her hair, she ran her hand over the comb and dropped the loose strands into the waste can. She then reached into her purse and got out her lipstick. The door to the stall opened and her companion walked out straightening her dress. She glanced at me and paused.

"Weren't you at Dr. Morgan's deposition?" She asked.

"Yes, I was."

"Aren't you his attorney?"

"Yes, I am."

I could see Carol's eyes close in on me. In her reflection in the mirror, still applying her lipstick, she said, "You're the one who called me."

"I am," I replied, as I eased my way past her companion into the bathroom stall.

I put the lid down and sat on the stool and waited. I could hear the sink running but neither of them said a word. I heard their shoes click on the tile floor and the whoosh of air as the big metal door closed behind them. I stood and listened. When I was sure they were gone, I left the stall and reached into the waste container and retrieved the strands of hair. When I got out of the bathroom, I saw them on the far side of the hall talking to the bailiff. He was pointing to the back door of the courtroom. He then led them over and opened the back door. I assumed she was used to being treated like that.

I picked up my briefcase and files and went into the courtroom to take my seat at the counsel table. Neither Dr. Morgan nor Noah was there yet. I opened my briefcase and took out two little plastic bags. In one I placed one strand of

Carol O'Malley's hair and in the other, the balance of six or seven strands. I placed the little bags back in my briefcase and took out a water glass and set it on the counsel table. I then waited to get started.

Within minutes the courtroom was full. Noah and Chris came in to take their seats next to me. Noah gave me a wink. At about a minute to nine, Becker came in and ignored us as he walked by and took his seat. The bailiff then brought in the jury and the Judge walked in, according to my watch, five seconds late. The first time all week.

"Good morning, everybody," he said. "Ms. Geroux, I assume you're ready."

"I am, Your Honor."

"Proceed."

"I'll call Carol O'Malley."

"Is Miss O'Malley here?" Judge Savano asked.

"I'm here," she said, and I could hear some rustling as she made her way through the spectators.

"You'll have to be sworn in," the judge said as he pointed toward the clerk.

Carol walked briskly and raised her right hand before the clerk who administered the oath. The pale blue outfit clung to her curves. I had not noticed it in the bathroom, but it was expensive, cut right above the knees to reveal shapely calves, thin ankles. For some reason as she stood there and took the oath, I recalled the comment of the young boy in the park, "Nice ass."

She took her seat in the witness box, gave a once around the courtroom and then her eyes settled on the jury. She nodded with a smile and said, "Good morning."

Some of them responded. I wanted to wipe the smile from her face. I stood, "Your Honor, I would like to have Mrs. Carol O'Malley declared an adverse witness so that I may cross-examine."

"So ordered," he said, without even waiting for Becker to respond.

"Thank you, Your Honor," I replied.

I could tell it had had the desired effect on Carol O'Malley. Her look turned serious as she fixed her stare on me.

"Would you state your full name for the record, please?"

"Carol Alice O'Malley."

"And where do you presently reside?"

"Boston, Massachusetts."

I don't know why it had not struck me before in the bathroom, but she spoke without any Boston accent whatsoever.

I continued. "But you're originally from Minnesota, correct?"

"Yes, I am."

"Born and raised in South St. Paul, correct?"

"Yes."

"Graduated from South St. Paul High School, correct?"

"Yes."

"And married to Benjamin Moore in Las Vegas on November 10, 1964?"

"Yes."

"And had a baby girl on May 13, 1965?"

"Yes."

"And you named her Cheryl Michelle Moore, correct?"

"Yes."

"And Cheryl Moore was the victim of a terrible murder on July 14, 1986?"

"Yes."

"And you know Dr. Morgan is on trial here based on an indictment charging him with that murder, correct?"

"Yes."

"And you were recently the plaintiff in a lawsuit where you were suing Dr. Morgan in what is called a wrongful death action. Isn't that correct?"

Becker was on his feet. "Your Honor, please, what relevance does any of this have."

"It's all preliminary, but move it along," the judge said.

"I will, Your Honor," I replied.

"You did file a lawsuit, correct?"

"Yes, I did."

"And that lawsuit has recently been dismissed on your own motion, correct?"

"Yes, it has."

"You were divorced from Benjamin Moore in Hennepin County on August 10, 1978, correct?"

"Yes."

"And you were granted custody of your daughter, Cheryl?"

"Yes, I was."

"You moved to the Boston area shortly after the divorce was finalized, correct?"

"Yes, I did."

"But Cheryl did not go with you?"

"No."

"She lived with her aunt, correct?"

"Yes."

"That was based on Cheryl's wish to stay in Minnesota, correct?"

"Yes."

"From the time you moved to Boston until her death, did she ever visit you in Boston?"

"No."

"Did you ever visit her in Minnesota?"

"No."

"Your only contact was by phone or through the mail?"

"Yes."

"You were aware that she was struggling with some issues that required therapy, correct?"

"Yes."

"Were you ever asked to attend any of the therapy sessions?'

"Yes."

"Did you?"

"No."

"You were aware that she made allegations that she had been sexually abused as a child, correct?"

"Yes."

"And you were aware that she had told her treating therapists that her father was the one who sexually abused her, correct?"

"That's what she said because that was the truth."

"Just yes or no, please," I replied.

"Yes."

"You never told any of her treating therapists that your daughter's statements were the truth?"

"No one ever asked me."

"And you never volunteered?"

"No."

"Your daughter told you that she was being counseled by Dr. Morgan, correct?"

"Yes, she did."

"And you understood that was to help her through a trial?"

"Yes."

"Did you talk to her often while that trial was pending?"

"I wouldn't say often. We talked."

"Did she tell you she was becoming romantically involved with Dr. Morgan?"

"Not in those words."

"But you understood that she was becoming sexually involved with him?"

"No, I didn't."

"Nothing in your discussions with her led you to believe that?"

"No."

"So, she didn't tell you that Dr. Morgan told her that he was going to be leaving his wife to marry her and that the two of them would move to California where he'd set up a new practice?"

"She never mentioned that."

"Do you recall the last time you talked to her prior to her death?"

"Not exactly."

I reached for the file of telephone records. "Is your number 555-494-8489?"

"Yes it is."

"May I approach the witness, Your Honor?"

"You may."

"Mrs. O'Malley, showing what has already been marked and admitted into evidence as defense Exhibit Nine; these have been identified as the telephone bills for your daughter for the period two months prior to her death. Will you look those over please?"

She gave them a cursory glance like it was no big deal and handed them back to me. "Okay," she said.

"Let's go to the month of June 1986, the month before her death. How many times do you think she called you?"

"I don't know."

"What do the records show?"

"I saw a few times in there."

"If I told you, Mrs. O'Malley, that there were nineteen separate calls in that month, would you agree with that?"

"Well, she may have called, that doesn't mean that I talked to her. Some of those are so short its obvious we didn't connect."

"Well, do you recall the times you may have connected?"

"What are you trying to get at?" she snapped.

"I'm just trying to find out how many times you talked to your daughter in the two months before she was murdered."

"Well, I don't remember."

"One would think that would be quite memorable."

Becker jumped to his feet. "Your Honor, objection, argumentative."

"Counsel, will you approach?"

Becker looked at me with his satisfied sneer as we stood in front of the bench.

Judge Savano leaned over, and looking at me he said, "Counsel, I have to agree. Unless you can come up with something better than this, I have to end it."

"Judge, all I need is a little leeway. I can't just confront her with what I want to know, I have to lead up to it."

He looked at Becker. "I'll give her a little bit more time."

Becker turned abruptly and stomped like a spoiled brat back to the counsel table.

"Thank you, Your Honor," I said.

I could feel Mrs. O'Malley's eyes on me the entire time. I wasn't sure whether she'd overheard any of our discussion.

As I resumed my seat, I asked her whether she would look at the telephone statement for the month of July.

She again perused it quickly and said, "Okay."

"I'm interested in the date July 12, 1986. That was two days before she was murdered. Did she make a call to you on that date?"

"Yes, she did."

"And the record indicates that that was for exactly fifty-nine minutes, correct?"

"Yes."

"And the record shows that that is the last call from her phone, correct?"

"As far as I can see."

"And those records also show that prior to that call, the longest conversation you had with her was four minutes, twenty-eight seconds, isn't that correct?"

"I have no way of knowing. If that's what it shows, that's what it shows."

"Do you want to look at those records again to confirm that?"

"No need."

"And in that fifty-nine minute telephone conversation with your daughter, two days before she was murdered, she told you about her relationship with her psychologist, Dr. Morgan, didn't she?"

"No, she didn't."

"And she told you that the therapy he had provided to her had been helpful . . ."

"We never got into her therapy," she interrupted.

"The question was going to be, Mrs. O'Malley, that didn't she tell you that to be truly healed, she would have to be honest with the doctor?"

"No, she didn't."

"And she told you that she was going to tell the doctor that you had sexually abused her in her childhood?" I said, hearing audible gasps from the jury and the spectators.

"That's outrageous!" she hollered. "Where would you come up with something like that?"

"Didn't she tell you that?"

"I'm not even going to give that the dignity of an answer. You know she said her dad was the abuser."

"I assume your answer is a no then, she did not tell you that?"

She tightened her lips, turned her face to the side.

"You're going to have to answer that, Mrs. O'Malley," said Judge Savano.

"Of course the answer's no!"

"Your daughter also told you in her last telephone conversation with you that the doctor told her the two of them were going to move to California, he would set up a practice there."

"She never said any such thing."

"And you had no way of knowing whether any of that was true, did you?"

"I already told you, she never mentioned that."

"So would it be fair to say, Mrs. O'Malley, that after that telephone conversation you had a real problem because you knew that if she, in fact, moved to California with her treating psychologist, at some point she was going to tell him the truth: that the cause of her problems was not that she was sexually abused by her father, but she was sexually abused by you."

I was staring right at her with as fixed a gaze as I could produce. She tightened her lips again and looked away.

"It simply requires a yes or no answer, Mrs. O'Malley," I said.

Again, she turned to face me and though she wanted to appear calm and relaxed, her eyes betrayed the turmoil going on inside, they darted around the courtroom and then settled on one of the jurors. "There's no truth to any of that," she said. "I loved my daughter."

I changed course. "Are you employed, Mrs. O'Malley?"

"No."

"It is my understanding that you were married to a John O'Malley, correct?"

"Yes."

"And your relationship started while you were in his employ as a real estate salesperson?"

"He owned the firm when I first started working for him, yes."

"And he died in a boating accident several years ago, correct?"

"Yes."

"And you inherited his estate?"

"Yes, I did. But what does that got to do with any of this?"

"It's fine, Mrs. O'Malley," said Judge Savano. "It'll work better if you just answer the questions."

"Well it hardly seems relevant to me if I inherited my husband's estate. Who does she think would inherit it?"

Judge Savano smiled. "I understand, Mrs. O'Malley. Go ahead, counsel."

"And according to the probate records, that was in the area of six million dollars, correct?"

"Somewhere in there."

"So you really don't have to work if you don't want to, do you?"

"Money has its privileges."

Becker jumped to his feet again. "Your Honor, I've been patiently sitting here listening to this diatribe. I have to agree with Mrs. O'Malley, what relevance does this have to our case?"

"Your Honor, if it pleases the Court," I said, "I intend to establish its relevance. It will all become clear if the Court permits."

"Go ahead," he said.

"You're also one of the directors for the Greater Boston Area Counsel for the Performing Arts, are you not?"

"I am."

"And you're also a member of the Boston Historical Society, correct?"

"Yes."

"And you're also involved in a number of charitable organizations and have been very generous with your donations to numerous organizations."

"I believe those that can—should, yes."

"And so when your daughter told you that she was going to tell Doctor Morgan the details of all of the years she suffered sexual abuse at your hands, you knew that it would be made public and the lifestyle you had become accustomed to would be jeopardized. Isn't that correct?"

"That's a total fabrication," she said.

"Your daughter told you that if she had any hope of having a normal life, she was going to have to tell Dr. Morgan that at puberty her mother threatened to cut off her breasts, remove her vagina, because she shouldn't have those. Isn't that what you feared Cheryl would do?"

"No way, it was her dad. He was the sicko who said that."

For the first time, in the word *sicko*, I thought I detected the slightest hint of a Boston accent.

"So you pleaded with her over the phone to not do that, to not disclose anything. You probably told her you would make it right with her; you just needed a little time. Isn't that true?"

"No, it isn't."

"So you told her that you would come to Minnesota, that you wanted to meet with her in person, that the two of you could work this out without her having to tell anybody."

"That's a figment of your imagination, young lady," she said.

"So you made arrangements to fly to Minnesota on Sunday evening, the night before she was murdered, and she was to pick you up at the Minneapolis International Airport?"

"Not true," she said.

"Are you familiar with Rogers, Minnesota?"

"Of course."

"That's near the Twin Cities, correct?"

"You know it is."

"And on Sunday evening, if your daughter was driving from her apartment to Minneapolis-St. Paul International Airport, she would pass through Rogers, correct?"

"If she took the same route we took yesterday."

"So you flew from Logan International to Minneapolis-St. Paul yesterday?"

"Yes, we did."

"And you drove on the interstate from the airport to the city here?"

"We rented a car, yes."

"So, isn't it true, Mrs. O'Malley, on Sunday evening, July 13th, 1986, Cheryl picked you up from the airport after you flew from Logan International in Boston?"

"I was never here."

"Are you aware that your daughter's charge card record indicates that she purchased gas at the Rogers' Amoco Sunday evening at 5:45 p.m.?"

"How would I know that?" she replied.

"Because she was on her way to pick you up."

"No, she wasn't."

"So she met you at the airport, the two of you drove to St. Cloud, and you spent the night at her apartment. Isn't that correct?"

"No."

"And in the course of the night, you pleaded with her . . . to what, forgive you?"

"There was nothing I had to ask her forgiveness for."

Again, a slight Boston accent stretched out the "for".

"That was the first night you had seen her in how many years?"

She hesitated for a moment like she was really trying to remember and then appeared to catch herself and said, "I told you, I wasn't here."

"Your daughter told you about her relationship with Dr. Morgan, that they loved each other."

"Why do you keep bringing that up?" she said. "I didn't know about any of that garbage until . . ." She stopped.

"Until when?" I asked.

She stared at me; I could tell her mind was racing, trying to remember what she might have said. "I told you," she replied, "after he murdered her. That's when I found out about how sick he was."

"Did you overhear her conversation that Monday morning when she was called by the prosecutor here, Randy Becker, to see if she wanted to testify at the sentencing of the man she claimed raped her?"

"I wasn't there, so how could I have overheard it?"

"Didn't she tell you after that telephone call from the prosecutor that she was going to tell the truth, that she couldn't carry through with sending an innocent man to prison, that she was going to have to tell the authorities that she made it all up to get even with you?"

"I wasn't there."

"How did you get her on the bed?"

She ignored the question.

"Did you ask her to just lie down with you for a few moments so that you could talk? Is that how you enticed her into the bedroom?"

She turned to Savano. "Judge, do I have to put up with this?"

307

"You have to answer the question, ma'am."

"I wasn't there."

"And as she was lying on her bed, talking to you, believing the two of you had worked everything out, you reached over with a knife you had brought along . . . you slit her throat so deeply that she died right there, without moving."

"You're sick," she said.

"How did you keep from being covered with her blood? Or did you have to take a shower."

"I wasn't there."

"And then in a real fit of anger, you started stabbing the body, wondering why she ever made you do this. Why wouldn't she just listen to you? Everything would be fine if she just kept her mouth shut. Isn't that what happened?"

During the course of my cross-examination, her arms had slowly come to rest across her stomach and her body seemed to shrink. Now her arms unfolded, her hands were placed on the front of the witness box and she clasped her fingers and in words as cold as ice, she said, "You have a tremendous imagination. Of course, that's what you get paid for, isn't it?"

"And then when the rage subsided, you looked at what you had done, your little girl lying in that pool of blood and you wondered how it ever got to that point. Isn't that true?"

"No."

"Then to cast suspicion on your ex-husband, Benjamin Moore—because Cheryl had, at your insistence, told therapists that her dad was the abuser, the one who threatened to mutilate her body—you took the same knife that you used to slit her throat and removed her breasts and jammed the knife into her vaginal area."

"You know, you're really sick."

"Isn't that what happened?"

She tightened her lips again and turned her head.

"When you left Boston, you knew that her death may be the outcome and you knew that you could not leave any trail. Isn't that correct?"

"That doesn't deserve an answer," she replied.

"So you were at her apartment, you had to get back to the airport, back to

Boston without anybody seeing you, without leaving any tracks, any record. So you disguised yourself. You even brought along a black wig just in case you'd need it. Isn't that right?"

"I'd have to be pretty clever."

"You've been here several times since the death of your daughter, isn't that correct?"

"I've made the trip twice.

"To meet with attorneys, correct?"

"Yes."

"And on those occasions, how did you get from the airport to St. Cloud?"

It was obvious she knew where I was going. It hadn't even occurred to me until that very moment that she may have been familiar with the service provided by Executive Express because she had used it on one of those two trips. If that's how she did get back to the airport, she couldn't admit it now.

"We rented a car," she said.

"Who are 'we'?"

"Me and my companion."

"You're referring to Suzanne Karcher?" I asked.

"Yes."

"So you found yourself in your daughter's bedroom. She was dead; you had murdered her. You had to get back without being seen, without leaving a record. So you put on a black wig and you walked from her apartment to the Holiday Inn where you signed up with Executive Express for a ride back to the airport, isn't that correct?"

"No, it isn't."

"Do you remember the gentleman who was driving that day?"

"How could I? I wasn't there."

"He remembers you. He remembers those eyes."

"He must have been drunk, I wasn't there."

"How about the two gentlemen passengers? If they can identify you, were they drunk too?"

"They'd have to be."

"So you bought a ticket to the airport under the name of Judy Severson and you flirted with these gentlemen in your best Boston accent the hour and a half it took to get to the airport."

"I don't have a Boston accent."

I paused to give the jury time to consider her last answer. I didn't know if I was hearing things, if it was just me, but that Boston accent was starting to come out in some of her answers.

I paged through my notes as if I was looking for something but I knew exactly what my next question was going to be. As casually as I could, I asked, "By the way, Mrs. O'Malley, you still have your two Persian cats, right?"

She gave me a surprised look, and then said, "What could they possibly have to do with anything?"

"I'm just asking. Muffy and Fluffy, right? Are they still with you? Who's taking care of them?"

"I have somebody who checks my home."

I said, "Persians. Aren't they ones with the long white hair?"

"Of course," she replied.

"What name did you use to book your airline tickets from Boston to Minnesota when you flew here on July thirteenth to confront your daughter?"

"I didn't use any name because I never came here."

"Shortly after Dr. Morgan was indicted, you came to Minnesota to talk to an attorney about a civil suit against him, isn't that correct?"

"Somebody recommended I do that, yes."

"Somebody here in Minnesota?"

"No, somebody in Boston."

"Who?" I asked.

"It's really not important," she replied.

"But on that recommendation, you came to Minnesota and talked to Attorney Ron Crane of this town, correct?"

"Yes, I did."

"And then you had his office sue Dr. Morgan for damages for the wrongful death of your daughter, correct?"

"Yes, I did."

"And in the process of that civil lawsuit, Mr. Crane's office obtained copies of all of your daughter's medical records from her years of therapy, including the period that she met with Dr. Morgan, and you had a chance to review those documents, correct?"

"I looked at them."

"Well, weren't you anxious to make sure that she had never told any of her therapists that you were actually the one who sexually abused her?"

"That's nonsense," she snapped.

Based on her voice, I thought this was the right moment.

"I'm sorry, Mrs. O'Malley, this has gone on longer than I expected. Would you like a drink of water?"

She gave me a wary look as if she was wondering why I had suddenly become solicitous as to her condition.

"Yes, I would," she said.

The bailiff immediately made his way to the water pitcher. I interrupted him. "That's fine," I said. "I'll do it."

I poured water into the glass sitting on the counsel table and proceeded to take it to the witness stand. I handed it to her; she took a long drink and then set it on the ledge of the witness stand.

She said, "Thank you."

I responded, "You're welcome," as I walked back to the counsel table.

"Mrs. O'Malley, Mr. Crane has an assistant, a Kay Schmidt, who provided you with a copy of your daughter's medical records. Isn't that correct?"

Again, the wary eyes, she was wondering where I had gotten all this information. "Yes, she did," she replied.

"You testified that you had been to St. Cloud twice for the purpose of discussing the civil lawsuit against Dr. Morgan, the first time was the end of July, to hire the Crane law firm to sue the doctor, isn't that correct?"

"Yes, it is."

"And the second time was during the week of August 25th. And as part of that trip, you were provided a copy of your daughter's medical records, correct?"

"I believe that's right."

"And those records revealed, as you had told your daughter to do, that she blamed all of the sexual abuse, including the threats of mutilation to her body, on her father? Isn't that correct?"

"It's correct that that's what the reports say but it is not correct that I told her to say such things. She said that because it was the truth."

"It must have been quite a relief when you found out that your daughter never told the truth."

"She was telling the truth."

"After reviewing your daughter's medical records, Mrs. O'Malley, why did you send a copy to me?"

"What? What are you saying? I never sent you a copy."

"Let me suggest, Mrs. O'Malley, that you wanted me to be able to use them in the doctor's defense. You wanted the authorities to believe that your ex-husband, Cheryl's father, murdered her, didn't you?"

"That's ridiculous."

"The only reason you sued Dr. Morgan was to divert any attention from yourself. Isn't that true?"

"I sued him because he killed my daughter."

"The money never had anything to do with it, did it? You have plenty of money. You wanted to pin Cheryl's murder on your ex-husband because he's the only other person alive who knows the truth."

"As I said," she replied, "you've got a wild imagination."

I walked to the edge of the counsel table and opened a briefcase. Inside was the original envelope that had contained all of Cheryl's medical records as well as the outside brown manila wrapping on which my address was written in black ink. I had recovered both of the items from Detective Kropp.

"May I approach, Your Honor?"

"You may," the judge replied.

As I neared the witness box, the envelope glanced the side of the water glass. "I'm sorry," I said, "I'll remove that." I picked up the water glass, my fingers as near to the bottom as possible, and placed it back on my counsel table. The two wrappers I left on the ledge of the witness box.

"Have you ever seen this envelope before?" I asked.

I didn't expect her to say she had, there was nothing distinct about the envelope. It was an 8 ½ x 11 manila envelope of which there's probably millions changing hands each day. I reached out to hand her the envelope. "Of course it wouldn't be stained like that. That's left over from when it was tested for fingerprints," I added.

She reached to take the envelope but as soon as I mentioned fingerprints, she withdrew her hand.

"It just looks like a plain envelope to me," she said. "How should I recognize it?"

"I guess you're right," I said. "How about the wrapper? Mrs. O'Malley, is that your printing?" I handed it to her but she refused to take it.

"I've never seen that before."

"You'll note the postdate, it's August 25th, 1986. I believe that's the week you were in St. Cloud to talk to Mr. Crane, your attorney, isn't it?"

"I told you, I've never seen that!"

"Thank you," I said, and took them both with me to the counsel table.

As I was about to ask my next question, Judge Savano interrupted. "This may be a good time to take our morning recess."

"Fine, Your Honor."

I was hoping he would take a recess soon anyway. I had to locate Brownie.

Mrs. O'Malley left the witness box quickly, rushed past the counsel tables to meet her companion in the back of the courtroom and immediately exited the back door.

As she shot by, I turned to Noah. "Is it my imagination or is that Boston slur starting to show?"

"It's not your imagination," he said, "it's becoming quite obvious."

"It's a sign of tension," said Dr. Morgan. "When her mind has to work fast to answer a question, her conscious effort is divided between answering the question and trying to maintain her Minnesota speech. Her mind can't do both at the same time, so her usual speech pattern slips in."

"In plain English," said Noah, "you got her nervous."

"Well, I'm only getting to the good part," I said. "What'll you think Savano's going to do?"

"I think he'll just let you go at this point," Noah replied.

I turned toward the back of the courtroom. I saw Brownie enter through the back door. Noah and I quickly joined him.

As we neared Brownie, he said, "He's here, Jackie. And he's here on his own volition."

"Where is he?" I asked, concerned that Mrs. O'Malley would have seen him.

"I have them both in a conference room for safekeeping," he said.

"Both?" asked Noah.

"Yeah, I had him bring the van driver just in case," I said.

Brownie led us to a conference room on the far side of the hall. As we walked in, Benjamin Moore and the van driver were sitting on opposite sides of the table.

I went to Mr. Moore first. "I really appreciate you coming," I said.

"Well, like I told Brownie, I'm not gonna testify, you're not gonna get me on that stand."

"I understand that," I said. "You don't have to. You just have to be here. Cheryl would have appreciated it."

Mr. Moore averted his eyes. I then reached across the table to shake the hand of the van driver. He stood. The smile he already had expanded as his eyes did a once over of my body, starting with my chest. The term "horny old fart" seemed appropriate. I guessed him to be in his early seventies with a full head of silver hair cut short and combed straight up. He had a pleasant face with a wide smile and bright white teeth, which I assumed weren't really his.

His eyes halted at my chest and that's where they were when I retracted my hand from his and said, "Thanks for being here."

"No problem," he said. "I'm not sure if I can be of any help. Like I was telling your guy there, your P.I., the only thing I really noticed was her eyes."

I couldn't pass it up. "Oh, I think you probably noticed more than you think."

He gave me a quizzical look. "All we're going to do, Mr. Bettendorf, is have you sit in the front row right behind our counsel table so that Mrs. O'Malley will see you. I don't believe, at this point, you will have to testify. Mr. Moore," I said, turning to him, "I've already made arrangements with the bailiff at the back door of the courtroom that when Brownie wants to bring you in, he can. Because court will be in session and all the chairs are full, you're probably going to have to stand in the back, which is better for us. That's exactly what we want you to do . . . and I promise, I'm not going to call you as a witness."

Noah and I walked back into the courtroom. Chris was at our counsel table. Becker was at his. Becker had taken to simply not paying any attention to us at all. He either acted like he was going through his trial notebooks or looked away, past the jury box, out the courtroom window.

I had my hands on the counsel table; Noah sat to my left. He reached out his right hand and covered mine, squeezed it a little bit and whispered, "You're doing great."

Brownie had been waiting for Mrs. O'Malley to enter the courtroom and take the stand. Once she was seated, Brownie came in the back door of the courtroom with the van driver, brought him up the aisle, and with some fanfare, offered him a chair right behind my counsel table. I watched Carol O'Malley's face. When the van driver was in the back of the courtroom, it didn't seem to register with her, but as he made his way up the aisle to stand behind my table, her eyes widened. I could see the heat crossing her face and she quickly looked away, out the same window that Becker liked to use.

I think at that point it dawned on her that she had no allies in that courtroom. There were no eyes she could look to for sympathy. Her companion was in the very back of the courtroom not visible from where she sat. Becker had appeared to have given up on helping her. So in her desperation, the only thing she could do was avert her eyes. She never turned her head back even when Judge Savano came in and she rose to the bailiff's command. Her eyes remained glued to the glare of a bright November day coming through the courtroom window.

"You can proceed, counsel," Judge Savano said.

"Thank you, Your Honor. Mrs. O'Malley," I asked, "you remember talking to Detective Kropp?"

The question seemed innocuous and she slowly turned her head to look at me. "Certainly."

"And Detective Kropp has testified in this matter how the forensic unit searched Cheryl's room and he told this jury about a theory of transfer and exchange. Basically, the theory is very simple: at every crime scene, particularly a homicide like this one, there's a possibility that the perpetrator's going to transfer something from his or her body to the crime scene or take something from the crime scene along with him or her."

"Is that a question?" She snapped.

"I'm getting there. The question, Mrs. O'Malley, is this: If you were not in your daughter's apartment the day of her murder, then there should be absolutely no evidence of your presence there. Doesn't that sound fair?"

"I have no idea what you're talking about."

"If you weren't there, there shouldn't be any evidence of you being there."

"Okay," she said.

"So you agree with that?" I replied.

She didn't answer and I didn't need an answer.

"Is your hair color now your natural color?"

"What kind of question is that?"

"Just answer the question, Mrs. O'Malley," the judge said.

"Yes, it is."

"So you haven't had it dyed or changed colors in the last year or so?" I said.

"Certainly not."

I reached into the briefcase and took out the plastic bag with the strands of hair I had collected.

"May I approach, Your Honor?"

"You may."

"Mrs. O'Malley, I want you to look at this," and I handed her the plastic bag.

"Mrs. O'Malley, what does that appear to be?"

"Hair."

"And you would agree that that hair is the same color, the same shade and the same length as yours?"

"It could be anybody's."

"You're right," I said, "but would you agree from just looking at it that it could be yours?"

"I suppose."

"Your Honor, I'd like to have this marked Exhibit Twenty."

Becker was on his feet. "Your Honor, I'm going to object to this. There's no foundation."

316

I turned. "Your Honor, I didn't indicate I was going to ask that it be admitted at this point, I just want it identified for purposes of further examination of this witness."

"It'll be so marked."

I then went back to my counsel table and removed the other bag from the briefcase. "I would like to have this marked as Exhibit Twenty-One."

The judge took it, looked at it and handed it to the clerk. She put her little tag on it.

"Now, Mrs. O'Malley, I want to show you what's been marked Exhibit Twenty-one and ask you what that appears to be."

"Is this some kind of game or something?"

"No, it's very serious, Mrs. O'Malley. What does that appear to be?"

"It's hair. Anybody can see its hair."

"Now I'm going to place Exhibits Twenty and Twenty-One side-by-side, and ask you if you see any difference."

She glanced at them quickly. "I can't tell."

"Well, Mrs. O'Malley, to the human eye, don't they appear to be identical?" She looked again. "I guess so."

"Mrs. O'Malley, do you recall meeting me in the ladies room this morning?" She gave me that quizzical look again. "We talked for a minute, yes."

"And you were combing your hair and putting on lipstick, correct?"

"Okay," she said.

"Do you remember cleaning off your comb and disposing of the loose hair in the trash receptacle?"

She didn't respond. She knew exactly what was happening.

"Mrs. O'Malley, the evidence will be that Exhibit Twenty-One is hair, hair that belongs to you, which I recovered from the waste can in the ladies' bathroom this morning."

"So?" she asked defiantly. "What does that prove?"

"By itself, nothing," I said. "But if the evidence were to be, Mrs. O'Malley, that Exhibit Twenty is hair recovered from the scene of your daughter's murder, hair found in the apartment by the forensic unit, and it matches perfectly with the hair in Exhibit Twenty-One, your hair, how would you explain that could happen?"

Again, no answer.

"There are experts, Mrs. O'Malley, who can microscopically examine hair and come into court and testify as to their similar characteristics. If we call in an expert who testifies that these two exhibits are microscopically similar, and from the same source, how would you explain that?"

"They must be Cheryl's."

"You know better than that, Mrs. O'Malley. Her hair was an entirely different color."

"They can't be mine because I wasn't there."

"Do your cats shed hair, Mrs. O'Malley?"

"All cats shed."

"Well, Persians have a tendency to leave hair wherever they go, isn't that right?"

"No more so than other cats."

"Well, then you'd agree that cats shed hair?"

"I already agreed to that."

"Again, Detective Kropp testified that the forensic unit vacuumed the carpet in your daughter's apartment and in addition to recovering human hair, they recovered hair that was identified as coming from a cat. Your daughter didn't own a cat, did she?"

"I don't know."

"Well, trust me, Mrs. O'Malley, the apartment manager told Detective Kropp that she didn't have a cat."

"So?" she replied.

I walked to the clerk's desk and removed the evidence bag including the cat hair. Without getting close to her, I said, "Mrs. O'Malley, I'm not an expert in cat hair identification, but the hair in here sure looks to me like it belongs to a white Persian cat. Would you agree?" And I held it up from a distance.

She did not ask to see the bag nor did she offer an answer.

"Do you know a Detective Eric O'Bannon?" I asked.

She gave me a cautious look.

"You remember Detective Eric O'Bannon?" I asked. "He investigated the

318

death of your husband in Boston Harbor, isn't that correct?"

"The accidental death of my husband."

"So you do remember him?"

"Of course."

"If Detective O'Bannon is executing a search warrant at this very moment at your home on the ocean front, the purpose of which is to remove hair from your two white Persian Cats, is it your testimony that under microscopic examination, the hair obtained from your cats will not be microscopically identical to the hair in this evidence bag, Exhibit Nineteen, found at your daughter's apartment?"

"How can he search my house when I'm not there? If he hurts those cats . . ."

"That wasn't my question, Mrs. O'Malley."

"He can't be digging around my house without me there."

"Mrs. O'Malley, listen. What if microscopic examination proves the hair to be similar? Can you explain how cat hair, white Persian cat hair, could have been found in your daughter's apartment?"

She turned her head to the side and stared out the window. Now the sun that streamed through the window to cast a bright hue to the room seemed to add years to her face.

"Mrs. O'Malley," I said, as quietly as I could and still be heard.

She ignored me.

"Mrs. O'Malley?"

She turned toward me, slowly, the sparkle of her eyes was gone, the blue was as bright as ever but the whites had turned sanguine, like all the little blood vessels had surfaced. Her gaze suddenly focused beyond me to the back of the courtroom, I assumed she was looking for her companion.

"Mrs. O'Malley," I said, "Detective Kropp also provided evidence regarding fingerprints that were found at your daughter's apartment. Are you familiar with fingerprint identification?"

"How would I be familiar with that?"

"Well, I'm sure over the years, Mrs. O'Malley, you've read books, watched television, or seen movies in which the criminal was caught because he, or *she*, left fingerprints at the crime scene. I'm sure you're familiar with that, are you not?"

"I don't read or watch that kind of garbage."

"Then do you mind if I tell you what Detective Kropp told this jury?"

"Do I have a choice?"

"Detective Kropp told this jury that they were able to lift and document nine separate sets of fingerprints. He also testified that five of those have been identified as prints from either your daughter or Dr. Morgan. Four prints, though, they have not been able to identify. Have you ever been fingerprinted, Mrs. O'Malley?"

"Do I look like a criminal to you? Only criminals get fingerprinted."

"So your answer is you've never been fingerprinted."

"I've never done anything to require it."

"Did you take any special precautions when you were at your daughter's apartment to not leave prints?"

"Do I have to go over this again?" she replied. "I've never been to Cheryl's apartment."

"So you're telling us your prints shouldn't be there?"

"Of course not."

"So, if one or more of those unidentified prints belong to you, how would you explain that?"

"I don't have to explain anything to you."

"Mrs. O'Malley," I said. "See this glass sitting on the conference table here?"

I could see in her eyes, everybody in the courtroom could see in her eyes, that she knew she had been had.

"Mrs. O'Malley, that's the water glass you used this morning. We're going to turn this glass over to Detective Kropp so that he can have his expert remove your fingerprints from it and compare them to the four prints, the four unidentified prints found in your daughter's apartment. We're going to find that one or more of those prints belong to you, aren't we?"

She didn't answer. She looked away again.

"Then, just to verify further everything I said is true, Detective Kropp will compare the fingerprints he took from the manila envelope and wrapper from the documents you sent to me, the documents meant to implicate your ex-husband. We'll find that those are your prints as well, won't we?"

By now she was starting to crouch over, her arms across her stomach, her shoulders stooped forward. Her body started to twist in the chair very slowly with her eyes still fixed on the window.

"Mrs. O'Malley, you were here in town the day your daughter was murdered. This gentleman here, Mr. Bettendorf, he's ready to testify that even though you wore a dark wig, he could never forget your face. He'll testify that he gave you a ride from the Holiday Inn in town to the airport within hours after your daughter was murdered. You murdered her, didn't you?"

She seemed to shrink even more. Her bottom lip quivered as she fought back tears.

Just then the back door to the courtroom opened and Brownie walked in with Benjamin Moore. I turned to look. Mr. Moore stood towering above the seated spectators.

"And your ex-husband is here, Mrs. O'Malley, Benjamin Moore, Cheryl's father, he's prepared to testify that Cheryl came to see him, to confide in him, to tell him how you sexually molested her as a child. That's why you murdered her, isn't it? You could never let that get out."

With her body still turned to the side, everything curled together, almost like a fetal position, her head turned slowly toward me, her eyes moved past me, past the spectators to Benjamin Moore, glaring at her. Suddenly she screamed: "You bastard! You dirty rotten bastard! You're the one I should've killed. You couldn't stand it that I might have a little happiness in this world. You put her up to it. It never came up between us until she talked to you. I hope you're happy, you bastard! You're the one responsible for her death!"

"Maggie, you should've been there. It loses too much in the telling, but in more than forty years of being in court, I've never seen anything like it. That woman, Carol O'Malley, she took the witness stand looking like a bright blooming flower . . . like a big blue iris. When she finally stopped sobbing and the judge asked the bailiff to lead her out of the courtroom, she had wilted to nothing . . . she couldn't even lift her head. She was led out like a little old lady, bowed over, her tears mixing with her make-up and running down her cheeks. She tried to hide her face. I looked at Jackie. I didn't see any pride on her face for what she had just accomplished, only empathy. It appeared she was on the verge of tears, too."

It was early evening; Maggie and I were sitting at the dinner table and I had just related the whole story to her. It did lose something in the telling. As Jackie cornered Carol O'Malley, the courtroom was dead air, no movement at all; then, as Carol O'Malley screamed at Ben, the scene turned to pandemonium, everyone there realizing what had just happened. The jurors were transfixed on the spectacle, wide-eyed, stunned. The press began elbowing each other to be the first one out. Judge Savano had motioned to the deputy to come forward and stand by the witness stand while Mrs. O'Malley tried to gain some composure. Randy Becker sat stoically at his counsel table staring at Carol O'Malley. I suspect he was already analyzing his case against her. I would have thought that Chris, once he realized he was a free man, would have been bubbling over with joy, but the words he'd uttered months before were prophetic: He had created a prison for himself, whether he was convicted or not. He could take little solace from a ruined life. Moreover, as a professional, I suspect he was also analyzing Carol O'Malley, attempting to decipher the psychological turmoil that had inexorably led to her collapse on the witness stand.

As the bailiff led Carol O'Malley out of the side door of the courtroom, Judge

Savano first glanced at the jury and then at Randy Becker. "Mr. Becker, do you have any motions?" he asked.

Without standing, and in a very flippant voice, Becker said, "Yeah, I move that the charges against the defendant be dismissed."

"So ordered," replied the judge. "Doctor, you're free to leave." Then he turned to the jury. "Ladies and gentlemen of the jury, I'm not sure what to say. We do thank you for your services and I'm sure you're just as happy not having to make a decision in this matter. I suspect this is something you'll talk about for years to come. I don't believe you'll be called back, so you're all excused. Have a good afternoon and thank you."

I watched the jurors as they filed out. I think I did see a look of relief on some of the faces. In the hall, before I left the courthouse, one of the jurors approached me. A professional man in his fifties, an accountant I believe. His demeanor in the course of the *voir dire* and trial had always remained rather inscrutable. Now, he introduced himself, we shook hands and he smiled. "I'm glad it ended up the way it did," he said. "I'm not sure how I would've voted. I think we would've been out for quite a while. There was just something about Dr. Morgan, in his testimony, the way he appeared, that gave me some trouble with the State's case. That young lady did a terrific job."

I thanked him for his comments and told him I would relay his compliment to Jackie. I looked for Brownie and Ben Moore; they were nowhere to be found. Jackie was on the far side of the hall where the press and the television reporters had her pinned in the corner, microphones shoved in her face while Johnny Connors stood just outside the circle wearing a big smile. What a change from the first day we walked into the courthouse, when she was completely ignored. Today, it appeared nobody wanted to talk to me—which was fine.

On the other side of the hall stood Randy Becker. He had already given his two-cents worth to the press. It was going to be interesting to see what excuses he gave. Now he was being confronted by Mrs. O'Malley's companion, who was waving her hands in his face, on the verge of screaming, and he was giving her a "what do you want me to do about it" look.

"What do you think is going to happen to that woman?" Maggie asked.

"With her money? She's going to hire some hotshot defense attorney. He'll hire himself some big-named psychiatrist and between them they'll come up with some psychological deficit she was operating under—plead her not guilty by reason of mental illness."

"I hope she doesn't get off claiming mental illness," Maggie replied.

"I'm not saying they'll succeed. I'm just saying one has to look for possible defenses. Truth is, if she hadn't broken down on the stand, they wouldn't have a thing."

"What about all that evidence you were telling me about? The fingerprints? The hair samples?"

"Maggie, you missed the point. Jackie made most of that up. Maybe some of it'll prove to be true. There were unidentified fingerprints found in Cheryl's room. As far as anything on those envelopes, there wasn't a print they could lift."

"The cat hair?" she asked.

"There was cat hair all right but not from a Persian."

"Her own hair?" Maggie asked.

"Taken right out of the garbage can."

"So you mean all she had to do was keep saying 'no,' keep denying everything, and you guys didn't have a case?"

"Not today we didn't. Maggie, that's what makes it even more astonishing. All she had to do was keep her mouth shut. Chris has his own theory and I think it's probably as accurate as any. She was guilty, and you have to wonder how many times she must've recalled the picture of what she had done to her daughter, and as she left, taking a last look at that bedroom, the body spread eagled, mutilated . . ."

Maggie interjected, "She has to be mentally ill to do that."

"Kind of fickle, aren't you?" I replied. "Chris believes just the guilt of it had to weigh on her; then, when she's in that witness box, and it appears that even though in her own mind she had planned it so well, had covered everything, she learns she *had* made mistakes. It just had to be overwhelming, the guilt, the fact that she had been found out. She might've even been thinking what her Boston friends would be saying about her. And as the realization set in, as Jackie started to wound her with each question, she started to retreat like an animal cowering in the corner, looking for some safe haven. Maggie, you could see it, it was like the incredible shrinking woman: she seemed to be disappearing before our eyes. I've never seen anything like it."

"The guilt she had to live with would probably do that," said Maggie.

The room went quiet as we both pondered the possibilities. I had read a number of articles on body language and how the body involuntarily sends out signals of what the mind is contemplating. This had been as vivid an example as I could ever imagine.

"I suppose Jackie was really excited," Maggie said. "What'd she have to say?"

"We talked for a while at the office. She was really happy for Chris. I know she was relieved. She had put a lot of pressure on herself. Once she believed Chris was innocent, she really struggled with how she could prove it."

We were quiet again as I thought back to my last conversation with Jackie, a long conversation, which for some unknown reason I didn't feel comfortable relating to Maggie. I was standing in the front of the office, at Linda's desk, telling her what had just happened when Jackie returned from the courthouse. After her interview by the reporters, she had disappeared and I had no idea where she was. I assumed she had returned to the office but she wasn't there. I could tell immediately that she had been crying. She nodded at Linda when she said congratulations and went straight to her office. I gave Linda a puzzled look, shrugged my shoulders, and followed Jackie down the hall. She immediately went to her desk, plopped down on the chair, brought her hands to her face and sobbed, her whole body shaking.

This was the first time in many years that I was completely at a loss for words. I thought I knew what she was going through, the realization of what had just happened and the resulting collapse of your entire system. I wanted to say something supportive, clever. Instead, I sat there mute, afraid to impinge on her feelings. After several minutes, the sobbing stopped. She removed her right hand first and reached for a Kleenex. She dabbed the tears running down her cheeks, then looked at me with a soft smile. "I must look terrible."

"To the contrary," I replied.

"I was doing fine," she said, "until I got by myself. I left the reporters and went to the ladies room. It was empty. I looked into the mirror; my face was bright red, my eyes bloodshot. For a moment, I wondered who that strange looking woman was. Then it was like everything came crashing down on me. I closed my eyes for a moment to a flood of memories: Cheryl at Clint's trial, pictures of her body lying on the bed, pictures during the autopsy. Trying to picture what happened that morning, how a mother could have done that. I had this image of Mrs. O'Malley curling up in the witness chair and then being led out, babbling to herself. None of it made any sense, Noah, and I just started bawling. I locked myself in one of the stalls; luckily nobody came in. When I finally composed myself, the courthouse was pretty much empty. I'm not sure I'm cut out for this stuff, Noah."

"That's not true," I said. "You were under a lot of stress. It had to be a tremendous relief to get it over with. And don't take the fact that you're sitting here crying as some sort of weakness, I'd be very surprised if you weren't."

"It's more than that, Noah, it's personal. All of my life, from my very first memories, I wondered about my mother, what she was like. My aunt Ruby tried to take her place but it was never the same. Everybody told me that my mother was just such a lovely, caring woman. They say I look a lot like her. Ruby told me that my dad was totally devoted to my mother and it took him years to recover from her death. Ruby thinks he blames me but she also thinks that he can't look at me without thinking of her and it's just too painful for him."

She turned from my gaze and hesitated for a moment, small teardrops slowly formed, rolled down her right cheek and stopped in the middle where she caught them with the sleeve of her blouse. She sniffled as she looked back at me.

"That's awful selfish of him, don't you think, Noah?"

She didn't wait for my response.

"You would think that I would mean even more to him. I don't understand that. And I can't help comparing my life to Cheryl's. She had a mother. How does a person become that perverse, Noah? What's in the human nature that allows someone to prey on their own young? See, Noah, it isn't just a case of defending Dr. Morgan, these thoughts now haunt me, and I just wonder, even with time, whether I can heal."

"Jackie," I said, "you're raising questions that people have spent their lives trying to answer. I've felt the same frustration and I can't give you an answer. What

I can tell you is, it would be a sin for you to give up and walk away. The system needs people like you, somebody who's willing to commit heart and soul."

She laid her arms across the desk and buried her head in her arms. The fluorescent lights gave her hair an ebony sheen. "I don't know if I can take the ugliness," she mumbled without raising her head.

I didn't argue with her. I wasn't even sure what I could say to console her. Her comment was a familiar lament I had heard from many criminal defense attorneys. Very few used it as an excuse to get out of the business, though. I considered it one of the ironies I had observed over the course of my career: part of the mystique of being a criminal defense attorney was dealing with evil on a daily basis, resulting in a peculiar kind of high for a peculiar kind of person, but it never quite got so ugly that you would say, "Enough—I want out."

I had no doubt that Jackie would recover, just like I had no doubt that she would remain a criminal defense attorney. She needed time to think, to heal, then she'd be back. Anyone else looking at her now would have found that hard to believe. She raised her head slowly from the desk. She looked forlorn. Then she smiled at me and I smiled back. It was one of those moments that didn't require any words; it was all in the eyes.

Throughout the time I was in her office I could hear the phone ring and Linda making excuses about why Jackie couldn't come to the phone. It rang again and a moment later she was on the intercom.

"Mr. Conners on the phone," she said.

Jackie picked it up. "What happened to you?" she asked.

"Well you could have waited around . . . I understand," she said. "Sure I will. About what time? I'll be ready." She hung up.

She looked at me. "Johnny," she said. "He said he didn't want to interfere with my moment of notoriety. We're going out tonight to . . ." and she hesitated. "I almost said to celebrate, but there's nothing to celebrate, is there? Noah, there are no winners in this."

She looked at me for an affirmation. "You're right," I replied. "There aren't. But that doesn't mean you shouldn't be proud of what you did."

My mind was wandering when I heard Maggie.

"Noah!" she said.

My eyes slowly settled on her. "I'm sorry," I said. "I was just thinking of my discussion with Jackie. "Where was I?"

"I haven't the slightest."

A moment passed as I thought. "Anyway, as the courthouse started to clear out, I got a chance to talk to Kropp. He was in a pretty good mood. Detectives like it when their hunches prove right. I asked him if he persuaded Judge Savano to let us call Carol O'Malley as a witness. He played dumb. I didn't expect anything different, but I could tell from the smirk on his face that he knew that I knew he was the culprit."

"You really think he did that, huh?" she asked.

"No question about it. It's no secret; judges always talk to people about your case behind your back—particularly criminal cases. There's always the information that gets in the file and then what might have really happened. Human curiosity being what it is, if you're the judge and at some point you might have to make a decision, why wouldn't you wanna know what the real facts are? Especially if you have a cop like Bob. I mean—there isn't a person who would question his veracity. So if he told Savano to give us a chance . . . well, I'm just sure that's the way it happened."

"Did Chris say what he was going to do?" Maggie asked.

"He said he was going to try and make it up to Elizabeth but I don't think that's going to happen. Do you?"

"Not from what she's told me. She has a hard time being in the same room with him."

"I think he knows that," I replied. "He's not going to be able to practice. He said he might just take some time off, travel, and try to write. Maybe he'll really go out to California, who knows. I'm actually a little surprised at his behavior. I expected him to be a little tougher. He became, I don't know, very fatalistic about the whole thing. Whatever happens—happens. I suppose that's normal, too, when you see your whole life crashing down around you. But I would've expected a little bit more gumption, I guess, from a psychologist. They're always trying to tell other people how to handle a crisis and then he couldn't even handle his own."

"Well, it was a little bit more than a crisis, Noah. It was more like a catastrophe."

DANIEL ELLER

"Even then," I replied, "that's what he's paid for."

"Have you talked to Brownie?"

"Yeah. I called him from the office. He said when Carol hollered at Mr. Moore across the courtroom, the guy's knees actually buckled. He wanted to get out of there, quick. Poor Ben never really believed his ex did it. Brownie said it was one hell of a shock. He said they hit the Sportsmen's and had a couple stiff ones. He said Ben plans on calling Jackie when this quiets down."

The room went silent. I don't know what Maggie was thinking. I was wondering what we were going to do for friends. In the last ten years or so, Chris and Elizabeth were some of the only social contacts we'd had. Nothing exciting, dinner and a few drinks, maybe a movie, a play, a concert. Maybe I would have to take up fishing with Brownie. I was picturing myself sitting out in a boat with Brownie on Pelican Lake, sipping my non-alcoholic beer, when the doorbell rang.

"I'll get that," Maggie said.

She opened the door and I could hear Jackie's voice. Maggie invited her in. Johnny was with her. Maggie was congratulating her all the way from the hall to the kitchen. I looked at them both. To be young, I thought. Their faces were beaming.

"I didn't want to get in trouble, Noah," she said, "so I thought I'd come and tell you. I'm gone until Monday. My calendar's clear, Johnny and I are going to Fargo. I'm going to introduce him to my aunt and uncle and my cousins. Do you mind?"

"You kidding? You can take off a couple weeks as far as I'm concerned."

"I don't need that much time. I just promised Ruby I would come and see her as soon as I could. This just seems like a good time."

"You're going to brag a little, aren't you?" I said.

"Maybe just a bit," she replied.

"What'd you think of that performance, Johnny?"

Johnny glanced at Jackie. "Awesome. All I could think of was, awesome."

"Johnny's thinking he's probably in the wrong area of practice," said Jackie. "He wants to talk to you about doing criminal work."

"Maybe," Johnny added quickly, a little embarrassed.

"We'll talk when we get back," said Jackie.

"Sure," I said. "Happy to."

Jackie came around the corner of the counter and I could tell it was time for a hug. She wrapped her arms around me and whispered, "Thank you." She then went and kissed Maggie on the cheek and said, "I guess we'll get going."

"Have a safe trip. See you Tuesday," I replied.

After showing them out, Maggie joined me at the kitchen counter again. "What a nice couple," she said. "Think he means it?" she asked. "I mean criminal law?"

"I've heard he's a good attorney but I can't imagine the two of them wanting to work in the same office side by side."

"Maybe they're in love," she said.

"They'd have to be to try that."

Silence again settled in. Maggie seemed to get this soft smile on her face.

"What're you grinning about?" I asked.

"Think they've ever done it in the office? You know, like you and I used to?"

"I don't know and I'm not going to ask." I laughed.

Her eyes seemed to turn even softer, her face flushed.

"What're you thinking about?" I asked.

She got up from her chair, came around the table and took my hand. "Come on, I'll show you."

"Do I need my nitro?"